WITHDRAWN

CALAMITY

Calamity
Heliosphere Books

Copyright © 2016 by John David Jordan.
Published by arrangement with the author.

ISBN: 978-1-937868-47-5
eISBN: 978-1-937868-48-2
Library of Congress Control Number: 2016935182

Cover design by John David Jordan.
Cover photography and illustration by John David Jordan.

This is a work of fiction. Names, characters, places, and events either are the products of the author's imagination or are used fictitiously. Any resemblance to actual persons, living or dead, corporations, or other entities, is entirely coincidental.

Heliosphere Books are published by Endpapers Press, a division of Author Coach, LLC.

The Heliosphere Books logo featuring a "bow wave" is a trademark of Author Coach, LLC.

CALAMITY

BEING AN ACCOUNT OF CALAMITY JANE
AND HER GUNSLINGING GREEN MAN

JO JORDAN

Heliosphere BOOKS

San Diego

For Jack and Malcolm,
come calamity or come calm.

ACKNOWLEDGEMENTS

Jane and the Green Man's journey through the Wild West has been a long road. So I'll start by thanking my parents, John and Jill Jordan, and my BFFs, Chris Bennett, Patrick Greer, Fleming Patterson, and David Werk. They entertained my early (and late) brainstormings and false starts and together we created a much larger world than even Jane travels through.

A number of talented authors helped me refine Jane's story, including Emily Horton, who probably saw the roughest cut, and Betty Emrey, who saw things in the text even I didn't see. But I never would've completed the manuscript without the amazing feedback of my peers in the Atlanta Writer's Club—Josh Bugosh, Emily Carpenter, Tom Leidy, Chris Negron, Jane Haessler, George Weinstein, and many many others.

You wouldn't be reading this without Andrew Zack and Rebecca Josephsen, who saw something they loved in this novel—and for helping it through publication. And to Donny Hamrick for driving to Wyoming with me in December to shoot video and still for the cover and website.

And thanks most of all to Ellie Decker. She offered to read the rough manuscript and fell in love with me in the process. Best. Review. Ever.

Lastly, thank you, awesome reader! You've got great taste. So let me know what you think, let your friends know how great Jane is, and share your favorite passages with the hashtag *#CalamityJD*.

BOOK ONE
SEEING THE ELEPHANT

ONE

So, you want to hear about the Green Man, do you? About how that green son of a bitch and me burned our way clear across the Wyoming once on thirty years? Well, reckon I can tell you my part of it. But that there's a story of some bloody goddamn revenge, it is. Against both men and worse. But if you're like to go through the mill, mister, reckon I'd be right obliged to take you. See, once on my name was Martha Jane Canary. That's Calamity Jane to you. And this here's the story of how the one become the other. And about the Green Man what rode through hell with me to do it. And that's the goddamn truth.

Part of it, anyways. Truth is, I heard him before I saw him—heard his ear-splitting roar all the way across the damn yard, even with my head pushed down in the hay, hot breathing in my ears and all. For a moment that queer howl of his right drowned out my own screams, if you'll believe that. No sir, you don't forget a thing like that—screams like ours.

See, Jimmy Burns was on me. I bit and I clawed at him. Did anything I could to get him away but he didn't back off none. No, he tore at my shirt with one hand and shoved my face sideways into the hay with the other. Fuck, ain't never been so scared. Was only a girl, see? Barely fifteen. And ain't nobody ever set themselves on me like that before, what with rape on their mind. And here was one of them doing it, too, what shot up Mister Harthra and the boys. Doing me worse than dead. So I screamed loud as I could from under Jimmy's muffling. And I thrashed all wild against him, swinging my knees and elbows into whatever bits I could.

Being in such a heap, the Green Man's howl wasn't all that frightening. Not to me. I'd heard Mister Harthra make such a holler once on when he was mad as all hell. So I drew hope from that roar, I did. Hope what I wasn't all lonesome out there in that barn. That someone else survived the die-up. That maybe what I saw done to Mister Harthra and the boys was some kind of bad dream what I was finally waking from.

But that roar? Well, Jimmy's buddy—Walker, I think it was—was might upset by it. And rightly so, I reckon. Was the last damn thing he ever heard.

I remember him clear as if he was standing right there beside you. Remember him hissing from them shadows by the barn door, "Shut that little cunt up. Reckon I heard something."

But, I tell you, them two boys didn't know what kind of calamity they was courting. Jimmy cupped my mouth with that filthy palm of his and breathed a loud "shhh" in my ear. Oh, I stopped screaming, all right. Flashed my teeth, I did. Sunk them deep into the meat of his hand, tasting dirt, blood, and bone. Tears might've filled my eyes and hay might've stabbed my cheeks but I was plumb glad to hear his screaming in my ears, I was.

Well, glad for a blink, anyways. Jimmy was mad as the devil, at that. He clutched his hand, reeled back, and, before I could free my pinned arms, he slammed that fat fist of his right into my face. Goddamn! Hurt something awful. The barn spun and I've got some weak recollection of my body flopping all around like a fish, whether from my own jerking or from Jimmy's manhandling, I don't rightly know. But was blood in my mouth, all the same. My blood. And as my wits come back, I felt Jimmy pulling at my belt, wrestling them dungarees over my hips. Boy, that's a terror you'll just never know. No man will. And no girl should. Turns my stomach even today, God knows how long on, to think on Jimmy Burns and how close he come to it.

But, of course, you was asking about the Green Man.

See, right then is when everything stopped. Jimmy stopped grabbing and pushing his hips into mine. Walker stopped his cussing. And in their stead, I remember some loud crash booming through that barn and the sound of splitting timbers mixed with cursing and screams. I felt Jimmy leaning into me, his arms fumbling at his own belt, letting me alone as he struggled for his gun.

And that's when I saw him. The Green Man, I mean. My eyes was all foggy and tear-soaked but I could still make out his tall, slender figure just fine in that open barn doorway. His long arm holding Walker's pudgy body two full feet off the dirt. Was a right beautiful thing.

I cried out but my words was muffled by all that blood filling my mouth. Jimmy heard me, though. Swung his elbow into my bare belly, knocking the wind right out of me, upturning my world all over again. Was a sight worse than when he punched me, too. Stars all flashing like powder before my eyes and the sounds of that barn all drowned by the rush of blood in my ears. The crushing volume of my own heart, if you believe that.

Shit, even them gunshots sounded far off. Jimmy's elbow, braced against my belly, stabbed into my ribs with every shot he squeezed off. And even while my senses was all fouled up, I could still hear the Green Man's roaring—that same haunted, other-worldly screaming I'd heard echoing across the yard just moments before. And damn if that sound wasn't rushing through that dark toward me—right damn over me, even! I swear, through eyes squeezed all tight from pain, I saw his long, dim shape fly like some avenging sprit right across me—like some answered prayer—arms and legs all moving like an animal's, some billowing duster blocking out the light from outside. And all of a sudden, Jimmy was gone. Ripped off me and cast beside. His fingers had done clutched at me for the last time.

Then silence. Shit, sudden as it begun, was all kinds of quiet. No heavy breathing in my ears, no tearing fabric, no curses. No inhuman roar. Just quiet like the damn Earth was new.

I remember, just lay there for a spell, right where Jimmy left me. Just watching ropes and hay hooks swinging from them barn rafters. Shock, I guess they call it. Bill used to call it sleeping. But that silence was un-nerving, it was, and Jimmy had showed himself to be a real curly wolf, if you take my meaning. So when my wits come back, God, panic took me. I scrambled to pull my clothes back on with no thinking for all that stabbing hay I swept up into my jeans. Was a right terrible mess, I was. My tits was all sore from Jimmy's handling, my thighs all bruised from his knees, my face all wet from his licking and my tears and blood, too.

But I barely had time to wipe them tears away and close my torn flannel before I heard voices in the dark behind me.

Quick as shit, I dropped back into the hay, thinking to hide, I guess. And looking across the dark of that barn, I saw two men locked together in some empty stall.

Now, Jimmy, he stood pinned, a tack peg wet with blood sticking right out through his shoulder. The Green Man stood over him—a towering figure in that long gray duster, his face all hid by shadow and the wide brim of a worn-out Stetson. His hand around Jimmy's throat, them long green fingers pointing that boy's face up into his.

Was then I heard Jimmy mutter through gritted teeth, "But we killed you . . ."

The Green Man pressed in real close. So close Jimmy's face was shrouded in that same shadow what hid his own.

"Where is it?" the Green Man asked him in a low, raspy tone. Now I can't quite speak same as he done. Or so well. No sir, I can only tell it with the words God gave me. But take my word, that Green Man's voice was a right dry thing. Rough like them stones what push up them Tetons. Like the growl of boots stepped in gravel. And, God, I didn't know him from Adam, yet, but I could just feel the rage in that voice. I don't think any of us—me, Jimmy, Jeb Boone, anybody in Piedmont that day—had any notion of what kind of passenger we woke up. But we'd find out soon enough. Goddamnit, we would. Not before half the town had gone up the flume but we'd know.

Point is, Jimmy didn't know who he was dealing with. "I don't know what you're talking—" I heard him start, his voice all shaking. But the Green Man just tore him off that tack peg easy as a man might toss a cut of meat. Threw him clear across the barn, he did. And that boy fell crumpled to the dirt, howling. That's when Jimmy and I both saw Walker, cold as a wagon tire, lying right there in the middle of the barn where the Green Man must've left him.

Pained as he looked, Jimmy still managed to scramble over to Walker's fat body, fumbling for the iron strapped to his bulging waist. Well, I got ready to move. If Jimmy started shooting I wasn't keen on hanging around and risking him finishing what he done started before that Green Man showed up.

But when I saw that green fella walk out of that shadowed stall, his breathing all hard and his fingers all curled in anger, well, I kept myself low. I'll never forget, when he stepped into the light, I saw them long bug stalks reaching up from his head through slits in his Stetson, bent forward like the feelers on a locust. And I saw his eyes, black dreadful eyes large as coffee cups, set like pools of oil against his rough green skin. Was a space man, he was, understand? Tall and lean and green and terrible. Was magnificent.

Jimmy lifted Walker's gun but the Green Man was fast as a colt, snatching it away by the barrel. I guess was then what Jimmy really saw The Green Man for the first time. I've never seen a boy's face go so white so fast.

"You ain't Harthra . . ." I remember him whispering.

The Green Man stood over him, thin lips pulling back over silver teeth.

"Where is it?" he growled.

Jimmy shook his head and cried. I think, by then, he'd figured how this was going to end. Maybe I didn't know yet but, looking back, I reckon Jimmy did.

"Where?" the Green Man screamed, his voice punching Jimmy to the floor—and me back into the hay—like a goddamn blow. If you've never heard a Green Man use his voice like that, well, it's hard to rightly explain. But you don't ever want to hear it. Not ever. My mind reeled with pain at the sound of it.

But bad as it was, that scream was worse for Jimmy. He was its target, see? And he just shook in terror, his back all pressed up against Walker's body. And while he done cowered, the Green Man towered over him, taking his sweet time turning Walker's gun around and pointing that barrel at Jimmy's shivering shape.

Now, I didn't know him yet. Didn't know what kind of man he was. But it was clear he wasn't like Harthra. I scrambled to my feet wanting to run but unable to step away. And when I moved, I saw that Green Man's stalks twitch, following me like Harthra's used to do. He turned to face me, that gun still held on Jimmy. And with no backwards glance, he come my way, them black eyes drilling all deep into me.

My heart just about turned to stone, it did. I clutched my shirt tight and watched him come. Reckon I wanted to run but wasn't a bit of me what could move under that stare of his.

"You know who did this?" Those were the first words he ever said to me. "You know who did this?" his voice booming, ringing in my ears and my head. "You know who killed these men?" he asked, pointing a shaking hand out that barn door at the dusty yard outside.

I backed against a beam, affrighted not by his strangeness, I reckon, but, well, by his violence. "I ain't never seen one of your kind do that to a man," I told him, thinking of the way he held up Walker in the doorway. The way he threw Jimmy across the barn.

He looked down at me, his gaze so goddamn cold. "Do you know who did this?" he asked again, his voice softer but somehow more menacing for it.

"I do," I told him, barely whispering.

He nodded and looked out through them open barn doors. In that harsh sunlight, I could see he was looking at the stilled boot of a man shot dead, his body lying out of sight. When I looked back at him, though, that Green Man was holding Walker's gun toward me, its peeling wooden handle just inches from my hand. Without thinking, I let slip my loose shirt and took that gun from him, that pistol stock all cold and rough. I can almost feel it now, thinking on it.

The Green Man looked over his shoulder at Jimmy, still crumpled on the ground, then back at me.

"Come outside," he said, "when you're through."

When I was through? Shit, he had such a calm way of talking about such things. About beefing a man. But, like I said, was just a girl. Ain't never killed nobody before. I stared down at that gun, so fixed on it I didn't even notice the Green Man leaving. How long I stared at that revolving chamber, that horsetail pin, and that long, long barrel, I don't know. But after a spell I cupped my left palm under that handle and lifted it, tilting that barrel up from the ground toward Jimmy.

Now, Jimmy's wits was dulled, see, by that scream the Green Man put on him. But his tears was slowing and his limbs stopped all their shaking. Blood dripped from his shoulder, urine from his chaps. Was all a mess, I tell you. All come a cropper. But when he saw me looking down that long barrel at him, my shaking hands waving that sight across his torso, belly, and groin, well, Jimmy caught a breath quick. He stretched out a hand toward me, shielding himself with the same palm I'd nearly bit in two. Was then I let my finger slip around that trigger. Was rigid as a damn railroad track.

"Martha Jane," I remember Jimmy sputtering, "It wasn't nothing to do with you, now. Was about Mister Harthra. About that flying engine."

I clenched my teeth and tried to steady that gun with both hands. I ain't never held a revolver before, see? And was a sight shorter than my squirrel gun. But I knew I could sink a bullet into him. Shit, I could pump half-a-dozen rounds into him before he hit the floor. And I wanted to. I wanted to make him hurt so fucking bad. He helped kill Harthra and the boys. He'd come back, on the prod, looking to do me worse. But still that trigger felt heavy, welded in place.

Jimmy rose to his feet and backed away, stepping over Walker's body without looking down, feeling behind him for escape. But he never took his eyes off me. I think if he had, I could've shot him.

"Martha, I'm sorry, now." he told me.

"Shut up," I whispered, every bruise and cut he left on me throbbing. I thought to pull that trigger. I really did. To scatter his blood as he would've scattered mine. But my finger just couldn't move that thin trigger. I wasn't like the Green Man. Wasn't no killer. Not yet.

"Martha—" he started.

"Shut up!" I yelled. Oh, shame added some steel to my voice, to be sure. And some fresh tears to my cheeks, too. That gun shook so wild—like I were aiming from horseback.

Jimmy's hand wrapped around the edge of a barn door and, without a word, he slipped away. I just held the gun on the opening he left behind, steadying the barrel and tightening my grip. I swear, was right then I could feel that trigger give under my touch. But he was gone. I dropped my arms, the gun into the hay. Maybe never been more Martha then right then, letting the man what made to rape me escape my sights.

Reckon I stood there in a daze for some long spell, holding my torn shirt across my chest and taking account of the barn around me. The bloody tack hook, the splintered wood. Walker's body in the middle of the floor. My blood in the hay at my feet. Felt like the last half-hour happened to someone else. That Jimmy done chased some other girl across that bloodied yard. That some other girl had tripped across the bodies of her friends before Jimmy finally caught her and dragged her into the barn. That another girl had nearly been raped in a half-eaten pile of hay before some green space man snatched off her attacker. But wasn't some other girl, was it? Was Martha Jane Canary. Was me. And it's a shame to admit it, still.

When I finally stepped outside, into the light, I saw the Green Man standing on the roof of Harthra's ranch, a short little scope held to his eye. When he saw me, he stepped to the edge of the shingles and dropped to the ground easy as a cat might drop from a table. But he didn't really look at me. Didn't even look at the dozen bodies strewn around the yard, none, neither. Them black eyes just bulged toward them brown hills behind me, watching. God, he was always watching.

He didn't come toward me none, neither. Just walked up to his horse. Now, that queer thing might be worth a whole story in your paper by its own goddamn self, I tell you. But right then, it just stood motionless at the porch steps, waiting, its harness dangling in the breeze.

"I didn't hear no shot," the Green Man said to me.

I couldn't answer him. Just looked away, afraid to see my bruised and swollen face reflected in them large dark eyes of his.

Well, the Green Man took a long rifle out from under his saddle. A magnificent Henry—perhaps I'll show it to you later. I got it in back. Its brass receiver so well worked and blinding in the high sun. Anyways, his eyes were fixed on the hills, see? And I watched him clip that short little scope to the top of that receiver and, with a flick of his wrist, lever in a round. And when he lifted the stock to his shoulder—against this polished patch of hide sewn into his duster, there—that little scope reached out and cupped his wide eye all around. I swear, it's like no goddamn gun you've ever seen.

Well, I turned and straight away found the Green Man's quarry. Was Jimmy running, stumbling through them tall grasses toward Piedmont.

"Wait—" I said. I still don't know why.

But a shot cracked the air, cutting me right off. Jimmy snapped sidewise and fell out of sight.

"Wait!" I screamed again. But still I didn't step toward the Green Man, none. I didn't really try to stop him.

But Jimmy, he wasn't dead. He started to stand and run, hands clutching at his punctured side. Was then a second shot rang out. And a third. Bang! Bang! Was like a dream, it was—one of them dreams where you can't move or scream, understand? I just stood there, looking through someone else's eyes, as Jimmy's body spun from a blow to his shoulder before his head broke open and he vanished into the high grass. Still there, for all I know. Just bones, burned and bleached.

And suddenly I could move again. I swung around and punched at the Green Man. Them stalks twitching as he caught my fist in his. First time I ever touched him, that.

"Why?" I cried, unsure why I was even upset. Unsure why I hadn't shot Jimmy my own damn self.

He looked at me for a long minute, holding my small fist in his. He had such a way of saying nothing that said so much.

"You're young, yet," he told me, "so I'll forgive you that outburst."

He threw my hand back at me, about spinning me around to the ground in doing, and pointed toward them hills and them tall grasses, saying, "Don't you ever let a man do that to you and live. You understand me, girl?"

I hung my head. I was spent.

"You understand me?" he kept on, his voice ringing in my head.

I nodded, my eyes locked on that brass receiver of his rifle. See, he taught me something then. Something I've never forgotten. If Bill was still around, he'd tell you. I ain't never forgot it.

"Best you kill him yourself, next time," the Green Man grumbled as he turned away from me, slipping that long rifle back under his saddle. "Can't count on no man to rescue you."

TWO

Well, that's how I met him. I expect he made a bigger impression on me than I did on him. But I'd make a mash on him before long.

I told the Green Man what happened. How that bastard Jeb Boone come riding in with his boys and shot up the place. "Mister Harthra and his didn't stand a chance," I told him. "Jeb didn't even say nothing. He just shot the whole place to- hell. Would've killed me, or worse, too, except I was up in the barn and small enough to hide when the time come."

The Green Man looked at them boys dead on the ground around us. Was a terrible scene, that. Reckon I've only seen worse twice else—at the hands of the Cheyenne above Deadwood and after we crossed paths with that gray bastard.

No. The Green Man looked around, his oily eyes searching and them stalks of his twitching. "Is that Lova Harthra back there by the trough?" I remember him asking.

I squinted at him, shaking my head and waving in the direction of the house. "Who the hell else do you think it is? Reckon he was the only green skin in the territory until you come along."

I'll never forget how he looked at me then. Surprised I didn't balk on seeing him, I reckon. Didn't scream or run off like a girl should've when confronted by some space man rode in from a fucking tall tale. But I'd worked for Harthra for six months. He didn't hide his face or bury his feelers under some boss hat like them Greens in Salt Lake. He might not've talked much about where he was from, or even what he was, but

Harthra never tried to blend in. So I'd seen green men before. More than most in the West, I reckon. Just not quite like the one I was seeing now.

I spat on the ground and told him, again, "Bastard Jeb Boone murdered the whole lot of them boys. He waited for that daddy of his to skip town before he made his move, too. Killed them all for that fucking flying engine." Turns my stomach to this day just thinking on it.

Now see, that's what got the Green Man's attention. Me talking on Mister Harthra's flying ship. The Green Man moved all quick then, forgetting me where I stood and taking off across the yard toward Harthra's big shed, where he'd kept that metal thing of his under tarps.

I didn't follow him. I'd been holed up in that barn since that gunfight the day before, hiding from Jeb's boys what come looking for me. So, first thing I did, I went over to Harthra's body beside the trough. You've never seen the like of what they did to him. Not even in New York City, I'd wager. Mister Harthra had been a godsend for me, see? Giving me work when the mess with the railroad cost me my job on the line. He didn't care I was a girl or that I wore dungarees instead of no gingham dress. He only cared that I could ride, knew how to use my Springfield, and could keep up with the boys. And I could. Don't let no one tell you otherwise.

But now he was dead. Stalks cut off. Burnt face pointing skyward. You hear me? Burnt. Burnt like a goddamn piece of meat. They burnt his goddamn face right off. And after all I'd seen and been through, I didn't even have a tear for the man. They burnt his face off and I couldn't even cry.

"Why'd they do it?" I asked the Green Man, figuring he'd hear me even over by the shed. "Why'd they do that to his face?" I asked him. "I ain't never seen no man or savage do something so grisly to another man."

The Green Man stopped walking. He seemed to think on it. I guess it meant something to him—not that Harthra was dead, mind you, but how they'd killed him.

"So the ward of heaven won't know who's come calling," he told me.

Awful ain't it? Awful what people'll do to each other. Don't matter none if they're white, red, or green. We're just awful.

"What kind of of savagery is that?" I asked him.

He just shook his head. And that was that. Never spoke about it again.

I watched the Green Man walk up on the open doors of that shed—great old big doors, like the kind a locomotive drives through into a wheelhouse. He stood on the charred ground, where the ship hung right in the goddamn air for a while before they took it off toward town. I remember he looked defeated there. All small and helpless in that big black doorway.

"You said Jeb Boone did this?" he asked me. "Took Harthra's ship?"

"Saw it myself." I told him. "Son of a bitch is son to old Moses Boone, the rancher what owns all them big railroad kilns in town. And I don't know where Jeb took off to but I reckon he didn't leave Piedmont. He didn't rightly know how to fly that damn thing. Didn't look like he could get it much off the ground."

The Green Man just stood there nodding. Was the way you knew he was having a kind of conversation with himself. Working things out. But when he started moving again, all that defeat in him was gone. Moved real quick back to his horse and, before I could get close, started off.

I remember yelling after him, "Wait. I'll come with you."

The Green Man jerked that horse of his away from me, though, turning toward the road into Piedmont. "I ain't got no interest in little girls," he said.

He sure didn't, that's for goddamn sure. But I stomped after him. "Well, I ain't got no damn interest in you, space man," I yelled after. "But I sure as hell don't want to die. Or worse," I kept on, thinking on what just happened in the barn. "I want to kill the fucker what done this to Mister Harthra and the boys."

The Green Man stopped and turned in his saddle. I could tell he was thinking about how I let Jimmy go. About how he had to shoot him as he ran away from us.

"Girl," he said to me, "I ain't got no time for some biddy who ain't got no sand in her belly."

Maybe he was right. But I told him, "I can hold my own," trying to sound all tough.

He nodded, having that talk with himself again.

"Can you ride?"

"Can you?" I snapped. God, I was full of piss. Wasn't no way I was going to let him leave me behind, waiting for the next Jimmy to come along and try his hand at me.

But the Green Man didn't say a wit. He just turned in his saddle and started off. And after he rode aways a bit, just when he was at the edge of hearing, he hollered back to me. "Then ride. And come heeled, if you mean what you say."

THREE

I think that was the meanest thing he ever done to me, riding off like that. Leaving me lonesome with Harthra and the boys. Without the least care.

Quick as he showed up, pulling Jimmy off me in the barn, the Green Man was gone. And I don't rightly remember what I did for a little while on his leaving, neither. I had a mind to see if my horse Bess was still alive. See, Jeb shot most of our horses same as he shot the boys. But I never got that far. I sort of wandered around, from body to body, taking account of the dead, I guess. But I wasn't really looking at them. I was just walking.

Harthra had a dozen hands working that ranch. He was a green man, too, understand? But he wasn't no longrider like this new fella. He ran that ranch just like any white man might. Better, I expect. And when the railroad come through and the Boones built them kilns, got in bed with the Union Pacific, Harthra didn't fuss with their business none. He kept to his and expected the white folk to do the same. But it didn't turn out that way, did it? Guess it's one thing to hear tell of Greens in California or Salt Lake and another entire to see one on your own main. Yes sir, some folks in town never liked a green skin doing so well while some of them did so poor. Even with them railroad workers all making a good living and all, some folks never could abide Mister Harthra.

But what Jeb did wasn't no regular hazing, like the kind me and the boys used to get going into town. Asking us how we could work for some green skin or some such. How we could stand him poking around in our minds with them stalks of his. People said some mean things—about me, in particular. Things what just ain't decent to repeat.

No, Jeb just rode up with his boys and waited for Mister Harthra to come out of the house and meet him. See, Harthra was an older man, I reckon. Never moved as fast as this new fella. So when Jeb pulled up and shot? Well, I don't know if Mister Harthra even knew what was coming. Me and the boys sure didn't. But was over in just a second, too, wasn't it.

God! I wish the Green Man hadn't left me there all lonesome. I remember dropping to the dirt in the middle of that yard, among all them bodies. My knees gave out. I just started bawling—bawling so much I couldn't see for the water in my eyes. Shook, too. I was a weak little thing in that moment. Weak and yellow. I remember kneeling in that dirt just wanting some arms around me. To keep me safe and unafraid. Was even Somers' squeeze I would've fallen into right then, finding lost sweetness in his holding. See, was the whole predicament what flooded over me, then. The murders. The rape. I remember realizing my jeans was still undone, my shirt still loose. What if someone else come along? Huh? What then? Jimmy had come so close . . .

I prefer not to think on it.

After a while, though, I come around. Stopped my bawling and began to get my head on straight. I was young but I wasn't dumb. The Green Man was right. I wasn't much good to him or myself lest I had some sand in my belly. So I decided, right there, sitting on the ground, surrounded by them bodies, cheeks wet and eyes swollen, that I wasn't going to be no goddamn mark. I wasn't going to just sit there. I was going to follow that Green Man.

And I was going to kill Jeb Boone.

Mister Harthra was nice enough to let me and two of the younger boys bed in the house. So I went inside and grabbed the only thing what mattered—my Springfield.

I tell you, each step through that house was like a step back through another life. Like how I felt after my momma died, riding the rest of the way to Utah with that great big hole in my heart. Like how I felt after Bill died. It must've happened to someone else. But there I was, in Mister Harthra's house, surrounded by his things. Reminders of a short life I lived with him. A life dead as he was. Plumb burned away.

I went looking for Bess. I think if she'd been dead it would killed me on the spot. The heartbreak would've been just too much to bear. I'd lost a lot in life, coming up on that moment. My momma and daddy dead; my brothers and sisters peddled off among them Mormons; Somers and my friends on the rail; and now Mister Harthra and the boys. Bess had been with me through it all, see? She was all I had left, tying me to those old lives.

But she was alive. She and a couple other horses spooked and took off when Jeb's boys opened up the barn. Took me a while to find her, grazing over the hill from the ranch, but she come to me right away. She wasn't no crowbait, neither. She was smart. I like to think that I was all she had left, too, and what she knew it.

So we went after the Green Man. But I should tell you, as I rode out, we passed that shed. The one where Mister Harthra kept his flying engine. Now, I told you this shed was big as a wheelhouse, right? Well, seemed a sight bigger now, empty as it was. Harthra was some kind of engineer. Or a pilot, see? He flew that thing fast as the damn wind, out over them hills toward Edmonton or straight up into the black to God knows where. I only saw him fly it once, truth be told, but God it was a sight! Thing never touched the ground, even when it was just sitting there. The boys took turns throwing shoes under it, at least until Harthra made them quit it. I would've given anything to ride in that thing, but Mister Harthra never allowed that. Him alone in that ship. Always. Before he was shot, Charlie Patch told me that Harthra and them greens done come to Earth in that flying thing and others like it. Across some kind of great divide in the sky. That someday he'd leave in it, too. But that most of the time, when he took off in that ship, he was just joyriding, like you and I might on horseback for the fun of it. What a thought, huh? Flying for the fun of it!

But it was gone now. Jeb took it, best he could, anyways. From where I hid in the barn, I could hear them fussing with the ship. Could even see them, some, between cracks in the dry old barnwood. But they couldn't figure it out, I reckon. Probably all them levers was written in some inhuman hand. Or maybe they was too goddamn dumb to reckon out the door. But it floated just fine, either way it was. So after a while they gave up and lashed the ship to some horses. Now that was a strange sight, I tell you. A whole team rigged up to pull that floating thing down the road toward town.

So I followed that same road. Followed the Green Man. And when I look back on it now, I guess I was a dumb girl after all. I should've seen what he was after. But I was so set on revenge I couldn't imagine that the Green Man didn't want the same thing I did. That he hadn't let loose that first howl for any reason other than seeing all them dead. Why, Jeb Boone had killed one of his own. Savaged him. Fuck the goddamn ship! The Green Man should've wanted revenge, same as me. Didn't matter if Harthra was friend or not. They were of the same people, like settlers standing together against a war party.

Well, that was my thinking anyways.

FOUR

Now, Piedmont wasn't much of a town, even then. The camp had sprung up around the railroad pushing through. Most of the folks in town, white and Chinaman both, come following that rail. Hell, that's how I ended up there. Before I took to working for Mister Harthra, I tucked my hair up into my hat and worked right alongside them boys on the rail. They didn't mind, none. Not until Tom Somers come along, anyways, and showed them all the girl they was missing. Right showed me, too.

So, I rode Bess into town. I remember it was quiet that day. The whole world was quiet after all that noise in the barn. But still, I was a might worried I'd be accosted in town before I found the Green Man or that bastard Jeb Boone. That folks would want to know where Jimmy was. I remember being torn, not knowing what'd be worse—the leers and sneers of them folks who reckoned Jimmy pirooted me, like he must've told them he was going to, or the rage of them folks who knew him and cared nothing for the little slut what saw him killed.

Now, as I rode close to Piedmont, I could see the Green Man's horse, plain as day, standing beside the Good Store, right in the center of town near the livery. I could tell it was the Green Man's horse from plenty far off, too. Hell, I was all the way out past the school house, see, but I could make out its perfect coat and that curious saddle, complete with this metal box perched right behind. But this horse—and I never could get used to this—it just stood there. It never needed tying up. It just stood and waited, still as a statue. And I remember, clear as I can remember when

Bill was shot, how as I rode close, that horse turned its head and watched me. Like the way a hawk watches its prey, see? Sent chills right down my spine. Watched me until I slipped up behind the store and tied off Bess out of sight. I tell you, no horse ever looked at a man like that one.

I slipped around the side of the store, down an alley, and worked my way close to the street. I remember kneeling at an open front window, concealed by some barrels and a display of shovel handles and plowing blades. Sure enough, the Green Man was in there. And from where I knelt, I could see him fingering through some mail-order catalogues, them stalks on his head doing some kind of queer twist over his hat. Didn't appear to be in no particular hurry but, when I look back on it, I expect he was waiting. To be found, see? Just not by me.

When Truett Good come out of the back room, saw them bug feelers twitching in the air, well the blood just drained right out of him.

He stammered something like, "Surprised to see you. Word was you was shot."

The Green Man strode toward the counter, staring at Good with those slick black eyes and them pointed stalks.

"I ain't Harthra," he said. Then he pulled this strange gun out of its holster and slammed it down on the counter, barrel pointed right at the shopkeeper's belly. It wasn't like no Colt. No sir. There was no chamber for shells or any such thing. Just smooth metal with some kind of red light blinking on it. And the barrel end was wide—big as a can of beans, almost, with a tiny little hole at the top of it where God knows what come out.

"Batteries." I remember him saying. "Vosh kind, if you have them."

Good jumped back from the counter, staring down at that black weapon.

"You ain't Harthra." I heard him stammer. "I'm sorry, sir. I truly am," he said. "Harthra used to come into town every now and again and, well, you look so much like him."

The Green Man, he just let slip a small screech. "Reckon I do," he said.

Good shook his head, though. "But, whoever you are," he said, "I ain't got no batteries. One of them Boone boys come in yesterday and bought the last one I had. They had themselves a whole cart full of stuff they got from Harthra's place after . . . well—"

The Green Man frowned and mumbled something I couldn't quite hear. Then he pulled a rifle strap over his head, them stalks of his curling down to let it pass, and held that long Henry rifle out in front of him.

Good backed away from the counter, hands out. "I ain't got nothing to do with that business up at the ranch, now. I ain't a part of no quarrel."

The Green Man cocked the rifle with a quick jerk of his wrist. I could hear the click of brass in the empty chamber all the way outside. "Cartridges?" he asked.

Good took a long breath, at that, and stepped back to the counter."Yes sir," he said. "Them boys from Fort Bridger just about cleared me out but I got some."

I squeezed up under the window then, just as Good looked down at the engraving cut into the brass receiver. I heard him ask the Green Man, "You fight with them boys in the 1st Maine, space man? Didn't know none of your kind got so far east."

The Green Man just snatched that rifle right back off the counter. "Not with them, no."

He threw some coins down and gathered up them rimfires Good laid out for him. But Good just looked past the Green Man and stepped away from the counter again.

"You're money ain't no good here." I heard him say.

"On account of my being green?" the Green Man asked.

"On account of your friends out there," Good told him.

Well, shit. I should've been more careful. More watchful, see? While I was watching the Green Man, some of Jeb's waddies was watching me. And I didn't get one step out from behind them barrels before one of Jeb's boys grabbed my arms and twisted me back against that wall. Damn, I wish I hadn't left my Springfield tied up, back on Bess. But it would've done me no good. Before I could catch my breath, there was three of Jeb's mudsills there, two holding me back against the wall and another coming up with a toothless grin. I recognized them plain from the ranch shooting. Was the same sick smiles they had gunning down Harthra's boys what they had now.

But they never even got a word out.

The Green Man just flew out of that store like some damn wind was under him. He grabbed up a shovel handle from that display on the porch and broke it clear across that toothless man's jaw. Blood blew out like water from a damn geyser, if you take my meaning. He was just so fast! The fellows holding me against the wall didn't know what to do. They fumbled for their guns but the Green Man stepped up on them too quick. He pistol-whipped that big gun of his across one fellow's face, cracking his nose and sending him down like a stone. The other, he put a Colt right into his cheek, pushing him right off of me in the process. Then he done lifted that big gun high, pointing it across the street at a saloon.

"Drop the gun!" the Green Man hissed, his voice about knocking me off my feet.

The waddy what'd been holding me was panicked. He raised up both hands, kept an eye on the Colt in his face, and begged, "I ain't got no gun."

Now pay attention. Your readers are going to like this.

The Green Man sneered and pushed that pistol into that feller's cheek. "Not you," he said. Then he flicked his space gun toward that far saloon across the street.

Now, I was pressed between them. But I could see what the Green Man was aiming at. He'd trained that big gun on a second floor window of that saloon where another of Jeb's boys stood inside, rifle at the ready. You got to understand, though, the Green Man never turned his head that way or nothing. He just felt it. Felt it on the air with them stalks of his. Shit, looking back, reckon he felt all these boys even before they had their ambush.

"Drop it!" The Green Man yelled, his pistol pressing under that first feller's check bone, his words giving him tremors.

Well, you can believe that feller yelled off the man in that saloon window to give up the gun.

But even with that pistol pressed into his jaw, that feller just kept looking at me, up and down. It wasn't no hungry look, like Jimmy had. Was sort of pleading.

"Where's Jimmy. And Walker?" he stuttered, scared so bad he was shaking.

My heart fluttered. This here was what I was afraid of. I didn't know what to say. Wasn't no answer I could give what wouldn't set half the town on me. Of course, half the town wanted me already, seeing as I was the last survivor of that shoot-up. Since I'd seen Jeb burn Harthra's face off, heard them awful screams.

I guess my silence was all the answer that feller needed.

"She killed them," he muttered.

The Green Man let out a small trill and sneered at him,"Wasn't her what killed them," he said, twisting that pistol a little as he spoke.

That feller was pissing himself then, I tell you.

"Who are you?" he squeezed out through blubbering lips.

The Green Man just starred at him, them stalks of his turned back around watching that window across the street. "I had business with Harthra," he said. "And if your boss has Harthra's ship, well, reckon I got business with him."

"What's this?" I remember asking. Remember, I was hell-bent on revenge. I come looking for this Green Man because I assumed he wanted the same. I didn't know things was about to get more complicated.

But the Green Man didn't look at me. Not that I could tell, anyways.

Instead, he pushed that feller out into the street. And ever he kept that big gun trained on the window across the road, never looking that way with his eyes, just with them twitching feelers.

"Take us to Jeb Boone," The Green Man told him. "And don't go trying to fag out, neither, or I'll have you for breakfast before you get across the street? Understand?"

Sure as hell that feller did. And he took us there. God help me, that scared bastard took us right to him.

FIVE

Was maybe the space of just a dozen buildings from Good's shop to where that boy done took us but wasn't a soul in that little town what didn't see us making our way. Any why shouldn't the whole goddamn world have seen us? Was quite a sight, we were. And every lady in her skirts or waddy or rail hand what was out on them boards got their eyeful. Saw them a green man—and not right the one they was used to none, neither—pushing some poor bloodied boy ahead of him down Main, a Colt pressed into his back, his long stalks and that queer gun of his searching them windows and doorways for more of Jeb's boys.

And me? I was following right along, peppering him with questions all the way.

"What the hell do you mean, you got business with him?" I remember hollering at his back as we moved down that road toward the Boone's saloon. I told him, "By business, I expect you mean to put that fat gun of yours clean up his ass."

But he didn't pay me no mind. Not even when I called him a lily. No, he just pushed that boy forward until I stopped behind them in the middle of the street. I'd worked myself up to a steam and I'd have been goddamned if this Green Man was going to do any less than have that son of a bitch Jeb Boone for breakfast. So I just stopped, my fists all shaking and clenched white.

"Then you go have your goddamn business with him, you fucking yellow belly!" I yelled. All manner of folks was watching us through windows and doorways but I didn't care, none. I just kept on, yelling after him, "I'm going to go back to Bess and grab my Springfield. While you're talking with that murdering bastard, I'll get the bulge on the both of you!"

He stopped walking right then. Those searching stalks of his, and that searching gun, they turned on me. Gun didn't look so big when it was pointed right at you. No sir. But I stopped my fussing straight away. Went cold all over.

"I won't have no biddy getting in my way after all this time," he snarled at me. Then those cold black eyes turned on me, his stalks turning back to his captive. "So hobble your lip, girl and fall back in. I ain't got no qualms about putting you down if you mean to come against me."

I didn't move right away. Just stared at that gun. At that little glow at the back of the barrel. This man had killed Walker so fast I didn't even see it. He'd shot Jimmy in the back as he ran across them hills easy as another man might beef a deer. And now I stood in his sights. He could've told me to fly to the moon, right then, and I expect I would've done it.

I stepped up to him slowly, watching that gun barrel sink toward the dirt with my every step toward him. And when I stood in his shadow, the gun lowered between us, I told him, "You ain't like Mister Harthra," I said. "He was a good man."

The Green Man just looked away. "Keep quiet, girl," he said. Didn't say another word to me after that.

So I fell in line, squinting in the brightness as drew up on the Boone's saloon.

Now it was nice and clear outside, if I remember. The sort of day made for shooting and smoke. Was a big open sky without a cloud in sight. Not like here. A dude like you might think this Dakota sky is something grand. But the blue over the Wyoming is so much bigger. So much clearer, like the sun is all that much closer. And from the middle of Main on a fine day, you could see as far south as them Rockies what ring that Salt Lake. And open plains and rolling hills all around under that wide, wide sky.

But stepping into that saloon? That was like stepping right into the abyss. Or into the black, as the Green Man might've said. That poor boy who'd led us down the road? Green Man kicked him right through them batwing doors. And as we stepped through on his heels, I couldn't see a damn thing. I could hear the scratch of chairs along the floor and the metal and leather sounds of guns unshucked but I was blind as a mouse. Walked right into the Green Man's back and clung to the flaps of his duster what to keep from falling.

Was a lot of commotion all around. And as my eyes adjusted to the dark, I got a notion of the tricky scene. The boy was scrambling to his feet in front of us, moving quick as he could to get behind the half-dozen or so men scattered around Jeb Boone at the far end of the bar. That smug bastard—not much older than Jimmy, to tell you true—kept to his seat while his boys trained their irons on me and the Green Man.

"Reckon it's true what they say, ain't it? Harthra wasn't the only green skin in the West," Jeb said, eyeing the Green Man, making a show of looking unimpressed. "You come to kill me? That it?" He asked, still sitting.

"Not today," the Green Man told him.

Jeb laughed at that. Surprising, really. But I reckon Jeb didn't know no more what this green fella was than Jimmy had before he got his. So he laughed like was all a goddamn joke. That same wicked laugh I'd heard after he burnt Harthra's face right off. Was like a knife stabbing into my head, it was. If I'd had my gun, I'd have put some shot into Jeb right then. I was so angry to hear him—goddamn!—the thought of getting put down myself never even occurred to me.

Then Jeb spoke again. A whiney little voice, like metal scraping on stone. "I don't suppose you'd tell me if you were?"

The Green Man knocked my hands away from his coat and stepped into the saloon. I stayed close as he moved, that duster blowing back and hiding me some all while showing them twin guns—one American, one green-kind—on his hips.

"Expect I would," he said. "I got what you humans call a weakness. I'm honest."

He stepped right up to Jeb's little table at the end of the bar and sat down. Never seemed to pay no mind to all them guns on him. But his stalks never stopped twitching this way and that, keeping track of what his eyes ignored.

Now, Jeb's eyes turned on me. I was standing beside the Green Man, trying to keep close to him and as far away from Jeb's mudsills as I could. And Jeb's eyes was hungry. Hungry like I'd seen them once on, when walking down Main after first coming to town. Made my skin crawl.

"Never mind the girl, just yet," the Green Man told him. "Come to talk business," he said.

Jeb seemed right annoyed at that. Suddenly his little war with Harthra had come to haunt him. "Then talk," he told the Green Man. "But keep your hands where I can see them. And none of that space-nigger talk, neither. When you're with me, you talk like normal folk. White folk. None of that screeching."

The Green Man reached across the table, setting all them boys on edge, and snatched away Jeb's shot of boss whiskey. He downed it quick and slammed that glass right back to the table.

"And none of that talking with your mind, neither," Jeb finished.

The Green Man just nodded.

Jeb's eyes drifted back to me. He smiled. Well, until that poor boy who led us here spoke up, anyways, saying, "They killed Jimmy and Walker. Beat the hell out of my cousins, too. Don't know if they're alive or not."

Jeb's smile faded fast. "That so?" he asked, his little eyes snapping back on the Green Man. He shook a little now. Like he was cold despite the sweat and the heat in that saloon. "Seems I left some loose ends up at Harthra's ranch, eh, green skin? Guess I'll need to attend to that."

"Little late for that, I reckon," said the Green Man.

Jeb nodded, "Reckon you're right."

Jeb's eyes found me again and that hungry smile returned. "Can't say I'm too sad, though, what this pretty little thing's still above snakes, eh? Even if she doesn't know how a girl should dress."

Jeb's boys was all set to laughing at me then—and not for the first time, I should say. They was pointing at my dungarees and bloody flannel. God, what I would've done to have my rifle on me, right then.

"I expect we can correct that soon enough, eh boys?" he kept on.

That laughter was like bullets. Could've withered under it, except I was so damn mad. If you've never hated like that, maybe you don't know what I mean. But it just fueled me. Made me hate them all the more.

The Green Man, he just waited. And when the laughter stopped and Jeb turned back to him, he didn't waste no time.

"I want the ship," he said. "The flying engine."

Again, Jeb's smile faded.

"Do you, now?" he said. "Well that's a might unfortunate, see? I went through a lot of trouble to get it."

The Green Man nodded. "I had a deal with Harthra," he said. "So now I mean to make a deal with you."

He tossed a small purse on the table. "I need that ship to take me home."

Jeb picked up the purse and peeked inside. Saw his little eyes widen something awful.

He chuckled all nervous like. Then shook his head and tossed the bag back toward the Green Man.

"Well that just ain't going to cut it," Jeb told him. "My daddy didn't bring us over from England for small-time jobs, space man. I plan to do more with that ship than ferry lost souls homeward for a few sawbucks."

Now the Green Man leaned across the table, setting all of Jeb's boys on edge. He leaned in close-like, pushing Jeb back into his chair.

"You misunderstand me," the Green Man said. "Seeing as you done already killed the only other pilot east of the Rockies, I'll need a sight more than just passage. I need the ship. And I won't be coming back with it, neither."

Jeb laughed again. But if he didn't look suddenly in over his head, then I don't know a damn thing. He took a deep breath, shaky as it was, and told the Green Man, "You've got to be kidding me, space man. Seems I've got the only flying engine between here and Virginia City." He pointed at the discarded purse. "You're going to have to do a hell of a lot better than that."

"I've got more," the Green Man said. "I've got her."

Now the Green Man didn't point at me but everyone's eyes found me straight away. No laughter now. No smiles or cruel stares. Just that sort of piercing look what makes you feel small. My anger melted away in an instant. And all of a sudden, I wanted to run—dash out of that saloon and not stop until I was back at Salt Lake. Back all the ways to Blackfoot, lying on the ground where my momma's buried.

Jesus. What kind of fella had I hitched myself too?

The Green Man just kept talking. He said, "You put us both in quite a spot, Jeb Boone. You stole my ride home. But you left a witness. So I suggest you take that fee and maybe I'll find space enough on Harthra's ship to take that girl away from this town. Else, I suppose we'll see if the sheriff in Evanston or the commander at Fort Bridger agrees with the means you used to get that ship from old Lova Harthra. Can't imagine your daddy would be too pleased to find the law waiting for him when he comes home."

Jeb laughed out loud, suddenly unafraid. "Your word against mine, space man. Or the girl's? Ain't no judge in the territory going to take the word of some green-skinned outrider or some little girl over that of a leading citizen helping folks make their way in the West. My family helps the community. We help the Union-Pacific.

"Matter of fact," he kept on, "I don't see why we can't solve this right now. Maybe I'll just take that girl off your hands, and your fancy coin, and fly you out of here in a pinewood box."

Jeb's boys steadied their guns on the Green Man. But he didn't flinch. And over the sound of a half-dozen firing pins snapping back, well, we all heard the distinct hum of something unearthly coming to life under the table.

That was the first time I ever saw the Green Man smile. He ain't human, understand? Things was different with him, from the way he showed anger to the way he showed compassion. So, whatever his intent, there wasn't no laughter in that smirk. No sarcasm, neither. Was like the devil smiling at you. Like whatever humor lay behind them thin lips meant damnation for all else.

Jeb saw it, too. And I expect he'd heard the hum of such a queer gun coming to life once on before. See, sometime along the way, the Green Man's hand had dropped below the table and now he had that big gun of his pointed right at Jeb's belly. Right where I'd wanted it pointed all along. I tell you, wish the Green Man had pulled the trigger right then.

"I wonder," the Green Man said "if any of yours can get a shot off before I put a hole in your gut the size of a rail head."

Jeb didn't say nothing. Didn't smile none, neither. Didn't even move except for the color running right out of him.

"I wonder, too," the Green Man continued, "if maybe my offer doesn't sound a little sweeter now then it did a moment ago. Seems you thought you had the upper hand. Seems you was wrong. Because I reckon you value your skin a little higher than that ship."

With little movement, I saw him unshuck his other gun, that Colt revolver. But he kept its barrel down. No one moved against him.

"If I'm wrong, you've got the chance, right now, to let me know," the Green Man said. "If you let me pay for the ship, or if I have to lay you and yours low, makes no difference to me. See, either way, I get what I come for."

Jeb's face was white as snow on the plain. But I remember him saying through trembling lips, "You'd never walk out of this saloon alive, space man."

The Green Man relaxed into his chair, the gun under the table singing its deadly song.

"One of us sure won't," he said. "But I don't expect that'd be me."

Jeb nodded. And then that goddamned smile come back. Ah! What I would've done for the Green Man to have pulled that trigger right then! But he didn't. Goddamnit, I'm still not sure what was going through his mind but he didn't.

Jeb waved off his boys.

"You bring that money and that pretty girl around by the kilns tomorrow morning. There's a big woodshed on the other side of the rail where we keep the fuel. We'll bring the ship there."

The Green Man stood, then, and he let them guns, both drawn, hang by his side. You're probably wondering, like I did at the time, if the Green Man could've taken all them boys, heeled as they was. And Jeb, too. He wasn't no slouch with a pistol. I'd seen that when he pulled up on Harthra. But let me tell you. After what I'd seen? Jeb made the right call. Damn him for not pushing the Green Man to violence, then, but he saved his own life there in that saloon. At least for a spell.

But as we started out of that room, eyes more on the Green Man now than me, Jeb's shaking voice followed us. "You keep careful, space man. Don't get so caught up in your little prize that you have yourself an accident between now and morning."

Jeb's boys laughed. Was half-assed but laughing all the same. And my heart jumped, blood boiling up in my cheeks. I started to turn back but the Green Man reached out to stop me. He turned on Jeb, saying, "You're welcome to come check on us, if you like. If you're so anxious to join Jimmy and Walker, I'd be happy to oblige."

"I ain't no yack, space man," Jeb told us. "Don't think you can pull one on me just because my skin ain't green or because my daddy's out of town. Harthra made that mistake. I offered him a fair trade for that flying engine of his. You've seen how I dealt with him."

The Green Man started to turn away but stopped, that silent thinking look on his face. "What I don't understand is why you needed to kill all his boys," he asked him. "I can understand you killing Harthra, to get his ship. But why all them human boys, too?"

Jeb shrugged, the color coming back to his face. "Harthra inspired some loyalty, I guess. Them boys wasn't about to just let us walk in and take what we wanted." He smiled. "So there was a little gunplay."

"Ain't nothing of gunplay I saw," the Green Man told him. "Murder's a better name for it."

And with that, he turned and pulled me out the door behind him.

SIX

The Green Man and me didn't say a lick to each other as we rode out of town, past the roundhouse and the hotel. Didn't say nothing, even, until we got a few miles into them hills south of town.

He led us to a wide-open spot between two slopes. Wasn't even a pecker pole for shade. Just brush and grass and dry dirt that'll freeze your bones after nightfall. But he hopped down and started through his saddle bags, hunting for God knows what.

I watched him for a minute—until was clear he meant for us to camp at that lonesome spot. I didn't know what to make of this green man. I really didn't. Harthra had always been kind. Took me in when I had nothing—when the railroad kicked me to the street and Somers got around to remembering he was married. But this Green Man? This longrider? Over the course of that afternoon, he done saved me from being raped, left me to fend for myself, saved me again in town, threatened to shoot me in the middle of Main, and dragged me into the devil's den to make a bargain with that hard case, Jeb Boone. Watching him now, as he pulled the bridle and saddle off that queer horse of his, I had no notion what he meant to do with me.

"So you going to rape me, like Jeb says?" I remember blurting out, my voice shaking a little, I'll admit. "Because if you ain't, you might as well go ahead and shoot me, Green Man. You're barking at a goddamn knot if you think I'm getting on any damn flying engine with you come morning."

"I ain't of a mind to do either," I remember him saying in that low, gritty voice of his. But he never looked up from his horse and saddlebags. I knew he didn't have to. Was watching me with them bug stalks, he was.

So I just sat up there on Bess, thinking to ride off if he went for firewood or some such. I didn't have no plan. Looking back on it, think I was still surprised to be breathing.

I told him, "You're a damn coot if you think Jeb's going to let you walk in and buy that engine off him. He's going to scoop you into some damn trap and lay us both low."

But he didn't pay me no mind. The Green Man just kept at his bags, pulling out a sleeping mat and some strange metal disc.

And suddenly I got madder than a wet hen—spit bubbling up on my lips, my face all hot. "You some kind of goddamn idiot?" I yelled at him. "You showed that bastard your hand. Now he knows we're coming. You killed us both in that saloon, you know that? Fucking killed us both."

"I expect you're right," he told me, then, finally letting his horse alone and turning to shape a circle of stones into a fire pit. "But he also told us where the ship's going to be." Then he looked up at me, those cold black eyes reflecting the sinking sun back into mine. "And he knows to be afraid."

He looked so small down there, crouching on the ground by that pit. All his strangeness suddenly nothing, his stature all small.

"Jeb ain't no damned fool," I told him. "Ain't fool enough to be afraid of one green man far from home or help."

The Green Man just stared at me, stabbing at me with them oily, bulging eyes. I wish you could've seen them eyes, I really do. Could cut a man right in two.

He pulled that rifle of his over his head and threw it at me. I barely got my wits quick enough to catch the damn thing. Nearly knocked me off Bess what it was.

"Who says I ain't got no help," he said.

That Henry of his felt huge in my arms. Weighed a bit more than my Springfield, to be sure. And with that damn scope set on top? Damn thing felt more like a cannon than a rifle.

"You told me you know how to shoot," he said.

Bastard was just getting my goat. "I sure as hell do," I told him.

"Then shoot. Or give up the gun," he said to me.

Oh, I snapped back. I said, "I'll put one through you, if that's what you want."

Ha! I remember him nodding, like he was thinking on the offer. Then, looking around them hills we'd settled between, he pointed at this small, wiry tree on the western rise.

"If you can quit yammering long enough," he told me, "then pick a branch off that tree."

Now the tree he was pointing out was right far away. Farther than nothing I'd ever pointed my Springfield at and hit. And what with that setting sun falling behind it, I just shook my head.

"Ain't no man can hit a branch that far off, space man," I remember telling him. "Not into the sun. You trying to make a fool of me?"

At that, the Green Man just chuckled. "Would you could pick it off with your tongue . . ."

"I suppose you could clip it?" I snapped at him.

Well, he stepped up to Bess, grabbed that gun right out my hand, and put it to his shoulder all in one quick movement. Wasn't nothing jarring in the way he moved, neither. All smooth and grace, you know? Like some kind of murdering angel. That black scope on the receiver reached out and wrapped around his right eye and with barely a breath taken between grabbing up the gun and pulling the trigger, he squeezed off a shot. And sure as I live and breathe, a branch popped and fell off that far off tree.

"Well I'll be goddamned . . ." I remember muttering.

He pushed that Henry back into my lap, almost grassing me, again. Then he was cruel, saying something like, "Now show me I didn't make no damn mistake bringing you along."

I hopped down off Bess in a trance—didn't even think to tie her off. In that moment, my whole world shrunk down to that dry pecker pole on the hill and that heavy rifle in my hands.

Now don't go thinking I was some little biddy back then just because I was a girl. I knew my way around guns. I grew up squirreling. And when we set out from St. Louis, Daddy bought me my Springfield. Taught me proper how to shoot from wagon and ground as we moved west. I knew about breathing and sighting and leading and all that. How to keep it clean and how to keep it safe.

So I settled down to a crouch, steadying my elbow on my knee and the stock against my shoulder. I took a few deep breaths to steady myself, too. But when I went to line up the shot, well, all of a sudden I was out of my ken.

I was used to sighting down the barrel, see, but the Green Man's scope blocked that sight. Well, I didn't know if that damn thing wasn't going to scoop the eye right out of my head but I bent my chin and put my eye up to it like he'd done, all the same. Was damned if I wasn't going to show that green bastard what I had the sand and the sight for shooting.

Now I expect a city dude like you has seen something of scopes. I'd looked through one at Fort Bridger not long before. And an old one Mister Harthra had, too. But neither of those was like this. It reached out and cupped my eye, blocking out all the light, see? And through that round lens, I could see that tree like it was just a few feet away. And that setting sun? Was like it was behind some smoked glass, its light not the least bit hurtful. And every branch and dead leaf on that tree was clear as I was standing beside it. And around it all was some little blue lights and queer letters flashing in the margins meaning God knows what.

So I let out some slow breath and squeezed off a shot. And I saw a clump of dry leaves explode where my shot blew through them. And was from there I started to figure out how that scope done worked, see? Was a smart damn thing. When you looked at different targets—the tree, the hill, a rock closer on down the slope—that thing's focus changed all on its own what without no twisting or adjusting done. And there was a little cross in the middle of the lens, too—a little red X that moved up and down as you focused on something closer or farther away, left or right as the wind picked up or fell. So while that first shot was a waste, my second one drove home the nail. Blew a branch clean off. Then I took off a few more, for good measure. To make a point, see? Was blowing branches off a tree, up hill, into the sun, with a forty-four at more than—I don't know—a quarter mile. You understand, don't you? No? Well, take my word for it. That all makes for a might impressive rifle. And a right good shot at the trigger.

I pulled the gun off my shoulder and that scope let go as soft as a momma's kiss. I turned to the Green Man, smiling ear to ear like some kind of loon, only to find his back turned, knelt over the fire.

I don't know what he was playing at. I really don't. I never could figure some of the shit he done.

I shouted at him, "You wasn't even paying attention!"

He didn't look back at me, though. Just stared into that little fire. "Not as bad as I'd feared, girl," he said. "I suppose that'll have to do."

By God, that made me mad as all hell. I threw his fancy rifle to the dust and stomped toward him, shouting with every step. I remember hollering, "I ain't no goddamn girl! I got a damn name! It's Martha Jane Canary!" I yelled. I kicked dirt at him, trying to get him to turn around. But he just kept at that fire. "You ever going to ask that?" I barked at him. "Or was I just going to be 'girl' to you?"

He just pocketed a small metal box and poked the fire with a stick. Didn't pay me much mind at all. Was plumb maddening.

"I shot your damn tree! Shot it all to hell. Just like you asked," I hollered at his back. "Goddamnit! Turn around when I'm talking to you!"

"You talk too much," was all he said.

Oh, Jesus. A stream of nonsense spilled out of my mouth then—I don't know what I was saying. I watched him stand and turn around, slow as the Earth turning under the sun, it seemed. And I couldn't get a word out straight, I was so mad. I wanted to punch him in the damn face—except I couldn't reach that high. I wanted to scream until his head hurt from the power of it.

He just watched my tantrum. Like he was waiting for a train.

Finally, I closed my eyes and took a deep breath. He was getting under my skin. Had been all damn day. The way he didn't care Harthra was dead. The way he was willing to deal with Jeb. The way he didn't seem to care about nothing but some damn flying engine. It all just ate at me. Kept my fuse short.

"What is wrong with you?" I remember snapping at him, my chest still heaving.

He just looked at me. Smuggest damn look. "You done?" he asked.

That lit my fuse all over again, that did. I just blew up. "You know, I met Buffalo Bill once," I yelled. "He was a hell of a lot nicer than you!"

But the Green Man just nodded. Kept that damn cool of his. "He here now?" he asked.

I screamed and stomped toward Bess. I remember, was only then what I even noticed I was crying. Man it was a day for crying. I threw my arms over Bess's saddle and leaned on her. My only friend left, it seemed.

"What the hell do you want that flying engine for so bad?" I asked him, my face pressed into that saddle leather. The smell of it—the musk, I guess—was so soothing. Always has been. But I kept on him. "Why the hell is it so damn important?"

I heard him walking around behind me, back and forth between that small fire and his motionless horse.

A long time passed, I think. Then he said, half whispering, "I've seen the elephant. Seen all and more of your little world than I care to. I want no more of it." But he said it all quiet-like. Without any of that grit or gusto or spit he'd had about him all day.

"That's it then?" I muttered into the saddle.

He didn't say nothing. Said it all, I guess.

Seeing the elephant. Was bullshit, it was. I remember when we first set out, Daddy right staring into that setting sun, telling how we was going to follow it west. Was going to see all America had for a free man. See the elephant, he said. And damn if there wasn't some smile at that what showed them cracked teeth of his in that red light. And that path what led to the elephant, so full of hope and promise and tomorrow, was a right bloody path, it was. Lost my mama on it. My daddy, too. Saw my brothers and sisters turned out. Was even me about laid by, left lonesome on that road.

This green man? He ain't seen all. Not yet.

"You just want to go home," I said, barely loud enough for myself to hear.

"Don't you?" I heard him say. From far away, sounded like.

I remember feeling—not seeing, see—the sun dip behind the hill. A sudden cold swept over me. I remember my own spit wet between the saddle and my cheek. I remember Bess shifting back and forth a little bit, upset by my outbursts.

No sir. He ain't seen no elephant what I could reckon.

"Got nowhere to go," I whispered.

He was quiet for a while. Long enough for me to wonder at what I'd see when I turned around. Understand, all of a sudden, he didn't sound so tough. And I wasn't sure I wanted to see him like that. Not tough. I didn't know him from Adam but my revenge rested on him. My revenge needed him to be hard.

But he spoke up after a spell, quiet though it was. "Been on your world for a long time, Martha Jane," I heard him say. "Come here in '49, worked a claim, fought some Injuns, rustled some cattle. Even went east once." Then he paused for a long while. And when he spoke again, well, it sounded like Daddy talking over Mamma's grave. "Didn't work out like I'd hoped," he said. "Seen a lot more than I bargained for."

I turned away from Bess and looked at the Green Man standing across that fire from me. His duster and Stetson was gone, draped across the back of his horse. An Injun breastplate hung over his shirt, some bit of them Northern Virginia colors making a patch between broke bones and a kerchief hiding the top of it. Scars crawled up and down his bare arms. Some round and ragged like the holes I'd seen left in buffalo after we gunned them down. I swear he looked sad, then. Defeated, almost.

"So you're just going to quit it, then? Run home?" I asked him. "You think bad stuff ain't happening to everybody all the time? My momma died on the crossing. Buried on some Blackfoot hillside. My daddy barely got us to Salt Lake before he passed. My brothers and sisters got split up between a bunch of strangers and I got left all on my lonesome," I told him. "But I still ain't seen your goddamn elephant. Don't even know if I will." And, I'll admit, looking back on it now, I'm a might surprised them words come out of my mouth, what with what I'd seen that day. What with what I'd been through. But it was true. It's just like I told him, then. "You can't just quit the world."

"It's different," he told me. "This world's yours. You can't quit it."

And it's like I said. All of sudden, he didn't seem so tough. Seemed weak. And I didn't care for it. "Oh, but you can," I remember saying. "because you're a coward."

Now he didn't react like I would've expected a man to react at being called yellow. The Green Man just started laughing then. Laughing! Like a damn fool! See, he'd transformed again. Once from a killer to a coward and now into some kind of loon.

"You're something else, Martha Jane. Something I ain't come across before," he said between these deep, laughing breaths.

That got me to laughing too. His laughter, like his yelling, got into you until you was right soaked with it. So you couldn't help yourself. But it felt good. Light. I tell you, I hadn't felt like that in a long while.

I told him, "Maybe you need a few more independent women in your life, space man."

He chuckled even more at that, saying, "Maybe you're too independent for me."

"Ain't no such thing as too independent," I told him.

"Perhaps," he muttered, his laughter fading all slow.

Then he just watched me. Like he was seeing me for the first time all over again—and wasn't the last he looked at me like that, none, neither. Like I suddenly warranted his notice. "The men in town said you're pretty," I remember him saying. "That true?"

I looked away from him, at that. His look suddenly made me feel queer. Not like when Jeb or the other men in town looked at me, understand? Those looks made me want to crawl right out of my skin. No, the Green Man's look was different. Didn't make me feel bad at all. Made we worry about my braids and the dirt on my face and the shabbiness of my clothes. Made me wish I was wearing my best bib and tucker, or some such, not some torn dungarees and a bloodied flannel.

"This is hard country, space man." I told him. "These men see a girl about as often as they see a green skin, I reckon. Girl what ain't a whore, I mean."

"How old are you?" he asked me.

"Ain't no goddamn business of yours," I told him.

I looked back at him. He was watching me in the growing dark. Having that private talk up in his head.

"I reckon you're pretty, Martha Jane," he told me, his words like music.

"Well, maybe you won't think I'm so damn pretty after tomorrow. After I splatter that bastard Boone all over the Wyoming," I said, my voice shaking for no reason I could understand.

He just nodded and, after another long time looking at me, pointed at his bedroll. "Best you rest up, then," he said. "Now I know you can shoot, I'll need you rested, heeled, and ready come morning."

I eyed that single bedroll, nervous as all hell. Wasn't the first time I'd been offered a fella's bunk, see? Sure as shit not since Somers took me into his. But this felt different. I wasn't afraid or nothing. It's hard to explain. I still had my wits about me. But I told him, "I ain't sharing your bed, space man."

"I expect not," he said. Then he stepped toward me, firelight shining off that Injun breastplate and those guns, otherworldly and earthly, on each hip. And when he stood over me, I thought my heart might explode. I like to think that it was just nerves. I think we both knew we had a heap of trouble waiting for us in the morning. But I was just a girl. Might've been something else.

He handed me that metal disc I saw him get out of his saddlebags earlier. Handed it to me all gentle-like, like it could've hurt me if he pushed it too hard.

"When you're ready to sleep, this'll help."

"And you?" I asked him.

"I don't sleep," he said. All the time I was with him, he never proved that wrong.

And that was it. He pulled the saddle and bridle off Bess then grabbed his rifle off the ground, collected his coat and hat, and stalked off up the hill. Keeping watch. Without me, I expect he would kept on horseback all night. But this camp was for me. I don't think he knew, yet, what he was going to do with me. I didn't rightly know what I was doing with him, neither. But I knew—felt it in my bones—that I'd be dead if I weren't with him. Without my murdering angel stalking them hills above me.

But I was nervous. Worse than a cat in a room full of rockers. And after a while not being able to calm myself, I took the Green Man's advice. As I lay down, I put that metal disc beside me. A little blue light come on at one end, responding, it seemed, just to my thinking on it. I remember jumping as some soft music filled my head, drowning out the crackle of that fire, the wind, the strange noises of the night that might've kept me awake, on edge as I was. Was right beautiful, it was. A sound like gold, rising and falling like nothing I ever heard. Otherworldly music, I figured. Found out later it wasn't.

And there, I drifted off to sleep beside the fire, my mind whirling. Thinking on the Green Man and me on the prod, walking into Jeb's trap, fighting like Kilkenny cats at each other's back, a rifle in my hands, those pistols in his. Dreamt about revenge, I did. Sweet dreams, indeed.

SEVEN

I remember, I woke up slow. Those last dreams in that early morning were of the light shining down on me, warming me, through those big old sycamores we left behind in Missouri. And my mom, her copper hair, those plump cheeks all buried under freckles. She was like some bell ringing from far off. Calling me back east, or to Blackfoot, or God knows where.

I thought I heard a shot ringing through that space between dreaming and being awake. When I did open my eyes that morning, wasn't no old sycamore tree in sight. Nothing worth shooting at, neither. Just the Green Man's horse, standing fixed, all like one of them stuffed beasts they've got in them traveling shows. And Bess, tied off to it since there wasn't no proper tree or post for such. And the cold. God, it was some kind of terrible cold that morning. If it weren't for Somers showing up when he did, I reckon I would've just buried myself back down in the bedroll, sleeping until the sun broke over the hill.

Stirring awake as I was, and with that pink morning sky behind him, well, I thought Somers was a damn dream when I saw him coming down the hill toward me. What the hell else could he be. Wasn't no one damn fool enough to come crashing the Green Man's camp after what he did to Jeb's boys in the barn and on Main the day before.

But Tom Somers was a fool. And I told him so.

I remember him stumbling when he got to the bottom of the hill, scrambling across the dust toward me. By the time I got my wits, I had some words for him at the ready.

"Are you some kind of idiot," I hissed at him before he could even get a word out. "If the Green Man finds you here, he'll have you for goddamn breakfast. Lucky, that, if he just kills you. You hear what he did to Walker and Jimmy?"

Somers smiled that wry twist of his. Dumb as a hammer, he was, but he was fine as cream gravy. Used to stop my heart when he flashed them teeth of his. Hell, I quit the damn rail and put on a dress just to win him. Shame I didn't realize he was bunko until after he'd won me.

"Martha," I remember him sputtering, his breath all heaves and wheezes after his run and tumble down that long hill. But still he cracked that smile between speaking. "Martha, you got to shin out with me. You go into town with this green skin and Jeb's going to beef you right alongside him."

Now I told that boy, like the Green Man and I done talked about the night before, "I know full well Jeb'll be aiming to bushwack us."

Somers grabbed at my arm then, hauling on the same bruised skin Jimmy'd pulled at the day before. "Come on then," he said, fixing to drag me with him. "I can get you south to Fort Bridger," he promised. "Get you far off from this mess."

I yanked my arm back. I've never liked being handled. Ain't no good ever comes of it, if you ain't steering yourself. Like the Green Man said. Can't count on no man to save you. Best, then, to never need being saved, I figure.

"Get your hands off me," I snapped at him. "And you get out of here before the Green Man comes back and you die for thinking you was being brave."

Somers knelt by me, looking at me like I was a coot or some such. "Jeb ain't going to hunt you once he gets what he wants from this green fella. Just let me—"

Now that caught me, there. "What he wants?" I cut him off. "What does that mean?"

He shook his head. His hair was like gold, Somers' was. Shame.

"I don't understand any of this mess," he started. And I've no doubt he was right. Boy was lucky to know which end of his rifle to point away. And dumb enough not mention his wife until, well, too late for his own damn good.

That's when I saw the Green Man.

Somers kept on talking, I remember that. But I didn't hear a damn word he was saying and he was too simple to notice I wasn't listening. The Green Man crested the hill, dragging a body with him. But when he saw Somers leaning over me, well, he dropped that body and took off like a blast of wind, he did. Came hurtling down that long slope like an animal possessed, running toward me on all fours, boots and gloves biting into the dust and dirt and rock. By the time Somers heard the rush of him racing up from behind—well, I've told you already how fast the Green Man could be. He snatched the pistol right off Somers's waist with one arm while scooping and throwing him with the other. Sent Somers right end over end through the air. Like he'd thrown Jimmy—like a damn doll. Threw him right out into the open, away from me and the horses, and crouched over him, screeching this god-awful trill toward the sky.

I won't lie to you. Somers screamed out like a girl half my age what with that space man making that awful noise right on top of him. I didn't know what the hell was about to happen. The Green Man was sometimes more animal than man, moving like a wild cat or a savage—and just as cruel when he needed to be. Wanted to be, sometimes.

I shot up to my feet, then, but my mouth and mind failed me. I'm not often want for words, as I expect you're figuring, but here, I didn't know what to say or do. Was like watching the Green Man take aim at Jimmy all over again. Except Jimmy deserved it. Somers was a twit and a cheat, sure, but he never meant nobody, me least, no real harm.

The Green Man looked down at him, his breathing hard and hot, steaming in the cool morning air as it blew on Somers' blubbering face. He flashed his teeth and leaned down close. Sharp teeth, now. Shiny. Like the bones on that Injun breastplate.

Then he pulled his Bowie and made to use it. Thank God I found my voice right then. I'd never have forgiven myself if it hadn't come back just then.

"Stop!" I yelled at him. And when he showed no sign of listening, I kept on, yelling, "Put the goddamn knife down right now!"

He held that arm up high, the Green Man did. Ready to strike. Somers turned his pleading eyes on me.

"He's come to warn us," I hollered at the Green Man, fearing even then that he'd feel out the half-lie with some more-than-human sense of his. "Jesus fucking Christ," I kept on, "you can't just go on killing and maiming any old folk what show up unannounced or take you by surprise. You were dead to rights yesterday, I'll admit, but this morning you're looking like a damn yack."

"Wipe your chin, girl," the Green Man hissed.

"Wipe it your own damn self," I snapped back. "And don't fucking call me girl, again, lest you mean to make it the last thing you say."

Now I knew I was walking a pretty fine fucking line, right there. This same fella had unshucked a gun in my face just the day before. Threatened to put me down in the street what if I crossed him. But I'd seen him weak that night. I'd seen him tired. And I'll be goddamned if he didn't respond to a strong hand then and now. He holstered that knife slowly, menacing Somers with them teeth of his the whole while. But he did it.

The Green Man stood all sudden-like, yanking Somers up with him. The boy looked rough, there. Dirty, bloodied, scared like I ain't never seen him.

"He's just come to warn what Jeb's gunning for us," I told the Green Man again. "Ain't that right?" I said, throwing Somers a bone.

He nodded, then. There wasn't a trace of that flashy smile left on his face.

The Green Man led Somers back to me, sneering the whole while. "Waste of his damn time, coming to tell us that," he said through those sharp teeth of his. "One of Jeb's boys followed him from town to this here camp," he said. "Bastard led them straight to us." He threw Somers down at my feet, saying, "Tie this helpful son of a bitch up."

It's something to see a man brought down like that. Somers wasn't clever but he wasn't no lily, neither. From the first time I saw him? My! I wanted to be with him something awful. I never wanted no damn husband—let's make that clear right now, so you don't go writing no lies—but Somers sure could cut a swell with the ladies, what with them looks and the way he carried himself. To see him broke down like, blubbering and busted up so quick? Well, I don't think I ever saw no shine in him after that.

The Green Man threw me some rope then turned his back on me, busying himself with saddling the horses. Somers didn't fight or nothing. Just watched the Green Man's back, all fear and trembling.

I tied him up tight, I won't lie. But as I did, I leaned in close to his ear. Close enough, I hoped, so the Green Man wouldn't hear me.

"Keep your mouth shut," I whispered to him. "Don't say nothing else he might just pick you apart yet."

Somers nodded a little bit, eyes locked on the Green Man.

I left him there, tied up and sitting on the bedroll. I stepped up beside the Green Man just as he was fixing that Stetson back on his head, his stalks fitting in them notches cut out of the brim.

"So who was it, then, you caught prowling after Somers, before you come racing back into camp?" I asked him.

The Green Man looked back up at the cusp of the hill, toward the body he left lying up there.

"Ain't nobody, no more," he said.

I remember wondering if that body on the hill was one of those boys Jeb had with him in the saloon the afternoon before. Can't say I was too upset about it, if it were. Like I said before, it's something different if they deserve it. And those boys what shot up Harthra's place, killed him and his? Those boys what looked at me with them wicked eyes? I reckon they deserved whatever God or the Green Man had in store for them.

"Give me some bug juice," I told him.

He looked down on me, silent as a bird.

I pointed at Somers, though the Green Man didn't look.

"You shook him up right good," I told him. "Now give me some damn whiskey to calm his nerves."

The Green Man looked back at Somers then. "How do you know that one?" I remember him asking.

My heart caught up. Don't really know why I didn't want him to know about Somers. Just didn't. Didn't want him to think less of me for, well—for nothing I done before.

So I just said nothing. And I suffered under his black stare for what felt like hours. Those black eyes, slick and wet. I could see myself in them, small and shaking and holding out my hand for a fucking bottle of benzene.

But he did what I asked of him. Responded to my strong hand. Be sure you note that in your paper. I reckon there are plenty of biddies back in the Old States what might need to take a strong hand with theirs, too.

Might benefit from the lesson.

Well, he handed me some dusty stoneware from inside that box behind his saddle. Label spoke of places I ain't never heard of. But when I pulled the cork—damn! The stink of it hit me like a wall.

I knelt by Somers and put it to his shaking lips. Just one swig was all it took. Looked like he was choking for a minute. But then his eyes were clear and his wits fought their way back to the surface. Was like a man suddenly woke up. Woke up coughing.

The Green Man stood over us both, then. I remember him asking Somers all about where Jeb would be, how many men he'd be bringing, if the flying engine was where it was supposed to be. The boy didn't know much. But what he knew settled the Green Man some.

Then the Green Man took one of them long pauses. The kind where he was having that talk with himself. Figuring to kill Somers or not, I reckoned, what that he couldn't follow us or escape and warn Jeb we was the wiser. But, truth be told, Somers wasn't one of Jeb's boys. Didn't reckon there was nothing to fear at all from this one.

The Green Man set his hand on his pistol, then cocked his head, watching Somers like the way saddle hands watch colts in a pen. No, the Green Man wasn't thinking to kill him. Turns out he was thinking something else all together.

So the Green Man asked him, "You got a wife? You got kids?"

The damn fool's eyes flashed toward me, just for a second. Long enough to make my heart leap. Then he struggled out, "Yes. Yes sir. In Denver."

The Green Man nodded. Oh, I knew he saw that glance Somers made. The yack!

"What's her name?" he asked Somers, his stalks bent close, feeling for a lie. God, I wish he'd found one.

Somers choked on his words at first, looking on me with a good, long, pleading stare. Bastard told me he was married just once and I was out of the room before he could get his next breath out. I didn't want to know no goddamn details. And when those boys on the rail found out I'd been bedded by a married man? Well, that's how come I ended up with Mister Harthra, see? Had to hide myself away from being branded a whore or worse. Had to hide myself off from the leers of men like Jeb and Jimmy, thinking I was all ripe for pirooting. Bad enough I'd given into to some pretty boy up from the fort. I remember thinking, back then, what it couldn't get no worse than all that.

But it could. And it did. That son of a bitch looked right up at the Green Man and said his wife's name. I swear to God he did.

Bastard told him her name was Martha. And fuck me—the Green Man just nodded.

I didn't know what I'd just heard. I couldn't get it straight in my head, at first. I just whispered back to him—saying it to myself, "Martha . . ."

Somers had that pleading look again. Only he wasn't pleading for help now. Pleading for mercy's more like it. The Green Man just stepped back, watching to see how I'd move.

"Sorry," Somers squeaked out.

Fuck him.

I lunged at him, knocking him flat. "Are you kidding me?" I screamed down at him.

He just closed his eyes and turned away.

No. I never saw no shine in him after that.

The Green Man just stood there, all smug. Did that green bastard know what he was courting when he asked them questions? Had he felt out the damn answer with that mind of his?

"How'd you say you knew this one?" he asked me.

"Shut your cock holster!" I barked at him. Then, not really thinking, I hauled that old dusty bottle to my lips and threw a full splash of the brown stuff down my throat. God! I'm no stranger to whiskey but this stuff burned the piss right out of me. Burned the sense right out, too.

I thrust the bottle back at the Green Man and stomped past him toward Bess. Wasn't going to give either of them no damn satisfaction, at that.

"Damn," he said to me, watching me go. Watching me like he'd never seen a fifteen-year-old girl with her back up. I remember him telling me, "this stuff is strong enough to float a colt."

"Well, bend an elbow, then. Or stop your yammering and mount up," I told him. I leapt right onto Bess, jerked my Springfield out, and laid it across my lap. Watching Somers all tied up on the ground down there, I'd half a mind to shoot it all. Shoot the whole damn world. With the hot whiskey still stinging in my throat, burning out through my nose, I was ripe to breathe fire. Burn the whole of Piedmont if it meant getting my revenge.

I still regret ever thinking that.

The Green Man mounted up, that long Henry across his lap. And he was watching me. Thinking on me. Debating. Well, I didn't have time for all that no more.

I started off for town, for the kilns. Where Jeb told us he and that flying engine would be. Where Somers told us the trap was waiting.

I was a dumb girl. I know it. Knew it then, I expect. But I was madder than hell. Felt like I'd been mad forever. I remember yelling back to the Green Man as we left Somers behind, "Let's go get your goddamn ship. Jeb's waiting and you and him got yourselves that devil's bargain." I told him, "And I hope like hell you shoot him when you see him this time. Like you should've shot him yesterday."

EIGHT

We rode in silence. Not saying a word at one another lest we set some kind of bomb off. I just kept thinking on him and Somers. On the words what come out of both their mouths. I felt like a goddamn fool.

But wasn't long until we could see them kilns north of town and all them self-pitying thoughts went right out of my head. Them kilns rose like little mountains from the plain, only they belched smoke like those volcanoes in stories. Like the brimstone God sent down on Sodom, I reckon. But instead of smothering sin, these kilns fueled it—satisfying the appetites of old Moses Boone and that wicked son of his. I remember caressing my Springfield then, the cold metal barrel wet with dew. I wanted to feed Jeb to them kilns so goddamn bad. Wanted to watch him smolder in that fire like the damned.

We come at them kilns away from town, with the sun behind us. That was the Green Man's idea, I guess. He led the way. Best to have Jeb and his boys blinking into the sun what if they had a mind to pick us off. But I expect the Green Man knew it wasn't going to go down that way. I expect he knew Jeb would want to yammer on and on, first. Expect he was counting on it. And, for my part, I kept thinking on how Somers said Jeb wanted something from the Green Man. I couldn't help thinking it had to be something more than the price they'd wagered.

We stopped a ways out from the kilns. Took it all in. Bess was skittish as hell, if I remember right. But the Green Man's horse might been made of wood it was so still. So was he. Still as a damn corpse.

He broke the silence, though. "I need you to keep your wits now, Martha Jane," he told me. "No flying off the handle. No losing your cool."

He didn't look at me. Just kept his eyes on them kilns. Me, though? I watched him like a hawk. I suddenly hated the sound of my own name coming out of his mouth. And I couldn't help wondering if he really was my murdering angel. Or if he'd sell me down the damn river for that flying engine of Harthra's. I mean, what was I to him, after all. Just a girl. Some weak human girl what got in the way of his exodus.

Well, he slid his Henry into its sleeve, between his leg and saddle, and pulled his duster up over his pistols. "If that friend of yours is right," he started saying, without a wit of irony, "and if this is a trap, then you let me handle it. And if we get to shooting, you get hid. You get quiet."

I corrected the Green Man right there. "Somers ain't no friend of mine."

He looked at me, then. "I reckoned," he said. Then he asked me, "so why spare him, then?"

I did my best to keep my cool, like he said. I needed my wits. Needed sand in my belly, not knots over some bunko what loved me for a minute then hightailed when he remembered his wife.

"He don't deserve dying," I told him.

The Green Man just nodded. Reckon he wasn't so sure.

"Don't start nothing here, Martha," he told me. "They might mean to bushwack us but I mean to know some things, first."

I know I was sneering, at that. Thinking on making a deal with Jeb made me madder than thinking on Somers and his wandering pecker. "Going to use that voice of yours on Jeb and his?" I asked him. "Like you done used on them boys in the barn or at Good's? Lay them low or make them do your thinking. Seems if I could make men do what I wanted, reckon I might do that right often."

The Green Man just scoffed at me, then. Said, "Seems you've no trouble making men act all queer, all your lonesome. You use that weapon right often, do you?"

"Fuck you," I whispered at him, my heart plumb racing and angry.

He just nodded, keeping them eyes and stalks trained on them kilns and else. "No. Some you put to the bullet. Some to the tongue. Reckon we'll have to see, yet, which way this is going to turn."

I snapped at the Green Man, then, telling him, "Well don't take too damn long with your deal, space man. Jeb's sharp and I'm on the prod."

"You just hold your horses and I reckon we'll both get what we want," he told me.

Well, I let him lead the way down by them kilns toward that big old woodshed where Jeb said that flying engine would be waiting. It was on the far side, see, toward town. And from the side we was coming, couldn't see no engine or Jeb and his boys or nothing. Just the shimmer of heat from the kilns and the smoke of unborn charcoal.

But as we rounded the first of the three big kilns I saw the Green Man's stalks stand straight as telegraph poles. Then I saw what caught him. One of Jeb's waddies was waiting by the third kiln and, when he done saw us, ducked out of sight. They knew we was coming, now. But the Green Man never slowed down. Never unshucked his guns, neither. He just kept on moving ahead, hunting for trouble.

When we come around that last kiln, the Green Man made sure to stand out of its shadow, the sun blinding at his back. And there, coming round the front of that big woodshed, was Jeb and half a dozen of his boys just like Somers told us there'd be. Now I never put my gun away, see, like the Green Man had. Needed to hold on to it. To know I had it when the time come. And I swear, I wanted to put it to my shoulder right then, snap Jeb's head right off. But I wasn't no loon. I did what the Green Man asked. I kept my cool. I'd give him a spell to do what he needed before I collected my revenge for Harthra and the boys.

"I'm right surprised to see you," I remember Jeb squeaking as he pulled up at the edge of the woodshed. "Thought you might've skedaddled with that little prize of yours," he said, eyeing me like a damn animal. "Or maybe I thought you'd have an accident on your way back into town."

His boys laughed at that. Laughed at the thought of him and me lying dead at our camp. Was the laughter of monsters, I think. Not men.

The Green Man didn't move a lick. Just stared at Jeb with those bottomless eyes of his. Just waited for the laughter to fade. And when Jeb's smile faded with it, the Green Man let the corner of his mouth creep up. Wry as shit, he could be.

"I should thank you for breakfast," he told Jeb.

I squeezed my Springfield tight in my hands, pressing the side of the barrel and the stock against my thighs. I remember expecting bullets to fly any second.

Jeb shook his head, speechless. But the Green Man didn't make him wait. See, he kept on goading him, saying, "That fellow you sent round my camp this morning, he was delicious. Wouldn't stop screaming though."

Now I knew the Green Man wasn't no cannibal—not that I'd seen—but I'm guessing Jeb wasn't so sure. He started to shake and just about stood in his saddle, pointing at the Green Man and screaming, "You don't fucking threaten me. You're outnumbered."

But the Green Man, he just looked down the line of Jeb's waddies and said, "Not sure that I am."

Shit! I remember Jeb looking at his boys then. Looked like he suddenly wasn't so fucking sure, neither. But I think he was in too deep to do anything but finish what he'd started. Damn fool had courted calamity from the beginning, with Harthra, with me, and now with the Green Man. He'd pushed it all right up to the edge of the cliff. And damn if the look on his face that morning didn't say all that. Said he already knew how this was going to end.

"Where's the ship?" the Green Man asked, his hands in his lap, close to those pistols under his coat.

"Where's the payoff?" Jeb asked back, shaking a little bit.

The Green Man's hand went into his coat. I remember all them pale-faced hands riding with Jeb just about shot us down then, twitchy as they was. But the Green Man come up with that purse of his, not them pistols.

Jeb nodded. And he pointed around the side of the woodshed. But he didn't make a move toward us to get the Green Man's little purse. He and his boys just stood like a wall between us and where that flying engine was tucked away.

My heart was beating so fast and hard what my ribs ached from the thud of it. Like the stomp of a thousand spooked buffalo. Or of one terrified girl, turns out.

But, damnit if the Green Man didn't just start forward, toward Jeb and his waddies. I tried to keep Bess as close on him as I could—closer than I'd ride behind any other horse but that queer mount of his. And as we passed by Jeb, I couldn't breathe. I couldn't blink or nothing. I just kept my eyes fixed on the Green Man's waist, waiting to see that coat blow back and them pistols come up shooting. Damn, my hand hurt from squeezing my rifle so tight.

But the Green Man didn't shoot. He didn't slow down. He just held out that little purse as he passed Jeb by and, as their hands come together, the Green Man let that pouch slip a moment too soon. Jeb tried to grab it out of the air and missed, nearly falling under our horses as he reached out. God, how I would've loved that. After all his posturing and shooting, for that bad egg to be trampled under by that queer mount and Bess.

The Green Man never looked back as we rode through Jeb's line. He only had eyes for the other side of the woodshed and the promise of Harthra's flying engine, there. And I kept close on him, believe me, but I also kept an eye back on Jeb. Man, he was cursing, swearing like a fucking mutton-puncher who done lost his flock, barking orders at one of his boys to get down and pick up the Green Man's purse.

Just about ran into the back of the Green Man's horse, looking back the way I was. He done stopped all sudden-like right around the edge of that woodshed. Hard to explain the look I saw on his face, then. From the side, I couldn't tell if he was in pain or ready to bust out laughing. Them stalks on his head stood straight up, three feet out of his Stetson, and his eyes bulged like they was being squeezed deep inside his skull.

See, right there in front of us, there was Harthra's flying engine.

Now, I didn't know nothing about them flying engines. What little I knew, I'd been told by Harthra's boys who'd seen him fly that thing around the ranch once or twice. But I didn't have to know nothing to know what the Green Man and I'd come across was all a cropper.

See, that flying engine wasn't like no stage or riverboat, now. It was all metal. Like one of them ironclads. Or a war wagon, maybe. Except it wasn't all cold and gray. Was sandy, almost the color of your skin. If anything, it looked liked some kind of bug. Its round body had these fat wings sticking out from the top of it. And it bulged in the middle and tapered as it pointed toward the ground. For the life of me, I didn't see no doors or windows on the whole damn thing. No man ever made nothing like this.

But ignorant as I was, I could see something wasn't right. Green Man sure as shit could. Remember, I told you Jeb and his boys had led that ship off by horse, dragging that floating thing across town. And God knows what they'd done in the meantime but one side of the ship was all black and ugly. Against that sandy metal skin, looked like a goddamn wound gone foul.

The Green Man's senses must've come back to him, then. He dropped off his horse and walked right up to the ship.

"What did you do?" he asked, his voice all distant. Like he was talking to himself.

Jeb didn't smile or nothing. He and his boys come up behind us, see? Walled off the open side of the shed, aiming to block the Green Man and me inside with that engine, I reckon.

"The boys and I couldn't figure out how to get inside the damn thing," I remember him saying.

The Green Man ran his finger along a black edge on the ship. The metal was all bent and torn like skin around a cut.

"What did you do?" he just repeated to himself, barely above a whisper. Was like watching a fuse burn down, watching him with that thing. Like watching a man standing under a noose.

Jeb never stopped talking though. I don't know if the Green Man heard him or not but the fool kept on talking, saying, "We looked all over for a damn door or whatnot. Then we tried to cut our way in. Nothing even made a damn scratch. Nothing until the dynamite, anyways."

The Green Man didn't say a word at this. Just kept stroking the ship's wounds.

"I expect we damaged it," Jeb said, then. "Now, we need you to fix it."

I was watching the Green Man when I heard the sound of a half-dozen guns being cocked. Jeb and his boys dropped off their horses, see, and leveled their pistols and rifles on the Green Man. Not one spared a barrel for me. Damn, guess I should've been pleased at that.

"Now you're going to fix this ship, green skin," Jeb told him. "You'll fix it and you'll show us how to fly it. I got plans, see? Plans for this ship what don't include you taking it back to God knows where."

The Green Man reached into a black scar on the side of the thing. The look on his face reminded me of the look on that Blackfoot doc when he was talking 'bout my mama. Like the way that Salt Lake doc had when he come to see me about my pa.

"I can't fix this, you fucking yack," the Green Man said, his back still turned on Jeb and his men. "Ain't no place on Earth what can fix this ship after what you done."

"But you will fix it," Jeb told him. "I need this ship. Daddy made his fortune on the railroad, see? Now he can ship cattle to St. Louis or Chicago in just a couple days. But with this ship? well, I can have cattle in New York by nightfall."

"You yack!" the Green Man screamed. God! He just about knocked me off my horse with that one. The words banged around in my head like shoes around a peg. Must've gotten into Bess' head, too. I had to fight something awful just to keep her from bucking me and fagging off. And Jeb's boys? Shit. They was all a might disturbed by it, grabbing at their heads and squeezing their eyes tight to quiet the noise in their skulls. Their horses took off running, spooked and swinging their heads around like they was suddenly made wild again.

"No one can fix this," the Green Man kept on yelling. "Not me. Not Harthra. Not no one. You blew it up. Right up the fucking spout! What the fuck did you think dynamite would do?"

Now I'll admit it. I was scared. The Green Man had been hunting down this ship since he come to Piedmont. It was why he went looking for Jeb in the first place. Why he'd kept me on. But if what he was saying was true? Damn. Ain't nothing scarier than someone with nothing.

Jeb was half bent over, clutching at his head. But he was madder than hell. He pointed his pistol at the Green Man and did his best to yell over the screaming in his brain. "You'll either fix it or I'll beef you, space man. I'll beef you right here." He hollered to his men and, once they'd leveled their guns on the Green Man again, he kept on, saying, "You'll fix it or you're dead. Got that? You green folk . . . You're just like us. Put a gun to your head and you'll do just about anything to keep that gun from shooting. Ain't that right, you green fuck? Fix it!"

Was right then, with the noise in my head finally dying down and Bess finally cooling under me, what I saw the Green Man's hands let go of that gaping wound in the side of that ship. Saw his fingers relax. Saw his long feelers drop down, curled close to his skull.

Was right then, too, I realized I was the only person still on a horse— that I sat up all high up on my Bess, like a goddamn target ready to be shot.

Well, shit. I bent down against the saddle, my Springfield held fast against my chest, and rolled off away from Jeb and his boys. Looking back on it, I expect I saved the Green Man right then. All them boys with their guns on him, they turned to watch me tuck and fall off Bess like I was full as a goddamn tick. And in that moment, the Green Man's jacket must've billowed out because he come up with them pistols. Now, I didn't see what happened. I just banged flat on the ground like I'd been grassed, the wind knocked right the fuck out of me. But I heard his Colt ringing out. And I heard that big Green gun of his shake the damn shed like a cannon.

All hell broke loose. I rolled away from Bess even as I heard her bolt. So many shots echoed through that shed, I don't know, still, who was shooting what. But when I scrambled back up to my hands and knees, well, two of Jeb's boys lay nearabout where they'd been standing moments before. One of them was clutching as his chest and crying. The other? I tell you truly now, wasn't no sign of his head. No blood about the neck, no mess about the ground. Just a burnt stump on his shoulders. I swear to God.

I scrambled beside that flying thing and pressed myself up against it. Jeb and one of his boys was crouched behind a woodpile not far away. They was shooting at something I couldn't see—the Green Man, I reckon. It was started. And, to be honest, there wasn't no fear in me, then. It was like after that first shot at that pecker wood the night before, with the Green Man's Henry—everything seemed so in focus. I knew what I had to do.

But before I could get my Springfield up to my shoulder, I got jumped. Was that toothless fellow what grabbed me outside Good's the day before. Only now with an awful scar across his face where the Green Man planted that shovel handle into him. He grabbed hold of my rifle and wrestled me to the ground, pressing me into the corner were that ship almost touched the dirt.

I fought with him for a second. Fought hard as I could to hold onto that gun. But he swung hard and punched me in the side of the face. I'd turned away on seeing the fist coming but, God, it shook my brain up. Enough for him to get the rifle out my hands and throw it off into the dust. And there I was again, on the ground, held fast under some man who meant me no damn good. I remember seeing the rafters and that toothless fella's silhouette through hazy eyes. Was like I'd seen Jimmy the day before. I might've been right back there in Harthra's barn.

That toothless bastard grabbed up both my wrists close to his chest and was hauling me off the ground, see? But soon as my eyes cleared and my wits come back, I pulled myself up on him—pulling myself right up close to him. And, well, thank Jesus I still had my teeth. I turned my head right into the side of his and bit down on his ear like a fucking bear trap. Then I just went nuts, swinging my elbows and knees and body as much as could. I was an animal. I was a monster. I could taste blood in my mouth, feel hair between my teeth. I could hear that mudsill's screams in my ears even as his tore off in my mouth like a leather poke.

I crashed to the ground and spat that bit of him right back at his feet. Oh God, he hollered like nothing I'd heard before, clutching at the side of his bleeding head with this look of horror that, well, I ain't ashamed to admit I plumb liked.

He pulled his gun on me, yelling some curses—what I don't recall. I was crazed, see? All my hate over these last few days, all the anger I had toward Jeb or Jimmy or Somers, it all spilled out on this toothless waddy. This creature what twice now tried to grab a hold of me. And I was so sick of being grabbed at. So goddamn sick of it.

I closed the gap between us before he could raise that pistol. I grabbed hold of his wrist with both hands and I sunk my teeth right into his flesh, gnashing and tearing like a fucking savage. He pulled at my hair but not before I ripped open his wrist and sent that gun of his to ground ahead of a gush of blood. He let go of me then and I fell on that pistol of his. His screaming was music to my damn ears. Like the symphony what lulled me sleep the night before. Was beautiful.

I come up fast as I could with that revolver. He was a mess, that toothless mudsill. Gushing blood from his head and arm. I put that gun to him like I should done Jimmy. Like I'd done Jeb a thousand times in my mind's eye.

Expect he saw the elephant right then. expect he saw it good.

I don't know how many times I shot him. Never shot a man before and the whole thing, then as now, seemed a dream. Like someone else done it. And before I woke up, he was flat out in front of me, spilling his stain all over the damn dirt.

But I didn't linger on it. I ran out from behind that flying engine, set on putting a bullet through Jeb what if I could. But he was nowhere to be seen. Instead, I remember seeing another of his boys running toward the kilns, screaming and begging. And I saw the Green Man. But before that boy got two steps what I could see, I heard the Green Man's queer pistol ringing out and I saw a flurry of red glowing shot blow that boy apart. Chewed him right the hell up. God, that gun could make a mess of a man.

Now, the Green Man stopped in his tracks when he saw me. Damn. What a sight I must've been—enough blood on my face and down my shirt for two men, I expect. I got that self-conscious feeling again. This wasn't what a girl was supposed to look like. Not like some damn rabid animal.

But I forgot those thoughts in a flash, I tell you. Forgot them right quick when I saw Jeb step out from behind the side of a kiln, behind the Green Man. The world just stopped right then. Cold and quiet. And before I could yell, that bastard shot him. He shot the Green Man right in the goddamn back. Was like a fucking nightmare. The Green Man's shirt bellowed and split where the bullet blew through his gut. And those long feelers of his just sank. His legs gave out. He fell to his hands and knees, dropping his Colt as he went down, still clutching that queer gun but unable to lift it. And blood, silver blood as shiny as quicksilver started out of his belly.

I threw down the toothless man's pistol and ran over to the Green Man's horse. That animal stood still and calm. Hadn't moved a step despite all the screaming and shooting. Was like there wasn't no damn row kicked up around it or nothing. Like its master hadn't just taken a bullet in the gut. And there, tucked into the saddle, I found the Green Man's Henry.

Thinking back on it, I'm not sure if I was crying or not. My heart was swollen and hurt, though. God, I didn't know what I'd do if—well—if the Green Man died. If Jeb walked out of this.

I crouched by that horse and set myself up just like I had when shooting that pecker pole the night before. I scrambled to get that gun up to my eye and to find that son of a bitch in its scope before he could put another bullet through the Green Man.

My hands were cold and clumsy, and my whole body was shaking, but I got that rifle up. That scope reached out and cupped my eye, just as before, and looking through that lens I found them, the one standing over the other. But before I could get my sights on Jeb, before I could steady myself at all, I saw him reach down and grab the Green Man's head by them stalks. Pull him up, blocking my shot.

And through that scope, I could hear their breathing all loud, like I was standing right there with them. I could hear Jeb sneering and spitting at the Green Man. I remember, clear as I remember this morning, Jeb saying to him, "This work out like you wanted? This worth a goddamn die-up? Worth your life and that of your little whore?"

The Green Man's face? Oh God, it was all twisted and pained. I was frantic to try to get a shot off. To beef that son of a bitch before he finished the Green Man. But I had no shot, understand? Nothing I wasn't sure wouldn't take the Green Man's head off with it.

So I had to stand there and endure that fucking scene. Had to watch Jeb stand over my Green Man. Had to listen as he fought to get words out, rasping as silver blood bubbled up at his lips. Was awful.

I heard him tell Jeb, "You should've given me the ship. Should've been more careful."

Jeb twisted the Green Man's feelers and pressed that pistol into the side of his head. And I heard him ask, "What you want off this world for, green skin? Want to tell me that before I butcher you like I butchered Harthra? What you done that you got to run from?"

I don't know how I knew it, right then, but the Green Man was looking right at me. Right down the barrel of that rifle, through them damn lenses. I could feel those black eyes on me.

And that's when I heard him say, "Nothing I done until now."

Was right then he twisted out of Jeb's grip and dropped flat to the ground. And I didn't waste a breath. I put a bullet right through Jeb's chest. I remember seeing his blood spray out. Watching his smug look fade and his face go white. If I close my eyes right now, I can still see it.

I ran out from behind the horse toward the Green Man, desperate and afraid for the first time since the bullets started flying. And as I ran close, the Green Man struggled to his feet and stood over Jeb. He kicked Jeb's gun away and just stared at him, debating in that head of his. But he didn't debate long. The Green Man was many things, see? And one of them things was cold. Cold as the Sierra. Cold as the devil. Strange as it is to think on, I don't think any of this was personal for him until he saw that ship fouled up. Not when he saw Harthra dead or even when Somers told us what this meeting was a trap. But now? Wasn't even God what could help Jeb Boone.

I remember seeing Jeb laying there, begging. And I remember seeing the Green Man reach down and snatch that little purse of his out of Jeb's coat. Then I saw him point that big queer gun at Jeb's face. I didn't yell for him to stop.

"The ward of heaven won't know you," I heard him say. And he pulled the trigger.

Was an awful thing to see. Awful to hear. Now, don't get me wrong. I know Jeb deserved everything he got—know it as sure as I know anything. But that don't really change it. Was a terrible thing the Green Man did there, no matter if the bastard deserved it or no. It's awful the things we do to one another.

And that was it. They was all dead. While I was fighting that toothless bastard, the Green Man beefed them all—Jeb at the last. And he took a bullet for his trouble.

I followed him back to the woodshed. He was hobbling, clutching at that weeping wound in his belly, but he only had eyes for that flying engine.

"Go get your horse," he told me.

I started to say something—don't remember what—but he cut me off.

"Go!" he snapped. I felt that word in my head. In my chest. I stopped fast, unable to fight it.

Without thinking I went running off, past them kilns and woodpiles. I could already hear a commotion rising in town. There wasn't much time for us to light a shuck out of there.

But I come running up on Bess right soon, thank God. She'd run out past the farthest kiln as soon as I'd dropped off her. Expect I scared her some, what with the look of me, then. I wasn't that same girl what rode west from St. Louis with her no more. I didn't know it yet but I reckon she did.

I led her back toward the woodshed, careful not to come up on the Green Man too fast. I didn't know what he might've become through all this. And I was careful to keep quiet. I just stood there watching him leaning against the front of that flying thing, a bulging round nose of sandy metal. He leaned his open palm against it, eyes closed, head down. And as I watched, that ship come to life. Lights glowed out from between breaks in the metal and a gentle humming filled the woodshed, like the sound of a train real far off. But smoke come out it, too. And an angry thumping from the wounded side of the thing.

I remember, the Green Man shook his head at that. His whole body slumped against the engine. I swear, I worried that he was dying right there with it. Maybe he was, a little bit. But then he stood back and drew out that big queer gun of his. Didn't say a word.

I backed away, then. I tell you, I didn't know what was going to happen. But that ship, being what it was—which is God knows what, really—I didn't want to be too close if things wasn't right. If they was going to get worse. I'd seen an engine after a boiler blew, once on. And that was just a train to San Francisco, not to the damn stars.

The Green Man pointed that big gun of his into one of the ship's open wounds and pulled the trigger. Pulled it over and over again. Smoke and fire leapt out of that hole and that humming stuttered and screeched and grew loud as a stampede. That whole damn engine shuddered and shook like a rattle.

He finally turned away from the ship and mounted that cool horse of his. I jumped on Bess fast as I could and followed him away from the shed and the kilns and the blood and the town. He didn't say a word as we rode back to our camp. Just clutched his stomach and hung his head. He didn't even flinch when an explosion rocked the ground beneath our feet and sent a cloud towering toward heaven. Wasn't nothing to say.

NINE

We rode back the way we'd come. Along the same trail. In the same quiet.

We come up over the hill, right next to that pecker pole I shot to pieces the evening before. I remember looking down on that small camp. I swear, it was like stumbling along someone else's spot. Didn't feel to me like I'd ever been there before. Not in this life, anyways.

The Green Man sat slumped in his saddle, clutching at that oozing wound in his gullet. But damn if he didn't made no effort to bandage himself up. Just grimaced and grabbed at it with his free hand. But didn't seem like he was on the verge of dying or nothing. Seemed awful hurt, don't get me wrong. He was shot through. But whatever them green folks is made of is stronger stuff than God made you and me from, mister. In all my days with the Green Man I saw him take some awful abuse. And don't think that this gunshot was near the worse of it. Oh, I didn't rightly know it then, to be sure. But snarl as he might, that son of a bitch was going to live. After all that happened to that flying thing he was so set on, I'm not sure he wanted to or not. But he wasn't going to kick it that day.

I remember him leading me and Bess down between them hills to our little camp. The black earth where he'd set a fire for me still steamed and the bedroll still wore a dent where my hips cut into it. And, sure as shit, Somers was still there, bound hand and foot, unable to shin out after we left for them kilns. Was like we hadn't been gone more than an hour. Maybe we hadn't. Sure seemed like a long damn time to me, though. Like a lifetime ago I woke on that mat.

Somers struggled to face us, tied up as he was. But we hadn't gagged him. My mistake at that. I remember him twisting my way and saying, "Martha!" God, that name just cut right through me like a fucking knife when he said it. "Thank Jesus you come back," he said.

The Green Man didn't look at him. Just pointed at a few scattered odds and ends on the ground.

"Pack your plunder. We can't stay here."

And, sure as the day is long, a deep boom rumbled over the hills from town, as if that dying engine needed to help make the Green Man's point. It'd all gone to pieces. The whole damn thing. Wasn't no one back in Piedmont what would shelter me now.

I remember looking at that stuff on the ground. The bedroll, the disc what played music, the whiskey. I didn't recognize any of it. I remember shaking my head and telling the Green Man, "I ain't got nothing."

The Green Man nodded and slid off his saddle, wincing as his feet hit the dirt. I thought he was dropping down to get that bedroll, see, but he pulled out that Colt of his and put it right to Somers's head. The boy tried to squirm away from him but there wasn't nothing he could do to keep the Green Man from putting a bullet in his brain.

"No," I told the Green Man. I didn't scream. Just kind of whispered to him. I know he'd hear me. That he'd lower that gun.

"There's been enough killing for today," I told him. And the Green Man? He put that gun down. Shucked it slow, snarling in pain a little as he bent at the waist to get his hand at the holster. Then he knelt down, grabbed up the bedroll and that music disc and stepped right back up onto that queer horse of his.

Somers, that poor bastard, he was shaking and pale. Like I'd seen him earlier. He didn't look like no kind of man down there, hog-tied and blubbering.

But he looked right up at the Green Man and stuttered out, "Ain't you going to untie me?"

The Green Man looked down on him, menacing, see? Those black eyes of his shutting Somers right up.

"I didn't shoot you, did I?" the Green Man told him.

Somers couldn't say a word back at that. He just froze up. At least until he gave me one last look and let slip a small, pathetic whimper. "Martha,"

I remember him saying. Martha. What are the goddamn odds at that, huh? His wife and all? No wonder he never said nothing about her.

I just turned my horse away, set to follow the Green Man off. But before I left, I told that bunko, "Don't you ever say my name again."

And, by God, if we didn't just leave Somers like that, tied up, miles from town, where no one with any sense would ever think to look for him. At the time, I was numb. His crying as we rode off didn't even make me look back. Ain't that cold? Here, just a day before, I'd fussed over the Green Man shooting Jimmy. Just that morning I was even frantic to save Somers. But then, as I rode off? Well, could've been my own daddy calling out for help there and I don't know if I would've turned back.

No. Now I need to wrap this bit of tale on up, eh? Probably got more than enough for your paper already. If you think your readers will stomach a story like this from an old bat like me. This ain't like your normal western, I guess. No posse or sheriff and certainly no rough riders conquering steeds and savages. Not like the stories I could tell you of me and Bill Hickok. But that was a lot later. And you did come asking about the Green Man in particular, didn't you?

Well, the Green Man and I took a wide ride around Piedmont, keeping the town out of sight over the hills but noting where it was, see, by the tower of smoke coming up out of it, rising almost to the clouds. And somewhere along that ride, I found myself in the lead, what with the Green Man following Bess and me.

So I led us back to Harthra's ranch—to the scene where I think we started this here story. Where the Green Man and I first met, him pulling Jimmy off me in that dreadful fucking barn. I tell you, when we got back to that ranch, there, I couldn't bring myself to go near that barn. Wasn't scared of it, none. But I think I was worried that something in there would remind me of the girl I was the day before. Some little girl what needed saving. And here I was now, that toothless man's blood still all down my chin and shirt, with sand enough in my belly for any comers. Seems to me, I wasn't the same girl at all no more.

So we spent the afternoon burying the boys and watching the smoke billowing up from town. I ain't never seen a fire burn like that. I reckon the Green Man got that ship of Harthra's to blow up like some goddamn dynamite. And from what I saw later, as we rode out of town, it took the

kilns out with it. Then the town. I swear, you go get yourself a map and
see if you can find Piedmont, Wyoming. You won't hit no pay dirt hunting
for that one, I promise you.

By the time the sun was dropping out of the sky, we'd only Harthra
left to bury. I remember coming out of the house, fetching something
to cover the poor bastard's burnt face with, and finding the Green Man
standing on the porch. Those black eyes, like oil, see, reflecting that wicked red sky. I watched his eyes follow that column of smoke rising above
them exploding kilns. Watched his long feelers twitch with every little
movement Bess made, tied up off the end of the porch as she was. And
damn if that Green Man wasn't still bleeding a trickle.

"You should let me dress that," I told him. "Harthra ain't going nowhere. There'll be plenty of time to dig that hole come morning."

I remember the Green Man looking down at Mister Harthra, his
shot-up clothes, his face burned away. Was like he was seeing him for
the first time.

He hopped down off the porch and put his foot to the shovel. Each
scoop with that damn spade looked like it was shooting pain through
his whole body. Might as well have been digging his own grave, I guess.

So I watched the smoke for a while. I'd lived in that town for months,
understand, and what with it now gone down the flume? Shit, I don't even
feel bad about it now.

When the Green Man was almost done digging Harthra's hole, I
remember mumbling to him, "I don't goddamn understand it." I asked
him, "what'd you do it for?"

He stopped digging, then. Just for a minute, see? And I swear I could
see him looking all far off. Farther than that long road ahead of us. Farther
than that long road behind him, from California and the War and God
knows where else. Jesus, farther still than all that black sky separating the
Green Man from his home. Was like he was in a trance.

He shook his head and rolled Harthra into that hole. "Guess it ain't
time for me to quit this world," he said, more to himself than me.

I saw him drop that little purse of his into the hole before he covered
Harthra up.

Then he used an old lamp from the kitchen to set the whole ranch
up, putting fire to the house, the shed where that ship used to keep, and

touching it to the hay inside the barn, where my blood still stained the ground.

I remember him standing in the middle of all that fire, looking at me. Remember how I said he was beautiful, before? Remember how I called him my murdering angel? He sure was then. Pulling me right out of hell.

"Best get a wiggle on, Martha," he said to me.

I winced at that, hearing that name. It was a burden, see? Martha was this little girl from Missouri. Orphaned, alone, and weak. She'd been taken advantage of. She needed to be taken care of. And seeing the Green Man there, all lit up like some damn devil between the flames, got me thinking on what he'd told me right when we first met. Can't count on no man, he'd said. Well damned if Martha hadn't needed a whole heap of men to rescue her.

"I ain't Martha," I told him. I remember, had to holler above the rising sound of the fires eating Harthra's ranch. Had to shout to him, "Guess I lied when I told you my name was Martha."

He just nodded, them long stalks of his fishing out my lie, I expect. Then he smiled a little—that infectious smile what I saw at camp the night before—and he told me, "All right . . . Jane."

And that's the God's honest. That's how I met the Green Man and how I ended up riding with him. At least for a while. He never really invited me to go with him. And I never really asked. We just set out together, riding away from Piedmont, guiding ourselves through the night by the glow of the town burning behind us. Riding in silence.

BOOK TWO

SOMEONE TO RIDE
THE RIVER WITH

ONE

Seeing as you've come calling for more, I suppose I should tell you how we come across that other space man—if you can call him a man. Wicked, terrible fella, that one. But first I should tell you about the posse what caught up on us after Piedmont. And about that other flying engine, of course.

After that mess with Jeb went all a cropper, we'd spent a week or two in the badlands up from Piedmont, licking our wounds and loosing our tracks in the hills well off the roads and rails. And damn if that Green Man didn't heal quick as a colt—wrapped some shiny bandage around his belly and wasn't but a week before all traces of that bullet Jeb put through him was plumb gone. But we had to come south after a while so I could run in on Green River and rustle up some supplies. It was there I overheard some talk about the burning of Piedmont and the posses Moses been rounding up to come hunting after us. See, hadn't been a week since we left Piedmont all smoldering when old Moses rattled his hocks back into town and found the mess we'd made of it. And of his son, Jeb. Shit, probably not enough of that boy left for buzzard food, what with how we both put the gun to him and left him to cook like some chuck in the fires of that exploding flying engine.

When I got back to camp and told the Green Man what for, well, he took a long time thinking—that quiet way he had of talking to himself, them long bug stalks on his head all curled in, concentrating. But wasn't too long before we took off east, zigging and zagging roundabouts the pilgrim trail. Seems the Green Man wanted one of them posses to catch us—or at least to catch wind of us. And sure as shit they did. Half a dozen or more of Moses Boone's boys picked up our trail about a day's ride from the Devil's Gate. And by the time they caught themselves up on us, the Green Man and I was already perched up in them cliffs, the horses hid, our rifles ready and waiting.

The Green Man settled that Henry to his shoulder and let that odd black scope stretch out and cup his eye. I looked down across that rifle from behind, watching the Green Man sight up on that posse. From all far off, I couldn't tell you if I recognized any of those boys from Piedmont or not. But I reckon it didn't much matter. We was going to beef them just the same. We was going to beef any what come calling after us. And I wasn't scared one bit, not then. Not facing some posse of men. Shit! I reckon part of me was excited, if anything. This was outlaw living. I was a longrider now, like my Green Man.

And when the Green Man set his finger to that trigger? Bang! He made quick work of them. Was like listening to a clock ticking off the time—snap, snap, snap—the way he levered them shells and squeezed them shots. When the first fella went down the rest unshucked their guns and hunted all around for us. But after the Green Man felled half of them, well, they fagged out as fast as any I've ever seen. Might've had a whole war party on their heels the way they lit off. But they didn't get two whoops and a holler before he dropped the last of those saddle stiffs right off his speeding horse.

Just six or seven ticks of that trigger—counting off their last seconds—what it was. Wasn't so long ago that the sight of bloodshed like that would've turned my belly. I remember begging off the Green Man from shooting that rapist Jimmy Burns or that no good fucking bunko artist Tom Somers. But here, watching them boys in that party dropping like flies, I didn't feel no sadness. They come hunting for us and they got theirs for it.

See, I was cold, then. Not some little girl to be pirooted in a fucking barn no more. The fires of Piedmont set my steel, I tell you. Or, at least, I told myself. See, was about to see things what would drain the sand right out of my belly, and the color right out of my cheeks, wasn't I? But up on that cliff with my squirrel gun and my gunslinging space man, I was cold and terrible just like them savages in the stories. Maybe nothing so much as the Green Man, I reckoned, but cold enough.

I was even thinking on that, I remember, when two of them dropped boys in that posse pulled up and started crawling after their scattered horses. Even from up on them cliffs, you could see the blood soaked through their clothes, staining them all red like pimples. The Green Man had just started to lower his barrel when he saw them and he wasted no time bringing that rifle back up again.

I swear, the crack of that Henry was even louder than before. One of them fella's heads popped right open, blowing its mess all across the dust. You don't forget seeing something like that, even as far off as we was. Goddamn.

The other fella saw that right good and up close, see? He started screaming so god-awful you could hear him all the way up on them cliffs. But the Green Man's rifle only answered him with the snap of the pin on an empty chamber. He pulled the Henry away and checked it. But he got that thinking look on him again, looking down at the rifle and out at that bleeding, blubbering boy. Then he just slung that Henry over his shoulder and started down the narrow path leading off the cliff.

Me? I stood there for a minute, watching that fella squirming in the dust, half a mile off.

"What, you ain't going to finish him?" I remember asking the Green Man.

Well, he stopped for a moment at that, not looking back with his eyes but taking me in with them long black stalks. You remember me saying how he'd watch you with them things, don't you? Well, he did just that and told me, "Man's dead. Just don't know it yet."

Well, when I didn't start after him, the Green Man turned around. I could see myself reflected in those big black oil pits of eyes.

"You don't much care about people, do you?" I asked him.

He nodded and looked down at them bodies and that crawling fella.

"Expect I care about them about as much as they care about me," he said. And I knew he was thinking on what that boy, Jeb Boone, had done to Mister Harthra. How he'd burned his face right off. No doubt the Green Man had a memory full of such hatefulness. People could be monsters, I knew it then and I know it now. Much more so to savages or space men. Expect the Green Man knew that better than most.

By the time we made the banks of the Sweet Water what cut its course through them cliffs like some damn knife cutting through the flesh of the Wyoming, well, that posse's horses was run off. Chasing their terror back to Piedmont or Green River or God knows where. But the Green Man, see, he hoped they'd make it back to Moses or them other parties searching for us. Might even lead them back to this here spot littered with blood as it was. See, he was setting a ruse afor all them boys, not just these here dead.

So the Green Man went to where we'd tied off Bess to his queer horse like it was some kind of hitching post. Then he stood there, stroking his horse's mane and whispering to it, like the way a man might whisper into the ear of a sweetheart. Like how Somers talked to me in such hushed tones, once on. Damn, I hated to think on that. Still do.

Then, with a smack, his horse took off south, leading Bess on behind.

You take my meaning, don't you? He sent them horses off, leaving us standing there not two shits from that massacre.

I remember barking up at that. "What the fuck do you think you're doing?" I hollered.

"The horses will ride south toward Ferris," he told me, calm as a damn mountain. "Any come following on this posse's trail, they'll catch ours heading that way."

"And what about us, eh?" I remember snapping. Damn, I tell you, that excitement of mine was turned terror and fury. Stuck in the mouth of that gate, on the banks of some river, without a horse to carry me off from the scene of the Green Man's slaughter? He knew more men would be following on and he stranded us. Seemed, all of a sudden, he was setting us up for a die-up.

He heard that little affrighted warble in my voice, I reckon, and just pointed west. Had this serene look on his face what made me feel the fool straight away.

"We walk," I remember him saying all easy, like some fucking stroll would solve all our problems. "It's just a few miles to Independence Rock." He kept on. "If you stop your yammering and get to it, we can make it by dark. The horses will meet us there in the morning."

Remember how I told you he whispered to that horse of his? Like it were a lover? Well, I asked him, "Suppose you told your horse this little plan, did you?"

He just nodded. Didn't say a word. Just nodded and started walking toward a rise of rock some miles off, just visible over the riverbank. And you know, I wasn't the least bit surprised. This fella, from somewhere up in that night sky, he was full of wonders. I reckon being able to speak horse was among the least of them.

TWO

I'm telling you this here part, I reckon, because it was one of the sweetest times in my life. That afternoon, I mean, not the killing back at that Devil's Gate. But tell you true, I honestly didn't think nothing about the Green Man beefing that posse. Was just men and the world's full of them.

No, I mean that walk along the Sweet Water what seemed to last forever and what ended all too soon. And the night what followed. Goddamn, that's a bright memory, I tell you. Maybe because of what happened the next day. But maybe because it was true and simple and good. Was a hog-killing time, if you take my meaning. With the weight of the chase lifted and the Green Man by my side, wasn't nothing, it seemed, could ruin that day.

Took us all afternoon to huff it those few miles to Independence Rock. We come quick out of the rocks where the Devil's Gate stuck up through the earth and made our way across these rolling meadows what curved in and out of the bends in that river. Reminded me of just a few years back, before I come West. Before all come a cropper. In fact, a lot of that afternoon reminded me of better times. Maybe that's why I'm so sweet on it.

See, once on, before Momma died, our train—wagon train, I mean—turned off the pilgrim road to fetch water from the Platte. Momma was sick but we had hope, yet. Well, was then I met Buffalo Bill Cody—the first Bill in my life, you might say. Now that was a man! I was just a little girl. Maybe only two years younger than I was standing there next to the Green Man, in truth, but a lifetime younger in what matters. I tell you,

I remember riding Bess for him, trying to make a mash on him. And he was a right perfect gentleman—charming as a fucking thoroughbred. That was a man to ride the river with if ever I'd met one. Someone who got it where it counts. Someone you can rely on. Wasn't bad looking, neither.

I remember stopping along the bank, splashing at those fast waters with my boot, and looking off all dreamy-like into the sunlight flashing off them ripples and eddies and whatnot. We wasn't much more than a mile or two off from Independence Rock, then. Close enough to see that thing squatting all tall beyond the grass like some giant damn tortoise. The Green Man stood between it and me, seeming miles tall by the comparison, and watched me playing in that splash. Reckon I looked quite the little girl to him then.

I figured to tell him about old Bill Cody but thought better of it. Just make me look more like a little girl, I expect, to go on yakking about some long ago encounter with a childhood hero. Nothing a proper longrider would prattle on about. But I was happy to think on it. Was a happy time, that. before we made Blackfoot and put Momma in the ground.

But it did get me thinking. About how I fell in with the Green Man. How he let me. Like how you might let a dog follow you on for a while, for the company.

"How many folk done ride with you?" I asked him. "before me, I mean."

He cocked his head a bit, I recall, and rolled them black eyes across the way we'd come rather than meet my look.

"A few," he said then. But after a spell he followed on, saying, "None alone, though. You're the first at that. I done rode with some fellas, even some soldiers, after a fashion, but never just one." Then he seemed to laugh a little, some queer smile bending his lip. "Sure not like you, Jane."

Well if that didn't bring a smile to my face, I don't know what could. Then, some dumb giddy laugh in my voice, I kicked a splash and said, "Expect I'm someone proper to ride the river with, do you? Reckon you think I'm just daisy!"

He laughed just a little at that. Fucking sunshine, that laugh was. Then he just nodded. "We'll see."

I ran after him and we walked, side-to-side, along that curving and bending river for an hour or two more. Maybe wasn't a mile on to the Rock but wasn't no straight course along that Sweet Water. Was pretty, though, what with that big sky and the tall grass. And I was happy. A couple times I looked up at that tall fella next to me, them stalks on his head reaching up into that cloudless sky, and counted myself the luckiest girl in the world. My murdering angel had pulled me out of hell back in Piedmont and with him, shit, wasn't nothing seemed could go wrong.

Happy as I was, was hot work, all that walking. Was nigh on the end of July, I think, and hot as a damn kiln under that open sky. As we approached that bare stone mountain, I was right ready to settle in for a proper sleep. But against the shape of the Rock I saw the outline of a long train. I remember it clear as I remember you coming by last time: The mountain was all red and bloody, lit up by the sun falling toward that Devil's Gate behind us. And in front of that red wash was a mess of wagons curled up like some damn snake a quarter mile long. Fires and smoke dotted around their wheels. And horses and children ran about like was some damn circus. Shit, wasn't much after I first saw them that I heard them laughing and squealing, echoing off the mountain.

I reckon the Green Man heard them well before I did. I saw him curl them long stalks of his down into the creases of his Stetson, almost flat out of sight even from just next to him. And he made to lead us off toward the south end of the mountain, away from the settlers, but I stopped on a small bluff and bit my lip, thinking. He knew what for.

"You go," he said, "but you remember, folks are looking for us. Men who know the name of Martha Jane Canary. Men who know the color of her companion."

I nodded, then. "Ain't no concern of mine," I remember saying. "I ain't seen no Martha since Piedmont."

Well, I guess that satisfied him. He watched me for a second, then started off south. "Watch your lip," he hollered back to me.

I started off toward them settlers at that. But damn if I wasn't running after a spell. Been a long time, seemed, since I'd been around other folk. And families, to boot. And as I ran up on them, well, was so goddamn familiar it just about broke my heart to see it. Boys helping their daddies work the wagons or hobble the horses. Bullwhackers raking hay in front of their oxen. And, shit, I saw little girls milking cows and helping their mommas whipping up supper. Put a twist in my damn heart, that did.

I walked right in among them. Some little boys ran up to meet me.

Damn if they wasn't all some swell folks. Out of Arkansas and Missouri, mostly. One family from Georgia. And damn if there weren't some folks with queer accents, too, from places called Sweden and Bavaria. Was headed to California or Oregon, depending on who you talked to. But none of that mattered to me none. I just wanted to talk and laugh and be among people. No strikes on the Green Man, understand? But I guess I was lonesome for people like me.

I introduced myself all proper like, and without one ounce of lying. Told them right what my name was, Jane, out of Salt Lake. Made sure to say I wasn't no Mormon, though, what with the looks talking of Utah earned me. But those was few and fewer still cared.

I ate supper with them and took to sitting among the children—wasn't comfortable around the men, no matter how nice they was or even if their wives was with them or no. I told them kids stories of my trip west. How was I met Bill Cody—that was still mighty on my mind, see—and how I learned to hunt and ride with the men. Lot of them girls liked that bit, I tell you. And no reason they shouldn't. Took special care to tell them how, on my 14th, was me, just some little girl, what rode out through the fog on some moonless night, across a prairie crawling with Injuns, to fetch back soldiers from a camp up on the Platte. Was the hero of the train, I was.

But, much as I wanted, said right little about what come after we got to Salt Lake. No point telling these little ones about my daddy dying and leaving us to be parceled out among strangers. Or about how I made my way to Piedmont and all the killing there. Their eyes was still filled with the excitement the road west put on you. It was hard traveling, don't get me wrong. But there was ever something exciting about what might be over that next hill or river or mountain. So long as it wasn't no damn war party or dust storm, that is.

I told them, too, how I once camped in that same spot. How the kids and daddies from near on sixty wagons carved their names in the face of the Rock, telling the world who had stones enough to make their way west. Well, that whipped them up proper. We ran over to the stone face of that thing and eyed the marks of a hundred folks. Shit, what am I saying—thousands, at least. Marks all up and across that damn rock. The stories of thousands of folks what made their way past that spot.

I looked for my old mark, the one Daddy and I made once on a time, but there was no way to pick it out. Even if the sun hadn't sunk by then, there was just too many to pick through. So I told them kids to fetch up some chisels. We made it to a clear bit of stone and worked in our own signs. A bunch of the men come to help their boys and girls spell out their names and the host of places what they was from. Was a right good time, that was. I even took off a chisel from one of the girls and made a new mark of me and mine in the rock. Read JCGM, if I recall. Carved in the ever-living stone, it was. Expect it's still there if that mountain is.

After that, them kids wanted their turn. They told me all about their trip west and whatnot. But I remember this one boy—not more than six, I reckon. Same age Lije was last I saw him. I remember him all excited to tell us of Injuns. They hadn't seen none on their trail, but they'd heard tell of war among the Lakota and of their chief, Red Cloud. Said that chief could work some wild magic, laying men and beasts low with fire and lightning. And that boy kept asking me if we was going to travel up near Powder River country, where them Sioux was burning the land, or so he was told. I tried to be coy for him. Tease him a little. Told them that if he wasn't very good, and if them kids didn't stay on close to the train, they might just get kidnapped and taken on into them tribes, raised savage. Shit! If that didn't make those little ones smile!

Around then the adults come and broke us up, sending the kids off to bed like they should've done hours ago. But I was glad for it. I missed my brothers and sisters terrible. Always have. Lena and Lije most of all. Was good to be around kids, again. I reckon, was the biggest reason I'm so sweet on that day.

Well, as I walked back among the wagons, back toward where I could see the Green Man's fire off to the south, one of them men come up to me. I'd seen him and his boy working on a wagon when I walked up to the train. But he surprised me some, then. Was like he was just waiting for me to walk back, see? And his eyes wasn't all sweet, neither. Not hungry like Jimmy's or even Jeb's had been—wasn't no meanness in them. But there was some hunt. Some wolf.

He stopped me there, blocking my way. I'd half a mind to run off. But this man wasn't no danger, I could tell that. Expect the wolf I saw in them eyes was mostly lonely, same as I reckon mine had been walking into his camp.

"We heard shots out of the west this morning," he said to me.

I know I flushed some at that. But I watched my lip like the Green Man said. Hell, I expect he was watching me, even then, through that scope of his. Or maybe with them stalks what seemed to take in every damn thing.

When I didn't say nothing, that fella just nodded and kept on. "I saw you walking up with that tall buckaroo. Walking out of the west. If you need some help—"

I cut him off at that. "I reckon we're doing all right, mister. I thank you kindly for your thinking on me but the Gr—, but me and mine don't need no help."

Shit! I almost fouled that up there, and I know he heard something amiss. Here I'd gone and let my damn lip get away from me. Almost, at any rate. And wasn't no doubt in my mind these settlers was going to ride across old Moses Boone's posses somewhere between South Pass and Fort Bridger. But this fella was thinking on other things, thank God.

"What I mean to say," he kept on, "is that if you want to take up with us, well, you're welcome." Then, I remember, he put my fears to rest if not the damn hairs on my back. "My wife fell back in Nebraska. I could take care of you, if you take my meaning. Silas and I could sure use a woman around."

Damn, I wish I could say this was the last time some dude took a cotton to me. But it was, right then, when I realized what I took for my own loneliness was nothing. Not like what this fella had. I didn't have none of that desperation or pain, no more, what come with being lonely. Oh, I'd lost. Shit, I'd lost more than most. But I had the Green Man. I had Bess. I had myself to rely on. No, I guess I wasn't lonely. Guess I come into this camp because I missed people, sure, but not because I needed them.

Well, I didn't say nothing. I just pushed on past that fella, heading for the Green Man. What could I say? Wasn't no meanness in him, like I said. Was just some lonely granger from back east taking a shine to the first young thing that walked across his path. Reckoned the best I could do, then, was to hightail it off that there path. I wish it was so easy to deal with men all the time, I tell you. Was like the Green Man said, some you got to put to the bullet. Some to the tongue. Often the latter, with me. But some, you just got to put behind you.

When I walked up on the Green Man he was sitting off from the fire a ways, watching the black country—for the horses, I reckon. He didn't say nothing as I lay out on the warm rock near the pit and watched the stars blink overhead.

Then, after a long spell, he spoke up.

"What'd that fella want?" he asked me.

Was barely a whisper, that. Could barely hear it over the crackle of that fire. But I smiled and kept my eyes on the black overhead.

"Asked me to marry him," I told him.

There was silence, then. Then he spoke up, asking, "What did you tell him?"

I couldn't help but smile at that.

"Told him I was already married," I said.

God, I howled at that. The Green Man didn't make a peep but I laughed well enough for both of us. When I looked across the fire at him, he was watching me, his black eyes all lit up red and yellow with firelight.

"Aw," I remember teasing him, "I reckon you think I'm just daisy, all right."

"We'll see," he told me.

We'd see, indeed.

I lay back and let sweet, exhausted sleep steal over me. But if I recall, I didn't fall off right away. I watched some far off thunder to the south as it rolled over the high plains. Far enough off that I couldn't hear no cracks or bangs. Just dim, cloudy flashes over distant grasses. And once, maybe, I heard singing from them settlers. Lonely songs of home, I think it was. Well, let them keep their loneliness. I was the luckiest girl. Don't you think because I didn't have no proper man or husband I was anything else. Wasn't no place I'd rather be than right there. Even now, I pine for that uncomfortable rock. Because he was watching over me and loneliness was some far off thing, echoing off the Rock from other folks. Wasn't nothing could ruin it for me.

Well, at least not until the next day. All went right up the flume then.

THREE

I woke late that next morning. The campfire was all cooked out and the Green Man off tending them horses what must've come back in the night. I remember walking over to them as they worked the short grasses what grew up at the edge of the Rock. Damn, I reckon I still had some yack smile on my face from the night before. Had me my space man and now I had me my Bess, again. Luckiest girl in the West, I was.

I remember putting my forehead up against old Bess's snout. That horse was the better part of all I had, see? Things was sweeter when she was with me. But even as I kept close to her, I looked after that wagon train. It was all but gone—just a thin cloud of dust leading west marked them. But I kept an eye on that fading cloud.

Well, the Green Man caught me watching that train. I don't know if he could read minds or see my thoughts but he always knew well enough what I was thinking. Maybe them stalks let him see more of me than I liked. Maybe I was just so easy to see through.

However it was, I remember him looking at me then, following my gaze off to the west.

"Hope you didn't get yourself too attached," I remember him saying.

So we set off north, not right sure where we was headed, I reckon, except away from men and guns and killing.

We'd rode the better part of the day in plumb near perfect silence—almost never talked from the saddle, we did—when all of a sudden I saw the Green Man stiffen up all like a corpse. Was about midday, I remember, when he pulled up that queer horse of his and stood in them stirrups, them stalks on his head straight as arrows aiming at the sky, I swear.

I looked all around, scanning them plains and hills for anything what seemed strange. Wasn't nothing but grasses and rocks and dust every which way. But still the Green Man stood stiff. Then he twisted fast, them stalks pointing on back south, the way we'd come, almost. And hanging high, like some shining bird, was this flashing point in the sky. Except I knew right away wasn't no damn bird. Couldn't barely see it for the bright blue all around. But it shined and flickered like polished steel—or a mirror, if you take my meaning. Hard to look at, so it was. Fast, too, coming all low and quick over the land.

Queerest thing of all, didn't make no sound. Not at first, anyways. Almost as soon as we saw it, it shot right over us, straight as a bullet but big as shit. And a few blinks after it passed over, BANG! Like a fucking cannon going off all around. Goddamn! Was one of the loudest things what I ever heard. Whipped the grass and the wind all up. Bess bucked and panicked, about grassing me. But the Green Man's horse kept cool and he just stood in that saddle, watching what way that flying thing went on.

No sir. Wasn't no damn bird, that. Was another flying engine.

Was some look of goddamn ecstasy on the Green Man's face on seeing that thing. On knowing it. And watching him follow that shining ship as it passed off toward the north? Well, might've been the end of this here tale before it began what if that ship landed itself all proper and took my Green Man up into the black and away from me.

But wasn't what happened, that. No sir.

See, all sudden like, up from the ground off to the west, in them Rattlesnake Hills, this long thin cloud reached up toward that flying thing. Glowed like some kind of flaming arrow, it did, climbing high on a chimney of smoke.

That flying engine didn't keep to its straight and true on seeing that arc of smoke reaching up for it. Turned east all sudden, it did. But fast as that engine was, that cloudy arc was a sight faster. And when them two met in the sky over the Wyoming, was a second bang I expect they heard half way to Cheyenne.

And over the noise of that god-awful explosion was another sound more terrible to hear. Something like the way the preachers describe

Gabriel's trumpets—like something out of the end times. Was the Green Man screaming. Some sick otherworldly howl like I ain't never heard from him before. And I saw this look of horror, rage, anger—all across his face. Then that scream was gone quick as he was. He took off racing north with all the speed that queer horse of his had in it. Leaving without one thought for me, I'm sure.

So, sure as shit, I took off after him. And as we raced north along the path of the flying engine, I saw some smoking mess tumble out of that explosion in the sky. Saw it twist and spiral, like some flotsam turning in a fast river. And I saw the Green Man pulling away toward it, racing that horse of his faster then Bess or I dreamed to go.

So we rode—rode like the damn wind all afternoon, else I'd have lost him. Sometimes we could barely see the Green Man racing out of some shallow crick or over some distant hilltop. Just enough of him to know we was still racing in the right fucking direction.

And when I didn't think I could push Bess no more, I saw that smoldering mess burning on the plains some miles ahead. I remember some gray plume rising up out of it like a damn tower—like how the ship we'd ruined in Piedmont burned high. And I remember seeing the Green Man, on foot, standing in front of that wreck. Was like the way a man watched his house burn, if you've ever seen such a thing. Was a sadness and hopelessness to it, I tell you.

When I rode up on him he didn't pay me no mind. Just stood there watching that thing smolder. And now I was close, I could see proper what it was. A flying engine, sure, like the one Mister Harthra kept in Piedmont. Had that same fleshy colored skin and bug-like shape to it. But was bigger. Big as a proper steamboat, if I recall. Fire and smoke poured out of some big hole in the side of it—a side I reckon was once the bottom of the thing. Now I knew squat all about these Green ships, see, what I hadn't already told you. But I could tell well enough, looking at this big thing, that it wasn't going to fly that night sky ever again. Just looking on it, you could see rips and tears all across what should've been some seamless skin. Bits was lying all around on the ground and sick noises—if you could imagine the sound of a machine dying—was spilling all out of it.

The Green Man stepped forward after a spell and approached a long straight tear near what I was thinking of as the back of the thing. When he pulled on it, we could see right properly that the thing was crashed on its side. He opened some kind of freight door and inside was some big dark room punched through in places by that explosion, letting in the sun. And all along the top of that room you could see cabinets and doors all fallen open, their contents spilled out like guts below.

I hopped off Bess and followed him into the back of that ship, eyes wide as ever they was, I reckon.

And as I stepped in behind the Green Man he finally turned, like he was just noticing me.

"Walk careful," I remember him telling me.

Was then I looked at what was fallen all across the inside of that ship. They might've come from some other world but I could tell straight away what them things was strewn about all around. Guns. Hundreds of them. And most stranger than that big fat-barreled thing the Green Man kept on his hip. So I stepped careful, to be sure. I'd seen the Green Man's gun rip a man in half, remember? No telling what some of these things could do if set off—especially the big ones.

The Green Man made his way to the middle of the room—was like some kind of barge hold, I reckon. He knelt there and picked up some long gun what looked like a kind of rifle attached to a sword. Just shook his head, saying, "I don't understand. These are all so old." And looking on that gun he was holding you could see wear like you might on an old firearm. Like most of them Green guns had already seen war.

I looked back out that opening we come through and saw the horses, his still as a damn statue, Bess wandering not far off. My heart was beating through my chest, see? First, I thought, from that race across the plains. But standing there among them guns in that ruined ship, I noticed my breathing was coming on slow. Almost stopped if I didn't think on it. And my stomach was like to chase up my throat. No, I was scared almost out of my wits, I think. And not because I thought this ship was dangerous. No sir. I kept on thinking of that cloud what knocked this thing out of the sky. How it reached up so fast and so cruel.

"What could've done this?" I remember asking the Green Man.

But he didn't say nothing. Just ignored me. Saw him pulling open some crates or whatnot, matching their contents against the cartridge what went in that big gun of his.

When he saw I was just standing there, heart racing, dumb as a yack, he looked around quick and pointed at a door farther inside that hold.

"Check the cockpit," he told me.

Check the cockpit? Well, I reckon I didn't know no fucking cockpit from no fucking cock but I knew sure as shit that I wasn't stepping one boot deeper into some space-man flying thing. Not without knowing what I was getting into. Shit, I wasn't right certain I could even move from that spot, I had the fright so bad.

"Why?" I remember asking him, my voice all shaking. "What's in there?"

He was back to sorting through that tossed mess. He sighed some and looked at the door, then back at me. To be sure, I think he was thinking same as me. Should be him checking through that door, if either of us. But he was looking for something, that was plain. Maybe something he'd been hunting for a long time.

"Jane," I remember him saying. Was the first time I heard that name with some scorn put behind it. "Jane," he said, "ain't nothing in there."

"Then you fucking go in there." I told him. Damn, my heart was beating so loud my ears done rung with it.

The Green Man sighed, all impatient, see? Told me, "Where the pilot ought to be. That's all."

Pilot? Well, fuck me. "What if someone's alive up there?" I asked him, panicked at the thought of meeting some injured green fella crazy with pain.

He just watched me, saying, "They won't be" like that was some fucking improvement.

Well, I don't know right sure what happened then. Seemed I was floating toward that door, sideways on the wall as it was. Had to fuss with it for a while, my fingers shaking all over the cracked side of it. Well, when it fell open—downward, see, as the ship was on its side—was just a black lightless room ahead of me. Lightless except for some flashing square of pale blue on the other side, that is. And he wanted me to go into that darkness? Jesus.

My throat closed right up at that. My breathing all fast and short. Was like looking into Hell—into some place even God wouldn't go. I looked back at the Green Man but he was busy, pushing guns beside and checking those unreadable labels on them cabinet doors he was standing on.

Well, don't ever let no one tell you this girl don't have no fucking sand in her belly. I swung a leg up and over and into that damned blackness. Was like what being in one of them ironclads must've been like. Dark as death. And when I dropped through that door, onto what should been a wall, well it was all uneven and slippery. Like mossy rocks on a riverbed. Had to reach down to steady myself, I did. Was wet, too. I remember lifting my hand up, back into the pale light following through that door, and seeing silver running down my hand. Was blood, see, like what I saw pouring out of the Green Man, once on. Fucking blood on the walls!

Had to close my eyes at that. Was a long while until I could move again. Blood on the fucking walls! And I couldn't see for shit. But somewhere in here was some other green fella, cold as a goddamn wagon tire. I could hear the Green Man outside, his muttering and the clattering of metal on metal as he went on looking for fuck all. Oh, I wanted to call out, see? I wanted to scream. But wasn't no voice left in me. Not yet.

So I opened my eyes. And damn if they hadn't adjusted a little bit to the blackness. I could see two chairs, bolted to the floor somehow so what they still stuck there even sideways, their occupants dangling down from straps across their bodies. Between them was this square of pale blue flashing all manner of queer shapes and figures. Greenspeak, I reckon it was. Like some kind of Chinaman writing what you might see in them shitty quarters of town.

Well, I found my voice then. I hollered out, still shaking as I was, "Them two dead fellas in here," I told the Green Man. "It's all plumb fucked."

Was silence for a while after that. Was then I realized I hadn't moved one lick since dropping in through that door. I was kneeling on some kind of instrument, like you might see in the boiler room of some ship—well, what if that ship could fly, anyways. That silver blood reflected some of the light back at me, it did, splattered across buttons and switches and the like.

"Check the bodies," The Green Man yelled back. "Bring me anything they've got on them," he said.

Shit! That got my heart all racing again. "You pulling my goddamn donkey's tail?" I hollered back. "I ain't touching no dead fucking Greens! You want what's on them, you can get your ass—"

Well, he cut me off at that. "Jane!" he snapped, "I need you to check them. We ain't got time for you to go yellow on me."

Yellow! Can you believe that? That's what he said! And there I was in some dark, ruined Green flying ship, squatting in their blood. You can be right sure that got my goat.

"Yellow!" I yelled back at him. "Fuck you! You can do this your goddamn—"

Well, he cut me right off again. Damn, I hated it, but he did. "Jane!" he hollered, "somebody shot this here ship down. And you can bet they'll be coming. Now we don't want to be here when they get here, do we?"

Now, if that didn't steel my heart. Visions of that wicked cloud come back to me then. The Green Man was right—didn't want to be nowheres near folks what could knock a ship like this out of the sky. So I swallowed a wad of spit and made myself move forward, fighting the urge to fag out something awful. But I moved. And soon, I think before my mind right knew what my body was doing, I was standing at the back of them sideways chairs. All slow and careful, like them dead pilots might wake up at any time, I leaned in between them, reaching down across the body in the lower chair. I'll never forget it—if I close my eyes, I can see it like I'm still in that god-awful room. His green skin and black eyes glowed in the soft light of that little blue square and its flashing symbols. Was half his face gone, looked like, and silver blood dripping all over.

I tell you, I think I'd been holding my breath since I started toward them dead fellas. And I had to breathe right then, all of a sudden. Scared myself half to death with the sound of my own breath, convinced as I was it come from one of them.

I felt around that dead green fella's waist and come up with a pistol what looked like a miniature of the Green Man's big gun. I remember, stuck that in my belt and felt around the pockets on that dead fella's chest, too. See, he was wearing something like an engineer's overalls, little pockets all over. Well, there I come up with some cards what I couldn't read, some metal and glass square about the size of my palm, and what looked like a pocketknife. That knife was daisy, too. Blade jumped in or out of the handle just by you thinking on it, humming some low tone all the while.

Was just about to pocket them things, too, when I heard the other pilot, the one above me, groaning. Barely had time to turn over, to look up, see, as I was beneath him, before he reached out a weak hand and grabbed me by the shoulder.

Now, in the dark, as it was, took me a second to see this fella for what he was. Remember, I'd seen green men before. Mister Harthra was a right wonderful man, green skin or no, and the Green Man, himself, had been with me for better than a month now. So when I saw that first fella, slumped all in that lower chair, I wasn't more affrighted than I would've been on seeing any dead man. But this fella in the upper chair, he was different. Even in that pale blue glow, I could tell, wasn't a spot of green on him. And the blood what ran out his mouth? Black as oil.

He was a gray man, if you believe such a thing. And not a stalk on his head, neither. His skin was shiny—not like it was oily, though, but shiny like the skin of that there flying ship. And his hand, the one what grabbed my shoulder, was cold as death. Like fucking ice touching your skin, sapping the heat right from it.

Well, I reckon I did the same as you would done in that there spot. I screamed. Screamed so loud in the little black room it hurt my own damn ears.

I tell you, however hurt that gray fella was, my screaming woke him up proper. He was suddenly alive, grabbing at me with them cold hands. Picked me right up off the floor, holding me over his dead companion, and screaming right back at me in some garbled speech I done never heard before. Was black blood on his shiny teeth—and in his words spit in my face. With one hand pulling me up by the shoulder and another wrapping around my throat, wasn't but a second before that dark room started to spin and go even blacker.

Well, I don't right remember what happened next. I could hear the Green Man running my way, to be sure. But I knew he wasn't going to make it. This gray thing meant to kill me and had the rage and strength in him to do it, too. I felt that metal and glass square drop out of one hand. But I felt that knife right true in the other. And without so much as a clear thought, I jammed that humming blade into that gray man's head. Stabbed like a wild cat, slashing fast and crazy. Wasn't easy, like cutting flesh, but still I made a mess of him. In the fading light, I saw that knife pop his big left eye, tear open his cheek, and slash his neck wide open from back to front.

That gray fella's screaming became some sick bubbling sound. His black blood spilling all out on me. And his grip slackened some, thank God, letting me get my breath back. By the time the Green Man pulled me clear, that gray man moved no more.

I fell back under the door, slipping on the blood where I squatted before. And, I tell you, scared as I was right then, still able to feel that gray thing's grip tight around my neck, wasn't nothing so scared as I was a moment later. See, when the Green Man got a good look at that gray fella, slashed all up as I'd left him, well, he backed away quick, afraid his own damn self.

"We need to get gone. Now," he said, all quiet like.

I was panting, see, and didn't right hear him. I remember stuttering out something like, "What was that?"

But the Green Man? He didn't pay me no mind. No sir, he just raised his voice and yelled, "Now!"

Well, that voice of his pushed me right through that sideways door and on through that big room full of guns. Never mind, no more, stepping on them firearms. We was tripping and rushing through them like kids running through dried leaves. That gray thing was dead and still the Green Man was quick for us to skedaddle. And what I didn't know why we was even running? Well, was the scariest part of all.

I'd been in that dark room for a while, understand, so when I come out and into the afternoon sun, I was right blinded. But I could still see enough to stop straight away.

Remember the Green Man warning me about us needing to move quick seeing as whoever shot this here ship down was going to come calling for it? Well, they was. And they did.

Mind you, here I was, a girl of fifteen stumbling out the back of some big flying engine, covered all in silver and black blood, with a Green gunslinger on my heels. And strange a sight as you should rightly think that would be, wasn't nothing next to what we stumbled out upon. See, out there on the plain, holding the reins of old Bess and the Green Man's horse, was a Lakota war party. And the warrior at their head, just a few feet from where I stood blinking in that blinding sun? Well, across his back was slung a long metal tube with little flashing lights all on it, still smoking from the barrel at one end. And in his hands, that warrior leveled this long black gun on me what could only have come from the Green Man's people. And when he got him a good look at me, he smiled this cruel grin—like what the snake must've smiled at Eve.

And then that red fucker shot me.

FOUR

I woke up plumb soaked. Not wet, if you take my meaning. Roostered. Like I'd been on a night-long bender, throwing back the Taos Lightning until I passed out in the saddle. Shit! Was only fifteen, remember, but I knew what it felt like to be properly soaked.

Except I wasn't soaked, to be sure. Took me a while to reckon my predicament, I'll tell you, but I knew quick enough wasn't no booze what set my head spinning. Was that warrior's gun what did it. Didn't scar or wound me none but plumb knocked me into a cocked hat.

You know, thinking on it now, I reckon that was the first ever some fool got a shot on me. Plenty of guns pulled, to be sure, but never before getting shot.

Anyways, I come to all slow. Was slung over Bess's back, head dangling down near the buckle. And my hair was all hanging around my head like some dark veil. So none of them Lakota was wise to my rousing. Which is all well, seeing as I wasn't wise to fuck all.

But my wits come back to me after a spell. So I let myself just hang there, afraid some little movement would spook Bess or them Injuns and, either way, I'd end up in the dirt. But hanging there as I was, I could see a lot. Saw maybe half a dozen of them braves riding around me, scarlet blankets over their shoulders, their saddles all heaped up with them old space guns we found in that ship. Reckoned there must've been another six or seven, too, on the other side what I couldn't see. And I saw the Green Man, that horse of his barely jostling him as it carried his limp form across its saddle. See he was all knocked out, same as I was, except they had a mind to tie his hands. What he was awake or not, I couldn't reckon from what I could see.

But that got me thinking, it did. Can't count on no man to rescue you, the Green Man told me. And sure as shit he was right. There I was with my hands free and no one else to save us.

So I started taking account. I could feel my Springfield tied up behind the saddle but wasn't no way I could undo the thong and get to it before them Sioux dropped me like a stone. Was that queer green knife I done that gray fella with, too—was in my back pocket. But wasn't no way I'd get close enough to them mounted warriors to use it.

But I had an ace, I tell you. Was that pilot's pistol, see? Was still stuck in the waist of my dungarees, under my flannel. Goddamn Lakota must not have thought I was much of a threat, see, being some little girl and all. Well, I planned to show them what courting calamity would get you, I did. This here girl was on the shoot now.

So I kept still, slung over that saddle with my arms and hair all dangling down, until the sky turned purple and a few more Injuns come into sight. See, much as I wanted to jump down and beef the lot of them warriors, I needed the Green Man to stir, show he was awake, before I could make my move. Needed to know he could ride off with me when the smoke was clear. Well, smoke or whatever goddamn thing come out of that Green gun in my belt—damned if I knew, I tell you.

Well, before long we was in a damn camp. And not like one of them camps you see made up in them Wild West shows. No, this was the real deal. A proper tribe and all. Warriors, horses, women and babes, to boot. And all around, leaning against teepees and whatnot, was them worn-out Green guns like what we saw in the belly of that ship. You understand? Them Injuns was packing space guns. Like what the Green Man carried. Fuck! This wasn't no damn tribe out following the buffalo or some such. This was a goddamn army.

And we rode right into the middle of that mess. Was all I could do to lie still as more and more of them Lakota Sioux crowded up around our horses, scarlet sashes and blankets on about them all. But, goddamn, the Green Man wasn't moving a lick, so what could I do? I tell you, my heart was racing. More so with every whoop and cry them warriors made, announcing their capture.

Then we stopped and, before I knew what was on, I felt a hand on my ass. For a second I was terrified they was going for that gun—my one chance at escape. I suppose I might've worried about my snatch some, like what when Jimmy jumped me. But, no. Wasn't the gun or my business they had in mind. Not yet, anyways. No, that damn Injun just shoved me right off Bess by the ass, head-first into the dirt.

The Green Man crashed to the ground next to me, shaking his head, looking around through gray, cloudy eyes.

We struggled up to sitting there in the dirt, watching them Sioux crowd up around us on all sides. I remember leaning back-to-back with the Green Man there, whispering to him, "Didn't think it was possible to sneak up on you."

I couldn't see him proper but I remember him turning his head toward me, whispering back, "I was distracted."

Well, my hands was still free and I didn't know how much longer that would be. There was near on thirty or forty of them Lakota crowded around us now, including some of them warriors what captured us. Not their leader, the fucker what shot us, but was most of the rest. They was all whooping and making to scare us. We was some kind of prize, I expect. Each of us for different reasons.

And it was thinking on that last bit—how there was no right way they wanted me for the same they wanted the Green Man—if you take my meaning—that got me moving.

I jumped up and, quick as I could, pulled that shining pistol out of my belt. Was a light thing, not heavy or solid feeling like a proper pistol. And it was slender, too. Right fragile looking though it felt strong enough stuck through my dungarees. And, seeing it in the light as I was for the first time, I was surprised there wasn't a cylinder or nothing—no moving bits of any kind I could make out. Just some little pulsing blue light above the grip and a little switch what I took for a safety. But more than anything, I saw that there gun wasn't all worn and old looking, like what them Injuns carried. This gun was right new, polished up and menacing.

Was some confusion among them savages, right then. Some ducked back. But more laughed or feigned fright. Even as I swung that thing around, most of them Sioux, the warriors in particular, acted like I was waving some fucking toy.

So I meant to put some fear in them. I pointed that thing right up into that purpling sky and squeezed the trigger. Shit, I didn't know if it was a toy or not. Like I said, I'd only ever seen the Green Man fire his big gun once. And it made a mess of men. Goddamn, a mess! But if this gun was made of the same stuff, I'd no idea.

Well, that gun didn't make no big sound like I'd hoped. No boom or blast like from a cannon. But made a strange metallic sound, it did. Like if you banged a taut piece of wire or something. It sang, like a banjo string struck sharp, then vibrating its long unbreaking hum constant as the stars so long as I held that trigger tight. And it didn't blow no hot shot into the sky. No sir, it shot some straight line of fire right up into the clouds—some long line of blazing white heat what cut up into that purple as far as the eye could see.

Now, that put the right fear into them Injuns, it did. Their own fucking fault for not tying me down, I tell you. In that second, I was on the prod, ready to take on their nation. My blood was hot, my heart was fast.

What happened next went down quick. I heard the Green Man screaming up to me from the dirt. Women grabbed up their kids and hustled away. And them warriors what were laughing at me just a tick before was all scrambling to get their own rifles and Green guns out and trained on me.

So I let off that trigger and lowered that gun of mine on the first warrior I could find. And they leveled theirs on me. And before my finger could squeeze that thing again, I heard the Green Man shout something—something I didn't right understand—and it froze my flesh, it did.

Remember me saying before how sometimes, when he yelled, it could knock you back or stop you in your tracks? Well, that's what he did right then. He yelled some queer word—"Inaji, inagy," or some such. And fuck me, I've no notion what it means but I stopped right where I stood—still as a damn statue—and couldn't help to move. And them Injuns froze, too. I swear. Was like that story about Jericho. You know the one I mean? Was like God reached right down and plumb stopped the fucking world. Except, wasn't no god what did it.

The Green Man stood quick and stepped between me and them warriors. And he started spouting such words as I never heard before. Not that shrill speak I'd heard him yell once on, nor that fast, mean speak that gray fella in the ship spouted when he was choking at me. No, this was Injun, I was sure. I'd never spoke no Lakota, and I couldn't tell you what all he was saying, but must've been the right damn thing because them guns aimed down, that crowd gave us a space, and a few warriors ran off to fetch their headman.

Took a minute before I could move again. The gun had dropped but I still held it fast. Had to watch my own, didn't I? And the Green Man's. So I took the chance to fish out the knife and free his hands. Was all black blood still on that knife, and plenty of it on me. Reckon I got some of it on the Green Man, too, when I cut that rope. But he didn't say nothing about it when I did. Just gave me a little look back, them big oily eyes clear of that fog what was in them before. Was like we was just the two of us, alone on the plain, right then. Never mind them savages or the horses or the darkening night all around. Was like we was alone, just for a moment. Took the heat right out of me, that did.

Was right then that warrior what shot us come back. Had some much older fella with him, too. Biggest toad in the puddle, he was. But, I tell you, that older fella was right impressible looking. Weathered like a damn mountain, dressed all properly savage in skins and beads, but carrying these shiny service pistols on his hips and wearing this tall feather sticking right up above his braids. Could've been old as the Earth, that one. But he moved like a young man—smooth and quick and like he wasn't afraid of nothing.

The younger fella—the one what shot me—was a sight, too. Young, fit, tan. If I close my eyes, I can still see them muscles of his straining under them skins he wore. He'd discarded them Green guns he'd been carrying but still wore this long, loose hair pipe breastplate what reminded me of the one the Green Man wore under his duster. And he wore the scars of honest fighting, too. But I tell you, if it were just the two of us there, I'd have repaid him the favor of that gunshot right then—with fist or knife, Springfield or Green gun, didn't matter. That fucker pulled a trigger on me and I reckoned I owed him the same favor.

So I started to push on past the Green Man and was like that whole tribe moved when I did, near to pulling up their guns all over again. But the Green Man stopped me quick, putting his arm right across me. Now

I've done killed myself plenty of Injuns over the years since then—and
damn few what didn't deserve it, neither—and, I tell you, I would've
made that young brave the first scalp on my belt, if I could've. Would I
could've beefed that young warrior with my eyes, he'd have been dead on
his feet. That whole tribe be damned.

Damn good thing the Green Man kept me down, though. You're
going to think me a liar when I tell it but this is the God's honest. That
chief we was facing right then? Was Red Cloud himself. Don't you laugh
now. I ain't no goddamn liar. I done met Red Cloud right then same as I
ever met old Bill Hickok in Laramie. You can take that to the goddamn
bank, mister.

This here was the self same chief those boys in the wagon train told me
about—the one what was waging war on the Union up in Powder River
country. And that warrior with him? The one what brought down that
flying engine and shot us in its ruin? Well, that was Crazy Horse. The
same what would butcher Fetterman and Custer. Was a demon, that one.

Well, for a while we all stood there all quiet. The Green Man and
me on one side, that chief and his hundreds all around. But I guess they
was as right impressed with the Green Man like I was with them. Them
Lakota just started on talking with the Green Man in that speech of theirs.
Hell, was more an argument than talking. The Green Man kept pointing up toward the sky and gesturing to that Crazy Horse fella—talking
about that ship he shot down, I reckon—and even gesturing to me a few
times. And there was this one word I recall even now—something like
"Wicate"—what was said over and over again.

Well, Crazy Horse was a hot fella, he was. Kept his voice up and arguing right back with the Green Man all while that chief just stood there,
all pokerfaced mostly but sometimes saying one or two words with such
authority that even I, not understanding a lick, took the meaning from
it. Was telling his and mine to hobble their lips.

I've never been much on waiting, see? Couple times I elbowed the
Green Man or pulled on his duster but he paid me no mind. Most of the
time, anyways. Was once, after some heated cussing between him and
Crazy Horse where they was all pointing at me, what I couldn't stand
being quiet no more.

I stepped around the Green Man and pointed right back at that red fucker and hollered, "Best keep them damn fingers folded, mister, else I'll snap them off!" Was just the Green Man grabbing my shoulders what held me back.

After an hour or more, Red Cloud stepped forward. That seemed to end all their talking. And the Green Man, taller than him by a good foot, left me in the middle of that circle of braves and bowed before their chief. Crazy Horse had his back all up at that—madder than a fucking hatter, he was. Even as the Green Man and the chief made their peace, that warrior was talking all in angry tones, pointing at the Green Man and me.

I looked him square, I did, and told him, "Let them make peace, them two. Not us."

Well, I don't right know if he knew real talking or not, but he met my look and, I reckon, he took my meaning.

But whatever the Green Man had been saying all that while, well, guess it satisfied old Red Cloud. He made them warriors hand back the reins of our horses and even gave the Green Man his guns back. When the Green Man come back to me, he took that pilot's pistol from my hand—I'd never let go of it, see—and led me and the horses right out of that circle of braves. Not even Crazy Horse made to stop us.

I let him lead me out of the shine of their fires, away from the rising voices what were responding to our leaving, before I shook off his arm and stepped clear.

"You going to tell me what the fuck just happened?" I snapped at him. I didn't like being kept in the dark. No sir. I was glad for the reprieve, to be sure, but I hated not knowing my lot in things.

The Green Man kept his eyes on them braves raising their voices behind us.

"Red Cloud owed me a favor," he told me, like that was all it took. Some fucking favor.

Well, maybe he did. I didn't give a damn. Wasn't what I wanted to hear, was it?

"No, goddamnit," I told him. "What the fuck happened back at the ship? What are these warriors doing here? And what the hell were you talking about all damn night long?"

"They blew up the ship after stunning us," he told me. "That war party meant to shoot it down," he kept on, "take what they could carry, and blow it up. You and I wasn't supposed to be there. The one they call Crazy Horse was supposed to kill the gray and bring back his scalp. Was he they wanted."

"What for?" I remember asking him.

The Green Man looked around, scanning that black horizon with them eyes and stalks of his, like he was all worried we was being overheard.

"We can't stay here, Jane," he said, his voice all low and quiet, like he was saying it just for me and didn't want even the damn wind to overhear. "They always operate in pairs," he said. "The other will be coming."

"The other what?" I asked him. Though, looking back on it now, I think I reckoned what he meant. They always operate in pairs, he said. And I knew that green pilot I found dead in that cockpit wasn't who he was meaning. No. The Green Man was saying there was another gray fella out there. That'd he be coming.

The Green Man was watching them braves again, still arguing as they was. "He'll kill them all," he said in that same hushed tone. "He'll be half mad, I reckon, what with his twin dead. And he won't stop killing, neither. Not until he finds the one what did his other half."

And I took that meaning right quick, I tell you. Still had that knife in my other hand, see? Still had black blood all on it.

I started to say back to him, "You mean that fella what I—"

But he shut me up right quick, covering my mouth with his hand. His skin was rough, there on my lips. Not calloused like a cattle hand's or nothing but rough, like how a stone might feel if you kissed it. Had grit to it.

"Don't you ever speak of it," he told me. And though his voice was low, them words rolled around in my head something powerful, quieting me proper.

And standing there, his hand on my lips, them big black eyes locked on mine, he told me something what still shivers my spine. Remember how I was all affrighted when we ran from that ship, not knowing what that gray thing was or why we was running from its corpse? Well, if I hated not knowing what for, maybe knowing was the worse of it.

He kept me close and said, just on above a whisper, "I need you to listen to me, Jane. And listen right. If you see another gray fella, no matter how far off you think he is, you run. Understand me now? Don't think on it.

Not for a second. You just run and you don't look back."

Well, that put the shakes in me. Here was the Green Man what felled a whole posse back at the Devil's Gate. What beefed a whole mess of Jeb's boys and put all of Piedmont to fire. The Green Man was a cold longrider. Cruel when he wanted to be. But never afraid, see? When all them guns was on us in that Piedmont saloon? When we was just now surrounded by a whole host of braves? Wasn't never no fear in him.

But was fear in him in that ship, what when he saw that gray I'd done carved to chuck. And there was now, what when he was telling me to run. And it wasn't no fear for me, neither. I wasn't right sure what the Green Man thought of me but I could see it in them black eyes—could hear it in them hushed tones—this was some kind of fear he wasn't used to. Was a fear for his own damn self.

Was right then that them Lakota took up a chant—"wicate, wicate, wicate." And Crazy Horse standing in the middle of them, a green rifle held high over his head. Was the nightmare of half the West, right there—them Sioux ready to take up the warpath. But wasn't against no settlements or white men they was going after. Even out beyond the firelight, just at the edge of seeing, I could reckon it in Crazy Horse's eyes. He was hunting for this other gray fella. The one the Green Man was so affrighted of.

"What's that word they keep using," I asked him. "What's 'wicate?'"

"It's their word for the Gray Man," he told me, his voice rising just a tick.

He just looked at me with them cold black eyes. And in their shine I could see myself standing there, in the dark, all small and covered with dust and blood. And that girl reflected in them eyes? Wasn't no Jane I'd become. Was a frightened little Martha I saw there. And I hated seeing her again. I could feel her, digging up from inside—helpless and needing.

That chant was like a heartbeat, it was. Wicate. Wicate. Wicate. Like the last heartbeat before the dark.

"What's it mean, you reckon?" I asked him.

"Death," was all he said.

FIVE

Was night when we set out from the tribe's camp, dark and moonless as being locked in a boxcar. But the dark didn't slow the Green Man none. He led us out of them Rattlesnake Hills true as a fucking compass. At a right good clip, too. Might've been his vision was even keener in the dark, I reckon, without them eyes to muddy up what them stalks of his was seeing.

Well, by the first crack of sunlight, I was as tired and hungry as I expect I've ever been. Been since we camped at the Rock what I'd eaten or slept. And while that might've been just a day before, seemed a lifetime. Was like I couldn't remember what bread felt like in my belly.

Reckon it was well on past lunchtime what he let us stop for the first time. About fell out of my saddle, half-asleep, I did. Got to remember now, the Green Man didn't sleep none. Never once saw him put his head down for a spell. No sir. But even as that was, he always let us pause for the night so I could get my shut eye. But not that day, I tell you. We stopped that once to let the horses eat some grass and for me to do some necessaries. That was it. Didn't stop again until the moon was up and the sky was purpling again in the west.

Was then, the first nightfall of our fagging out of them hills, what we saw smoke. Was coming from where we'd been, see? From the direction of that Lakota camp. And thinking back on it now, I could hear that faint popping of gunshots and Green guns on the wind. The weak sounds of dying far off. Was like the Green Man told me. That gray fella come for the tribe what felled his other half, see? Come for them to burn them up, same as they done to his.

As we stood there watching that smoke, the Green Man didn't say a lick. Didn't need to. I remember turning them sleepy eyes of mine on my own hands and that black blood what still caked them—in the grooves of my knuckles, under the tips of my nails. That fella was coming for what did his in. Wasn't going to find them among them savages, none, neither. Was going to find them right here, in me. Goddamn, was one of the scariest times of my life, that was. Didn't need no boy fixing to rape me or holding a gun on me to feel that kind of fright. Was the fear before a storm or an execution. No matter what you did, wasn't nothing you could do to get out of the way of what was coming.

The Green Man turned his horse around a couple times, scanning that darkening horizon every which way. Was anxious, he was. That same unsettling unease I saw the night before in the Lakota camp. And that made me all the more unsteady, my own damn self.

After a bit of looking, I remember him dropping off that horse of his. "We'll camp here for a few hours. Let you and the horses rest."

Well fuck me. Was nigh on two days, I reckon, since I'd eaten or slept but with that smoke over them far off hills, wasn't a bone in my body what wanted to hop off Bess or risk some shut eye.

"Are you fucking kidding me?" I snapped at him. "What with this gray demon right on our ass, you want to stop for a . . . for a fucking rest?"

"You need to sleep," he told me, his voice cool as ever despite his quick looking all around. "So do the horses," he kept on. "Just for a few hours."

I pointed at that smoke, dim as it was in that darkening sky. Was a growing plume, too. That Gray Man was working wicked among them Sioux. "Do you not see that goddamn burning?" I asked him. "We ain't got time to hang no fucking fire in sight of that die up. Or didn't you tell me to run what I saw that gray fella coming?"

He looked at me, blank as a goddamn statue. And I remember him asking, "You see him?"

All I could do was shake my damn head. Was barely a thought I could keep in it, I was so tired. "Don't you?" was all I could say.

We was on the side of a hill facing south, there—some wide swath of them sinking hills off before us. And beyond, through them flat grasses,

God knows. Salvation, I hoped. Anything what would calm the Green Man's nerves and shut that affrighted little Martha up in my head. And I wanted to get on. I was desperate to get on. Things wasn't right, see? Fear was on us and I wanted out from under it—to squeeze Bess tight and race away from it on the damn wind. Wasn't no time to think on sleeping.

"Rest," was all he said back to me. "We've got a day on him and plenty of time for running." Then he just watched me, the way a hunter watches a buffalo—waiting for me to make the move what would fell me. And when my eyelids sank, he knew he'd won out.

"Three hours. For the horses," he said. "Use what you can of it."

And goddamn if I did, too. Hopped down off that horse, hot as shit for being talked down to like that. Wasn't a bone in my body that I thought could sleep in sight of that mess. Hell, I didn't even hobble Bess before I sat on the loose dirt, facing the smoke peeking over the side of that hill. But I was out, faster than you could snuff a wick.

Seemed like it wasn't a blink later my eyes cracked open again, the Green Man in the saddle high up over me, holding Bess's reins. Was barely a shape against the dark, he was.

"Rattle your hocks, Jane," I remember him saying down to me. "Time to move on."

"Goddamnit!" I snapped, waking in a flash and pulling up to a sit. "Wasn't no three hours . . ."

"Reckon not," he said, dropping Bess' reins on me and heading off. "More like four. Now let's light a shuck."

Damn, was like I was floating, not walking, when I stood right. And wasn't like I knew up from down when I mounted, neither. Felt I was drifting off that saddle, left or right, as Bess hurried after the Green Man.

But we kept on fast, no chuck or sleeping to slow us, neither. I ate what bread I had to quiet my talking belly before the sun was up that second day of running. Lost the fight with sleep in the saddle more often than not, too. This was real longriding, I reckoned. And, over them long years since, I've done my share of hauls in the saddle, to be sure. Longer and hungrier than that, true. But here I was, just on from being a girl, and moving at speed, making the struggle of it all the harder. And once we got out of them hills and started south across them grasses, Bess' canter kept off sleep well as a nail in the ass.

Around mid morning, what with dew still on the grass, we stopped again. Was along some shallow crick and Bess dropped her snout in the water like she'd never tasted that wet stuff before. Shit, nearly grassed me in doing.

The Green Man rode past, never once letting that horse of his dip its snout in the crick, and mounted a small rise on the far side of the stream. Was a small copse there, thin but green and casting some shade across the Green Man and down onto the crick. He stopped beside them trees and got to scanning the horizon again, nervous as a rabbit among wolves. Made my heart shudder, that did.

He pulled a bundle off the back of his saddle—I hadn't seen it before—and tossed it down to the crick's edge.

"Put these on," he told me.

Well I didn't know what to make of that, none. Just looked up at him, barely a squeak forming in my mouth. Yammer as I'm wont to do, was barely a thought I could shape to say right then.

He watched me like a hunter again. And I saw him doing that queer thinking of his, talking to himself, looking inward instead of out. After a bit he turned his horse around, their backs to me, and called over his shoulder, "Need you to strip down. Wash up in the crick. Need you to put them bloodied clothes of yours on the bank. That little knife, too." Then he looked back at me, them big black eyes flashing in that morning sun. "Understand? Need you to wash all that black stuff off you. Every damn bit."

I saw the sense of it, to be sure. And looking down the sleeves of my flannel or down at my dungarees, I saw I was marked worse than some blood caked under my fingernails. Was black stained down the plaid across my chest, bleed into the stitching and rivets around my waist and legs. Reaching up, even felt it dried up in my braids. Was a right mess, I was. If that gray fella was a hound, I was some bloodied beacon for him to trail on.

And that rose the fear up in me something awful. Was a panic to claw them clothes off me what gripped me. But I wasn't no trollop, neither. Had the Lord's healthy dose of shame, I did. What I had, only Somers had ever seen of my choosing.

I hopped down and tossed that bloodied knife onto the far bank. But before I even made to pull off my boots, I looked up at that Green Man, him looking back at me with them cruel eyes, and I told him straight, "Don't you be no Nosey Parker, now. You keep your eyes peeled for that gray fella, not what I got, you understand?"

He turned away and never once did I see my nakedness reflected in them black eyes. But he said, quiet and with a bit of nerves in it, "Be thorough, Jane. Be quick but be thorough."

So I did what he said. I set my boots beside and pulled off them bloodied denims and that blackened flannel. I let out my braid and stepped out of my drawers. Tossed them all, except the boots, anyways, over by the knife and stood there, naked as my momma made me, by some quick crick between the grasses.

You might not think much of me now, to look at me, but once on I was a right young thing. And like I said, I wasn't no trollop quick to steal off my bloomers, none. So I knelt there in the stream and washed quick, afraid of the Gray Man, afraid of the blood, afraid of being seen buff even by the wind, much less by some murdering space man. And there was blood all on me, like I said. Tough stuff, too. I remember, my heart was beating fast as I knelt in that cold crick. I used some smooth river stone to scrub that dried stuff off my hands, arms, and collar, scraping at them goosebumps as much as at the blood. Clawed that cake out of my hair, too. Was a rough sight, I reckon, scratching at myself like that, turning that young skin of mine all red from the stoning. Hell, the only sign of that gray thing I couldn't scrub off was the bruise he left around my damn neck from choking me.

God, I found blood in places I would've never of thought. Must've bled through the flannel, it did. Felt like forever it took to clean myself off. And when I was done, I knelt there in that shallow flow, my feet near on to numb from the cold water, and hugged myself round the chest, pulling my arms tight against my little tits. Was trying to squeeze some heat into me, I reckon. Trying to offer myself some comfort, too. The Green Man was many things but he wasn't nothing for my nerves right then. I remember thinking, maybe, if I squeezed hard enough, I could push that weak little Martha out. Right out through my pores. Didn't want to feel the way she'd felt ever again. Didn't want to need nothing. But maybe I did, you ken? Maybe, without the Green Man to lean on,

I still was that scared and angry little girl, ready to be pirooted by any pecker with a strong arm or a Sharps.

Can't count on no man, he said. Kneeling there in that crick, wasn't right sure I could count on Jane, none, neither.

I moved toward that pile of clothes the Green Man what dropped down for me. Looking at it, a thought took me what might well have crossed your mind by now. Was a pair of dungarees, not as trailworn as mine, I reckon, but similar. Was a khaki shirt, too, and a man's drawers. All a sight big for me but I could make them do. Thing was, wasn't nothing of the Green Man's. Of that I was sure. Since I'd been riding with them, I'd seen the Green Man in precious few changes. Was always the same long dungarees, chaps, and Injun bone shirt. Was that same notched Stetson and bandana. Same duster and gloves, too. And rolled on the back of his saddle, near that little metal box of his, was naught else. A vest, maybe. A red shirt to replace his gray one.

So I stood there naked, that khaki shirt in hand, and felt the blood rush hot through me. Them goosebumps sank right quick, they did, warmed by all that anger sudden in me.

"Where the fuck did you get these clothes?" I asked the Green Man.

He kept his back turned. Never once looked at me. But he said, plain, "Ain't got time for yammering, Jane. Get on."

But I was more scared then what I'd been even when kneeling in that water. More than I'd been watching that smoke the night before. And as my blood began to boil, Martha slipped away some, I reckon. Can't count on no man? That's God's fucking truth.

"When did you get these clothes?" I yelled at him, shaking that shirt in his direction. "When the fuck did you ride off and pull these off some granger's line?"

"Ain't no mind," he said all quiet, trying to calm my wrath, I reckon.

"Was it last night?" I snapped at him. "Was it when I was passed out on the dirt in sight of that damn smoke?" I threw the shirt his way, right then. And watching it catch the wind and sink to the grass just a short ways off made me even hotter, it did.

"Did you fucking leave me alone, with that gray thing coming after?" I screamed at his back.

"For land's sake, Jane—" he started. But I didn't let him finish. No sir.

"You cocksucker!" I hollered. The world was shaking red to me, right then. My murdering angel indeed! More apt to get me beefed, it seemed. "Was you hoping he'd come along and snatch me up while you was off on your errands?" I kept on. Then I pointed at them damn clothes. "You beef the homesteader what you got these from? Like you beefed that posse back at the Gate?"

Well, he just sat in that saddle with his back turned. Didn't say a damn word.

I expect my heart slowed a bit at that. Kicking up a row does me well sometimes, I tell you. Then as now. But I couldn't pull my eyes off the Green Man. Would I could've shot him through with my eyes, his bones would be bleaching in that Wyoming grass even now.

Was then I remembered my nakedness, forgotten in the heat, I expect. Well I stood straight, then, and swept my hair back behind my shoulders. My whole body was tight, angry from the curl of my toes to my fists and pressing teeth—and all what in between, if you use your imagination some.

"You might've kept your back turned," I snapped at him, my voice lower but meaner, I hoped. "But I hope you got a good fucking look with them stalks of yours. A right good fucking look!" I remember cupping my little tits at that last bit, even. And I saw them stalks of his twitch some. Right they should've, too. Was fifteen years old that summer. Wasn't the same looseness I keep hidden' under high collars nowadays, no sir. Might never been much next to them Old States girls you grew up wanting but half them boys in Piedmont had pined after what I once had, I tell you.

So I dressed up quick, shaking again as I did, too. Was angry, sure. That didn't pass out of me until well after was too late to help it. But the fear was still there. Was still between Martha and Jane, then, I was. Between the girl I was and who I wanted to be.

I dressed, scrubbed what little black was staining my boots in the crick, and mounted up. That rage woke me proper, it did. Wasn't no tiredness in me no more. And when I rode up next to the Green Man, my blood still hot, I told him, "Next time you decide to fucking leave me off on my own, you better make sure it's for goddamn good."

He didn't say nothing at that. Just hopped down off that horse of his and grabbed some small silver tube out of that box on the back of his saddle. Then he plucked up that bloodied knife and swept my clothes up into a pile beside the crick. And with a touch of that silver thing to my stained flannel, it all went up in a flash, burning hot like coal in an engine for a short minute. Then gone. Cooked down to a circle of ash the Green Man kicked into the crick and away.

When he mounted up again, I saw dirt on his hands. "Anything else you ain't been telling me?" I asked him

But he just rode off, not looking at me. Not with them eyes, anyways.

SIX

When that Gray Man caught up with us? Well, I reckon that was one of the right scariest things I done lived through. And there's much I would've done different if I could. Was one of those times you never stop thinking on. About how things could've been different if you had a little more sand in you. A little less Martha.

Was nightfall when we rode into Alcova—some little pimple of a town with maybe half a dozen buildings and maybe twice as many grangers. We rode in single file, me bringing up the rear and none too close behind, neither. I was fighting sleep again, to be sure, but was still madder than an old wet hen at the Green Man. I remember, we crossed some dried-up crick what ran by the town and saw a sign tacked up on that first clapboard building, read, "thirty miles to water, twenty miles to wood, ten miles to hell and I gone there for good." Shit, I expect the dude what wrote that was off by a few.

Well, was night, like I said, but not late yet. Some folks was out on the boards as we rode in. And damn if they didn't look like they was seeing the elephant right then. Some was staring at the Green Man's Henry, slung in front of his right leg, some at that dull metal box with its faint blue lights all stowed behind his saddle. But most was staring at them long stalks of his and them dark, pupilless eyes, the green skin and the short spines what sprouted up from behind the collar of his long duster. And once in a while, one of them waddies or their biddies would glance back at the dark haired girl on the Green Man's rear, wearing men's clothes a few sizes too loose and about ready to fall out of her saddle, asleep or dead.

Now, why the Green Man would've led us into some town like that, what with us being chased, I couldn't reckon right then. Maybe he was thinking to bushwack what was following? Maybe even his queer mount needed rest on occasion? Right then, I didn't care a fucking continental. I was plumb done, ready to sleep through until winter if the Green Man let me. Right then, I might've laid down next to that pursuing gray devil himself if it meant a few hours sleep out of the goddamn saddle.

I followed the Green Man up to the hitching post in front of the only saloon in sight. Some shabby two story thing with the sound of a maybe a half dozen men echoing inside. But the Green Man didn't right look at it, he just kept looking all around at everything else. The Green Man was a cocksucker, to be sure, but he wasn't no damn fool. Ain't never walked into a trap he didn't set.

Well he hopped down off that horse of his and started working on the saddle right away. After a spell, he looked over it at me and nodded once, like that should've said something. Maybe it should've but, mad as I was, had it in me to be difficult.

So I just sat there in my saddle, watching him but doing nothing. He just shook his head and pulled that saddle off his horse and set it down on the boards near the saloon door. Dropped his horse blanket right over it, too. Then, as he was giving his horse a little rubbing where that saddle had been, he leaned in close, whispering to it like he had back at the Devil's Gate. And when he was done, he told me plain, "Set your saddle on the boards, Jane. Across the door from mine. Give old Bess a breather."

He watched me for a minute but I didn't move. Just shot him with those high caliber eyes of mine. After a spell he just shook his head again and walked inside, calling back as he hit them batwing doors, "Once you're done having your goddamn back all up, why don't you join me."

I looked at that shoddy place again. Felt the bile up in me and I liked it. I just wanted to be mean, I reckon. So I asked him, "What the fuck are we doing here? Sure ain't for no boss whiskey—not with that strong stuff you got in that box of yours. You a little trail worn, is you? Maybe craving a poke after watching me in the crick this morning? Hoping some fat whore here won't mind them stalks or them shrill screeches if you balance the right coin on your pecker?"

"You want to kick up a row with me?" he said back at me, cool as if we was talking about the fucking weather, "then unshuck that shit horse of yours and see me inside."

Oh, God! He ain't never spoke to me like that before. No sir. And sure as shit not about old Bess. But he was through them batwings before I could drop out of the saddle and start after. I made it all the way to them doors, I reckon, before I got to thinking that stripping off that saddle might be a kindness to poor Bess, insulted and tired as she was. So I just yelled, "Fuck you, Green Man!" through them doors and turned back to my girl. She was the best thing I had, remember? To this day, I'd have cursed my own damn self if I let something get between doing right by her after all we'd been through.

Didn't mean I wasn't quick about it, though. I stripped off that saddle and tossed it on the boards fast as I could. And as I checked that she was tied right to that post, I looked over at the Green Man's mount. It just stood there watching me, still as a damn statue. But I tell you, was the first time I ever saw a line tying it to the hitch.

"Fuck you, too," I said to it. God I hated that horse.

And with that I punched through them batwings, my back up as ever.

The Green Man was standing at the bar. He was handing the barkeep his Henry in exchange for a bottle of bug juice. What for, I had no damn idea. And the other folks what in the bar—some roostered waddies playing faro by a quiet upright in the corner—they was keeping a good distance from the space man. Reckon none of them had seen a Green before. Probably thought them Greens was just some Injun story like I did, once on.

But I was all blind to the scene there. Was hot, see? And ready for a fuss.

Before I could open my mouth, the Green Man turned his back to the bar and said, cool as before, "Hope you didn't get too attached to them settlers back at the Rock, Martha?"

Martha? Jesus! He was just trying to get my back up, wasn't he? Shit, I wasn't thinking at all clear that night, to be sure. But looking back now, I should've seen what he was trying for. Wasn't mean, the way he'd said that, see? More like he just knew how to say what I didn't want to hear. Like he was just trying to keep me riled.

But, like I said, I wasn't thinking clear. Was mad, tired, and hungry.

And baffled, I reckon. Where had this talk of settlers come from? So I snapped at him, "What the fuck is that supposed to mean?"

He just turned back to that shitty benzene he was drinking and said. "It's called Independence Rock for a reason, little girl. You don't make it here by July 4, you don't make it across the Rockies before winter catches you." Then he threw a glance back my way, those black eyes reflecting them loose clothes hanging off me. "Was August when we saw them there, wasn't it?"

Well, my mind lit up with images of them boys and girls, their mommas and them lonely men. They had that excitement, remember, of taking the long road west. And here the Green Man was setting their sentence like some damn prophet.

"Wait just a goddamn minute," I hollered at him. But he just turned away again, like to ignore me. So I rushed up to that bar, yelling as I come, "If you knew they couldn't make it, why didn't you tell me? Or tell them, for God's sake. Let them know to camp it for the winter shy of the mountains?"

But that cold son of a bitch, he just took a drink, never even looking at me.

"Reckon I don't care," was all he said.

God, that lit me up! In the years since, had to tell myself, surely, them settlers come across some town or some buckaroo what warned them what we should've. Or that they'd sense enough of their own to stop for the season at Fort Bridger or Evanston. But I pray those kids didn't end up frozen, or worse, in them mountains. I like to think them boys grew up fine and had them a whole mess of kids to fill up the streets of Eugene or Sacramento or whatnot. Like to think but I don't know for sure.

But I did know, then, I was right when I'd done accused him of caring not at all for men. And I told him so, I did. Told him, "You're a goddamn monster, you are. Green and ugly and mean. Maybe people would care a little more about you and yours if you showed a little fucking care for them and theirs."

But he didn't say nothing. I told you he was a cold one, that Green Man. Cold as I liked to fancy I was, wasn't nothing I had on him.

Then he did something wicked, he did. He turned to me all slow, them eyes and stalks training on me like barrels, and told me, "You got something you want to say, girl, then say it."

And damn if his voice didn't hit me like a punch in the goddamn gut, them words rolling around in my head something awful. Was an echo, see—"say it, say it"—bouncing though every which part of me. And every mean or sour thought I'd ever had for the Green Man rose up like bile in my throat, burning and choking.

And as I started talking, saying things I regret still, I knew I couldn't stop myself. Was the way of his voice sometimes. Hit you hard, it did. And with each punch, took a bit longer to get your wits back.

"You're fucking yellow!" I hollered, my voice all shaking with rage, my face all hot with blood and sweat. "A goddamn lily on the run from what? Some gray piece of work? Some silver ghost hunting us across the plain? Shit! How bad could it be, huh? Seems to me some girl got the better—"

He shot off the bar and thrust a long finger right in my face. And more powerful than before, his voice cut into me, stabbing and slashing its way with every damn word. He said, "Don't you ever speak of that! Not ever!"

And goddamn! The room was set to spinning. I was pissed, though, and tried to keep on. To show what I could beat him. To remind him I could do what he was so afraid he couldn't—I'd killed a Gray, goddamnit. I'd cut one to shit in that dark cockpit. And if I'd had that knife in my hands, reckon I could've done that other Gray right then and there, the one chasing us.

But not a word escaped my mouth of it. Try as I might to tell him of that Gray I cut to ribbons, wasn't nothing what come out. Reckon them words of his give me some pause on it, still.

No, I wasn't able to squeeze out more but bile and spite and hate. Even when I heard the sound of horses outside, of spurred boots clanking their metal way down the boards toward the batwings, I still had words in me for him and I couldn't help myself but say them, like the Green Man's voice done commanded.

"You fucking left me! With that thing on our heels, you left me lonesome!" And tears was on my cheeks right then. I thought they was tears of rage. A rage that wasn't right all my own, to be sure. See, I didn't want to keep on talking like this. God, I wish I could've stopped. To this day, it breaks my heart what I couldn't stop. But them words of his were still rolling around in my brain. "You got something you want to say . . .

then say it," he'd said. But what I was saying, I didn't want to say no more. Was the last things I said to him, right then. Should been words of sweetness. Should've been thanking him for saving me from them boys in Piedmont—for pulling me out of the goddamn fire. Should've been words about how this last month in the saddle was the happiest of my life. How I loved them quiet nights around the fire, with him watching over me as I slept, or them quieter rides when we'd go for hours without saying a word. Without needing too.

But that ain't what I said. No sir. I said something terrible.

"I wish you hadn't come back," I told him. "I fucking hate you."

Was right then I heard them batwings open behind. Sounded like a whole troop of boots coming through, too.

And then it was his turn—the last damn thing he said to me. Except he did it with that same evil voice of his. Looking back, I was a goddamn yack for not seeing what he was doing. Was an ambush he'd been setting, all right. Just not for that Gray Man.

The Green Man's words was powerful, then. Strongest I'd ever heard him shout. And his voice boomed when he said them, as much for everyone else in that bar to hear as for me.

"Why don't you sit down and wipe your goddamn chin," he said. "I ain't got time to waste with little girls—in their daddy's clothes or out of them."

Them words knocked me back. Three times real quick, there, he'd hit me right in the damn mind with that voice of his. One-two-three. And this last one? Right knocked the wind—and the wits—plumb out of me. I barely remember stumbling back, my anger all but gone in a flash, and falling into a wobbly chair against some window sill.

Was right then I knew what'd happened. Was then I saw the Green Man had bushwhacked me, made me a weapon all unto my own damn self. See, because was right then I saw them fellas what'd come into the bar behind me, who'd heard that last bit of yelling. Shit, that last bit had been all for them, I reckon. Was at my cost, see, but for them.

Was about a dozen federal cavalrymen. Galvanizes Yankees, most of them—or so I'd learn. And right in the middle of them, standing a full head above the rest like some kind of wicked reflection of the Green Man, was that gray fella in a blue cavalry uniform covered by some queer black duster what shined in the gas light almost as much as his skin. And I was right afraid. Afraid like none of that running or rushing across the hills and plains had prepared me for. See, because the look on that Gray Man's face wasn't one of anger or revenge or even cold hate, like I right expected.

Was the look of a madman.

SEVEN

What happened next happened fast. Though nigh on to senseless as the Green Man left me, seemed to last forever. Like the length of a blink in Hell.

The Gray Man was queer, to be sure. Tall and thin as the Green Man, like I said, and had them same big black eyes. But he didn't have no stalks on his head and wasn't no little bulge at the back of his duster from any spines like what the Green Man had. Was more like he was the skeleton of a Green, it was. Only covered with this shiny gray skin crisscrossed with shallow creases.

But to look at his features? Excepting those big black eyes, his silver face was that of a man—nose, ears, chin, the lot. Some poor copy of man, anyways.

Well, on hearing that gray fella come through them batwings, the Green Man turned around and, quick as shit, unshucked his Colt and that big gun of his. Was a cruel looking gun, that thing. That big soup-can barrel punched through the end by some little hole the size of a penny glowing like red death ready to spring out.

The Gray just smiled. Was then I saw the worst of him, see? That silver skin and dead physique, that mockery of a man's face? Wasn't nothing next to that grin. No. Them teeth was a whole row of pointed triangles, interlocking and ready to bite through, it seemed. And they was silver, too. Except even shinier than his skin, see? Was like they had some light in them. Like they was some killing mirrors all lined up in a row waiting to reflect your blood.

And when he spoke? Shit. Would've sent chill's through me what if the Green Man hadn't struck me still as a statue with them words of his. Was like there was some laughter behind that terrible voice. Was madness.

So the Green Man had his Colt and that big pistol unshucked, see, and that Gray Man just smiled his deadly smile and spoke in this laughing voice—I can't do its terrible justice. Said, "You go for them guns, you know what'll happen."

I remember the Green Man just nodded and said, "Reckon I do."

And what happened next? Fast ain't quite the right word for it.

The Green Man pulled up them guns of his and let fly a tornado of lead and red fire. Was loud, too—like a damn Gatling gun banging out lead. Boom boom boom. Except was so fast it was almost one constant sound, see? Like a freight train. But that Gray Man, he was faster. Ain't never seen nothing like it. He ran forward, closing the gap between him and the Green Man right quick. But what was so fast was his dodging, shifting left and right, ducking low and jumping high so quick you couldn't right see it. So fast the Green Man's shots hit empty air, killing ghosts but not Grays. And them cavalrymen what come in with that gray devil? They was all sent diving for cover. Seems I saw two or three of them fell shot, red fire punched through their shoulders or chests.

But, like I said, that gray fella was fast and not one of them shots found him. And in a flash, he was on the Green Man. With one arm, that gray fella knocked that big gun right out of the Green Man's hand, sending it flying across the room toward me. And with his other, he threw the Green Man up into the air, sending him end over end and over the bar. I remember my heart all tightening up with some dumb horror as I saw the Green Man slam into the mirror behind the bar—so hard that Stetson popped right off his head. Wasn't nothing I could do, was there? The Green Man had seen to that, hadn't he? All I could do was watch, still as fucking stone and silent as a goddamn mouse, as he crashed to the floor with some rain of shattered glass falling all on him.

And that gray fella? Wasn't no wind in him at all. He just stood at the bar looking over at the Green Man. Was an almost bored look he had about him. excepting for this little twitch he had, curling the left side of his lip and squeezing on his left eye some, you might've even reckoned him to be some majestic thing, all towering tall there and shining. Not some crazed rip. But there wasn't nothing right about him. Not one bit. And standing over the Green Man like that, was clear as ever was something foul behind them eyes. Shit, wasn't even a look back for his boys none, shot up as they was, or for the barkeep rushing out a back door. Just cold crazed hate for the Green Man felled before him.

Then that gray fella, he vaulted over the bar like some kind of circus performer and landed astride my senseless Green Man. Picked him up, he did—like how I once saw the Green Man, himself, pick up Walker and Jimmy in that barn. Like a goddamn ragdoll. And holding him up like that, that gray fella leaned in close and took a long, loud breath. Like a bloodhound sniffing its quarry—testing it.

Was right then that gray fella took the Green Man's wrist in his hand and sniffed it—an even louder snort then the last. And I knew right on what for. Was the wrist I done got some black blood on when untying the Green Man back at that Lakota camp. Was me what marked him. And with all that attention on me to wash myself clean, the Green Man left that stain on his own self. On purpose.

Well, the Gray Man howled at that. Not like no animal, though. Wasn't no howl like sounded on Earth before, I reckon. At least not in the Wyoming. And black and pupilless as they was, I expect everyone in that saloon saw the madness in that Gray Man's eyes right then.

He tossed the Green Man out from behind the bar, throwing him near halfway back toward them galvanized Yanks. Was like the Green Man got his wits back mid-flight, too. Where he'd been all knocked galley west just seconds before, now he reached out to break his fall, coming down on a bunch of tables. I tell you, them card-playing waddies in the corner what hadn't already, they fagged out then. Might've been dumbstruck before but they was right pissing then. I was scared, too. No shame in telling it. You put yourself in my place now, and tell me your heart wouldn't have been on the verge of busting.

See, I still couldn't move a lick. Didn't right know if I ever would again. The Green Man's last words to me, "sit down and wipe your goddamn chin" was still ringing around inside my head, freezing me. My mind was quick as ever but my body didn't listen none. So as the Green Man groaned and tried to pull himself up, wasn't nothing I could do to help him.

Or myself.

That Gray Man rounded the far side of the bar, eyes locked on my Green Man. My murdering angel laid low. Then he looked at me. God! He turned them crazy black eyes right on me. Mister, I couldn't tell you what it was about them what made them eyes look so mad. They was black through and through like the Green Man's. But there was a darkness in him. Something right darker than black, if you take my meaning. Something not all color and light. Like what was behind them black eyes was blacker still. Blacker even than the blood what I knew ran through him.

So he looked at me, he did, and he said, "Girl, hand me that gun."

Was then I noticed the Green Man's big gun laying against my boot. Right there on my goddamn boot. But as much as I wanted to fetch it up and fill this saloon with its killing fire, wasn't a bit of me what could move to do it.

"Girl!" that gray demon snapped, "I said fetch up that gun and bring it here!"

But I was froze, like the Green Man must've wanted me. Froze so I wouldn't do what I meant to do and pick up that gun and use it—or some other fool thing—and get myself killed. And there's no mistaking how it would gone right then, neither. No sir. Having seen that Gray Man move, wasn't no way under the sun I could've even grazed him. Was right then I understood them warnings the Green Man told me. Oh, I wanted to run.

But I was relieved at one thing. Wasn't no command in that Gray Man's voice. Not like there was in the Green Man's. No sir, the Gray's was just words. And that was a kindness in that wicked saloon. To have two set of queer voices rocking round in my little head just might've burst it.

Well, that gray fella started toward me, see, mad as piss what I hadn't moved to help him. And as he come, I remember him spitting some venom at me, saying something like, "Listen, you little cunt, you'll want to start being a little more cooperative else I'll let my boys piroot you to their fill. And not for any coin, none, either, you little whore. Now give me that fucking gun before I—"

Before what? I never knew what he was about to say. Because right then the Green Man jumped him from behind. Maybe he wasn't so done as it seemed. I hoped not, anyways. And in his hand, the Green Man held that little knife, the one what murdered the other gray, still caked in black blood.

Well, they fell to the ground, rolling round and fighting like Kilkenny cats among them barstools and broken glass. And everywhere they rolled, was stripes of silver blood left behind. The Green Man's blood, it was.

And when they stopped rolling, still all locked together and fighting just under the lip of that bar, well, the Green Man was pressed up against the kickboard. But he had that knife inching toward the Gray Man's face, he did. And as ferocious a snarl as I done ever seen carved on his green face.

"You smell this?" he snarled at the gray. "This here's the knife what cut your other to pieces. Carved his face so the ward of heaven won't recognize him—not that your kind go to heaven, you fucking—"

But the Gray Man started screaming that mad howl again. And, Goddamn, I wish I could unsee what happened next. I really do. The Green Man's words pushed that gray fella beyond madness, I reckon. He just set to screaming this even, evil tone like no howl you'll ever hear in the wild. And, in a flash, he twisted the Green Man backwards and snapped his knife arm in two, bending it in half right between the wrist and elbow. Was a god-awful sound, that, like timber popping, and you could just barely hear it over that gray howl. But if the Green Man screamed, I couldn't tell none. And then, with the Green Man all but done, the Gray Man just set to wailing on him. Punching and kicking and smashing and gnashing and all manner of cruelties. No man would've survived a lick of it, I'm sure. And that the Green Man was made of tougher stuff, I'd seen before. Seen him take a gut shot and walk away, hadn't I. But for that toughness, I was sorry right then—would've been better for him to die.

And I tell you true, mister, all the while that gray monster was destroying my Green Man, I was right screaming a howl in my own brain. And louder than all else it was, trapped behind my locked lips. And before that bloodying was through, was plenty of tears what joined it on my cheek. Tears for both of us, I reckon.

The Gray Man's howling didn't so much stop as fade away, like it was fading off into the distance even with him right there in front of me. And as it faded, seemed his hitting and kicking and biting slowed, too. And after a forever, he stood over the Green Man, silver blood all on his fists and clothes and face.

But the Green Man wasn't dead. I could see that straight away. Wasn't much of him you could recognize right then, bloodied as he was, but he was moving still.

That gray fucker wiped silver blood off his mouth and spat on my Green Man. Then I remember him saying some queer stuff. He said, "You Greens are so weak. Weak!" he screamed. "Reckon that's why you hate us. We're smarter, faster, stronger—"

But the Green Man interrupted that gray fucker, coughing up bubbles of silver blood as he did, if you can believe that. Interrupted him, saying, "Not so strong I couldn't gut your twin like an Earther pig on a spit."

Oh, I expect I knew what the Green Man was up to. Wasn't so different than what I was apt to do, time on and again. Being mean for mean's sake. Getting a rise just to see it. Letting the anger take over. And he was trying to make that Gray Man even madder than he was—to make him blind, so he wouldn't see the fifteen-year-old girl sitting still as buzzard food right behind, tears wetting her cheeks. So he wouldn't see her little handprints in the dried blood on that knife's handle or think on about why the Green Man had been arguing with her not two minutes before.

And the Gray Man didn't. He just shook and twitched and clenched his fists instead. And he reached down, grabbed up that fallen knife, and plunged it deep into the Green Man's leg—deep enough the handle was stuck half in.

Was then I heard the Green Man scream for the first time in that brawl—that slaughter.

But the Gray knelt close over him, close enough I almost couldn't hear him saying, "What are you even doing here, you antennaed fuck? Gold? Cattle? Oil?" Then, looking at me and, perhaps, thinking on that yelling he done overhead, added, "Pussy?"

The Green Man was shaking like he was out in some winter storm. Was done, he was, and close to death, it seemed. Was a lot of his silver blood on the floor and them stools and that gray monster what loomed over him. But I saw, too, how riled he got when that Gray Man looked at me. God! It made me sick to see that what with all I'd said to him at the last. I wish he hadn't made me say none of it, I do.

"Well . . . what the fuck . . . are you doing here?" the Green Man asked back at him, his voice all wet and small, shaking and feeble. Was blood bubbling up at his lips when he talked. Was just god-awful. But he kept on, turning that gray fella away from me with each word. "There's nothing . . . here for your kind."

The Gray Man hissed at that and leaned in even closer. And as he did, was impossible, I suppose, but his face changed. Changed from being some mask of a man to being like the Green Man's. His chin pointed, his nose and ears all but gone.

And he said, "You're wrong. There's blood here. More than enough for us." His head shook at that, like he was struggling to fight off some thought. Or, maybe, was more like the way them boys in them opium houses shake when they're turned out, penniless and short a fix.

"More than enough for me," he kept on. "There's more than one way to profit from the West."

Then he stood, that Gray Man did. Was like some calmness come over him for a moment. And I reckoned the gambit was up. He'd finish the Green Man now, and perhaps all else in that pecker of a town out of spite. I tell you, I was screaming inside. Was desperate to move, to fight, to run to my bloodied Green Man. Shit, didn't even care if I died doing it.

But I just sat there, still as a goddamn stone.

Well, thank Jesus fucking Christ almighty, the Gray Man didn't do what I right expected he would. No, he stood there, looking down on the Green Man, and said, "You killed half of me. expect I owe you the same favor." And at that, he reached down and grabbed the Green Man's stalks in one hand and hauled him to his feet. Now, there wasn't no strength left in the Green Man's legs—that was plain to see, even the one what didn't have a knife stuck into it—but that gray fella held him up by them stalks. Shit, I kept waiting for them to rip right out of his bald head.

A bunch of them cavalry boys rushed over to grab up the Green Man before he fell to pieces. Grabbed up his big gun, too, still on the boards at my feet. And as the Gray Man started out them batwings, them boys of his carrying the Green Man behind, I remember the Green Man raising his weak voice enough for me to hear over all them clanking spurs. Said, "Do what you want, you metal thing. There'll be heaven for me when my time is done. Not just cold darkness and nothing."

The Gray Man stopped in them batwings at that and smiled that razor-toothed smile of his, crazy as a loon. And he said back, barely more than a whisper, "Oh, yes. There's blood enough for me in you. Blood aplenty."

And then they was gone and I was alone. In that saloon. In the whole fucking world.

EIGHT

Wasn't another soul in that saloon. Just me, still as a fucking corpse. I couldn't even tell you how much time passed before I got my fingers to start working or before I squeaked some quiet whimper through them stilled lips. Just that it was plenty after hearing all them cavalry and that Gray ride out of earshot. Ride off with my Green Man. Plenty of time to start panicking that I might never move or speak again.

But that first twitch of a finger and squeak of my voice was a blessing, it was. Even as the tears kept coming, was a right wonderful blessing. And bit-by-bit I got my moving back. Tell you true, was like my whole body was waking up—like how your arm does after you been sleeping on it all night. Except none of the prickling but all the slow movement of dead weight. And wasn't just my arm, none. Was all of me. But soon as I had enough in me to drop myself out of that chair by the window, I did. Then I done shuffled myself across the floor like some dying man making for water. And that breathless squeak through my lips turned into a proper blubbering as I went, I tell you. Wasn't a word I could've formed, then, but I was moaning and crying enough to say all I had in me.

And after a forever pushing across them sanded boards, I got to where I was going—the Green Man's Stetson, lying among bits of glass and slashes of silver blood behind the bar where that gray thing first felled him. I remember pulling that hat to my chest, never minding the cuts on my fingers and hands from the glass. Pulled it close. Was bad as when Bill was taken from me, it was. Was like my whole world had gone up the flume and all I had left was some notched hat.

But before I got all my wits back, all went plumb black. Passed out, see? And maybe it was for the best. Put me out of my misery, it did. Better to sleep than lay awake wondering where that gray fuck had taken him. Of what cruelty the Green Man might endure. Of what future a penniless girl in some pecker of a town had, on the run from old Moses Boone's posses or not.

But wasn't no restful sleep, none. Was like blinking, not sleeping. And when I awoke, was a blue sky peeking between some gay curtains what first I saw. And quick on after, realized I was naked as the day Momma made me.

That'll wake you right quick, it will. I reckon there was a time when waking up buff seemed a sweetness. But that was once on when I was Martha and Somers was my bedmate and that memory was long since soiled, I reckon. No, wasn't no pleasant state this time, I tell you. Was plumb naked in a strange bed—lonesome, thank Jesus—but with no notion how I got there. And looking around that little room, I didn't see any of them baggy clothes I'd been wearing, neither. Just the Green Man's Stetson hung over a bed post, like he should've been lying there beside me.

Then, I reckon, the Green Man and the bloody night before all come rushing back to me, it did. I swear, I sat up like a bolt when I got thinking on that. How long had I been asleep? And what of him? Could he still be alive? Was he suffering under some Gray? And why—for fuck's sake, why—had that dumb son of a bitch let that gray bastard have at him like that? Sure as shit the two of us could've done that gray thing according to Hoyle, couldn't we? No gray man could dodge bullets from the two of us.

But of course he could. He did, didn't he? I saw it my own self. That gray thing was fast. Faster than else I'd seen. And another gun in my hand wouldn't have made no difference at all. Shit, haunts me still thinking on what the Green Man did. How he set his own self up. Why didn't he take his own goddamn advice and run—keep on running until the whole of the West was between us and that gray devil. Then he might be here with me, belonging to that hat. Wouldn't that have been a sweetness.

But all that thinking was a sight worthless long as I was just one lonesome, naked girl thinking it.

And running? Was done with that, wasn't I? The Gray Man done caught us. But what now? The Green Man never said what come after all. Shit, I remember feeling this crazed flutter in my chest, I did. The urge to keep on. And with a quickness. To get out of bed and just run until my legs gave up—or Bess's did. I didn't know what to do or where to do it but I knew I had to get out. Had to keep running from what just happened.

So, balled up as I was, I wrapped that bed sheet around myself, keeping hold of it at the shoulder with my left so I wouldn't trip over no loose bit of it and leave myself all buff. I remember checking the window and seeing I was up on some second floor. Was still in Alcova, I was, but I knew, quiet as that dirt track outside, wasn't no way some girl wearing nothing but a bed sheet was going to scale down the side of no building unnoticed. Or unshucked.

So I went to the door. Was clearly a woman's room, from the doilies and mirrors and frilly things about the place. And as I put my ear to the wood, listening for what might be waiting outside, I got to thinking about why some pretty place like this might be in some pecker little town like that. And farther on that train of thought, I got to thinking what else might've got done in that bed I woke up in—or even under that sheet I was done wrapped up in. Gave me the fucking chills, that did. Was like having Jeb or Jimmy or even Somers' hands all on me. Goddamn, I had to get out of there.

But standing at that door, wasn't no thought of the Green Man what stopped me. Was thinking on men again. Was thinking on how I tried to make my way after Daddy died and them Mormons cast me to the world. Thinking on the last time I was in a room like this, dressed all in some black spangled thing—the last dress I wore until I was nigh on to fifty years along, I reckon. Thinking on how I was pushed out of that little room into some dusty Helena saloon where them men laughed at me with their toothless mouths—raped me with their hungry eyes. On how I wanted to run then, too.

But that was Martha, that was. Was some helpless girl what lost her momma and her daddy and her way. Was before Piedmont and Mr. Harthra and Somers and the Green Man. Was before putting a bullet to that toothless man at the kilns and shooting Jeb Boone through. Was some other girl, that was. Not me.

Well I'd had enough of Martha. The Green Man was gone. Was Jane

I needed to be now.

So I slipped out that door onto some balcony over that dusty saloon. And quiet as I meant to be, the barkeep saw me right away. Was sweeping up glass and silver-stained sawdust from behind the bar, he was, but he stopped what he was doing and looked right up at me. I grabbed that dirty sheet tight, I did, careful so his upturned eyes didn't spy my snatch between the skirts. But he wasn't looking on that. He didn't say nothing to me. Just smiled a weak, thin thing and called out for some biddy.

Well, this woman, maybe twenty by years and forty by living, took one look at me—and the panic in my eyes, I expect—and took me back into the room. She told me how she and the barkeep plucked me up out of the glass and put me to bed. Was almost a whole day ago when they done it, too. Seems I stirred not a lick as she stripped me out of them man's clothes and went right on sleeping through the whole damn day. Seems, too, the Green Man left a few dollars with the barkeep before I stormed in and kicked up a row with him. Heh, that sweet tramp offered to run out and bring me some gingham dress from the general store but I put her straight. Told her, "Some boy's clothes would fit me fine, as ever."

Was a well-thought ambush that Green Man laid for me. Seems, while I was yelling my fucks on the boards outside, that Green Man done gave his Henry and a few dollars to the barkeep. I reckoned then, as I still do now, that the Green Man used that voice of his on the barkeep, staying any greed to make sure that gear got back to me.

Well, was a busy hour or two, right after I woke up. And all that busyness was good for me. Kept my mind off what just happened and what might happen next. Kept my feet from running off, too. But when that time was up and I stood in that saloon wearing proper boy's clothes and my boots, holding the Green Man's Henry and wearing his notched Stetson over my fresh braids, was then when the weight of all what might come next hit me. Two dollars in one hand, a rifle in the other? What was I supposed to do? Where the fuck could I go?

I remember standing on them sandy boards, silver stains still showing where that gray thing nearly had my Green Man for breakfast. That barkeep and his whore watching me like parents.

"You're welcome to stay, if you need. For a little while or a long one, if you like," that barkeep said to me.

But I couldn't stop thinking of that try at being a dancing girl in Helena. Of that fucking spangled dress and that laughing. And of running—then and now. Wasn't no part of me meant to stay in that town—or any town. Oh, was what Martha might've wanted, it was. But not Jane.

So I did like I had with that fella back at the Rock. Some you got to put to the bullet, some to the tongue. And some, you just got to put behind you.

Was nice folks, them two. I didn't know where to go but I knew I had to fag out of that town. Wasn't no bit of me what could've stayed there, anyways. No bit of me that could work or walk everyday on boards where the Green Man spilled his blood, where I sat frigid and watched, where that gray thing laughed his maddening cackle.

Yes sir. Some you just got to put behind you.

So I didn't say another word, right then. I just turned and pushed through them batwings into the long shadows outside. They called after me from inside but I didn't hear them. Well-meaning folks, like I said, but with nothing, it seemed, for me. And once I was through them batwings I knew I was headed the right way. I was moving, after all, and that's all I knew to do, right then. For that one second, not knowing what I needed to do or where I needed to go, I knew all the same that I was going in the right direction.

But only lasted a second, that feeling did. Because was just a second after I turned to pick up my saddle and head for Bess. Except my saddle wasn't there, piled beside the batwings where I done dumped it. Was just my Springfield lying in the dirt at the edge of them boards where it must've fell in my hurrying to undo Bess the night before. And looking around in a panic, was the Green Man's horse blanket I saw. And peeking out from under it, the stirrups of his discarded saddle.

Was then I heard what the barkeep was calling out to me. Was an apology, see? Was saying, "We tried feeding that mount of yours but I swear I ain't never seen a horse so stubborn on taking feed or water."

Well, I turned around at that. When I saw the empty hitch where Bess should've been, my heart done more than skip—come right close to stopping. And when I saw that queer horse of the Green Man's standing there, following me with them terrible, unblinking eyes, well, them beats started right up again and leapt clear up my throat.

"Well I'll be goddamned—" I remember muttering.

And, fuck me if that horse didn't turn its head down, bite them reins tying it to the post, and pull loose the knot its own damn self. Then turning a hair as it backed off from them boards, it fixed a piercing stare on the Green Man's saddle and just stood there, waiting.

I remember spinning right back toward that barkeep, now leaning on an open batwing. Oh, panic was up in me then, I tell you. First the Green Man, now Bess? "Where the hell is my horse?" I demanded of him.

That barkeep just shook his head, looking back and forth between me, the Green Man's horse, and where Bess' ought to have been. "I don't understand you, miss. Them cavalrymen put that green fella up on his horse when they took him off to Platte Bridge Station. Left this here horse as yours."

I turned back on the Green Man's mount. Bile was crawling up the back of my throat, it was. Reckon I was nigh on to spewing all over them boards. But that fucking horse, it didn't care none. It was just watching me again. And soon as it saw I was turned back, it starting looking back and forth between me and that saddle, like to tell me what it wanted me to do.

Reckon the goddamned Green Man planned out that bit, too.

NINE

Damn if that horse didn't stand still as a fucking statue while I saddled it up. A might unsettling, that was. Not a hint of life in it. Not until I was done, I mean. Then, soon as I adjusted that last stirrup, that goddamn thing just started off, cantering on down Alcova's shitty little main like I was already on it.

Hell, I wasn't even right sure I wanted to ride that queer thing. Green Man once told me it was a Mustang—some wild thing he done tamed in some unnatural way. But right then, with it all starting off on its lonesome, like I done served my only purpose in saddling it, I didn't care a continental if that thing was Mustang or Bay or fucking crowbait. I only remember yelling after that goddamn horse, "Where the fuck you going?" And did it stop, none? No sir. Just kept on until I had to run after to catch up.

Must've been a fucking sight for whoever was watching. To see some girl in boy's clothes trying to scramble up the side of some queer horse what'd started out of town without her, ignorant to her clamoring up into the saddle. Must've trotted off a hundred feet before I got good hold of that horn and pulled myself up, what with that Henry I was clinging to and how desperate I was not to drop it—or grass myself on account of it.

Was a strange thing sitting up in the Green Man's mount, it was. Was a sight bigger than mine, to be sure—I felt that straight away when I tried to pick the damn thing up! Felt it in the spread of my legs, too. Was a bittersweet thing. Here was leather worn from his dungarees, shaped to fit his seat. Here was the holster I'd seen him shuck that Henry into and the metal box from which I'd seen him pull forth all manner of things. Felt like I shouldn't be perched up in that saddle, it did. Like I was some kind of interloper, trespassing where no human being was meant to tread.

But there was time enough to deal with them feelings later, I reckoned. See, by the time we cleared the last of them clapboards out of town I realized that queer horse was taking me the wrong way. Was heading south, the way the Green Man and I'd been headed before that gray thing caught up with us. Shit, I didn't know what way was right, like I said, but it sure as hell wasn't any horizon what some horse picked for me.

So I pulled up on them reins, trying to stop that queer thing. But it didn't respond none. Might as well have been pulling on a goddamn stone. Now, I could feel the little give of flesh as the bit pulled in its teeth. But damn if the thing didn't just ignore me! I squeezed it, kicked it, hit it. I yanked on then damn reins like we was going over some fucking cliff. But it didn't matter none—was like trying to rein in a fucking river. That goddamn horse just kept on the way it willed.

Finally—and after not too long, to be sure—I remember getting all hot and yelling "Jesus! Goddamnit! Stop!"

And like I'd hollered some magic spell, that horse pulled up so fast about threw me over that horn. Well, I wasn't too sure what I'd done or how, but we was stopped. And, I tell you, that horse didn't flinch a bit as I near went over it—just stood there, waiting.

But with the whole flat world around me, I couldn't think of a single point on the old compass to head for—except not back into that town, anyways. Seemed every which way I looked was just dry hills, wind and grass and dust and nothing. Except I just knew I had to keep moving else I'd end up having to think about what I was doing. About how I got here. So I made the only sensible choice. The choice my daddy made years on before, for all of us. The same choice them folks back at the Rock had made, gladly. The same choice tens of thousands of folks had before me in that same spot—lost on the plain with nowhere to go and nowhere to retreat. The only way I could go.

I decided to push west.

But was then, see, I had the differing problem as before. Here I'd done stopped that damn horse and I wasn't right sure how to get it moving again. Must've spent ten minutes kicking and prodding it, just trying to start it off. And you can bet I was muttering and cursing the whole goddamn time. I tell you true, mister, that horse stood still as death in the afternoon sun until I just up and said, frustrated as I was, "Fucking thing! Just go west."

And damn if it did. That horse turned right around and took us west—straight as a compass, too—past that pecker of a town and on toward them hills darkening on the horizon.

Fucking thing . . .

Well, and I swear what I'm saying is the God's honest, I spent the next two hours, until the sky was so dark I couldn't see no trail to follow, getting a handle on that damn horse. And in that time, I plumb reckoned how to drive it. And you and your readers might as well not believe me but it's true. I could kick and pull all I wanted but the horse wouldn't mind me none. Was only when I told it what I wanted—where I wanted it to go, how fast, and whatnot—that it obeyed me even a lick. And it seemed to know what the difference between me just muttering to myself and when I meant for it to hear, too. And was when I realized that, well, was when I really learned to steer that mount. See, I hardly ever saw the Green Man talking to this horse so I knew there must be more to it than yammering. Was the thinking on it. Thinking a simple girl like me had to put to words for that queer thing to reckon. Yes sir. I swear to God Jesus it's the truth. And after a good while, well, I just thought, "trot" and it would set off at it. Like to think, "right" and that queer thing would turn. Except it was more particular than that. You could look out across the ground and eye a route between some rocks or across a crick and, without a word saying it, that horse would follow the way you wanted. I swear! And after an awkward little while of trying it, damn if riding that bizarre thing wasn't like having four more legs trotting on the damn ground. Was a right queer feeling, it was.

But was dark after long, and right soon I had to stop that thing again and make camp. Was then what things really started to hit me, see? All this while I'd been busy, more or less. Been with that barkeep and his whore, been dressing or braiding or chasing this damn horse down main. Then there'd been trying to ride it and trying to figure which way to go. But wasn't until after I made camp and settled myself down by a fire that I really had time to think on things.

Wasn't no sleep for me that night, I tell you. I don't know if it was because I'd slept so much the day before or because that queer horse was standing unhobbled across the fire from me, watching me like some goddamn hawk. Reckon, more than anything, was just the quiet and all them memories catching up on me. On the predicament I was in. What a fucking calamity I'd become—no family, no home, no horse—of mine, anyways—and now no fucking Green Man, neither.

Goddamn, I missed that Green Man. Barely was a thought in my head for all that trouble between us on that last day. All I could think on then was them long silent rides or them nights around the fire. All that cursing him I'd been doing? About how he done gave himself up to the Gray Man? About how he'd let himself take the blame for my killing of that other gray? Was just me beating the devil around the stump—just me avoiding what I'd done, see?

Shit. As that fire cooked down and that long arc of milk glowed out of the sky overhead, was all I could do to think on all them times I should've done more. Like how I should've kept my wits in that bar so the Green Man didn't need to set me quiet with that voice of his. How he might still be here beside me if I hadn't overreacted in that cockpit and stabbed that first gray thing to death. How if I hadn't been so mad, I might've insisted he wash himself in that crick, same as me, to clean off that black blood I'd got on his wrists.

And when I did slip off to sleep, wasn't none better. Must've been early in the morning before sleep finally took me. And when it did, was all nightmares and ghosts. Was Somers remembering his wife. Was Jimmy ripping open my shirt, punching me in the face and tearing at my dungarees. Was that toothless man pinning me up against the wall or kicking me to the ground beneath Mr. Harthra's spaceship. Was watching all them boys get shot to hell by Jeb and his—was Mr. Harthra getting his face burned right off.

But was worse than all that, it was. Every evil vision that night was chased by one worse. Was Momma, pregnant and weak, in the back of the wagon. Was that corpse baby she squeezed out and Momma's last, crying breath echoing off some Blackfoot hillside. Was Daddy coming back one night, pale as a ghost. Was me waking up in the chair beside his cot, his body all gray. Was Lena and Lije and the others taken off by strangers. Was me, all alone, on the banks of that Salt Lake with Bess, a few dollars in my pocket and fuck else to call my own.

And I woke crying at that. And that fucking queer horse was still standing there, unmoved a tick since I hopped off it. Sure as shit reminded me that even Bess was gone now—taken to God knows where by the Gray Man and his cavalry. I threw them two dollars I had left into the smoldering remains of that fire and, I swear, I just about lost it. Was bawling like I never done before. All that talk about me being some cold longrider? Wasn't none of that to be seen then. Just calamity and ruin, I reckon. Just the mess life had made of me and all I loved.

Reckon I fell off back to sleep after all that crying and when I woke again it was light out. And all them thoughts of death and rape and lonesomeness was long gone. Was just the dust stuck to my cheek where my tear-wet face had pressed in the dirt to remind me of that terrible, restless night. Was a lot to be ashamed of in them reminiscences. Lot I should've done. I should've kept my head low and avoided them boys in that barn. I should been awake when my daddy passed. I should've been a good enough nurse to save my momma.

I should've been Jane, them times.

Well, goddamnit, I was Jane now. Jane Canary. And my life, calamity or no, wasn't through yet. You be sure your readers understand that bit of this story, mister. Don't matter none how bad it gets sometimes. You can always turn this shit around.

See, I might've failed all them times before but there might be something left this time I could save. I didn't know if the Green Man was live or dead. Didn't know what, if anything, there was of him left to rescue. But I knew one thing for certain:

Can't count on no man to save you. Or to save yours.

So I hopped up fresh as if I'd slept solid all night and broke camp with a mind to ride up to Platte Bridge Station and rescue my Green Man my own goddamn self. And if he was done when I got there, then I'd satisfy myself with killing that Gray cocksucker. How I was going to do it? God knows. But I had the fire in me, then. Felt like I could take on the whole world.

So I wiped them dirty streaks off my cheeks and mounted up. And was right then, with that dirt from my face all on my hands, that I remembered something. Something what meant the difference between this little adventure succeeding or ending in me dead by that same gray thing what got my Green Man.

See, looking down on them soiled hands, I remembered the Green Man's dirty hands what after he burned up my clothes back at that crick. They was dirty from what he'd done when he'd gone off to fetch me some clothes, I reckoned—from doing something he hadn't told me about.

So I leaned over that saddle horn, right close to that queer horse's ear, and told it straight, "Take me to where the Green Man went that night you two left me. Take me to where he buried something."

And, I tell you true, that horse started off like it knew just where to go.

TEN

Took us a whole day of riding to get to where that horse reckoned the Green Man buried something. Wasn't until the last hour or so I recognized where we was heading, neither. Why should I have? Last I passed through these parts, was madder than an old wet hen at the Green Man for sneaking off on me, leaving me lonesome with that gray thing on our heels. Reckon I hadn't been paying so much attention to the scenery as I ought to have.

But when we come up over that little rise and I saw the crick below us, I knew where we was straight away, I tell you. Could see the burnt spot on the bank where the Green Man cooked up my clothes. Could still see the little scoop in the crick where I done knelt in that cold rush and scrubbed myself clean of sin.

And there that horse stopped, lowering its head and snorting. So I dropped out of that big saddle and looked around, bewildered as shit. When we was here last I didn't never see the Green Man dismount to bury nothing. And was a good long ride from the spot where I right reckoned we'd been headed, too—where he done left me sleeping unprotected that night before. Could it be he'd ridden ahead all this way that night? To bury something so I might find it here abouts later? Shit, I began to wonder then if that wasn't why he left me with his horse instead of Bess—so I could find whatever it was. If there was anything to find, that is.

So I hunted around the ground, looking for any old spot what looked scratched at or disturbed. But wasn't nothing to see? Just rocks and dirt and scrub between that horse and the crick.

And as dark slipped up on me again after an hour or more of looking around the ground, I just dropped to the dirt and watched the sun touch them westward hills.

Now, I'd gotten familiar with the notion of talking to a damn horse by then, I tell you. A horse what listened, anyways. Bess might've cocked her head or jumped when I hollered but wasn't no listening in that. Not like the Green Man's queer mount. It fucking watched you and kept them ears primed, it did. Like to wait its turn at talking, too, except was only huffing or snorting what it said. But it listened, all the same, and lonesome as I was by that crick, reckon an ear of any shape's all I needed. So I spoke my mind to it, saying, "You sure you brought me to the right spot?"

Thing just snorted, it did.

So I snorted back. Here I'd been thinking all the livelong day that there'd be some treasure buried here. Something to help me win the day and rescue my Green Man—if there was anything left of him to rescue, that is. Was like losing him all over again, it was—that feeling of failing before even beginning.

But that queer horse just kept snorting. Fucking got my back up, that did.

"What!" I remember snapping at it. Now Bess would've jumped if ever I'd raised my voice at her like that. Reckon most horses would've. But not the Green Man's horse. It didn't move a hair that the wind didn't stir. Just stood there, head down, snorting. But right then, watching that thing huff at the dust, I remember seeing something I hadn't before. Something I should've if I'd any sense in me. See, that horse didn't do nothing you didn't tell it to. Not that I could see, anyways. So when I done told that horse to take me back to where the Green Man done buried something, it brought me back to that very spot. Didn't mean for me to hunt around none. No sir. That queer thing was particular. And so it stood all along—head down, pointing with them snorts at the precise fucking spot I was hunting for.

I remember kneeling beside that thing's head and scratching away the dirt it was snorting at. Was some torn grass on top, see, and the soil was all loose. Fresh dug and dry as a bone. Didn't take but a minute to dig out what the Green Man buried there. And when I saw it—shit, when I held it in my hand—I couldn't believe I hadn't missed it. Goddamn thing had been buried in the waistband of my dungarees the whole ride off from that flying ship. When the Green Man had lifted it off me, God knows.

Was that shiny gun I pulled off that dead Green pilot, back in that ship what the Lakota shot down. Was the gun I done fired in their Injun camp.

Still felt light in my hands, it did. But having seen it fire off, once on, that gave it some weight. Here was a gun that could kill a Gray Man. But, of course, if that was true why hadn't the Green Man kept hold of it?

I took that shiny thing and pointed it at that crick, at the spot where I once crouched buff as momma made me, and pulled the trigger. Was that snap—that metallic twang like a banjo string—and some line of white hot fire leapt out of the pistol, cutting a beam straight and true as a rail. And the whole while I held that trigger down, that hot beam kept its shape, searing the water at the other end, boiling it up into the air.

And, tell you true, when I let off on that trigger, I remember seeing them rocks at the bottom of that crick was cooked white and cut right in two. Was a powerful gun, it was. But power on its lonesome wasn't enough, I reckoned, or the Green Man would've kept hold of that thing. Was speed the Gray Man had in spades, wasn't it. Speed enough he might could dodge a dozen or a hundred of them guns like that. So why secret it away like some treasure? Why bury it here hoping I'd the wits to come find it?

Well, sir, I'll tell you now, it took me some thinking that night to figure it right out. Made me a fire on that spot by the crick and sat there conversing with a goddamn horse, I did. Not that it answered me none. But I knew it was listening, so I talked to it. And in them watching eyes, and in its queer quiet, I reckon that horse done helped me feel out the answer. By morning, I had myself a plan.

See, this here was a gun what could bury a Gray Man. Just not by shooting.

So I told that horse where to take me. And to get there under cover of night, I did. And, damn if that horse didn't head off straight and fast.

ELEVEN

Was morning the day after we set off before I saw my first sign of them Lakota. That first day after digging up that pistol was all anxiety and hurrying, like there wasn't enough rushing forward I could do to make up for dragging my boots out of Alcova. But when I returned to them Rattlesnake Hills and I saw them burn marks in the dust and them shot-up bodies—men, women, and children, all—that cooled me right quick. Was hoof prints and spent shells and blood every which you looked. Was the Gray Man's work. Might've been the camp we'd seen burning from that hillside that first night on the run. Maybe was another war party caught by them cavalry and their Gray boss. Truth is, I don't know who them Lakota was what died there. Just lingered long enough to reckon none of them was Red Cloud or his warriors before I kept on my way.

See, that burned up camp wasn't where we was headed anyways. And that horse seemed to know it just fine. Knew right where to take me, it did, and we made good time, too. Thing never stopped to eat, sleep, or do its necessaries. And wasn't nothing what could spook it none. When we rode into that massacred camp I was ready to fight it from bolting like I would've with Bess. But that horse was calm as a summer's day, it was. Shit, even when we come up on a snake and it snapped them fangs at us, that horse just kept its cool and swung wide around. Queerest damn thing.

Right quiet, too. That horse didn't make hardly a noise. Even its stepping was a quiet thing, which was right and swell given' what I was planning for that nightfall. So when the sun set and my nerves told me

we was getting close to Red Cloud's camp, I told that horse to keep on.
To keep quiet but to keep on. Wanted to find them in the dark, see? Was
like to be the only way some little white girl was going to get so far into
a savage camp as she needed.

See, wasn't the first time I done seen Injuns. I'd seen a few in towns,
of course, as I made my way west that first, terrible time. But wasn't the
first I'd seen warriors, neither. Sure, back at that ship was the first one ever
done shot me. And after that, the first I'd ever seen one of their camps.
But not the first time I'd ever come across a war party and certainly not
the first I'd gotten the better of them.

Back when I was just fourteen—shit, was just little more than a year
before, wasn't it? Seems like a whole another life looking back on it now—
that wagon train we was riding west with got plumb surrounded by a war
party. Was right on the edge of Mormon territory, I reckon. I remember
all them men getting settled for an attack come morning. But I'd just lost
my momma and wasn't like to lose my daddy and my brothers and sisters,
none. So I rode out in a huff, angry as a stampede at them men what were
settling in for a die-up when pushing on could bring us to rescue. Was
dark and moonless and in my awful terror I plumb forgot my Springfield.
Shit, riding through them Injuns in that dark was the scariest damn thing
I'd ever fucking done—and would be until that Jimmy made to raping
me in that barn where the Green Man found me. But I went all the same.
Rode right through them circling Injuns, I did, thanks to dark and fog
to hide me. And when I come back the next morning with fifty cavalry
to free up the train, well, was the hero of the party I was. An instrument
of God, Daddy called me.

Well, that as long time ago and I had myself a different notion this
time—but had sneaking to do, all the same. So after nightfall that queer
horse and I kept on, quiet as could be. And wasn't too long before I could
see the shapes of men and horses off in the dark a ways off, lit by the fading
embers of dying fires under some cloudy sky what hid the glowing moon.
Wasn't no teepees for this was a camp on the move. But was plenty of
folks. Hundreds, it seemed. Was just what I was looking for.

How nobody saw me? Well, was that horse to thank for that. Quiet
as death, it was.

Took forever to get deep into that camp. Couldn't have been more than a few minutes, to be sure, but felt like I'd been sneaking on that quiet horse all night. And soon we got ourselves to a point where there was too many folks around in the dark—some what must've seen us. Reckoned, then, couldn't count on sneaking on any further else I'd end up with an arrow poking out my chest and my errand plumb fucked. So I stopped the Green Man's horse and pulled that shiny gun from my waist.

Now, mister, them Mormons talk about God coming to them Injuns, they do. That's the truth. Well, was right time for that camp to come to Jesus.

I pointed that shiny pistol straight up into the night and squeezed hard on that trigger, holding it tight. And, like some wire struck, a twang rang out through the camp same as that rail of fire leapt right up into the black. Straight up into them clouds, it went, lighting them all up like some firework. And as I kept hold on that trigger, keeping that beam alight, it cast some glow all around me, too. Was a beacon, it was. Was a message to all them savages around abouts. Was an instrument of God come calling.

And, goddamn, you can believe that set off one hell of a commotion. Women and babes scrambled off to the dark while them warriors grabbed up whatever weapons and torches they had nearabout and rushed close. And when I saw the first of them coming, I started shouting over and over, "I come to see Red Cloud! I come about the Gray Man!"

Looking back on it, I was like to end up beefed right then. And the look on your face says you're thinking the same. Shit! I don't think the thought ever crossed my mind, mister. But I was young and stupid and, besides, I was good as dead if I went after my Green Man alone, wasn't I? Worse if the Gray Man fed me to his boys like he done promised back in that saloon. Wasn't no way this could end up worse than all that now, was there?

Shit. Might be. See, was screaming and shouting aplenty from them savages. Enough to tear me up. But I didn't understand a lick of it. So I kept shouting my chant and they kept shouting back. And after a spell I saw that red son of a bitch Crazy Horse, naked but for some leather britches, step out of that wild crowd right toward me.

I stopped my shouting when I saw him. Told him plain, "You know who I am! You know who I ride with! Fetch me Red Cloud. I've come to see him about the Gray Man!"

Well, that son of a bitch sneered at me like he was some kind of wild animal. Put his hand right on a knife strapped around his waist, he did. And them eyes? Goddamn, he was killing me with them eyes. I remember wishing, right then, I had that Henry across my lap instead of shucked away. But if I went for it? Damn. That host of savages would cut me down before I could touch skin to stock.

But he didn't draw that knife, none. No sir. He turned to them warriors all around and started shouting his own cries over mine. Always one hand pointing back at me, too. Now, I couldn't speak a word of Lakota but in them cheering replies Crazy Horse got, well, I reckon I knew well enough what he was saying. Was whipping them warriors up. Was blaming me for all the misfortune that gray thing had heaped on them since we parted ways. Was reminding them who was brought this calamity to them.

Thank Jesus Red Cloud showed up when he did. Them warriors stopped their shouting straight away. Me, too. But I kept my finger on that trigger, pointing that rail of light as ever up into the black. Shot all the way back to the Green Man's world, it might've. But was likely that glowing halo it cast around me was all what was keeping me alive.

Now, Red Cloud didn't say nothing. Just stepped next to Crazy Horse and looked at the Green Man's horse for a spell. Was doing my best to keep my cool, I was, so I held my tongue. But once his cold, dark eyes drifted up and met mine, didn't waste no time getting started. "Red Cloud," I said to him, trying to sound all tough and strong. "I pray you understand my words because I come seeking a favor."

A couple of them braves around us chuckled at that. Reckon I was more surprised that many of them savages understood my English. But Red Cloud didn't laugh none. Just kept them dark eyes on me and said nothing.

So I kept on, hoping I wasn't lying and that them words of mine was understood. Told him, "You let the Green Man and me go a few nights back. He told me you owed him the favor of it. Well, he needs you still. So do I. The Green Man's been taken by that gray fella. Taken back to that fort of his up at Platte Bridge Station."

Red Cloud raised his hand, like to quiet me.

"If he's taken to the fort, he's dead." Red Cloud said. And my telling ain't worthy of his speaking, no sir—that chief's words was clear as any

Old States boy I ever heard. Told me, "even if that silver still pumps in his veins, you can't save him." He stepped close to me, then, with Crazy Horse closing up behind, and kept on, "Them are war-hardened Southerners what ride with him. What hole up with him in that fort. Many of my braves have died facing them. And they've better than cavalry arms, girl. They ride with the Gray Man's guns in their holsters."

And at that, I did reach down and unshuck that Henry, turning it so the scope was plain on the register. Well, them warriors all around started shouting at that but I ignored them, talking only to the chief and his man.

"Reckon I ride with the Green Man's gun in mine," told him.

But was just some pitied look he had as an answer. "Ain't nothing one girl can do," he told me. "The Gray is death."

Damn, I hated that. Wasn't nothing one girl could do? Ask Jeb Boone about that one.

But I fought to keep my cool, I did. I remember taking a deep breath and making my proposition. "You get me close enough to that fort, I can best that gray bastard for you. If he's hell-bent on revenge for the murder of his kin, I can draw him out."

But Red Cloud just shook his head and looked like he was about to turn away. But my blood was up. And every second spent yammering was time the Green Man was loosing, if he was still alive to lose it. So I let my finger off that trigger and let that Green gun's firelight die. And in that fresh dark, I dropped off that queer horse quick as being grassed and ran right up to Red Cloud. Now, them warriors were scrambling, ready to finish me, I'm sure. But I didn't have time for them—was a war I was meaning to wage.

So I scrambled in front of Red Cloud, stopping him from walking off, see? And with just them savage torches to light us now, I told him, "I mean to go after my own. And I need your help to do it."

I tell you, in what little light there was, I could see a kindness in that chief's eyes. Warrior and headman what he was, could see plain he was kind man, too. Shit, was the first kind look I'd seen from a man in a long while.

"There was two Grays, once," he told me. "They gave us weapons. Weapons from the stars, they said. From the green people. They asked for nothing in return. So we took them and made war on the white man. And we had many scalps." At that, was a whoop from many of them braves. "But it was just a trick," Red Cloud kept on, "same as we've seen before. For no man—white or gray—gives anything for free."

Red Cloud turned to face his warriors, shouting, "Them guns was bought with our blood!" Then he said something in Lakota, repeating that thought, I reckon, what with how he said it. And the cry what rose out of the tribe at that was a sorrowful thing. Was angry and sad and vengeful all at once—the cry of a people who know what it was what was killing them. And from the look on Red Cloud's face, was something they should've known from the start.

Turned back to me, he did, and kept on, saying, "For every weapon the gray men gave us what we might war against the White Father, they turned another against us. Sold guns to the soldiers in the fort that they might have slaughter. And when we was bloodied and the land was burning around us, them gray twins returned. They offered us more guns, better than them of the men in the fort. But was a mighty price attached. A cost too dear."

And was some knowing look passed between that chief and Crazy Horse, right then. I've long wondered what price them gray men might've demanded for their arms. Was blood enough in the West, I'd heard that Gray Man say. Was a profit to be made from it. But what price was too dear for a people fighting off wiping out? What price could've been worse than Armageddon?

But wasn't time for what was. Was time to settle up the future.

"You're at war already," I told them, chief and his warrior, both. "Help me and I can give you revenge. The Gray Man can be beat. Them soldiers of his, too." I reminded him, "Your warriors brought down his flying ship, taken weapons meant for his cavalry—better weapons than they have."

But when that chief started to shake his head and turn away, I stepped up so close my breath about fluttered that feather in his hair. Shit, would he could've felt my heart about to punch through my chest when I raised my voice for the whole goddamn tribe to hear, calling out, "Y'all know I—"

And there I choked—right in the middle of talking—my throat catching with such a quickness that chief was right to wonder what I was dying. Was the Green Man's words, "Don't you ever speak of that! Not ever!" echoing up out of the dark and rattling around my brain as if they was fresh said. Freezing my tongue fast here same as they done in that Alcova saloon. But I'd be goddamned if the Green Man was going to interfere with his own fucking rescue. No sir. I closed my eyes, clenched them little fists of mine tight enough to cut my palms on my nails, and pushed out them words like they was something vile fouling in my belly.

"Y'all know I . . . killed a gray man with my own two hands!" I struggled out. And, opening my eyes at the last, I fixed them not on that proud Red Cloud but on that son of a bitch Crazy Horse and I kept on, shouting, "Surely your braves ain't afraid of an enemy what some little girl's already bested?"

Well, Crazy Horse leapt at that—angry, face all flushed. I tell you, mister, if there's anything good about being a hot-tempered bitch, it's knowing right well what buttons to push in others seeing as they're the same ones what get your own back up.

But I didn't pay that warrior no mind. I just took that shining gun and pushed it into Red Cloud's hands. And I told him, in quiet measured words so I'd seem all the wiser what with Crazy Horse ranting in his savage gibberish behind me, "The Green Man gave me weapons, taught me how to use them, and pointed me at my enemy. I reckon he's done the same for you now."

Then I backed away, giving him room. Was the moment, I tell you. It'd all go up the flume right then if I'd been too heavy handed or not strong enough. But I wasn't afraid none. Hadn't been this whole time I'd been in their camp. Might I should've been but I knew what I needed to do. That shining gun could fell a Gray Man, to be sure. But not by the beam it shot out. No sir. By the army it could win me.

Backed right up to the Green Man's horse, I did, and shucked that Henry in its holster. And I told them all, plain, "Reckon I just walked into this war of yours. But they done took my Green Man and I mean to finish it."

Red Cloud was watching me then like he was seeing me for the first time, he was. Even Crazy Horse was quiet now, one eye on that shiny gun in his chief's hands, the other on me. And I could see that chief was thinking. Thinking on all that blood them Grays and their cavalry what spilled. Thinking of all that pain delivered and all that promise stolen. Was the same thinking you might've seen in me once on, when Jeb Boone still loomed, my vengeance yet repaid.

But Red Cloud only asked me one question. After that, his decision was made. And tell you true, I answered it right perfect I did.

"You can draw out the Gray Man? You can kill him?" he asked me.

"I can," I told him. Then, without missing a fucking beat, I looked straight at Crazy Horse and said, "With his help, I can."

I remember Red Cloud nodding. And looking at that shining gun I gave him, he muttered something in his tongue what I couldn't reckon. But Crazy Horse nodded to it. Wasn't no argument left in that warrior. See, he was on the prod for that gray thing and here was some white biddy offering him up. So they spoke for a spell, their eyes drifting to me time and again. And that was the first I was nervous that whole time, I tell you. But didn't last long.

No sir. Was right soon Red Cloud stood straight, not much taller than me, in truth, but could've been a mile high right then. Of the first water, he was. Hell, I remember that single feather in his hair glowing like fire in the torchlight. And in that gravely voice of his, with them dark eyes on mine, he said, "My riders will go out tonight. We'll leave for the fort in the morning. If you speak true, we'll have that gray demon's scalp before two days are out."

And, looking at Crazy Horse, I planted that seed even deeper, saying, "And we'll have that scalp on your lance."

Well, guns was raised at that, Red Cloud's among them. He lifted that shiny thing and pointed it at them same heavens I once shot through. And was whoops and cheering what joined that rail of fire, filling up the night. And so lit up was them clouds, that Gray Man must've seen it shining over the horizon. And to that, I remember thinking, Fuck him. Let him see it. Let him see what's coming.

I done had my army. And I meant to come for my Green Man.

TWELVE

Was a whirlwind, that next day was. The tribe was all activity, women and kids helping the men ready for war. And the weapons they had? Goddamn! Never was an army on Earth armed like them savages. Queerest mix of bows and rifles and Green guns you ever saw. And some of them weapons they took out of that ship? Hell, I've seen them in action and I couldn't begin to tell you what they was. And right to say them Injuns didn't plumb understand them guns, neither. But they knew which end was the business and where to aim them.

And before the sun was a hand span above the hills, that whole tribe was all on the move. East toward the Platte and bloodshed. Crazy Horse rode with me most of the morning, talking through the plan with me. Wasn't no talking as clear as Red Cloud's, understand, but was proper words, all the same. And all the while, that warrior kept eyeing that horse of mine. Of the Green Man's, I mean. Reckon I caught him watching me a bit, too, when he figured I wasn't looking. Seems a lot of men never saw one such as me. A girl what could keep up and fight and ride and curse with the best of them. A girl what ain't trapped in some dress or some house or some bed. A girl what ain't waiting on some man to do what she ought to her own damn self.

Was a little after noon a group of Cheyenne rode up. Seems them Grays was fucking with more than just the Lakota. Looking to make the whole West a bloodbath, them gray fellas was. Giving space-man guns to them savages so they could force the Union to pay top price when their time come. I reckon a Gatling doesn't hold much water against guns like what these Lakota carried. And I reckon them Army boys would pay just about anything to keep them savages from getting revenge for a century of blood.

But riding with that tribe, on that eerie, silent horse, I'd my moments of pause. Got to wondering what I was getting these braves into. Was just one man I was caring about here—a green man what might already be dead. And here I was betting the lives of a few hundred braves against his one. I'd done seen these men with their women and their babes just the night before in camp. And here I was risking making a bone orchard out of them if my plan didn't go off. But, goddamn, I'd have done just about anything to get my Green Man back. By hook or crook, I'd pull him from that gray fella's clutches, even if it meant setting the Sioux nation afire. Even if it meant burning all the Wyoming.

So that night—the night before I faced the Gray Man—we camped a few hours' ride from the fort. Was a steady stream of braves riding up to join us all day until there must've been a thousand or more warriors in that camp. And they was all fine red men, too. Fine as cream gravy. How we ever won their West away from them, God knows. And watching them make their preparations, wasn't no army on Earth I reckoned could best them.

Course, the Gray Man wasn't of the Earth, was he?

But that night, I was full of hope and promise, I was. And nerves. Here I was just hours from facing that gray fucker what took my Green Man from me. And like that other night—the first out of Alcova—wasn't hardly a lick of sleep to be had. Except wasn't all fright in me now. No sir. I was ready to fight. Ready to revenge.

I remember going over to that little metal box what the Green Man kept on the back of his saddle. Seen him take all manner of things out of that box over the weeks we'd been riding together—things what wouldn't all rightly fit in there together. But I wasn't thinking on how or why that box was. I was thinking on what I needed from it. And just like that queer horse and how it responded to my thinking, that box was the same way. So I opened it and found just what I needed right there in it, all alone—that music disc the Green Man done let me sleep with back before we burned out Piedmont. Just the thing I needed to set my mind to quiet for a little sleep before the fighting.

I lay back down by my fire with that disc in hand. Across the way, some brave done up like a squaw—some berdache, I mean—was whipping them warriors up, leading a scalp dance and whooping loud enough even for them soldiers to hear all them miles off. Was a queer sight, that—the only dress in the war party worn not by the little white girl leading them but by some Injun man prophesying their victory. But when I turned that disc on, wasn't a lick of that war whooping I could hear. Just sweet music filling my ears, drowning out all else, see? Calming me and taking me off to sleep even as it rose and fell like the wide open under hoof. And, for a time, I watched them warriors do their terrible dance, moving in and out of shadow like nightmares, naked but for paint like blood on their skin, rifles and Green guns flashing in the firelight. And in the middle of their dance, that berdache—that would-be woman—raising his arms to the heavens, evoking their savage gods.

Well, let them Injuns call on wolves and ravens and thunderbirds. Let them pray for blood. Christ Jesus wasn't one to lend aid to killing, I reckoned. And killing was what I meant to do.

THIRTEEN

Crazy Horse woke me before dawn. Was dark as damnation, it was, with just the faintest firelight on his red cheeks so I could reckon who he was. But he knelt close—close enough I could smell the bitter stink of oils what he'd rubbed on himself—and whispered to me. Said, "Did you kill a Gray? Truly?"

Well, my head was right swimming with sleep, it was, but I knew this was a test of sorts. Was a reason he woke and asked me all abrupt.

But I didn't need to pull no bunk—I'd done right what I said. So I told him, again, struggling with every breath against them words the Green Man put in me. "With my own hands," I said, plain. "Not a pistol in them, neither."

That Injun nodded a little, thinking about what I done said. Of course, he'd heard this before. From the Green Man that first night in their camp and again yesterday when we was riding, making our plans.

"He is fast," Crazy Horse whispered. "Too fast."

Well, I remember I nodded at that. And why shouldn't I? I'd seen that bastard move like lightning across the plain. Faster than the eye, he right was. But it didn't change what I done. Or what Crazy Horse needed to hear.

"Not when he's got ahold of you, he ain't," I told him.

Well, he didn't say nothing at that. Just stood in the darkness—all but vanishing into the black. Then, when all I could see of him in that far off firelight was his moccasins, I heard him tell me, "Follow me. Stay quiet."

So I did like I was told. I scrambled off that bedroll and followed his faint shape through the dark toward that far off fire pit. Except, wasn't so far off as it first seemed. Was the same fire that berdache led his whooping dance around just hours before. But was so crowded with braves now, they all but blotted out the light of it. Hundreds of them, there was, in all manner of savage dress, kneeling in front of each other, taking on their war paint.

And now what we was in the proper light of that fire, I could see the red and white paint stretched across Crazy Horse's face, striking down over them cheeks and chin of his, making him into some frightful visage. And looking around, better than half them braves was already painted likewise. Was the nightmare of a million settlers, there. Was one I once shared.

Crazy Horse pointed at the ground and nodded, directing me to kneel in front of one of his braves. Now, wasn't no bit of me that could right imagine kneeling to no man of my own free will. But wasn't no menace in this what I could reckon. Was the right opposite, it seemed. So I did like he wanted and took knee. See, I wasn't kneeling as some girl, was I? This was a host of braves, it was, making their last preparation. And they done welcomed me in. Was a warrior there, I was. Nothing else.

That Injun put his fingers into that red paint and just about dragged it across my cheek before I pushed his wrist off, stopping him. Well, that right angered Crazy Horse, it did, him thinking I was rejecting his honor. But I ain't no yack. No sir. I knew better than to reject honor, least of all from a thousand war-whooped savages. No, I pushed away that red paint and pointed—never saying a word, like I was told—at a little bowl of paint lying in the dust behind them.

When Crazy Horse saw, he calmed. Was a fire in him, there was. Was like looking in a mirror—all rage and anger and no reason, it seemed. And I caught myself wondering where his green man was. Where whatever squaw or whatever companion it was kept him cool was holed up while he made war on space men and the Army. Made me ache for the Green Man, thinking on that. Ache for how, mad as I could be at him, was more often his company kept me calm. Kept me Jane.

So Crazy Horse knelt before me with that new bowl of paint. Green paint. And with two fingers at a time stroking across my cheek, my forehead, my chin, he changed me. I could feel it deep in my chest, in that

heart fluttering behind my breast with every touch, in the steel of my
bones bent kneeling around that savage fire. Was become a green man,
there. A longrider. A murdering angel, my own damn self.

And so painted, we warriors mounted up and rode off through the
dark, finding our way first by fading starlight then by the gray glow of
that earliest sun. And when the light broke over the long low hills on
the horizon, well, goddamn, was a sight no White ever proper saw what
wasn't his last, I reckon. A sight I share with the likes of Fetterman and
Custer. Was a thousand braves, painted and armed and riding behind
their chiefs and headmen. And until we crested the hill above the river,
wasn't nothing I could see any which way but war paint and feathers and
bareback horses making for war.

Then, in front of us, down a long sloping hill, curled the Platte all slow
and cool. Was trees and brush all growed up on both of them banks, with
long rich grasses stretching back for a mile off either side. And crossing
between them was the Platte Bridge, the last such crossing between here
and Oregon what wasn't a ford. But my eyes was on the fort sitting at
the far end of that bridge—a dozen small wooden buildings behind a
stockade where was hiding my Green Man and that gray devil what took
him. And, I tell you, I was right glad to see no wagon train pulled up
alongside that wall. The whole scene bathed in red dawn like it was, was
right easy to imagine the bloodshed we was bringing down from them
distant hills on this remote station. Easier still without no settlers to soak
up our arrows and shells and worse.

Most of them savages started riding fast and wild, circling and swirling
around our side of the bridge like a tornado, never stopping. And right
quick, too, them started shooting bullets and red fire cross the river at that
fort. I followed Crazy Horse beneath that gunfire to a bluff over our end
of the bridge where Red Cloud and a mess of braves was all surveying. I
took out the Green Man's Henry and put my eye to that scope. I could
see them boys in that fort hustling, all running and panic. But never did
I see the Gray Man among them. Even when some officer come out to
scope the scene with his glass, that gray fella never showed his face. And
no matter how much I hunted for Bess among the horses or the Green
Man through them windows or the like, I couldn't spy neither of them
I come for.

But what else I could see from up on that vantage was encouraging. Was the Lakota all riding like a storm on the north bank around me. And was maybe as many dog soldiers on the other side, harassing the fort from right up close. And though there was a couple thousand Injuns, was barely a hundred of them galvanized Yanks hunkered down behind their stockades. But with what manner of Green and Gray weapons in their hands? Well, we'd no way of knowing. Well, except for the Howitzer, that is.

Damn! When that thing cracked, I bet they could hear it clear across the territory. Might've been going off right next to you. And the cruel whistle of that shell through the air, and boom of it blowing all to hell? Was a terrible thing to hear. Was the only time I was ever on the receiving end of such artillery, I tell you, and more than time enough at that. Except for soldiers tromping through our farm back in Missouri, wasn't much all I'd seen of war, see? And that all through cracked cellar doors behind what Momma hid us. Wasn't nothing like this.

But when that cannon shot off, was a scramble among them Lakota and Cheyenne. After a few shots, we got so we could reckon where it was pointed, which was a mercy, but each blast was still enough to stop your heart with terror. Because run as you might, when you heard that whistling on the incoming, wasn't no escaping it.

And that's how the fighting started. The crack of that Howitzer and the return of a thousand rifles and Green guns echoing off the river. And them queer space-man weapons, they was a terror all their own. Was red and yellow fire launching out of dinged up metal from both sides, blowing men in half or searing them like they'd been dropped in a fire. Was one come out of the fort what looked like lightning, burning both ground and flesh as it cut its way through that savage host. And was one them Lakota fired back what looked like a dozen flaming arrows streaking across the scene—like what felled that Gray flying ship, I reckon—each blasting against that stockade and them buildings like a bomb.

Well, each what wasn't stopped in mid air, that was. Them soldiers had them some kind of invisible wall, they did. Didn't stop every shot, that's for sure, but a right many of what them Injuns shot at that fort seemed to . . . something . . . just short—exploding or crackling or burning all harmless shy of their targets. Was a queer thing to see, that. But showed me, sure as shit, that the gray fella was inside that fort. See, I figured if that gray devil really was selling guns to these savages and them soldiers, was right sure he'd have some protection from them he was selling to.

But how'd I know for sure I'd found that Gray son of a bitch's station? Well, I remember seeing an Injun wade out into the river below the fort, making to sneak up, I reckon. But this long line of fire leapt out of that fort at him—a long rail of light like what I done shot out of that pilot's pistol I gave Red Cloud. And all what was left of that brave was smoke and bubbling froth on the water. So every time some blast or bomb was stopped short over that fort, or some long straight rail of flame cut down an Injun, well, I saw the Gray Man's hand behind it. Sure as shit.

And by the time the sun was climbed up high, well, was about my turn to ride into that mess, it was. The tribes was riding their circles around the fort and choking up any troop what tried to shoot their way across the bridge. And was clear dying on both sides, I tell you. Once or twice that Howitzer even fell silent and I got to hoping they was out of shells. But was always a fleeting thing. And when it cracked again, was a dozen braves blown to chuck all unsuspecting to reward that delay.

Now don't think I ain't noticed how you been looking at me since I done started talking about riding with them savages. Like I was some kind of traitor to my race or the like. Tell you the truth, the thought never crossed my mind, mister. Fuck my race, I say. What all had I seen of any race? Was death and greed and rape and murder. White or yellow or red or gray, didn't make no damn difference to me right then. Was green I was after and I'd have taken any side what would've helped me get him back. If Red Cloud had been the one to take him from me, well, I reckon I'd been riding alongside them boys from the fort as we massacred them savages. But wasn't how it played out, was it? So wasn't the troop I went to war with.

Red or white, this was a lot of killing I'd set out for. And if I was going to go through with the plan what Crazy Horse and I was counting on, I reckoned I was going to need to be cold. Cold as the Green Man picking off that posse back at the Devil's Gate. Colder. And I knew hiding behind some green paint and some red war party wouldn't turn my heart to ice, none. I knew it. But hoped it would make me cold enough to let them Lakota and them soldiers do their killing all around me while I focused on the blood what I come for.

But wasn't a lot of time for thinking what with all the shooting echoing around. When the sun hit noon, them dog soldiers and them Lakota braves took one last pass against the fort before pulling back. And was the first real silence, then, what fell across the scene since that first round of shooting and that first crack of the Howitzer.

Crazy Horse and his riders was long gone, rode off for their part of the plan. So was Red Cloud himself what rode up to me. He held out that Green gun I gave him but I remember just shaking my head and squeezing that Henry across my lap so tight my fingers chilled cold as snow.

"Better to face him with the Green Man's gun," I told him. "Better so he knows me with it."

I'm sure Red Cloud said something more to me right then but I don't remember it. Just handed me some long war lance wrapped around one end with feathers and some bulging medicine bag and around the other with a crude white flag. My heart done jumped right up into my neck, holding that thing, and I started shaking. I know I did. Goddamn, doesn't sound like a girl cold as a green man, does it? But I made my way down the hill toward that bridge, all the same, that white flag slapping the wind above me. Lonesome except for the Green Man's horse beneath me. And thank God that horse was made of strong stuff. Took some comfort from that, I did. Like having a little bit of the Green Man there to calm me.

Felt like it took hours to ride down the slope to that bridge but just a few blurry seconds for me to cross it. And, I tell you, I could feel the eyes of all them braves and all them soldiers on me. On some little girl dolled up in green war paint with dark braids spilling out under the Green Man's notched Stetson, some Injun peace offering held over her head, its white flag kicking in the wind. Could feel that gray devil's eyes on me, too. Black and crazed. Sent a chill through me, it did.

But might be the Green Man was watching me from somewheres unseen. Had to hope he was, didn't I? Hadn't come all this way and spilled so much blood for naught else, had I?

So I stopped at the end of that bridge and looked up at the fort some hundred yards off. At them blasted holes and dark windows and gun slits broken by barrels pointing my way. And I tell you, mister, was shaking something awful in that saddle, I was. But I'd sand enough to stab that lance into them boards, I did. The sound of wood splitting loud as that

Howitzer, it seemed. Dismounted, too, though that wasn't part of the plan—and was a damn foolish thing for me to have done. But it felt right, it did. Was a gray-killer, after all.

Was then I knew there wasn't no cold core in me. Knew I'd never be cold as the Green Man. No, my core was a hot one. Steaming red and angry, it was. Ever had been, I reckon. And behind that mask of green war paint, wasn't nothing to keep back that anger—nothing to stop my blood from boiling hot or to hobble my lip. Let the Green Man keep his cold, killer gaze. Right then, on that bridge facing that fort, I was a Green Girl, all heat and revenge and all the more powerful for it.

So I held that Henry in both hands, ready to raise it in a flash when the time come, and raised my voice to that fort. Tell you true, I sounded small over the roll of the river below and the rustling of a thousand savage horses on the far bank. Shaky, too. But I knew that gray thing could hear me. Felt it sure as I felt that summer sun on my shoulders. So I shouted out my hate, nerves or no.

"Gray Man!" I hollered, "I come from that ruined ship of yours!" And then, steeling myself against them echoes in my head—the Green Man's long ago voice trying to keep me quiet—I pushed on, yelling, "I come from aside the corpse of your twin, I do, and I mean for you to hear me!"

Wasn't no movement from inside that fort. No answering call or no emerging Gray. Just them rifles and Green guns swaying as they kept their sights on me. But fuck all them guns. Was whites what held them and I didn't come so far so no galvanized Yanks could hear me yack.

"Get you out here, you gray coward," I called up to that stockade. "I come for my Green Man and I mean for you to bring him to me your own damn self, I do." And shaking though I was, was anger pouring out, too. Like the rage the Green Man drew out of me in that saloon, I reckon. "Else I'll hunt you down and do you like I done your brother." I hollered. And, shit, I was started now, wasn't I? Was heat in my blood, warming my cheeks and setting fire to my tongue. "I murdered him like some goddamn butcher does a pig," I yelled at them walls. "Took my knife and put it right through his eye, I did. Carved a fucking smile on his face from the side of his cheek down across his neck. Jesus! How he bled a fucking river at that. Screamed worse than a girl, he did!"

Still wasn't nothing from that fort. Just my own noise echoing back.

But I'd seen the Gray Man quick to anger in that saloon, hadn't I? Seen
how the Green Man played him. Was like how I'd prodded on Crazy
Horse, it was. And, sudden, was easy for me to keep on, shaking or no.
Was smoke rising in my chest thinking of that gray bastard raging behind
them walls with each word I hollered true.

"I wonder if you'd known it, you gray fuck?" I screamed at that stockade. "I wonder if you'd felt them straps holding your other down as I cut
him up? Huh? If you felt that eye pop or that throat slit? I reckon you
did. Little else to explain why you're madder than a rabid dog! Reckon
that's why you're too yellow to come out of that fort. Out from behind
that invisible wall you got. Afraid some little girl will cut you down like
she done your brother—easy as shit and laughing my ass off as I do you,
too! So I'll give you a second to explain to them boys you're holed up with
why you're so goddamn affrighted of a little girl."

Then I waited a second, I did, and said again, "Go on now. I don't
mind waiting while you tell them."

Goddamn! Was hot, then, I tell you. But I waited a spell at that,
smiling some wicked thing and hoping them words was eating at him.
Wasn't a man from either world, I reckoned, could stand some uppity
biddy calling him a coward. Men are fools about such, don't matter if
they're white, red, or gray. But I expect your lady readers don't need me
telling that bit of wisdom.

Well, was just about to start up yelling again when I heard this high
voice roll down the hill. Was a piercing thing, it was. But was no guessing
who it belonged too, see? Was just enough crazy in it for me to pick it
out anywheres.

"Ain't no place for little girls," the Gray Man yelled out of that fort.
"And ain't no place for tall tales. You best ride on, child, else we'll shoot
you down to quiet your yammering."

Well, was shaking some fresh tremors on hearing that voice, to be sure.
But I stilled them, I did. Hadn't come this far to hobble my tongue on
account of some little Martha's trembling. So I took a right deep breath
and laughed at that stockade. A laugh a sight bigger than me, it was, too.
And I yelled at that wall, "Tall tales? Tell you what, you gray coward, you
go check that little knife you took off the Green Man back in Alcova.
You go get it and give it a good looksee? Reckon there's human prints on

that handle, I do. Little human prints in your brother's dried blood. Little enough for my hands, I reckon."

Was a while passed after that. A while where I right expected some shot or some bolt of light to come out of that fort and fell me. To spare me the rapid fire drumming of that heart under my ribs. But wasn't no such shooting. Just silence and the sounds of men nervous behind their rifles.

Then, after a spell of minutes, that stockade opened just enough and that Gray Man stepped out into the sun. Looked like he was about to say something, too, but I had a ways yet to draw him out. So, nerves or none, I cut him off before he could say a word.

"You're a goddamn loon, you know that," I told him. "Here you made all that fuss back in that saloon, beating on and abducting the Green Man. Probably done all manner of cruelties to him, too. And all the while, you had the wrong fucking murderer, didn't you? Just like a goddamn Gray, ain't it. Doing dumb shit without thinking on it. Like your brother, I reckon. He wasn't thinking, neither, when he messed with me. Would've thought you might've learned something from his mistake. But since when does a gray fucker learn nothing?"

Well, that Gray Man was smiling the whole time I was talking, see? Smiling like a goddamn coot, them pointed teeth of his shining in the midday sun like a hundred mirrors. And, I tell you, the sight of him made me hotter still—madder than anything I could right remember. And, mister, all them little nerves and tremors in me was gone in blink, they was. Was just hate in my blood, then. Just vengeance.

"You're a lot of talk, girl," he told me. "Not like that affrighted little biddy I saw in that saloon. No, you're full of piss, ain't you? Like that Green was until I cut it out of him."

That set my heart to beating even harder against my chest, it did. Hard and hot. All this while I'd been keeping myself going with thoughts of the Green Man, rescued and riding with me again. Maybe it was dumb but I had to hold onto them images—had to think I was spending all these lives for something more than just revenge.

Took a few steps toward him, I did. Away from the Green Man's horse. And I told that gray bastard, "I'm done running from you. I mean to put your head over a saddle and bury you alongside your twin."

The Gray Man laughed at that, he did, and told me, "You go for that gun, girl, and I'll put you down."

I remember swallowing hard at that. But I nodded, saying, "Reckon you'll try."

And what happened next, mister? Happened fast, it did. Sometime after, Crazy Horse told me he thought our little adventure was over right then. And, tell you truly, was a bit of me what reckoned the same.

I moved fast as I could manage. I brought that Henry up to my shoulder and took to shooting. And soon as I did, that Gray Man did something I never expected. He crouched quick and leapt into the air. Like some kind of bird taking flight. Was maybe a hundred yards between us there, and he was covering it in one solid jump from that stockade toward me. Goddamn, I don't think I breathed the whole while he was in the air, terror took me so much. I'd imagined him running at me, like I'd seen him run in that saloon, or even sprinting on all fours like I seen the Green Man once on. But this almost flying, shook me right up it did.

But wasn't so scared I stopped shooting. No sir. I must've fired four or five rounds at that gray demon as he flew through the air. And damn if some of them shots didn't punch holes through his jacket or even his person. I swear they did. But that mad look on his face, them wild, huge black eyes—they never faltered or strayed from me. I was a mouse and he was the owl swooping down. And in that last second, after my last shot and before he hit me, I knew I'd lost. He'd bested me faster than I'd ever expected. I'd let the fire in my blood bring me too close and now my plan was up the flume and I was plumb fucked.

He hit the bridge so hard them boards split under his boots. And in one lightning fast move, he knocked that Henry out of my grip with one hand and hit me square in the chest with the other. Shit, was my turn to fly through the air. Felt I was lifted off the ground for a good while, too. Until I hit the Green Man's horse, that is. Crashed into the side of that horse something awful—the edge of that saddle stabbing me right in the kidneys, knocking the wind out of me and just about busting my back. Hit it so hard one of them saddle bags burst open, spilling sundries all over, and my Springfield was ripped right out of the boot-top holster it hung from under that saddle.

I hit the boards of that bridge like a damn corpse, the whole world spinning around. Them sundries and that Springfield fell down all about me, the rifle done knocking me in the face, even. And for a long spell, it seemed, I was dead to rights—broken, lying under that queer horse.

But my wits come back as I heard that Gray Man walking across them boards toward me, some mad cackle echoing off them bridge joists and the water below.

"Oh you're some mighty fucking warrior, ain't you, girl?" he said as he stepped close. "That Green of yours wouldn't say a lick about that little whore I saw him with in that saloon. No matter how much I cut or broke or tore. Wouldn't say a goddamn word. Now I see why. Wasn't nothing to say." Oh, he was a talker, that gray fucker, was. And, he kept on for a spell, saying, "That's what I like about your kind, girl. You're all noise. Ain't no substance." Then, through eyes was only just seeing clear again, I saw the Gray Man pull out that little knife. The same what I killed his twin with all that long ago. Was silver blood caked on it, down to the hilt. The Green Man's blood, it was. And as that demon stepped over me, he laughed some cackle right up from the brimstone. And damn if that face of his didn't twist with each screech. Right softened, it did, coming womanly, until he wore a fucking likeness near to mine own like a goddamn mask. And laughing that same crazed shriek from between reshaped lips, he said plain, "At least that Green had the decency to keep quiet while I killed him. Expect I'll need to cut that yammering tongue right out of your head to shut you up before I gut you."

Was something happened right then. Something terrible. Was something blew up inside me I only felt one other time in my whole life—when that murderer Jack McCall killed Bill, I reckon. And same as then, wasn't no bit of reason left me in. Was become a creature of all hate, I was. Was like the last bit of humanity was taken from me, replaced with the devil's love and naught else. And if this gray monster was telling true, and the Green Man was dead, then wasn't no bit of me wanted to be human no more, anyways. I'd be Green without him. Not cold but hot. And if revenge was all I had, then I was goddamned if it wouldn't be enough.

I grabbed that Springfield what fell by my head. Took hold of it by the barrel and as that gray thing stood over me, knife ready to cut me up like I done his, I swung that gun like a war club. Swung the stock of it at the side of his knees like an axe head into timber. Wasn't really no aim to what I was swinging. But was all the hate in the world behind it—and hundred times more strength than I right should been able to muster. Was the Green Man's strength, it was.

Well, one of his knees bent all the wrong way when I smashed it. And was a cracking sound loud as a thunderclap, seemed. He screamed, he did—in surprise, not pain—and fell flat on his back, cracking more of them boards when he hit them. And like some fierce force of nature, I was up and on him. I let the swing of that rifle through his legs carry me up to my feet. And screaming some terrible, anguished, angry cry of my own—like a savage in my own right, I reckon—I followed the swing of that rifle around, over my shoulder and down on that fucking gray's throat like I was chopping wood. Was just a tunnel of vision I could see, was all. Shit, was my head throbbing from the blood boiling up in me. But was all my hate channeled into the swing of that rifle down onto that Gray Man's neck. And when that stock struck below his chin, felt it smash through his flesh all the way to them boards beneath.

Black blood splashed up on my face and all across that bridge. And sparks, too, struck out every which if you believe such a thing. Not like you get off a flint, neither. Was sparks like you might get off a smashed telegraph. And that Gray's body bent wicked, curving at the spine so much I reckoned he'd snap in half what with the stock of my Springfield anchoring his neck to the bridge and his back rising two or three feet up off them boards.

Was a huge whooping cry echoing down from them Lakota on the north bank, right then. Some joyous noise, I expect. And was just about to yank my rifle back, confident that I'd done better than planned by a mile, when that gray thing reached across its own wrecked body and grabbed hold of that rifle. And them black eyes pointed right at me and that cruel, jagged mouth opened, speaking gasps and bubbling pain where his voice might've been once on.

You'd be right to think he should've been dead—I done smashed his neck right through, and that's the God's honest. Sparks and black blood was spraying out of that crushed mess. But dead as he ought to have been, he snatched that rifle out of my hand. And in that second, all that heat and hate drained right out of me and I remembered what the Green Man told me so long ago in that Injun camp.

He told me to run.

I leapt back just as that Gray was reaching for me and grabbed the Green Man's horse by the horn fast as ever I moved before. Had that horse off at a full gallop before I had little more than one foot in a stirrup, too. And by the time I sat myself across that saddle and looked back, I saw the Gray Man on his feet running after me—closing the distance between us, too, if you can believe it. Here I was on the Green Man's queer horse, a beast faster than any I'd ever seen a man ride, and that gray fella, with one leg broke all the wrong way and a throat crushed next to flat, was closing on me. And to heap terror on top of terror, I saw him raise my own rifle on me as he ran.

I leaned low across that horse's neck and spurned it on faster and faster, concentrating every anxious, hurried thought I had into it. Was about at the far side of the bridge, too, when I heard the crack of my Springfield. And while it was a mercy, I expect, that I didn't feel no punch and heat of no shot tearing into me, was a terror to feel that horse buckle beneath my saddle. The Green Man's horse reeled with the shot, almost spilling over. But it kept on, despite whatever wound it'd taken. Least until I heard that rifle bang out two more times. Bang! Bang! And wasn't nothing the Green Man's horse or I could do to keep us going down at that. All three of them shots found their mark, punching through muscle and bone of both that horse's leg and trunk. And in a whirl of light and flesh and pain, that horse and I was grassed something awful in the brush just off the north end of the bridge.

Was the second time that Gray Man about knocked me out. Only this time, was for good. We come all a cropper in the tall grass just off the bridge, all tumbled and ruined. The Green Man's horse lay heavy on my legs and waist—and I was sure one of them legs was broken, too. I remember coming to all screaming, clutching at a thigh I could just barely reach under the heaving side of that mount. And the horse? Its head was back, eying me, and labored breathing sending waves of pain through its body and mine. Shit! Its blood was even mingling with mine in the dirt and brush underneath.

Was laying with my head downhill some, too, so every struggling breath that horse made threatened to roll it down across even more of me, smothering or crushing me if it did. And right made it impossible for me to sit up none, too. I remember thinking, maybe if I could reach that little metal box on the back of the saddle, maybe I could will something out of it. Something to save me or kill that Gray Man. But every time I stretched toward it, some thunderbolt of pain shot through me, leaving my body as some animal howl.

But I didn't have long to suffer. Soon that smashed Gray Man stood over me, blocking out that midday sun. Can't say the look on his face was a smile—looked like wasn't enough control left in his face for that. I done proper damage to him, that was clear. Damage enough to kill him, I reckon, given how much blood was running out of that crushed neck. Hell, that gray color of his was even turning a pale silver. But right then, wasn't time enough for him to bleed out before he finished me. No sir. I was finished and wasn't nothing to be done for it.

Except, of course, I'm sitting here in my dotage talking to you, ain't I? Close on to thirty years after that dread shadow fell across me. But wasn't no miracle that saved me, none. No sir. Can't count on no miracles. Sometimes, you just got to have a plan.

See, it's like I told Crazy Horse. The Gray Man's fast. Faster even than I right expected. But he ain't so fast once he's got a hold of you. And right then, standing over me with my own damn rifle, well, he had as good a hold on me as he ever would.

Was a sudden thunder of gunfire, there was, as Crazy Horse and his men opened up on that gray fucker. Rifles and arrows and Green guns emerging from the brush all around the end of the bridge. Must've shot that gray demon a dozen times in that first blink. Just about blew him limb from limb, they did. Hell, his shirt and coat were all blown and burned to pieces; black blood and sparks raining all down on me and the Green Man's horse. And as his body shook and shuddered under that terrible hail, that Gray Man let loose my Springfield and dropped it onto that horse's side.

I'll tell you the truth now: Ignoring all the pain and the blood, I pushed myself up, grabbed that rifle and, just as a second volley of Injun fire wrecked that gray fella, I raised my own barrel—the same I once used to pop gray squirrels out of trees—and put a shot through that Gray Man's eye and right out the back of his head. And screaming like a mad woman, I didn't stop shooting none until that hammer fell flat and was just the sound of metal snapping on metal answering my frantic pulls of the trigger.

Them Injuns rushed the Gray Man's body as it swayed and started to fall back from me. They swarmed all over him like dogs onto carrion, they did. I fell back into the dirt, still pinned by the Green Man's horse and lying on that downhill, spent. Was just the wide open peaceful blue overhead and that cruel sun burning down out of. And the whooping of warriors what felled the devil himself.

The war started right up again, at that. All manner of fire rained down on that fort. And my view of that cloudless sky was all of a sudden streaked with smoke and red fire. And after a spell, Crazy Horse knelt over me, his war party all around. They pulled the Green Man's wounded horse off me and helped me to sitting up. One of them savages even moved quick to wrap up and splint my broken leg.

But before that, Crazy Horse took my hand in his. Was black blood all over both of us, there was. The Gray Man's blood. And into my hand, he thrust a rough circle of silver, thick as leather and covered on one side with a web of dark material and black blood. Was the Gray Man's scalp. Was proof of revenge delivered.

Crazy Horse smiled from behind his wicked war paint and howled a war whoop to the sky. And all them savages took up with him. Then he looked me square and made sure my fingers was curled around that scalp. And he said to me. "You're quite the little war party. All yourself."

And I remember squeezing that scalp, all right. Remember feeling that black blood squish between my fingers like my throat might've squeezed between that Gray Man's if things had gone different. And, I tell you true, I started to cry right then. In front of all of them braves, too. See, was revenge right there in my hand. Was victory. Was all mine. And was the least of what I wanted.

FOURTEEN

The fighting wasn't on for much longer, if I remember.

Without that Gray Man and that invisible wall of his, wasn't nothing to stop that rain of god-awful Injun fire from tearing through that stockade. Red Cloud and his warriors kept to their word, they did, sparing the fort itself from their heavy fire in the hopes my Green Man might still be living. But perhaps I knew better than them savages. Perhaps that gray demon hadn't been lying when he said he done killed my murdering angel. Butchered him with that same little knife I done his gray twin.

Crazy Horse and his left me to lie in the brush just under the north end of that bridge. They had them some scalps to win, I reckon, and no time for some wounded white girl, whatever she might've done to help bring down the gray devil. To conquer death.

And left there all alone, the boards of that bridge affording me some cover from the fighting, I done cried for a while. Put my face into the side of that wounded horse, its breathing all struggling and wet, and I let them bottled up tears pour out. Understand, wasn't the same crying as that night camped all alone, what when I made my mind to come after the Green Man. No, was different. Was how I reckoned that sad fella from that wagon train must've felt. Was the sadness what propelled him to propose to some strange girl tromping through his camp. See, was lonesome, I was. If the Green Man was dead then wasn't no one left in the wide world for me, was there?

So I cried. Wasn't no heat left in my blood. Just chill. And, I tell you,

I might've been back on that hillside in Blackfoot, watching my momma lowered into some shallow grave, some plank with chicken scratch on it to mark the end of her journey. Or I might've been back in Salt Lake, waking to find my daddy all gray and gone or watching them fucking Mormons parceling out my brothers and sisters like chattel into new, alien families. And me? Lonesome. With not a soul in the world to turn to.

But wasn't back in those terrible places, was I? All that done happened to Martha, didn't it? And was Jane now. Jane who didn't need no man to save her—and none to ride with her, neither. I remember hearing a mess of braves riding by, across the planks of that bridge and into the firefight at the fort. And right about then, I put a stop to that blubbering. Maybe I'd lost something. Maybe I'd lost a lot—more, even, than I could suffer—but I still had my own self. And lonesome as I might be, wasn't no force on Earth or from above what could make me less. Had that gray scalp in my hand to prove it.

So I stroked the mane of the Green Man's horse for a spell, letting the rhythm of that petting calm us both. And when its breathing was slower and mine done steadied, I leaned in close, imitating what I'd seen that Green Man do once on. And I remember the horse stopped its moving and seemed to bend its ear to me, listening as I spoke.

I ain't ashamed to say that I told that horse, "Thank you." Wasn't no regular beast, that thing.

Was a spell, then, what I thought to put that queer thing down for a mercy. To still that pained breathing what I just calmed. And if there'd been a pistol lying on that bank nearabout, or rounds for my Springfield, well, reckon I might've just done it, too. But wasn't no such and was a better mercy for us both.

I remember hauling myself up the bank on my ass, pushing with my good leg, dragging the broke one gentle as I could. And, shit, that hurt something awful, it did. One of them Injuns had set it against a split below the knee but, still, each jostle sent a damn knife of pain up my thigh. Bad as it was, though, only time I stopped was scooting past what little was left of that gray man, all sparks and black blood and ugliness what he was. Wasn't nothing what resembled a man in that dead mess and I was glad for it. But I stopped long enough to pluck off him that little knife what caused so much trouble and naught else. Wasn't nothing else of his

I might want except that and his dying.

I pushed myself up to the end of that bridge and struggled up onto my good foot, my Springfield serving as some clumsy cane, and I started across. I kept to the side, grabbing onto them joists wherever I could, leaning on that rifle the rest of the way, keeping my broke leg bent up off the boards. Might be I'd lost all I'd come for but I'd be damned if I was going to lose all I'd come with. And, while crossing that bridge was a right quick blur before I faced the Gray Man, was a right terrible eternity then, hauling my broken body along them boards to where that gray bastard knocked away the Green Man's Henry.

Was all the way at the other end of the bridge, it was. In the shadow of that shattered stockade. And as I knelt to pick up that rifle, the scope on its register knocked askew but still clipped, was a sudden flurry of activity from the fort. Was hardly aware of the fighting and dying up on that hill until then. But all sudden, was a rush of men and horses bursting out of a hole in the stockade—a mess of them soldiers making their break out of the charnel house their fort had become. And as they rushed for the bridge, right at me, a tornado of bullets and red fire cut them boys to chuck, dropping them off them horses—and some with them horses—into pieces no momma would recognize.

And out of that mess, a few horses broke loose. And I tell you true, mister, my Bess was one of them. Some stranger's saddle on her back and some scorching in her mane from where green gunfire cut her rider away but was Bess all the same. And in her panicked, crazed eyes, I saw her recognize me. I swear I did. We'd been through a lot, that horse and me. She done started this road with me in Missouri and I'd be goddamned if she wasn't going to finish it with me.

I risked getting right trampled, I did, stepping out into them oncoming beasts, yelling after Bess to see she didn't pass me by. And spooked as all the gunfire and killing what made her, I managed to grab her bridle as she come by and turn her out of that group of rushing horses. Was some fella's blood all over the horn and splashed through the hair on her neck. But didn't stop me from hugging her none. Nothing could ever stop me from loving on Bess.

Might've started crying again right then if it weren't for the explosion. Reckon some of them Howitzer munitions up in the fort finally got

sparked. Went up like the end of days, it did. But right before that fireball
ate up half the fort and just about laid Bess and me flat, was a familiar
sound I remember hearing. Was a fast register but loud like cannon fire.
Like the Green Man's big gun.

The fort lit up like a second sun, it did. Was a hundred yards away or
more but that fireball and the splintered wood and metal about knocked
me off my feet and near spooked Bess into bolting. But, try as she might,
I held on to her, fighting against her instinct with every bone in my
body—even them what broke. I'd be damned if I'd lose her again.

And about the time I got her under control, I looked up to see some
big dark cloud—the smoke off that explosion—going up, curling into
the sky and blocking out the sun. Like some great big mushroom, it was.
And all about, splinters and what not was raining down on the dirt and
planks what so I had to shield my head and eyes from it.

And when I opened them again, was a sight I'll never forget up on that
hill. Not until the day I take my last goddamn breath. No sir.

Was the Green Man, covered all in his own silver blood, walking toward me. Had that big gun of his in one hand, the other all clutched and
bloody at the end of his broke arm, resting some on his holsters—Colt
and all—ripped where he must of stole them back from some soldier what
meant them as a trophy. He was naked above the waist, too, except for
that bone shirt of his hanging by a thread. And his face and body was
all scarred, bruised, and bleeding. Even them big bug stalks on his head,
they was snapped broken between his scalp and the first joint, lying all
limp and lifeless against the side of his face.

And as I watched him, wasn't much of a walk he was doing, to tell
you the truth. More stumbling. And the way he was gritting his teeth,
favoring the leg what that Gray didn't break, and peering ahead with one
big eye, the other contracted all tight like some kind of squinting—well,
it told the story, it did. He was plumb fucked up, he was.

I kept Bess's reins in hand and started limping toward him my own
damn self. What a sight we must've been, we two. In a sea of savages
riding bareback and running all around, murdering and scalping their
way through them soldiers in that fort, we was one pair of fucked up
unlikelies. A little white girl with a broke leg, all covered with red and
black blood, and her Green Man, broken and abused, limping their way

toward each other in the whirlwind.

When I reached him, I didn't say nothing. Neither did he. Wasn't nothing to say right then, I reckon. Some folks might've wanted him to apologize for them harsh words back in Alcova or for all that deception on the run before the Gray Man done caught us. Not me, though. Was a long time ago, all that, and not for no reason, neither. No, wasn't nothing at all to say right then. Was the two of us together again. That spoke all what needed said.

I remember falling into him. Burying my face in his chest and hugging him round the middle, my fingers finding their home among them long spines on his back. He winced some, he did—must've been bruises and broke bones deep inside what I didn't think on. But he hugged me right back, wrapping them long arms of his around my shoulders, cupping the back of my head in one of them long-fingered hands. Might've been a whole war going on around us right then. But all that shooting and dying and screaming coming out of that fort was silence in that moment. I had my Green Man. I had it all.

I closed my eyes and lost myself in him, I did. Oh, I try to be strong. All my life I've had to try and since meeting the Green Man I done a sight better at it then ever before. But right then, I didn't mind being weak. Of being nothing but happy to have him back. I might've cried a little. Reckon I did. I took in the smell of him. The feel of his rough skin. And, by God, in that moment all them feelings of loneliness and anxiety and rage was gone.

And when I opened my eyes, I looked across the scene beyond him, my head still pressed against his chest. I couldn't see the fort at all. But I could see a mess of butchered boys and savages, their blank faces and empty eyes all fixed on that afternoon sun and wide open blue sky. And it's like I told you before, mister, was fate what brought me against these boys. Was fate what set me with a host of savages. And would the tables was turned, I reckon I'd have found myself peeking across the Green Man's chest at a wrecked Injun camp, not some frontier fort. But was a lot of death I brought on them savages and soldiers, alike. Was war I'd made to get my Green Man back. And standing there, holding him, I didn't regret a single drop of their blood or mine. No sir. But it didn't make it any easier, none.

I remember mumbling, to myself, really, "It's a terrible thing I done here."

The Green Man stroked my hair some at that. I could feel him looking around at that mess. At them Injun warriors whooping and slaughtering the last of those soldiers. At the quieting gunfire at the end of fighting.

"Was hoping you'd find that gun," he said, his voice rougher than usual. He never told me all what that gray fella done to him in that fort. What all happened between that saloon in Alcova and that reunion on the bridge. In truth, I don't think I right wanted to know. But you could hear it in his voice and see it in his walk—and else. Was terrible things done to him.

His left hand was on the small of my back, it was, and felt strange there. And as much as I wanted to stay in them arms forever, I pulled away and took that hand in mine. Was two fingers all but gone on it—his trigger and middle cut off just shy of the knuckle. Was a mess of burned flesh and silver blood all matted around them nubs. But he didn't show no pain when I took that hand or handled what remained of it. Just watched me all intent, seeing me anew.

"What's he done to you?" I mumbled.

"Nothing what can't be mended," he said. And looking at that crude splint on my leg, he kept on, "I can mend us both."

Then a queer smile broke his lips. I remember seeing there was silver blood on his teeth, too. Wasn't a bit of him untouched, I reckoned. But that smile was a light, all the same. Under that cloud of smoke, with all that death around, that smile was fucking sunshine.

"Expect you're someone to ride the river with after all," he said.

I remember laughing at that. A good goddamn laugh what made my whole body light. And I remember smiling my own damn self and saying back, "Reckon you think I'm just daisy."

And goddamn if he didn't just nod and say, all hushed, "Reckon I do."

Was another eruption of fire and smoke out of the fort right then. And the largest war whoop of all from them Lakota and Cheyenne. The day was won and their enemy was scalped, their bodies and their fort put to fire. Was right burning my way across the West, I was. Lighting signal fires from Piedmont to the Platte.

But for now, I'll just tell you how I hugged my Green Man again. And he me. And I watched the fires eat up that fort and them savages ride their whirlwind around the flames. And I told him, "Don't you ever fucking do that again. You hear me? Don't you ever leave me."

And his arms relaxed around me a little and he kept his good hand stroking my hair. And he said nothing.

BOOK THREE

A MAN FOR BREAKFAST

ONE

A lot of folks say I'm a liar.

Now don't you shake your head. You know I'm telling it true—at least about this. I hear what folks is saying around town about them stories of me and the Green Man you been printing. Right fantastic they is, no doubt. But ain't no fucking hogwash. No sir. Ain't no one can nail this to the counter. Shit, it's all the same folks what tried to brand me bunko after Bill was shot, saying he and I wasn't nothing special. Saying I was just some hanger on. Them folks, I could tell them it was raining and they'd look up into the wash and complain about the sun. Some you just can't do right by. No sir. And, shame is, we're long past the time when you could resolve them disputes with proper steel and gunfire. We're civilized now in Deadwood, ain't we? All we've left us is talking.

But that's what you come for again, ain't it? Talking. To see how my story ends. Well, I reckon I can give you that. But it ain't no lie. Never has been. Been the God's honest from that first meeting in Harthra's barn to that last one on the Platte. Was the most important time of my life, I reckon. Ain't nothing of it I'll forget so long as I breathe—and, thanks to your retelling, maybe a forever thereafter.

But I should get to it, I reckon. The end of it. Of it all, really—of me and the Green Man, of Boone and Somers and Martha. Of how that Gray Man buried us all, in a way. Never did get out from under his silver shadow. From under the smoke of it.

But the end wasn't right in sight. Not after what happened at the Platte.

Them Injuns made a mess of that place and we fagged out right quick. Wasn't worried about my safety none, understand—had Red Cloud in my camp, remember?—but didn't see no need to hang around for when the cavalry come calling to answer them savages. Them Green weapons the Lakota carried wasn't going to work forever and when they ran out was the Union what would win the day. So I intended to take what I come for and be a sight on over the horizon before that reckoning come.

We was right banged up, if you recall. The Green Man was a sorry mess of blood and bruises and even missing two fingers. Had myself a broken leg all fouled up. And the Green Man's horse was shot three times in the trunk, all right mortal if you ask me, but it kept on, slow but steady with some queer Mustang strength borne of wildness and these shining metal bandages what the Green Man done wrapped it with. We stole ourselves two cavalry horses and what gear we could and escaped the slaughter. Rode off east with no particular place in mind. Was a rough damn ride, that. Was heaven to have my Green Man back but, damn, if we wasn't a sorry, slow, and right feeble pair of longriders.

Was days out of North Platte Station—or what was left of it, smoldering as it was—before we come upon a sod hut left abandoned some seasons on. Wasn't nothing to look at but was right what we needed. Was a roof over our heads—after a fashion—and place enough for the horses. Was right unremarkable, too. Wasn't no one wouldn't ride right past such a place and give it the least glance. Well, except us.

And damn if we didn't take up in that hut like a pair of proper homesteaders. I tell you, was months we spent in that dirty hut, mending what ailed us and letting the smoke clear from that whirlwind Red Cloud done kicked up. And except for these two scouts what come by about two months in, I reckon we passed close to four months in that dirt hut without a single visitor.

The Green Man was ready to beef them scouts, he was. Was all setting himself up against the back wall of the hut, all gone into shadow, taking aim with them splinted stalks of his—not quite healed up but sharper than an eagle's eye all the same. But I wouldn't have none of that. I let my hair down and went out, playing all the part of some dumb biddy. Like I done told you, mister, there's more than one way to put off a man and sometimes words is a sight better than bullets. Sometimes it's all what's left you.

We hunted game in the hills nearby and cooked over pecker wood left piled outside by whatever poor soul done walked off this place. And damn if we didn't mend proper. Well, except them two fingers the Green Man lost to that gray devil. Seems even he couldn't mend back what was missing, just what was broke. And there was plenty broke to occupy us both, besides.

We never much talked much about what happened back at the Platte. Shit, wasn't much talking at all between us. Except one time the Green Man told me I shouldn't have come for him. At the time, I took it as a sweetness—a concern for my safety, see, as I should've been killed in that rescue a dozen times over. But looking back on it now, I don't think it was a sweetness. No sir. Think there was another meaning altogether. Was regret, maybe.

But I didn't think too much on it, then. I'd won my space man back and I was in heaven keeping home with him in that sorry little hut. Been a forever since I had anything close to a home, felt like. Was where I grew up in Missouri, of course, and I expect some folks would call their wagon trains home for the spell you live on the crossing. Hell, the closest I'd come to a home between setting out with my momma and my daddy and this here sod house was when Mister Harthra took me in. And that seemed a lifetime ago, it did. Someone else's life. Martha's life, I reckon. No, that filthy hut I shared with the Green Man that fall, well, that was a home alright. And maybe wasn't because it had walls or some leaky roof none, neither. Was the company I was keeping. Shit, looking back on it now, might've been I was home since we put Piedmont to the fire. Reckon I was home wherever I was with him.

But wasn't all sweetness. When we set up in that hut was still the height of summer on them plains. Hot as a whorehouse on nickel night, it was. And I remember lying in the shade back, in the coolest corner of that hut, watching them clouds track across the sky through holes in the sod roof, just sweating like I had the fucking consumption and cursing every little twinge from that broke leg. Miserable, it was, at the start.

And banged up as the Green Man was, didn't keep him from complaining none. I remember waking up one night—a month or more before them scouts come by—and seeing him sitting in the doorway, stars ringing his smooth head, holding up them snapped stalks with their starlight. Was pissing a weak rain earlier that night and was water still dripping down through holes in the roof and over the eaves by the door. I remember hearing him muttering in that queer language of his and I could tell it was just plain grumbling.

I propped up on my elbow and yelled to him over the dripping, "What you grumbling about?"

He seemed surprised at my calling out to him. His senses wasn't as sharp since that Gray Man fouled them stalks of his and was a few months yet until they was healed up. Anyways, he looked around on me all quick—though not affrighted any. And he just watched me in the dark for a spell. Something about how he looked at me was different after that rescue at the Platte. Was always looking longer than before. Was always more thinking before his talking to me.

No, he just watched me for a spell. Then I remember him looking up at that ceiling what was still leaking all around us even though the rain had pushed on an hour since.

"This ain't living, is all," he said after a spell. Then, looking back on me, he kept on, "Shouldn't be hiding out in no dirt hole."

And I reckon it was one of the first times I really saw him for what he was. Understand, I'd been riding with that Green Man for better than two or three months by this time and I knew, plain as to look at him, what he wasn't no man of this world. But wasn't ever what I really thought on that. It's like how you might meet a fella from the Old World in some dusty camp. Like them Jews or Chinamen we got here in Deadwood. But you just never think on what they was or where they was before they come west. Reckon I was always too busy with the present, see, to worry so much about his past. Especially haunted as I was by my own.

But that night, sitting all small in that door, looking on me with them big black eyes like he was needing something, I guess I saw the Green Man for what he was. Was a space man, after all. Was a man from some other world. One what didn't belong in no dirt hole at all.

I remember asking him, "Are the homes where you're from like them ships of yours? What when they're not all blowed up, I mean. They all shiny and clean and flashing lights and whatnot?"

He took to looking off out that door again. "Some of them," he said.

Then, after a spell, he bowed his head and looked down at himself. Looked even smaller then, he did, like he was being crushed under all that starlight.

"I reckon when you're healed up, we'll find you a flying engine yet." I told him. I didn't know how or where to even start looking. Reckoned he'd have a notion. But I remember how crazy he'd become when he lost Harthra's ship. How he blew a whole town to Hell over Jeb's fuckup. And how he'd right lost his reason, too, when he saw that gray fella's ship shot out of the sky. Was a desperation to it. Said he'd seen the elephant, he did. Said he didn't want no more of it. Well, maybe this was a good enough home for me—what with him in it—but I was starting to reckon maybe it wasn't enough for him.

He just shrugged and turned them big black eyes on me. Wasn't no light to see myself in them, then, just enough to see their outline in the starlight leaking through the roof on them trickles.

"Reckon time's up for that." He said. "Fewer and fewer of mine on this world, seems. Never many to start. Just didn't play out." Then he started fingering them severed knuckles on his left hand, where that Gray done took his fingers, and kept on, "Reckon I'll have an easier time finding a bullet—and right quick, too."

And I'll tell you, true, I didn't want him to find no ship. I just didn't. As mean a thing as it might be for me to think it, I did. And with all my heart, too. I didn't want him to disappear off up into that starlight, none. I was home enough with him right here. But was terrible seeing him on the slippery edge of giving up. Or so it seemed. Looking back, I think his thinking was a bit different. I reckon he was already thinking on some tomorrow I didn't see, yet. But I never done thought too far ahead.

"We'll find you a ship," I told him. "In Salt Lake or San Francisco or San Antonio or fucking New York City, we'll find you a ship." He didn't nod or nothing at that. Just sat there watching me. "I'll stay with you until it's done." I told him. "I'll stay with you long as you like."

And I prayed he'd agree to that. That'd we'd ride this wide world together until we found him a ship or found lead. And maybe he'd take me off to that shiny world of his or he'd be satisfied staying in this dirty one with me.

And for a moment my prayers was answered. He smiled that infectious smile what seemed to glow with its own light and, I tell you, my heart just swelled.

"I'd like that, Jane," he said. And in that second—that barely-a-moment before he started talking again, I was the happiest I'd been since Daddy gave me Bess for my own. Broken leg and leaky roof—none of that mattered a tick. Just that I had my Green Man. That I was home.

But then he turned his back on me, he did, and looked out that door across the grasses and the blackness and the starlight. And he spoke almost a whisper to them distant flickering lights overhead. "But what I like and what I need's two different things."

TWO

Took a hair more than four months but time and quiet got us all proper healed up. Even the Green Man's stalks didn't need splinting no more but stood proper off his head all on their own. Was a good sight to see, I tell you. He'd come all back to me now, excepting them two fingers.

And that was the biggest change I done seen in the Green Man. Remember how, once on, he'd pull them two pistols—that Colt and the big space-man gun—and lay low a whole mess of hard cases, if needs be? Well, them days was gone, I reckoned. That left hand wasn't going to hold no pistol again. Not and pull no trigger, too, if you take my meaning.

But still he carried both them guns on his hips. And was one day he caught me spying that Colt, he unshucked it like lightning and put it right in my hand. Scared holy Jesus right the fuck out of me, he did, pulling that pistol on me so fast. But was an education he meant to give me, you see? I was just dandy with a rifle, as I've told you, but with a pistol? No sir. And the Green Man meant to change that.

We had a few revolvers what we'd brought out of North Platte with us on them horses. Cavalry pistols, all, and fine ones, too. So we took to shooting firewood and cans and all else the Green Man could set up for me to take aim on. Even worked on my drawing, some. Got to be fast, he told me. Targets come big, he said. Time comes small.

So it was that last morning we was at the hut, see? I done brewed us up some Arbuckle—not that he needed it, any, what since he didn't sleep at all—and the Green Man made us some bully breakfast. I remember sitting outside the door all wrapped up in a blanket. That sun was just over the hills, warming all the cold world up even as that Arbuckle cooked my insides. Was a right good feeling, that. And I remember the Green Man took that empty coffee can from me and walked out aways from the hut waving on me to follow.

Well, I kept that blanket on tight and followed him to the top of a little rise near on. And when we got there, he done handed me one of them cavalry pistols and started tossing that can in his left half-a-hand. And, shit, I remember him smiling like a goddamn loon, I do.

"What's going through that green head of yours?" I asked him.

He just smiled for a spell. Then he said, "Reckon we're going to see what sort of crack shot you've become." Then he stopped tossing that can and held it out for me to see. "First to let this can hit the ground's going to feed them horses."

Damn if that gun didn't feel a sight heavy in my hand at that. My heart started beating like a steam engine. And not from the Arbuckle none, neither. He'd set up all manner of targets for me to learn pistol shooting at. But nothing like this.

He saw them nerves in me, no doubt. With them stalks of his plumb healed he was sharp as ever at seeing through me. But he didn't laugh none or make fun. Just shook that can and told me, "Keep your eye on the can. And remember, it ain't just aim what does the shooting."

I remember nodding at that. "It's speed, too."

And without no more jawing the Green Man chucked that can all up into that morning sky. In a flash, he took his turn, unshucking, aiming, and shooting his Colt faster than a blink. And damn if it wasn't true, banging that can on higher toward that wide open.

Well, was my turn next, see? I let that blanket fall off and pulled my heavy pistol up fast as I could manage. Tracked that can through the air as it started to come down again, leading like you would a hare or a man on the run. And with my guts all atwist and my heart all aflutter, I pulled that trigger and was fucking rewarded. Bang! Knocked that thing right square up into the sky.

The Green Man squeezed his off just a second later, before the can even had a chance to start down again. That shook me up, it did. I shot too fast and missed by God knows how much. Then I panicked, aiming all hasty and landing a lucky shot just as that can was halfway to the ground.

But I barely had time to catch my breath before the Green Man shot again—a perfect ding, popping it up almost as high as it ever went before I missed and let it fall down so far. I hit it again, myself, and the Green Man one more time, too. But was drifting down, it was, and my fifth shot was off the mark. Before I could aim up my sixth, that can dropped into the grasses.

"Damnit!" I remember yelling. But as twisted up as that game what made me, was a smile on my face so damn big made my cheeks hurt. Went three-for-three with the Green Man, I did. With a cold longrider. With a murdering angel. For three shots I'd kept pace with a space man!

The Green Man, though, he just nodded, shucked that Colt of his and started back toward the hut. "Make sure you check the shoes," he told me.

Well, goddamnit, I wanted a little more than that. That warmth in me turned right quick into some damn heat, it did. "I did right goddamn well, don't you think?" I yelled after him. "Hit that damn can three times!"

He just kept on away, he did, calling back, "Except you shot five."

Goddamn he could get a rise out of me like no man—and in a flash, too. So I yelled after him. "Means I got one to spare for you, don't it!" But he wasn't listening, none, and I didn't care. I was right pleased with myself and if he wanted to be a mean old rip, let him. Was just his way, sometimes. Like he meant to get my goat.

But this, here, is where things start to go ill, see? And I reckon it's no accident, neither. Reckon we was being watched already. It's the only right way to explain how I done got bushwhacked.

See, the Green Man headed back to the hut—inside, even. He'd been fussing lately with some white metal thing he kept in that saddle box of his. Had some little glass what showed all manner of queer symbols—like them ones I saw in that flying engine of the Gray Man's. Reckoned he was hunting for sign of more such ships. Picking a direction we might set off on before winter stole in and we was stranded.

But the thing for you to understand, mister, is that he went inside the hut, set into the hillside as it was, while I went around back. A couple hundred yards off, I reckon, where we done made a rough pen for them horses to mend and meander. Was peckerwood and them cavalry horses got out as often as not but Bess and the Green Man's horse obeyed it

proper. And they was all there, still, that morning. The air was cool and
the sun was hot and them horses all nickered when they saw me.

Was then I saw the rider coming my way through them tall grasses.

Now, I should've called out to the Green Man. I know it. But he'd
got my back up all proper and I wanted none of him. Besides, that son of
a bitch was as likely to shoot this stranger as he was them scouts and we
was trying to keep out of trouble.

But this fella coming through the grasses was a rough customer, he was.
Certainly not the kind no girl should try to manage on her own unless
she's packing. So I made sure my pistol was plain on my hip and made
out to meet him before he got too close to the horses. And I'll be honest
with you—was something about this fella what at first glance rose some
alarm in me. But damn if I didn't ignore it. I done conquered the Gray
Man, after all. What was some dirty saddle stiff to me?

Was a bit farther off the hut than that corral when that rider come to
a stop. Was an ugly smile he put on for me, full of dark and rotten gaps
between yellow teeth. And was this way he looked me over, skipping right
past that gun hilt to drink in all manner of ugliness what sent a shiver right
through me. Was that hungry look. Except wasn't like the way Jimmy or
Jeb ever spied on me. Was something worse in it.

Well, that fella leaned out of his saddle a ways with them leering eyes
and that rank smile and said to me, almost laughing as he did, "Morning,
missie. Was wondering if you might spare some kindness for a tired buckaroo." Then that smile widened all menacing like and he pointed on past
me toward the back of the hut. "Was wondering if you could spare a
tired man a dip in your well. My canteens ran out two days ago and I'm
a sight parched."

I just stood there, silent as a stone waiting to see that mean smile fade.
But it didn't. And that cold gleam in that saddle stiff's eyes was only
getting crueler as he watched me, waiting. I tell you, I could see, plain,
wasn't nothing parched about this fella. Wasn't a chapped bit around them
lips or any gaunt hint in them cheeks. So was right then, mister, what I
realized my mistake. What I should've called out to the Green Man. I even
looked back toward that hut, wondering if them stalks of the Green Man
could peer through earth and sod and distance enough to reckon us out.

"You hear me all right, girl?" he asked, almost snickering as he did.

"Oh, I hear you right fine," I told him. "But I don't reckon we've water enough for you." Then I put my hand on the hilt of that pistol I was carrying and told him, "No sir. I reckon you ought to just turn around and ride off. Forget you saw this place."

And he did laugh at that, that waddy did. Laughed like I told some damn joke. Then I remember him saying, "Now that ain't no kindness, girl. None at all." Then he sat back up in that saddle and looked all around the scene—the corral, the well on the far side, the hillside what made the back of the hut. And, not looking at me, he kept on, "Your daddy around here, girl? Maybe I'd do better talking to him."

Was then his eyes fell on me again. Them mean, hungry eyes.

"Sir," I told him, my voice shaking a little, I admit. "You turn that horse around and ride on out of here, now. Trust me. I'm doing you a kindness sending you on."

And goddamn if he didn't nod even as he cackled a little bit. Turned that horse halfway round before stopping again. And when he did, that smile was gone, it was. Wasn't laughing no more, neither. Every bit of his face went dark, it did. And I knew I was in trouble. Jesus, I wanted to call out for the Green Man. Wanted to know he's seen us with them stalks of his. But who knew what this waddy would do if I screamed. He was heeled, that was sure, and the Green Man was a long ways off.

"Hey, now," that waddy said, them dark eyes on me again, "I think I done seen you before, I do. I'm certain of it." He leaned over the horn of his saddle some right then, squinting in the morning sun at me. "Yes sir. Damn certain. Ain't no way a man's going to forget a sight pretty as you. You're one of Lova Harthra's, ain't you?"

Shit, the color must've dropped out of me something awful right then because I didn't even get a swallow down before he started nodding. Jesus, was like all the heat rushed right out of me, too. Felt the cold stab right through me. And, I tell you, looking on this waddy, I couldn't tell if I'd ever done seen him before or no.

But he didn't wait to let me think on it. Just kept on, saying, "Yes, sir. I remember you just fine. Think I might've seen you on Main one or twice. Might've even been one time I saw you on the heels of some green fella. The same what buried Moses' boy, Jeb. Same what burned that whole damn town."

"Mister," I started but I didn't have no damn words. Who the hell was this? How had he found us? We'd beefed a whole posse back at Devil's Gate. Sent the horses south to lead off our trail.

"Yes, sir," he said, not a lick of laughter left in him at all now. "I reckon that's you. Martha Jane Canary, ain't it?"

Well, I found words right then, I did. The heat come back fast on hearing my name on his ugly lips, like water suddenly hitting a boil. "I reckon you're mistaken, mister," I told him. "And I reckon you better fag out of here before I put you down."

"That right?" he said, his eyes wandering the property again. Then, almost talking to the air, he said, "Tell you what. Why don't I have a look in that shit hole sod house of yours. If there's a green man, maybe I'm right. If not, maybe I'll just water my horse and move on." Then them eyes was on me. "But I don't think you want to try and stop me, girl. I can do worse than put you down."

Shit. I was in it now, wasn't I? But wasn't no more time to waste waiting on the Green Man to come out shooting. If he was even ken. Was time to get rid of this waddy my own self.

"Mister," I told him, "I ain't never heard of no Martha or no green man. But I'll sure as shit beef you where you sit if you don't skedaddle right now."

"That right?" he said again, licking his lips as he did. And damn if he didn't start that horse of his forward. So I did it. I pulled my pistol and brought it up fast as I could. Went for his, too, he did. But I did like the Green Man taught me. I took a step to the side as my gun come up and, before I right had it aimed, I started squeezing on that trigger. So before that waddy's gun even cleared his waist I put my bullet right through one of them hungry fucking eyes of his. Right into that rotten brain and all onto them grasses behind him.

And if he'd been alone, might've been the end of it.

As that gun shot rolled off and out of earshot, was a rustle in them grasses all around. Must've been a dozen boys hunkered down out of sight what stood up fast and quick, pistols and rifles at the ready. Was one not ten feet off what rose up, gun right at me. But I was quick. I stepped off, started my aiming true, and squeezed my trigger, ready to see a splash of red and yellow to reward my shooting.

Was a bang, alright. Except wasn't no smoke coming out of my barrel. See, I'd shot five at the can. And the sixth at that beefed waddy. But this fella what rose out of the grass in front of me? Was his gun I'd heard so well, not mine. Was his bullet what split the air.

I stood there for a second, pistol leveled on that buckaroo what bush-whacked me, and all I could hear was this distant clicking as my hammer fell on an empty chamber. And was all other sounds drained out of the world, right then. Them buckaroos in the grass was all yelling, that waddy's horse was bucking all panicked right next to me, but I couldn't hear a lick of it. Was like my head was in a river, it was. Just some rushing sound of water filling my ears. And after I pulled that clicking trigger a few more times, I stopped and looked down at the hole in me.

It's a terrible sight to see yourself shot. I hope you never know it. To see your lifeblood pouring out. And that's what I saw right then. Saw a hole in my belly big enough to put a gun barrel through. Was all torn and ruined skin and gushing blood what could stop your heart. That's terror, mister. Cold fucking terror. Cold because whatever heat was rushing through you drains away right quick. Terror because you're done. Because there's nothing to do for it but die. Because there's no such thing as a good death. I'd seen my momma and my daddy and Mister Harthra die. Hell, I'd seen Jimmy and Jeb and a mess of others, too. Was right there with some of them, I was. It's a singular thing, that. It's the loneliest a person can be. And the last.

I remember dropping to my knees but I don't recall falling back on the ground—that just happened some point along the way. I dropped my gun somewheres. Was trying to hold my blood in. But my hands was too small and the blood too much. And that rushing sound of water in my ears was deafening. Was the sound of Armageddon, that. Was the sound of them trumpets calling for the end of my days.

I looked around where I'd fallen and was surprised to see the fella what shot me dead himself on the ground, half his face burnt right off. And was then I saw red streaks of fire shooting over me, cutting grass and flesh down in equal measure. Was the Green Man's gun, it was. That big space-man pistol was come. Just too late.

A few of them buckaroos took shelter behind the waddy's horse—dead in halves now, and lying just a few feet from me. And the Green Man?

I saw him hurdle that horse on all fours, like an animal pouncing on its prey. Was that big pistol on one hand, that pilot's knife in his half-a-hand. And when he fell on them, was red fire and slashes of blood in such a wild fury as I'd never seen. And I'm sure the plains was loud with screaming and gunfire and death but I couldn't hear a lick of it.

Last I saw was a cloud pass over the sun. And the whole world seemed to freeze up. Wasn't a drop of heat left in me, seemed. Was pouring out on the dirt and my finger's wasn't enough to stem it. I might've been crying, I don't know. I know I was gasping. Was getting harder and harder to breathe. And, at the last, I realized it wasn't no cloud hung over. Was the Green Man. Covered in blood and yelling at me God knows what. And wasn't no way I could tell him all I needed to before my life bleed out of me.

Was then all went black. And the sound of that rushing river carried me off, lonesome.

THREE

Well, mister, suppose I don't need to tell you I was right surprised when I woke up. Should've been buzzard food after that shot through the belly. But there I was, like I was waking up after some long damn sleep, all bleary-eyed and groggy. And stiff as a son of a bitch, I tell you. Like how you feel after a long ride—every damn joint all rigid and pained.

Was dark in that hut when I woke up, too. Just some weak little lantern burning inside the open door, casting them long dancing shadows all around. And me? Was propped on the Green Man's saddle with one of them queer metal bandages wrapped around my guts. Had one of the Green Man's shirts on, too, open halfway down showing that bandage. And when I made to touch that queer thing, was a storm of pain what swept through me like I done never felt before. Was like some rod digging into me, all deep on the inside. I tell you, I howled like a damn beast at that. Howled in such pain what I surprised my own self.

But I was alive. And awful as that pain was, was a blessing to feel it. Goddamn agony never felt so fucking good. But that pain put a rush of tears in my eyes and got me all shaking. Was lightning, bright and terrible, what blinded me and put that terrible rush of water in my ears again. I hope you never feel nothing like that, mister, I really do. Should've been dead and that's the wound what should've killed me. Wasn't meant for no one to live with that kind of hole in them. That's the kind of pain it was—like no man was meant to endure.

But beyond my stirring and screaming and that rushing sound, was another noise I reckoned in that dark hut. I wasn't alone, see? But wasn't no Green Man in there with me. No sir. Was the fast scampering sounds of someone scared shitless, it was. And as my wits come back, I saw some poor waddy, not much older than me, all bound up in the corner.

Wasn't much of him I could see in that firelight. Just these big, open, terrified eyes wet with tears. And I could make out the shine of blood off his clothes, Especially around his knees. The way he was looking at me was all desperation and fear, it was. Like he was shocked just to see me breathing or afraid of what I might be.

Soon as he saw me looking on him, he started up, just above a whisper, "I done saw you shot. I done saw them kill you," he said.

Wasn't no wit in me to answer. Hell, even thinking on talking hurt my punched-through gut. But wasn't no need for me to say nothing, neither. Right then was some god-awful scream echoed though that open doorway. Like you might hear in a nightmare.

"Oh, God Jesus," that boy started blubbering, watching that door. "What's he doing to him?" Then he was all looking back on me, as scared a look as I ever seen. And he was pleading, "What's he going to do to me?"

Was then I found my voice. Much as yammering was going to pain me—I knew it—was a pleasure to croak out some dirty words at this boy. Pitiful as he was, he was one of them what come hunting us, wasn't he? Was just fine to put the fear in him, some.

"Reckon no worse than you would've done us," I told him. And god-damn if every word didn't feel like another fucking gunshot. Was like my whole body tried to curl up on itself—or at least into that gaping wound under that bandage. But when I looked up again, the dark all lit up with fireworks in my eyes, I could see that boy squeezing his eyes shut, crying like some babe, and that right succored me, it did. Right soothed that agony like the devil's own balm.

And like to make my point, was right then another demon scream echoed in through that door. And that boy? He could hardly blubber as fast as he was shaking. Said, "I didn't think the old man was telling true," he did. "Figured we was on some fool's errand. Ain't no such thing as a green man. Everybody knows that. Just some story them miners made up to keep folks off the rivers, is all." And at that he started looking around all in a panic, like he was living some nightmare he couldn't wake from.

And I remember him hollering out, "Ain't no goddamn thing!"

Like I said, I ain't never seen a man so in the grip of it. Not even at Little Big Horn did I see such terror—not with a hundred mad savages rushing for your scalp. No, this boy was on the edge of madness. So I obliged him that gentle push, I did.

"Oh, he's real," I struggled out through the tightest goddamn teeth I ever had. "And you come calling on him."

Well, he was watching me again, all affrighted. Shaking so hard he was almost a blur in that dim firelight. "And you," he said, "I didn't right believe in you, neither. But he kept saying you was real. Kept saying you'd bring us all calamity if we wasn't careful. And, damn, the way you shot Rooster, out there? I ain't never seen no girl shoot like that."

Now I didn't recognize this boy any more than I recognized that waddy what I done shot off his horse. And, to tell you true, I'm not sure how I felt about what he was telling me. My head wasn't so clear as it should've been. Was pain all tearing it up. But was something he was saying then what ate at me. Was something that spoke familiar.

"Who told you?" I asked him. And, Jesus, if each breath wasn't a struggle to suck in and push out. I wondered how much of me was even left under that bandage. But I had to know. So I kept on, "who told you about me?"

That boy looked on me like he was right afraid of what he might say next. Like them words coming out of his mouth might rip him up sure as the Green Man's gun.

"If you expect any manner of kindness from the Green Man, best you tell me," I told him. And damn if all that talking didn't just about put me out with the pain of it. But when my eyes cleared again I saw that boy nodding right quick, like I was telling him what he already knew too well. And, shit, if I didn't know them words what come out of his mouth before he even spoke them.

"Was Somers," he said. "Boone's man, Somers."

Well if that didn't set my mind reeling. That son of a bitch. Somers sent these boys after us? After me? Boone's man Somers? Somers never worked a day for old Moses Boone or his boy Jeb who we done put in the ground. Burnt down to ashes, more likely, what with how the Green Man blew that whole town to hell on top of him. But Somers? We done left him miles from town. Was a fucking kindness I didn't let the Green Man beef him right there. A fucking kindness twice over! I done saved that boy. Why'd he be coming after me? For Boone, of all people?

But like some kind of answer to my thinking, was some screaming outside and the crack of a gun to answer it. And was quiet thereafter. Set that young waddy tied up next to me all thrashing in a panic, it did. Could've felt sorry for him what it weren't for that painful blast through my guts to remind me what he done come for.

Then that boy stopped his squirming and weeping. And was a darkness fell over the dim hut. The Green Man was in the doorway, see, his duster blocking out that weak lantern. And in the pitch, I swear I saw him watching me, them eyes bulging my way, them stalks pointing toward me in the dark. And we watched each other for a spell like that, all quiet, not a drop of light between us. And all through, that bound-up waddy lived some black nightmare in the corner, I'm sure.

Now we didn't say a word to each other. But in all that silence between us, I knew he was taking me in, measuring out my injuries and taking stock of my wits. Was his handiwork what was keeping my guts together—what was keeping me alive when I should've been otherwise. So I sat quiet and let him listen to my pulse and watch the light in my eyes. Even standing off as he was, I knew he could feel me living.

After a spell, the Green Man stepped inside, letting that light bleed around him, and stood over that terrified boy, smothering him all in shadow. Then, all casual, like he might've talked to me, even, the Green Man said, "You're in luck, boy. Your friend told me what I needed to know," and without the least pause between word and action, he drew his Colt and shot that boy right through the head.

The crack of that gun filled that small cabin like some fucking dynamite, it did. And was just the muzzle flash to illuminate the Green Man's cruelty—the terror mask of a boy facing his devil, a blast of blood and brains all on the wall. Was right dark again afterward. Darker then before.

I swear, right then, I forgot all about what them boys come for. Just remembered how terrified that boy had been of whatever evils the Green Man was executing outside. Of them screams echoing in from God knows who.

The Green Man shucked his Colt and knelt over me, them long fingers of his touching that bandage all lightly, queer blue lights flashing off the metal.

Was shaking, I was. Not from pain but from fear, I expect. Was a cold longrider, this one. Colder, here, then I done seen him before. Colder than I cared to.

"You didn't need to kill him," I whispered, loud enough for him to hear but so quiet I almost couldn't. And the Green Man stopped his fidgeting with that bandage and looked at me. Stared right through me, he did, them black eyes red in the lamplight.

"They come for us, Jane," he said. "They come to put us down or drag us back to Moses Boone. Letting him live would've put them that much closer to finding us again."

I shook my head but didn't say nothing. I'd seen my share of men killed over these last few months, to be sure. Was always an ugly business. But was something different about how he shot that boy. About how he'd been all tied up and terrified. Was more like how you slaughtered a hog than beefed a man. Was like them stories of the Injuns, or from the War, where folks was captured and killed for meanness. For anger. Killed when they could've otherwise. Wasn't no proper killing, that. Was murder.

The Green Man felt out what I was thinking. Was a way about him, being able to do that, Especially now what them stalks of his was mended. "Shouldn't feel no pity for them what was trying to kill you," he said.

"Wasn't him what shot me," I whispered back. And the pain struck through my gut like a locomotive, bringing fresh tears up from below.

"They meant to kill you," he said, barely a whisper.

"Wasn't him what shot me," I said, tears softening the crack of my voice.

"They meant to kill you!" he hollered. And I swear, was a hint of that queerness in it—that echo in your brain. But then he sat back from me, looking on me like I was some kind of loon. Like I couldn't see the plain darkness all around. "Might not have been this one, today," he said, his own voice shaking, I swear, "but might've been if the draw had been different. It's what they come for, Jane. Don't—" But he never finished. Just shook his head and looked off from me. Off into the unlit corners of that black hut.

And that made me think on Somers, it did. Made me think of that night I lay with him. On how he'd looked off across them dark hills after we'd finished, thinking clear for the first time since he took his shine to me, I reckoned. Maybe thinking on that other Martha of his. Maybe not. And it made me think, too, on what that boy said about him being Boone's man. And, for the life of me, I couldn't reckon on Somers coming for my blood. After all the bunko and betrayal—after the mercy we showed him when we left Piedmont—wasn't a bit of that boy I could imagine coming after me with murder in his heart.

I remember asking the Green Man, painful of the mind and the flesh as it was to ask, "What was you doing out there? What was all that screaming?"

The Green Man looked back down on my bandage. "Talking" was all he said.

"Talking?" I asked, squinting from the pain of it. "Didn't sound like no talking to me," I said.

The Green Man shrugged and stood up, towering. "Was talking enough," he said. "We lost them at the Devil's Gate like we planned. But they picked up our trail from the stories out of Alcova and the Platte. From the settlers you fancied at the Rock. Stories folks was telling of a green man, a gray man, and some little girl what brought the Lakota nation down for a slaughter." Then the Green Man started packing up our plunder, pushing pistols into saddlebags and rolling up my bedroll. And as he did, he kept on, saying, "All they had to do was follow the smoke."

But that still didn't answer me, none, who the Green Man was torturing out there. If it was Somers I'd heard silenced by his Colt.

So I asked him plain as I dared. "You recognize any of them what come after us?"

The Green Man looked up from them saddle bags, peering through me to feel out what I was really asking. Maybe he did, too. But if so, he never let on.

"None of them," he said.

I let my head fall back at that. I reckon I was glad for it, though I wondered at the time if he was being honest or just telling me what I wanted to hear. But I let my head rest on that saddle all the same. Goddamn, I hurt but I was so tired. And laying there, staring at that dirty ceiling, I could see stars winking through the slats and the sod. Was thin roots reaching down between the boards in the dim lamplight toward me like I was in some grave.

"What now?" I asked him. Just a whisper, it was. Hurt less to whisper. The Green Man started packing them bags again. "We make for Cheyenne," he said.

"Hell to that," I snapped, wincing as I did. Goddamn, if it kept hurting like that, the Green Man might've finally found a way to stop my yammering after all. But Cheyenne? That was suicide, it was. And I told him so. Said, "If they were able to find us here, sure as shit they'll find us in Cheyenne."

But the Green Man just stood with my gear on his shoulders—my saddlebags all packed, my bedroll already tied behind the seat.

"Ain't nothing to be done for it," he told me. "There's a bullet in you and it's got to come out. And the closest doc worth a lick what don't work for the Army is in Cheyenne."

I let my hands reach up and touch on that metal bandage around my middle. Was tender to even let my fingertips brush on it—and a damn lightning storm of pain to touch it proper. Like some crowbar working on my insides, prying out kidneys and what else.

"I'd rather you let me die here," I told him, halfway hoping all this yammering would do the job. "We go to Cheyenne, we're both dead."

The Green Man stopped in the doorway, already headed out, see, to rig up Bess. How the hell he thought I was going to ride, I honestly don't know. I was in agony lying on the ground. The thought of bouncing on a horse was right beyond me.

"Maybe so," he told me. "Maybe so." And though I wasn't looking on him, I knew was starlight around him where he stood, pierced by them mended stalks and blotted out by all the gear he was carrying. And in the saddest tone I done ever heard him speak, he shut me up sure as he used that voice of his on me.

"But I reckon what you like and what you need is two different things."

FOUR

Must've been near on two hundred miles from that shitty sod hut down to Cheyenne. Without that hole in my belly, and with four horses to rotate under us, we might done that in two or three days. But wasn't no way I could ride at a trot, what with all the jostling of my torn up guts it would do me. Shit, if it wasn't for the Green Man's horse, I doubt I could've ridden at all.

No, was that queer horse what made riding possible. I swear, that saddle shifted not a wit on that thing's back. Like riding a damn river skiff, it was—all smooth as water except when the ground broke and got rough. And wasn't ever that horse got uppity, none. Might've been a Mustang before it met the Green Man but was obedient as a locomotive now. And as steady, too.

But I was in rough shape, like I told you, and needed a sight more than a smooth ride if I was going to get anywheres out of that hut, much less across the damn territory. And I still think was a damn fool idea of the Green Man's to take us so far south to Cheyenne. We should've been making for them Black Hills to the north or to them fairytale lands up on the Yellowstone. Anywheres we could disappear into the woods and grasses and mountains out of the sight of white men. Anywheres old Moses Boone couldn't come after.

But the Green Man had his mind set on taking me off the plateau and into that goddamn lion's den. And wasn't much all I could do to resist him, was there? Was a damned invalid, I was. So he set me up on that saddle right in front of him like I was some captured prize to be carried away. I tell you, him pulling me up onto that horse was one of the most god-awful moments of my life, it was. Felt my whole body stretch as he lifted me up, that big old hole in me pulling tall and opening wide under that metal bandage. Should've killed me all over again. Right then, wished it had. But once I was in that saddle, I was thankful for him behind me. For them arms of his on the reins framing me in. See, took us more than a week to make Cheyenne and I reckon I was awake—or clear-headed, at least—for nothing more than a few hours of it. No, I spent most of that ride drifting in and out of reason, leaning back on my Green Man as he carried me south, cantering along all day and all night except for when I needed to do my necessaries. And that I tried to fight off so long as I could seeing as I'd have to go through the agony of mounting up every goddamn time.

But I don't right regret that agony, I guess. At least it gave me my wits back for a bit. before I slipped away again. No, what I regret is that I was out of my reason for so much of that ride. Rather wished I'd no hole in me, no pain weakening me what so I couldn't keep my damn eyes open. Then I might've had that time with my Green Man. Might not of wasted it on healing.

No, instead of having my senses was some dreamland I traveled through. Was a liquid place my mind would drift off to, full of mountains and hillsides and vast fucking plains what moved like water under my feet. Like the dreams them Injuns tell about, I reckon. But wasn't no peace pipe what sent me there. No sir. But was a sweet and swimming place. I remember drifting off from that pained damned world on that queer horse's back into that there dreamy one. Was Bess under me there and a whole empty West all around. And was the Green Man, too, riding beside, ever hunting for some flying engine to haul us heavenward. And wasn't no need for shooting or running or gray things what might haunt you. Was just room enough for the two of us and everywheres we could go. And time on again in that misty place was the stars themselves what come down out of that sky so the Green Man wouldn't need no ship and so he wouldn't have to leave me none, neither. Was home in that dream, I was. Home forever.

But was a fairy tale, it was. Some fucking cruelty formed up in my fevered brain. It's a wonder I can remember it at all except every time I closed my eyes I was there again. Was just about all I can remember of that miserable ride except waking on some empty stretch of plain or plateau, the Green Man's arms holding me up. Holding me up like they been doing for months, I reckoned.

But I do remember this one time, after we'd come down onto them plains what lead off into Nebraska, waking in that saddle to see some town all around us. My face was buried in the Green Man's arm and I remember peeking out over the sleeve of his duster at some sleepy clapboard camp. Was cold as hell, I remember that, too. Seemed the only bit of me with any heat at all was that aching cavity in me. So I shivered there, all cold under my coat, and asked the Green Man through clattering teeth, "This Cheyenne? We make it?"

He was quiet for a bit. Felt like forever, it did, but I reckoned was because I was just waking. But he told me, true, "Not yet. Maybe tomorrow."

Was folks coming out onto them boards, there was, staring at some queer spectacle riding down their main. A green man riding right out of some tall tale and into their pecker of a camp. Was women hiding their children, men checking their guns. But no one moved against us. Might've helped I was awake, I reckon, and not begging for no rescue. Held as I was in front of him on that saddle looking the part of some captured little white girl. But awake, was certain I wasn't no prisoner.

At the time, I wondered why we rode through that town at all. We didn't stop for no reason. Watered them horses on cricks aways from towns and ranches, we did, never in no settlement. But I didn't have the strength to ask him about it.

So was a week of that slow, dreamy riding south, night and day, before we come on that magic city of the plains. Was a queer thing, Cheyenne. There you was riding through these dry damn prairies, barely a ranch or house anywheres in sight, when all of a sudden, over some hill or around some copse, was a city of thousands squatting in the grass, hugging some shitty little river and some railroad twist like them Chinook winds was going to up and blow it all away.

I remember, was cold when we rode into town but wasn't no snow on the ground yet, just frost hiding in the shadows. And like in that little camp we rode through, people was clamoring to their windows and onto them boards or into the street to see a green man, real and in the flesh, riding into their town. I remember some kids playing out by the rails when we rode in, beyond the edge of the settlement proper. Them boys spied us and come running about half-way to us before stopping and gawking like a bunch of loons watching a tornado. Was a right funny mixture of excitement and terror them boys had at seeing my tall Green Man with them long stalks growing out of his Stetson, carrying a little white girl and leading a trio of horses into their town. Shit, wasn't more than a couple seconds they must've watched us before they turned tail and went running home to fetch their playmates or their mommas. I remember hearing one of the boys shouting how them "green men is real!" and how he "done seen the elephant now!"

He hadn't seen nothing yet.

See, Cheyenne wasn't no Salt Lake, that was right sure. Was maybe a dozen Greens living in or near Salt Lake when I rode in there with my daddy two years before. And was tell there of maybe a dozen more Greens living in Nevada and California, too. And was Mr. Harthra in Piedmont, of course. But all them places was older, see? This here Cheyenne was barely two or three years old when we rode in on it, sprung up from the damn dirt out of nothing, it was. Right missed the coming of the Greens, it did. And already there was fewer and fewer of them. Soon, excepting mine, might be none at all left in the West. Was played out, my Green Man said. They was going home or being put under.

No, them folks in Cheyenne ain't never seen a Green before. So was quite a commotion when we rode into the heart of that town. Must've been a thousand people if it was ten on them streets watching us ride by. And I was right awake to see them, too. After all that sleeping in the saddle, I was a sight better—able to sit up and speak without screaming, at the least. Was a right good thing, too, because was some marshal and his boys what rode up on us in the middle of the street and I reckoned quick I was going to need to do the talking.

Was a right fine looking marshal, if I recall. All crisp and clean and well shaven—a sight different than any man I'd seen in nigh on half a year. Was something right fatherly about him, too. But I felt the Green Man tense up behind me, one arm squeezing in some to hold me better, the other moving down toward the hilt of that big gun of his. But I set my hand on his leg and sat up well as I could. Wasn't no need to make no trouble, I reckoned, not with a row of lawmen and a wide host of town folk on us. Not when I could heel myself with words as well as bullets.

The marshal and his blocked the road, they did, and we stopped maybe twenty feet shy of them. Close enough they could see the Green Man plain and, just as likely, the shine of that metal bandage around my belly.

That marshal smiled and tipped his hat to me, like a proper thorough-bred, he did. And said to me, right ignoring the Green Man, "Morning ma'am."

I tipped my hat right back to him, trying to smile, hoping I didn't look as wrecked and weary as I was. Reckon I knew what these boys come for. Was the rescue, wasn't it? Some little girl in the arms of a savage or a nigger or a space man. Would've been surprised if they hadn't stopped us. Would've been a might surprised, too, if I hadn't seen that spool of rope over the back of one of them deputies' saddles, too. But wasn't going to be no hemp party today if I could help it—certainly wasn't going to be no hemping at all if the Green Man unshucked them guns.

"Morning, marshal," I remember saying back, my voice all cracking and dry like I hadn't said a damn word in days. Shit, maybe I hadn't. And damn if it wasn't a kindness to feel just some dull ache when I spoke instead of that crowbar in my belly.

But was quick to business, this marshal was. He got right to it, looking at the Green Man over my shoulder and asking, "Ma'am, you need any help?"

And was right then all them deputies what flanked that marshal showed their guns, see? Ready for the rescue, they was, never mind the girl was square between them and the space man they'd be aiming at. And the Green Man tensed all anew, his hand right on that hand cannon of his. But I kept my hand on his leg, I did. Reckoned if any bullets was to start flying what I was right in the middle. And I'd had my taste of lead. Wasn't anxious for a second helping.

No, I answered that marshal quick, I did. Said, "No sir. Reckon I'm just fine. My green man was just being so kind as to take me to a doctor." Then I pulled back my shirt a bit—the Green Man's shirt I was wearing—and showed them that shiny bandage around my belly. "Some Injun put a bullet in me and if my Green Man hadn't wrapped me up and carried me this far, well, reckon I'd be cold as a wagon tire."

That marshal nodded some at that. "Your green man? That so?" he asked. And I could tell he was watching the Green Man out of the corner of his eye. Watching for some ruse. So fixed on the notion I needed escape, he was. Or maybe I was lying, with either a gun in my back or out of wickedness all my own. But the Green Man sat still as a statue, he did, never moving a tick toward them guns of his. Not that he needed to. Was fast enough to unshuck them before these lawmen knew trouble was started, he was.

So I kept my eyes on that marshal, I did. Told him, "Marshall, it'd be a kindness if you'd point us in the direction of a doctor. I've got a shell in me just begging to come out."

That marshal took out a cigar and popped it in his mouth right then. He smiled some, too, saying, "You say an Injun put a bullet in you?" Looked around at his boys then and kept on, "We've all heard of some girl and a green riding with the Lakota. How do we know that ain't you, darling?"

Damn. Was right afraid of that story riding ahead of us. That's why I told the Green Man we shouldn't come here. That this place would be the death of us. Might've shot our way out of Piedmont, all right, but this was a proper town. Nigh on a city by plains' standards. Wasn't no way even the Green Man could shoot his way out of here.

So I did my best to lie. "Heard tell of them, too," I said. "But if we was riding with some braves, why'd you reckon they put a bullet in me? Or the rest of our party? Was just the two of us rode out of there, marshal. Was half-a-dozen boys what didn't make it."

Now, the marshal never lit that cigar. Just chomping and nodding. Deciding, right then, if I was bunko and if the Green Man wasn't no devil. Ain't never been a group of folks assembled what didn't want a fucking hanging, was there? And it's a damn trick talking them out of rope and fire, ain't it? Now, don't go giving me that look. Ain't no different in your Old States than in my new ones. Some queer stranger comes on and it's a first instinct to see wrong and fetch rope. Well, if that stranger ain't heeled with green backs, anyways.

Expect I was holding my breath, I was. But the marshal was looking around at that gathering crowd, he was, and I saw him doing the damn arithmetic. Was an awful lot of women and kids watching this encounter and no telling what a wild green man would do if pushed. So he nodded at me, smiling. "Alright," he said. "Alright. If you're shot, like you say, I reckon it's Doc Cobb or old Doc Crowder you'll be needing."

"Doc Crowder," the Green Man said, breaking his silence. I swear, some of them deputies just about jumped out of their saddles to hear him speak. And that crowd what formed around us gasped on him talking like a white man.

But the marshal kept his cool. "Alright," he said. "How about we show you there. Make sure no one causes no trouble."

"Ain't us going to start no trouble, marshal," I told him.

And before the marshal or no one else could say a thing, the Green Man spoke up again. "But it'll be us what finishes any," he said.

And was the first, right then, what the marshal looked right on the Green Man instead of me. Watched him over my shoulder, he did, and said, "I reckon you would, at that."

FIVE

So that marshal and his boys led us through town, making a half circle of sorts around us. A couple times it seemed like them boys of his was trying to close us in but the Green Man, or his horse, was wise enough to jockey them out of position, keeping a way out. Was a queer dance, that. Queerer still because that marshal, watching us like a hawk, only spoke up twice the whole ride.

The first was just a few minutes into riding. They was leading us into the middle of Cheyenne, they was—deep as we could go into that town. Was a grand building rising up out of what must've been hardscrabble just a few years back before the rail pushed through. The timbers was still yellow and raw as the earth it grew out of. Barely a lick of paint on it yet and hardly a door hung in place, too. But that marshal, he looked on that big wood skeleton like he was looking on the Pearly Gates, he did. Like he didn't want to be there in front of it but was right in awe all the same.

"You know who built this here territory, darling," he said, looking at me like the answer ought to have been plain. "You know who raised this town—timber by timber—and all them others from nothing but the dust?"

I watched him over the sleeve of the Green Man's duster, I did, that big raw building casting its shadow on us. "No sir," I told him.

The marshal laughed at that. Most of them deputies did, too. Got my blood up, that did. Fucking hate feeling foolish, I do. Expect that's true of every man or woman or child, ain't it? But it got to rise out of me all the same, that chuckling. The Green Man closed them arms of his on me some, trying to calm me, I reckon. Like how you might put the squeeze on some heifer with its back all up—to calm it and keep it from hurting on its own damn self.

That marshal didn't pay me no mind, though. Just laughed a bit and kept on, saying, "Was ranchers. Was them what drove out them savages, cut across the country with iron rails, and make of cattle what others might have made of factories or cotton in them Old States. Them ranchers is the real authority, you understand? The real power. From here on to Green River, I reckon. Or to Piedmont."

And that marshal let that last hang in the air between us for a spell— all heavy like them unfinished rafters, ready to come all crashing down if I wasn't a might careful. And the way he was watching me gave me the goddamn chills, it did. Was Moses Boone I was thinking of. Them ranchers was the real authority, was they? I knew that was God's fucking honest. Was why Jeb ought to have been untouchable even after what he did to Mister Harthra. Was why them posses was still chasing us across the territory. And, seeing the glint in that marshal's eyes, was all this he knew too well.

We was made. Since before we even rode into this goddamn place, we was made.

I tell you, I wouldn't have minded if the Green Man started shooting right then. On horseback and heeled as we was, might've just made it if we started shooting and fagged out of there right quick. All might've turned out different.

But instead I held my damn tongue. And the Green Man never budged toward that big gun of his. And after a spell we rode on and come upon some squat little house squeezed in by saloons and whorehouses and what else. Must've been the oldest damn shack in town, it was. And at our coming and raising all kinds of ruckus, some gray-haired old man stepped out of it, all dressed in black like a goddamn undertaker and wearing some long skinny beard on his chin so thin you could see scars crisscrossing his jaw.

Well, that marshal sent off for a boy from the livery to take our horses and tipped his hat to me, them knowing eyes shining out from under that brim. Oh, I was bunko, he knew it sure. Was writ clear in them thoroughbred eyes of his. We was made.

The Green Man dropped me down easy as he could. Wasn't no damn torture like it'd been even a day before but the aching and tearing in my gut still hurt something awful. But wasn't what mattered right then. Was that look from the marshal what pained me more. So I made quick to Bess and took her by the bridle, stroking her muzzle and fixing on them big lovely eyes. I'd rid this horse from Missouri through Hell and back again. Done rescued her from the bloodbath at Harthra's and from that gray devil on the Platte. But was now more than ever I feared I was going to lose her for good.

Some boy from the livery come up and tried to take her reins from me and I just about bit his fucking hand off, I did. Just wanted a goddamn blink without no marshal or Green Man or nothing sneaking up and taking her away. Just wanted to hug that horse close, feel the heat of her snorting on my sleeve, hear the rumble of her breathing deep against me. So I closed my eyes and put my cheek to hers. And for a moment, I wasn't in Cheyenne no more. Wasn't no marshal or deputies or Green Man none, neither. Was just nothing but me and her.

"Jane," I heard the Green Man calling. But for a spell I didn't mind him none. I just kept there, breathing deep of Bess' musk.

"Jane," he said again. And this time was a hint of that echoing voice in it, such that I couldn't help but pull away from Bess and look over at the Green Man. Was standing there with that old doc, watching me like I was hanging fire. And maybe I was. Reckon we was both anxious to get out from under this marshal and his but, damnit, this was my Bess he was tearing me away from. And I reckon the Green Man knew he was about the only what could pull me from her.

So I let that boy from the livery take my Bess. And I stepped up close to that marshal, surprising him some to do it, too. I even took hold of one of his reins as I stepped close, wincing a bit from the pain of lifting my arms up to grab it. And I told him, "I thank you, marshal, for bringing us here untroubled. I reckon we'll be well enough on our own from here on. We've got business, as I'm sure you understand."

The marshal watched me careful, he did, chomping on that unlit cigar. And was a surprising bit of honesty he showed me right then. Said, "Darling, I think you need to separate yourself from that Green of yours.

I think you need to do it right soon, too. Ain't no one going to be looking for a girl like you on her lonesome. Ain't no need for you to get mixed up in any of this."

Well, I let them reins loose at that and stepped away, back toward my Green Man and that doc. Was one hand already on my belly, cradling that bandage, and the other on my pistol. And I tried to be polite when I told him, "I appreciate your thinking on me, marshal, but ain't no trouble of his what ain't trouble of mine, too."

And he just nodded at that and motioned for his boys to head out. Then he said back to me, at the last, "You have a nice day, ma'am. And a careful one."

Me? I just turned and walked back toward the Green Man and that doc, passing right between them and on into that shitty damn shack. But as I passed them by, I told them plain, "This is a right fucking mess you led us into. I hope you know that."

The Green Man didn't say nothing.

The inside of that place was dingy as the outside, it was. Dark and dirty and with tell of all manner of unpleasantness. But was clear, too, why the Green Man wanted old Doc Crowder. Was some sketches on the wall of green men, some showing their bits and insides, like the kind you might find of cattle by some butcher. Except the insides of these Greens was all manner of strange, with nothing in them drawing at all familiar or in the right place, as I understood it. Was a few things lying around, too, what could've only been of the Greens. Shiny metal things what looked just big enough to fit in the palm of your hand or with handles like pistols but with business ends nothing resembling a firearm.

And the doc himself? Why he wasn't the least interested in me. He was busy looking at the stumps of the Green Man's severed fingers, he was, mumbling such about knuckles and healing and regrowing and the like. And the Green Man indulged him for a spell, he did, but was watching me the whole while. Watching like he was waiting for me to say something.

"What?" I asked him. But he kept quiet, letting that doc examine that left hand of his.

"Goddamn, what're you fucking looking at?" I snapped.

He pulled his hand away from the doc and gestured to me. Not a word passed between them right then. Must've been some talking out

front while I was hanging on Bess but not a word right then. And that
doc went over to one of his dingy tables and gathered up some of them
space-man tools.

"Don't you worry about that marshal," the Green Man said after a bit.

God, I hated it when he talked to me like I was some kind of yack.
Or worse, some little girl. Like I hadn't seen what men was capable of or
like I needed some sheltering from what was true.

"Bullshit I don't need to worry about him," I said. "He made us.
Knows who we are. Shit, like as not he's getting word out to Boone or
Som— and his right now!"

The Green Man just aimed them black eyes at me like rifles. And I
don't know if he caught my slip or what all but he said, quick, "Then
maybe you should've gone with him."

Oh, that got me in a twist, it did. So much words couldn't right form
up in my mouth. And seeing a break in the battle, that doc took me by the
arm and sat me by some greasy brown window, never saying a word. He
started waving some queer whirly blue thing over my gut, all lights flashing
and little bell noises. And I remember looking at him like he was waving
some goddamn bones over me or the like—some savage medicine—and
snapping, "Jesus, what the fuck is that thing? I thought we was looking to
pulling out that damn bullet? Not to waving some fancy lantern around."

The doc just shook his head and went on paying me no mind. Looked
back at the Green Man, he did, saying, "Bullet's in too deep and I ain't
inclined to make a hole what where there ain't one already. Maybe if I
had some better tools—"

The Green Man howled at that, swinging an arm wide, sweeping all
manner of sundries and cruel surgeries onto the floor. Right scared me
something awful, that outburst did. Scared the venom right out of me
for a breath, too. His roar filled the whole damn shack. Even made them
greasy windows rattle in their frames.

But that doc's meaning wasn't lost on me just because I grew up
some hick. We'd just come two hundred miles to find no help at all. Put
ourselves in the path of some deadly goddamn train doing it, too. So I
snapped at the Green Man, never mind the aching in my belly kicked up
by every odd word.

"What the fuck did we ride all this way for?" I snapped at him. "We've done rid to our own hemp party, we have. And for what? What the fuck kind of doctor is this that he can't even pull out a goddamn bullet?"

That doc looked me in the eye for the first time, like he was just noticing I had them, and said, "Well, most of my clientele is whores, not gunfighters."

"Jesus fucking Christ," I yelled and leapt up out of that chair, the hole in my gut stretching and screaming through my whole body. Tears leapt out of my eyes right then, they did, but they didn't stop me from yelling, "Have I been sitting in crabs and French pox there, too, doc?" Then I turned my rage on the Green Man again, blood cooking up from that shredded pot in my belly. "This was some proper goddamn idea you had, now, ain't it?"

"Now it ain't all that, girl," Doc Crowder said. "I've dealt with my share of bullets and yours is healing up all nicely. Aside from some lingering pain from that bullet moving around in you, you should be right healed in no time. Especially with that shiny bandage to mend you."

I swung back around at that doc, yelling, "So I get to keep it like some fucking prize in my belly. Well ain't that all proper and good."

"Jane—" the Green Man made to interrupt me. But I kept on.

"Don't you fucking, 'Jane' me," I hollered back at him. "Weren't them stalks of yours listening to what that marshal was saying out there? They know us. They're coming for us. And you brought us right to them. For what? For some whore doc what can't do shit but wave around fancy tools?"

"Jane—" he tried again.

But I wasn't finished. "No, goddamnit. You listen to me. If I'm going to lose you and Bess, or get beefed my own goddamn self, I don't want it to be for some fool's errand. Now if this doc ain't the one to cut this fucking thing out of me, then lets us find another, like that Doc Cobb or—"

"Doc?" the Green Man said over my shoulder. Was a plumb frustrated wrinkle on his brow, too, when he said it. Like wasn't no fight in him right then. And damn if I wasn't so caught up in my ranting and raving what I didn't hear that old doc step up behind me and put some little pricker to my neck. Was some loud hiss it made, too. Like steam escaping an engine. And, I swear, all I managed out after that hissing was a single "Goddamnit!" before the room began to spin all around. Except wasn't swimmy like them sweet visions I had on the trail. Was more like when

Crazy Horse done shot me with that Green rifle of his. Was like going from straight to plumb soaked in blink.

Then all went black.

SIX

I woke on some hard damn table, sunlight bleeding in through one of them greasy brown windows. Smelled like a damn slaughterhouse in that shack, it did. Don't know if that's from the whores or from the cutting and proding docs is prone to but it stank something awful. And wasn't nothing to hear in the whole place excepting the sound of horses passing on outside and the soft clanking of that doc fussing with his tools.

Was all the fire slept out of me by whatever put me down. And before it could fire up again, was the reckoning what my gut didn't hurt none no more. My hands drifted over to that bandage, they did, and was the first damn time I'd been able to handle it proper without no bolts of pain cutting through me. Even what felt like that crowbar stuck through my guts was quieted. Excepting for the bandage itself pinching at the edges, wasn't nothing what felt out of the ordinary at alls.

Well, I must've made some noise because that doc looked over at me. No smile or nothing on that old face. No, his lips was just another god-damn wrinkle. But he come over to me with that same damn space-man tool he use before and started waving it over my belly.

I told him, not that he asked, "Feeling right fine, doc."

He didn't pay me much mind. Just watched that little thing of his and the queer blue lights it was flashing. Then, after a long spell, he started, "Gave you something for the pain. But you'll need to keep that bandage on a while longer. Not sure how long." Then he stepped back to that table full of tools and got back to paying me no mind.

Was then I noticed the Green Man wasn't around. Just me and that old doc and the afternoon sun angling through them filthy panes.

I sat up on that table—felt like I was flying up, it did, what with no pain to slow me or well up no tears. But damn if that doc wasn't ignoring me so much as I imagined. Right sudden he broke that silence of his and told me, "He's around back giving all a looksee."

Should've reckoned as much. But I wasn't worried, none. Not because he'd never left me on my lonesome, mind you. Done that to ill effect a few times, hadn't he? No, was because there was a whole town outside waiting for us, wasn't there? Sheriffs and posses and God knows what else. Where was he going to go?

But this doc? He was a queer one, he was. Most of them folks in Cheyenne acted like they ain't never seen a Green before and here was this doc among them what looked at the Green Man same as he might've on any old granger or buckaroo—niggers and Chinamen the same. Gave me pause. Spoke to familiarity.

So I straight asked him, I did. Said, "How'd you know the Green Man?"

The doc stopped his picking about them tools and seemed to stare off for a spell. Then he turned around and gave me this look what made me feel as well as a burr in his boot. But I didn't blink, none. I right wanted to know and if that made me some damn chore, well, didn't bother at all.

But he told me. Said, "Was in Sacramento at the same time. '49 or '50, I reckon it was. Was a bunch of Greens what come for the gold, same as we did. Excepting was some trouble. A Green doctor tried to break up a fight between one of his what got shot and a group of prospectors jealous of the Green's gold-finding gear." He shrugged some at that. "Well, that Green doc ended up with his head cracked. Me? I ended up figuring out his doctoring tools. Right quick, too. Shit, can figure out most anything fast enough with a gun to your head."

Made me think of them first talks I ever had with the Green Man. Him saying he'd been here a long time, worked a claim and whatnot. Said he'd seen the elephant, he had. Seen it all.

And was right then the Green Man come back in. Like he was right summoned up by my thinking on him. And as he stepped through that doorway, I tried to imagine him twenty years younger. How he might've looked in them California hills, just arrived in the West, surrounded by a whole mess of his kind—not just some lonesome soul played out as them once-golden rivers. Was a hard image to muster up, mister. The cold, hard reality of him right in front of me made it right impossible to see back to what was.

And like to answer my thinking, bringing me on back to the there and then, the Green Man spoke up, saying, "There's a dozen—maybe two—in the street and windows all around. All heeled with rifles, a few with pistols. No Green guns but plenty of steel."

I turned around on that table and spied out through that grimy brown window, barely able to make out the shapes of men and horses on the other side. But keen on his warning, I reckoned I could see a few folks what weren't walking up and down them boards, minds all on their shopping or getting to some saloon or a whore. Was folks standing around, all watching and all in sight of the doc's front door. I couldn't see any of them clear, and was a knot in my gut thinking one of them might be Somers—or, worse, old man Boone himself—but ugly as that window rendered that view, uglier still was what I could still see plain. Was a shooting gallery setting up out there.

The Green Man stepped up and pulled some filthy curtain across the window. Our eyes met for a blink as he leaned across the table and I could tell he was proper concerned. Wasn't like at the shed in Piedmont where rage put his caution beside, or even at the Platte where we stood safe as a whirlwind of arrows and bullets and fire blew itself around us. Wasn't even like at that saloon where the Green Man talked around Jeb, short of shooting that whole place to hell. Was something different here. Maybe was the number of folks out there, maybe was where we was holed up. But thinking back on it now, I reckon it was me what worried him more. All them times in Piedmont, wasn't a second thought given to me. Was only his own safety, or that ship's, what troubled him. But now they was shooting for me, too, and I expect that slowed his gun a bit. Made his living and fighting a bit more complicated, I did. Like I had back at that hut, when I took that bullet. Or like when we first rode into Cheyenne, with me all saddled between him and that marshal. Might've been the first time I really thought he'd be better off without me, right then. So focused on how much I wanted him to stay on with me. Expect I'd never thought he might want any different.

I could see him thinking it through all careful like, hunting for some way out of this mess. And after a bit of that inward talking, I remember him asking the doc, "What's the tallest building around here? Anything three stories?"

The doc was watching us careful, he was. And he shook his head at that, saying, "Nothing three stories, no sir. But there're a few two-story saloons and hotels down the boards a ways. Out the front to the left, near the end of the road, is one what might be a hair taller than the others. Nice and open on the inside, too."

The Green Man nodded at that. But not me. They was talking about going to some hotel with as many as twenty or so boys out there aiming at us? Crazy as coming to Cheyenne might've been, this was right near suicide, it was. The doc's shack was a shit hole, true, but wasn't no one aiming a barrel at my brain in it. So I told them both, "Damned if I'm going outside into some shooting gallery. Better off digging in here, ain't we?"

The Green Man looked at me then. Wasn't no smugness in him. Just concern. And the clear look of someone trying to make it just one more step before tripping.

"Can't hole up here," he said. "Ain't no way to defend it and ain't no reason to put the doc in harm's way." Then he stepped toward the front door and peeked out by cracking it. "There's a mess of folks still going on about the day, out there," he said. "Ain't no one going to start shooting at us."

I laughed at that. I swear, I did. Told him, "Lots of figuring they care about shooting them folks, ain't it?"

He shut that door and stood there looking at me. And in his silence I reckon I saw the truth of it. Was a tiny shack, this was. Maybe two rooms and as many doors. Lots of dirty windows and taller buildings all around, too. Was a death trap. Might be shooting outside but sure as shit was dying in here.

"They'll tighten a noose around this place, Jane," he said. "Tightening it all up until we got nothing left but to bust out and it'll be too late then." Then he walked over to me and stood right close, just inches from where my knees bent over the edge of that table. Was barely a whisper he spoke, too, like he didn't want that doc to hear him say what else. And he went on, "You and I'll both die if we stay. But if we get to that hotel, to some high ground . . ."

And I surprised myself, right then, reaching out and taking the crease of his left duster sleeve between my fingers. Was cracked and dirty, that coat was. But was thick. Like you might not even feel the rain beating on you or the horseflies scampering around on it. And I swear I could hear the jangle of that Injun bone shirt underneath. Was a story in these, there was. Some long journey what I didn't plan to see end here. So I told him what I reckoned he wanted to hear. Told him, "I ain't worried. I know you'll get us through."

He leaned close to me then, he did. Sent my heart right leaping through my shirt. And that sleeve I'd been holding on to? He pulled it away and reached out right for my hip, that half-a-hand brushing my leg just the littlest bit as he did. Couldn't hardly breathe, my heart was choked up so high in my throat.

He unshucked my gun. And he lay that cavalry pistol right across my lap, that long metal barrel weighing a goddamn ton across my thighs.

"I ain't worried neither," he said, whispering just for me. "'I got you with me."

SEVEN

Standing just inside that doc's door, ready to bust out onto the street and face God knows, well, reckoned right then I'd follow my Green Man anywheres. Hadn't I already, after all?

No, to Hell and back again suddenly didn't seem so far to stick with him.

But we was about to test that, wasn't we. Yes sir. We was as ready to step out into that mess as we was ever going to be. Me with my pistol, hanging heavy as a rail in my hand. Him with his space gun shucked but with his duster thrown back behind it, showing that queer hilt all shiny and otherworldly next to his whole hand hooked over the holster. Both with our rifles slung across our backs. Both, too, with our hats pulled low, shadows across our eyes, braids and stalks busting out.

He put his hand on the knob, he did, then turned to me and, calm as a conductor giving directions, told me, "We go out, take a left and head for that hotel like the doc said. We don't make no trouble, now, understand? If it's going to start, we let them start it. If we can get where we're going without no shooting, all's the better."

I nodded, not saying nothing. And I hefted that big cavalry pistol in my hand. Once on, that gun would've felt plumb wrong there. Like that first gun the Green Man handed me in that barn a lifetime ago. But after them months in that sod hut, him and me practicing our draw to pass the time, seemed I'd carried that pistol since I was a babe. Felt as proper in my hand as Bess' reins or that old Springfield Daddy gave me what

I used to pop squirrels and that Gray Man. Except was the Green Man what put this pistol in my hand. Was him what taught me how to shoot it.

And then, without no damn warning, the Green Man pulled open that door and stepped out like a man in no hurry at all. And following him out into that street? I swear I saw better than a dozen boys standing straight all up and down the other side of that road. Was some rough hands, like them what found us at the hut, and some proper looking gunslingers, too. Even some of them marshal's deputies, though I didn't see that marshal himself. Was an army waiting for us, it was.

But we didn't stop to give them no time to look on us. We just started down them boards toward that hotel, wherever it was. Was a few folks walking on our side of the street, there was, and I saw their eyes go wide when they seen the Green Man with his coat open and that long Henry across his back. Some even did their doubles seeing that long pistol I was carrying out of its holster. Plenty of them gave us a wide berth, they did. Hell, we wasn't even one block down before seemed like all them folks on our side of the road up and raptured, leaving us all lonesome in the shooting gallery.

But wasn't none of them waddies or deputies across the street what bothered us, none. They was all following and making their own guns plain to see. But wasn't none of them what drew on us. I looked up at the Green Man and saw them stalks of his working themselves wild, pointing this way and that, taking in them boys all around. Shit, the way them stalks would go pointing up at some second floor windows, I reckon he was keeping a mark on some fellas I couldn't even see, too.

And true to the Green Man's word before we stepped out, we didn't start nothing. Was one of them what started it. And, goddamn—the mess he started.

See, we was just stepping down off them boards, making to cross some little alley, when this rough waddy stepped out from around a stack of crates and grabbed me by the damn braid. Near about yanked me right off my feet, he did. Might snapped my damn neck, too, if I hadn't been so goddamn tense already. Shit, took me a second to realize just what was happening, it did, and damn if I didn't feel more the fool than the victim when I did, too. There I was with my gun drawn and this boy got the drop on me anyways.

That waddy done yanked me back against the wall. Had my hair all held up near the back of my goddamn skull, he did, so what my head was turned up toward that blue sky. And, shit, was barely out of the corner of my eye what I saw the Green Man spin round to face us.

Now I tried to end it, I did. Tried to point my pistol at his foot or leg or anything else what I could put a bullet in but he was quick. Just as soon as he yanked me back, I felt that terrible cold of a barrel push against my temple and I heard that waddy say, "Don't you get no ideas, darling. I mean to end this all quick like and I'd hate to have to scatter your pretty little face all over your friend, here."

Well, now, that slowed me some.

But not the Green Man. Was a right calm look on his face. But when that boy started talking about blowing my brains out, well, was some frightening transformation I saw right then. His big black eyes bulged toward me. And his lips curled up, releasing this shaking kind of growl what seemed to rise up deep in him. Was some kind of terrible animal noise it was. And damn if even I didn't want to run screaming from the sound of it.

Well, that boy started to say something. I swore I heard him mutter, "Stand back, now, or the girl—"

But he never got to finish that muttering. Quick as some viper, the Green Man unshucked that space-man pistol of his and, before I right knew what was happening, I heard that whipping snap it made when he pulled the trigger. Was near blinded by that red shot what come flying right at me. Damn! The heat of it near burnt my cheek as it snapped over my shoulder. Felt that waddy jerk back off me, like he'd been torn away by a tornado or by some bolt of God's own lightning. Heard his body crash against the wall and caught a whiff of some chuck-house stink, too. Burned flesh and blood and bone, you ken? And before I could even turn around, saw him crumple to the ground beside, some smoking hole where his face had been.

And right then, like we'd blown the damn bugle, was a clamor of gunfire what filled the street. All them boys across the road done took their cue from the Green Man gunning down that rip and was letting their lead fly.

I dropped behind them crates, just about sitting on that waddy's chest in doing. The Green Man stood his ground for a spell and let fly some wicked arc of fire from that pistol, each whipping snap of that gun being answered by some horrible crash or scream across the street. But after a few long seconds, he leapt into that alley, behind some barrels.

Was a hail of bullets what started raining down on us then, chipping at them wood crates and barrels like axmen working a stump. But for my part, seemed like that shooting was happening all far away. No, was the sting of sunburn on my cheek where the Green Man's shot had passed me by and the stink of burnt hair where it done passed me close what had my proper attention. And sitting there behind that crate, I swear I was shaking like I was in a blizzard.

The Green Man was watching me from behind them barrels across the alley, gauging my condition, I reckon.

"Jesus Christ!" I remember yelling at him, the sound of them bullets whizzing by or biting into wood just about drowning me out. "What if you'd missed?"

That son of a bitch just shrugged, hollering back, "Never occurred to me."

And was right then one of them marshal's deputies come busting out of some alley door behind the Green Man. Quick as I saw him, he brought his pistol up on the Green Man's back. And what happened next was all instinct, it was. Not a bit of thinking in it. All that shaking of mine was gone in a blink and I yanked up my gun. Was just like shooting them cans back at the hut. I started squeezing that trigger before I had my aim true and by the time my gun was up and pointed, my finger had done its duty. Damn if I didn't shoot that boy right in the arm, throwing that pistol of his clean out of his hand. And hearing my shot, and that deputy's yelling, the Green Man spun around and pulled his own trigger. That gun of his snapped red fire and, I swear, that deputy flew off his feet near ten damn yards.

And that there was the start of the running. Craziest damn run of my life, too. The Green Man stood behind his barrel, raining his god-awful red fire on them boys across the street. That afforded me some cover and I ran for the door what that deputy come out of, the Green Man on my heels. Once inside, though, wasn't no goddamn shelter to be had. Was bullets shattering that store's windows and tearing up all manner of goods.

I remember some bullet shot in what hit a barrel of shovels and ricocheted around like some murdering bee. And with the Green Man shooting back out of them blown windows, was all manner of hell in that place. Was bags of flour burst by incoming bullets, set afire by the Green Man's outgoing shot. And low as we tried to keep, seemed them bullets coming in was just missing the tops of our heads—such I kept feeling the wind of their passing in my hair.

But long as it might've seemed we was in that store, couldn't have been more than a few seconds before we got across it and Green Man kicked open another alley door. Had to keep moving, see, else them gun thugs outside would tighten the noose and end us right quick.

So we were in another alley. And don't think I wasn't doing my share of shooting none. Shot on that deputy, hadn't I, and at least one more while we was crossing through that store. And now, in that second alley, we could see, plain, some of them boys running across the road toward us. I just kept thinking to myself, was like shooting cans in the air. Got to hit them before they crash down, ending me. And with that, I dropped two of them buckaroos in the middle of that street. And the Green Man? He never stopped running but kept that space gun of his shooting its red fire, knocking a couple of them gunslingers right up into the air, all burnt and blown through.

Now, this second alley didn't have no door on its other side. So, like damn fools, we ran up onto them boards again, in plain sight of them shooters across the way, and took to running like the possessed. Heads down and guns shooting blind off across the road. Was like we was running through a hailstorm. Troughs and windows and all else throwing splinters and shards and splash on us. And right before we made the third alley, was another stack of barrels waiting. I swear, mister, I dove behind that stack like a man diving out of a mine about to blow.

And for a second there, I reckon the Green Man and I both figured we was going to get a breather. Maybe even a spot from which we could return fire from cover. I even remember starting to say something like, "Fuck, I thought you said was only a dozen or—"

But was right then we heard something clattering against the wall and boards toward us—tossed over them barrels and back at us off the front of whatever business we was sheltering on. And we heard this hiss, like a snake making to scare you. Except wasn't no snake. Goddamn, what I would've given for the sensible fright a rattler puts in you. No sir. Was a bundle of dynamite sticks landed between us.

And I swear, my heart stopped right then. Might not have started again if the Green Man hadn't pushed me.

Was a terrible drumming of bullets on them barrels behind us, there was. Terrible as the drumming of my restarted heart. And I tell you, mister, I took off running down some third alley like Jimmy and Jeb and all the rest was right on my heels. Like the Gray Man himself was running me down. And I don't know where the Green Man went, just that he wasn't with me when that dynamite blew, taking up half that building with it.

Shit, you taking my meaning here, mister? They threw fucking dynamite at us. And not just one, neither. I reckon the Green Man's reputation as a cold shot must've right preceded him with this here posse. They must've heard well of what happened to them what chased after us at the Devil's Gate and at that sod hut. Or maybe what befell them soldiers on the Platte what crossed paths with us. We'd done burnt up every bit of the Wyoming where some fool—either of them Boones or that gray fella—meant to cut us down. And seeing as how well these gunslingers and buckaroos and deputies was faring in the streets of Cheyenne, I suppose I can't blame them for bringing out the big stuff and making to end us quick in a blast to all Hell.

But, however that dynamite ended up between us on that porch, I must've been damn near the end of that alley, fixing to come around the corner of some other building, when them sticks went up. Loud as that fucking Howitzer I tell you, except was like it went off right in my goddamn ear, it did. And that explosion? Lifted me plumb off my feet. Threw me through the air like some rag doll and tossed me into the dirt and sharp grasses, tumbling me like some log down a hill until I slammed right plumb against a bucking livery door. And thank God for that. If it'd tossed me a hair to either side, might been a solid wall or even a pile of barn tools what would've ended me proper. As it was, I come near to breaking my whole body, I reckon. But I lucked out at that, just getting cut all the fuck up on my arms and neck. Shit, felt cuts all under my dungarees and the Green Man's shirt, too, from God knows how many splinters punched through. And damn if the ringing in my ears wasn't some god-awful wailing in my head. Was even blood I felt running down one cheek.

Was all balled up, too, but some big chunk of lumber what crashed down next to me snapped me out of that. See, was bits of boards and furniture and glass and metal raining all down from that building blown up into the sky. So I clamored out of that hay pile and ran for whatever cover I could find—some little porch top back across this new alley. Couldn't hardly tell up from down there for a spell, neither. But sheltered there, over the sound of that terrible ringing in my ears and the crashing of that building and its bits back to Earth, I could hear gunshots echoing from far off. Gave me some hope, that did, what the Green Man wasn't in bits and pieces now, all blown to hell. He was still fighting.

Was right then the back side of that building—the half not blown right up to heaven—fell right the fuck over, like some drunk dropping all over himself. Wood and all else crashed and banged out every which, blocking all the way I'd come. And damn if I didn't have no idea where I was, no more. My shaken brain couldn't make no heads or tails of which way I should be headed.

I just wanted back with my Green Man. If he was out there fighting, then damned if I wasn't going to be shooting by his side. So I went back the only way I knew—back toward that blasted heap. And when I come round the corner and saw what was left, well, Jesus Christ ain't never seen a mess like this, I reckon. Was like them stories of the War, see? Like from that battle in Richmond or where else. Was just some crater where the street used to of been. And just some perched on the edge of it. And on the far side away from me, back out in that street, was the Green Man, his duster all blackened but that space gun of his still whipping out shining bits of red death. And he was running again. Running and killing like a whirlwind.

Maybe that's what brought my wits back. Seeing my murdering angel on the run, I mean. Wasn't no way I could get to him through that crater, though, so I took off down the alley I was thrown into. Reckoned it ran parallel to the street the Green Man was fighting on and, sooner or later, I'd rejoin him or even meet him at that hotel. So I took off running.

And right there, around the back of that next building, I saw an alley what should've taken me back to the street. And soon as I rounded that corner, saw something else what stopped me cold.

Somers and three well-heeled boys was coming my way. And at seeing me, they raised them guns up in a flash—all but Somers that is. He raised his arms quick, yelling for them boys to hold their fire. And damn, I was having a hard time hearing it all over the ringing in my ears—from the bleeding one, especially—but I held my fire all the same, too. Shit, reckon I'd begun to believe my own fright, that the Green Man had done Somers back at the sod hut. That it'd been Somers' screams I'd heard on waking after getting shot.

But here he was, beautiful as the day I first saw excepting some dirt all on him from where he must've been thrown to the ground by that explosion. And, damn. Holding a pistol like he was, was something I could see in him of that Army boy I once took a shine on. Something but not much. Them buckaroos running up with him dispelled any bit of that lost longing, they did. No, this wasn't no Somers what cut a swell through my heart. No sir. This was some Somers what Moses Boone put on the hunt. What was on the hunt for me.

I remember him running up to me, saying, "Martha Jane! Thank God almighty. After that explosion I right feared—"

Goddamn it stung to hear that name out of his mouth again. Martha! But, I didn't let him finish his talking, none, for the sting of it. I raised my pistol on him, pointing it right at that goddamn beautiful face of his—that face what was once part of my ecstasy, it was. Shit, I didn't even know if I had any bullets left. I'd lost track of my shooting long before some fool tossed dynamite at us. But I raised my gun on him all the same and told him square, "You stay right the fuck back, Somers. You and your boys done shot me once and I don't reckon I'll let you put a hole through me again."

Well, he stopped just like I hoped he would. And he put his hands out so I could see them. Even the hand what held a pistol he opened up all but one finger so he wouldn't drop it. Waved off his boys, too. And damn if the look on his face wasn't as sincere as it'd been that morning he snuck into that first camp I shared with the Green Man.

"Martha Jane," he said, "Shit, girl, I've come clear across the territory to rescue you."

Damn, my blood was up at that. And that ringing in my ears seemed to rise with my heartbeat, it did, the first hammering on my brain while the other beat against my chest.

"Hell you have," I told him, waving that gun all menacing. "That why that boy of yours put a bullet through me? That why another just put a gun to my head and dozen more tried to shoot me down or blow me to Kingdom Come!"

"It's the Green Man," he said at that. "We're trying to get the Green Man, not you, Martha—"

Now, that set me over the edge, it did, hearing that name coming out of his mouth again and again after all this time. His wife's fucking name! I stepped so close I buried that barrel of mine in his chest, I did. "Don't you ever fucking call me that," I spat at him.

He covered his head like I was raining blows on him. Was a right pathetic look he had, too. Almost disarming, you might say. But my blood was afire, it was, and was going to take a measure more than some pitiful look to bring it back to a simmer. Was pain all through me—from the running and the shooting and the explosion—to take the place of that gunshot in my belly. And wasn't no bit of me what could forget who this was I was talking to and what I had to thank him for.

But he kept his head half bowed, so low I half expected him to take a knee, and told me, "Now, Martha Jane, I'm plumb sorry about all that mess before. I tell you true, I ain't never come gunning for you. Damn, girl, I reckon it'd kill me to see you come to some bad end on account of that green fella. You got to come with me. Let me get you safe."

Shit, the Green Man done told me you couldn't count on no man, didn't he? Sure as shit didn't plan to start counting on this one. So I put a little weight behind that gun barrel in his chest and I told him proper, my voice all still cracking and angry, "I don't fucking cotton to any man telling me which way to run or aim, lest he's my papa or he's green, you understand?" I told him, "I reckon you done forfeited your right to looking after me, one way or the other, when you done pirooted me while calling out your wife's fucking name."

And what he was going to say next, I'll never know. He opened his mouth to say something right about the time the sound of the Green Man's gun snapping out red fire cut him short. Them boys behind Somers folded like buffalo shot, they did, never even screaming as red shots burst clean through them. And Somers? Well, shit, was my standing so close to him what must've saved him. Shots streamed by us on either side but seeing as we was standing right in front of each other, the Green Man couldn't hit Somers without hitting me, too.

Well, Somers crouched low and pushed us both back around the corner. But before he could say nothing, I whipped him with my pistol and told him, "You get the fuck gone, now, you hear? I can only save you from the Green Man so often and I reckon this here's the last of it." Then I whipped him with that pistol again, driving him back off me. "Get gone."

"Now, Martha—" he said.

Well, I leveled that pistol on him fresh, at that. Was enough fucking hate in me right then I should've beefed him where he stood. Should've sent him right to Hell right there. And he saw every bit of that hate, he did. And damn if he didn't look as scared as I ever saw him.

"Don't—" was all I could muster. And he took the gist of it, fagged out quick as a mare.

Well, I didn't waste no time watching him off, neither. I ducked back round that corner and near about ran over the Green Man. Or him, me, is more like it. He was bounding down that alley on all fours, pounding them hands and feet in the dirt and dust fast as a fucking colt, until I come round that corner. Couldn't have been more than a few feet off when we saw each other. I pulled up fast but he kept on coming. And the reason for it was plain, too. Was boys crossing the street he done left in ruins, chasing him down that alley toward me. They was shooting, too. So the Green Man damn near scooped me up as he ran over me. Carried me right across the alley and behind another building, he did.

Was the back of some undertakers, it was. Was a dozen or more coffins in various states of build in that yard. Shit, that sight will give you pause any fucking time, it will. But the Green Man and I didn't even slow down to breathe. We was across and around them coffins before the first of them pursuing buckaroos and gunslingers rounded that corner behind us. And the Green Man put a number of them boys in them coffins, he did. Shit, I was scrambling to reload my cylinder—turns out it was empty—and before I was even done at that the Green Man finished his shooting and grabbed my collar, moving me on.

We ran a spell, there. Some kind of nice respite, I guess you'd call it, until we come up on the back of that hotel. The Green Man kicked in the kitchen door and pulled me through all rough and blind. But once inside, he stopped right quick and put a hand out for me to wipe my chin and keep still. And was plain why. Was the sound of boots on the boards overhead.

I remember starting to whisper at him, "Could be any folks. Doesn't mean—"

But he just fingered the collar of his duster, poking a finger through a bullet hole there, and whispered back at me, "Two shooters upstairs."

And then he drew that little pilot's knife from his pocket, holding it in his half-a-hand like I done seen him back at that sod hut, the blade sticking out the bottom of his grip, below his pinky.

"Stay close," he told me, "cover my back."

And at that he was out of the kitchen and into the hotel proper. We done slunk through some dining room and into the lobby, an unpainted, dusty place with a two-story ceiling and a long stair going right up from the front door to some U-shaped balcony connecting all the rooms. I remember, clear, what when we stepped into that lobby, the Green Man was padding quiet as a cat in his boots—quiet as I never seen no man creep in such. Was a good few seconds before the hotel's keeper, looking to spy some action out the windows, marked us on his rear. About screamed, he did. And if he had, I reckon the Green Man would've quieted him. But the old coot had his wits and didn't need me to tell him to skedaddle. But watching him fag out through the front door made it plain we needed to move right quick. What was left of that posse outside was fixing to know right where we was hiding.

But I didn't need to tell the Green Man that, none. He was up the stairs and around the left side of that balcony in a blink. And when the Green Man made his move? Well, was a nice gesture he made asking me to cover his back but wasn't no way I could've kept up and kept quiet. But I moved fast and silent as I could.

See, them shooters the Green Man saw from the street was in them two front windows, each in a room on either side of that U-shaped balcony, what with the gap of that open lobby between their doors. So when I saw the Green Man making for the door on the left side of that balcony, I pointed that pistol of mine at the room across from it.

But the Green Man was faster here than even I seen him before. He crouched outside that first door and pounced through it like some wildcat setting on its prey. Was a terrible loud crash, and the cursing from the gunslinger inside that room was near drowned out by the Green Man's own shrill trilling. And wasn't a second later that gunslinger, rifle and all, done flew out that door and into the space between the ends of that balcony. Was blood all across his chest where the Green Man done slashed him and, as he hung there in the space—between flying and falling, it seemed—wasn't a sound he made or I seemed to hear. But was the snap of that space gun what broke the silence, punching that falling buckaroo in the chest like cannon shot, kicking him clear across the gap and through the railing on the far side of that balcony.

Was right then the sharpshooter in that other room done threw open his door, a long rifle riding to the ready even as his partner crashed through the rails next to him. And for a second, his eyes met mine. Was some kind of frantic confusion in them, like he couldn't believe how some little girl done tossed his buddy clear across that open lobby. And right he should've been balled up over it—I would've been by such bosh. But the Green Man didn't let him think on it too long. No sir.

That Green Man burst out of the first shooter's room like a goddamn bullet. Was on all fours again, he was. He leapt onto the balcony railing on our side of that lobby and soon as his feet caught up, he done propelled himself clear across that gap. Was time enough for that sharpshooter to pull up and fire off one quick round before the Green Man crashed into him, tossing them both back into the far room.

And was near about then a couple of the marshal's boys pushed through the front door of that hotel, down on the floor below us. I remember unloading my pistol on them as they come inside. Reckon I winged or worse a couple of them, too. But they kept pushing in until that sharpshooter done flew out of his room and crashed down on them. The Green Man had made buzzard food out of that one, too, see? Was right cut up. But them deputies didn't have no time to think on it before more of that Green Man's red fire rained down on them from the balcony, driving them out.

I ran around that balcony, meaning to get back to my Green Man's side. I remember leaping over that first gunslinger—the one threw and shot clear across the gap—and just about diving into that room. Was a little bedroom, it was, with the window right broken out so that sharpshooter could take his aim down the street. But was the Green Man what took his place by that window now, his big alien gun on the floor by his feet, that Henry shouldered and shooting across rooftops and down into the road.

I knelt inside the door, watching him do his deadly work. Wasn't no thinking or pause in him. Wasn't nothing but killing. Was a cold longrider. Cold as they come. And for that, I was plumb glad, right then. Back at the Devil's Gate, it maybe scared me a little to see him kill with such ease. Especially seeing him beef boys nearabout my age. But here, on the other end of some bushwhacking what just about shot and blowed me to Hell, I prayed for rain, understand? Prayed that lead rain from his Henry would fall on every fucking head in the world what was chasing us.

After a round of shooting—and some shots coming back, too, I tell you—the Green Man knelt back from the window to load another cartridge, his hands all work and business even while them stalks kept their watch on the road and them eyes kept their gauge on me. I smiled at him, then, and he at me. And I saw silver blood running down the left sleeve of his duster from a little hole that sharpshooter must punched through in his last gasp.

I started to move toward him, meaning to tend him if I could, but he stopped me with a gesture. And he didn't need to use them strong words for me to listen. Not this time. I knew he was made tougher than any man. Was made of sand, this one.

I remember him asking me, "Where's your hat?"

Talk about being balled up! I near dropped my pistol in my rush to feel my own head. And goddamn if that hat of mine wasn't nowheres. Must been blown clear off my head by that dynamite.

He laughed a little. Goddamn, that made all the fear and shaking in me fade to air, it did.

"No matter," he said to me. "We got the high ground now." And he let them big black eyes of his linger on me for a spell. Lingered long, too. Long enough to make me worry about more than my missing hat. Shit, what could I look like to him right then? Blood running down my cheek from some painful ringing ear, little bits of splinters sticking all out of my clothes, powder burns on my fingers, my braids all tossed and burnt, dirt everywheres.

"Shit, Jane," the Green Man said to me, still smiling. "Whatever happened to that girl I met in Piedmont what couldn't pull a trigger?"

Might as well have asked him what happened to that cold son of a bitch what left me at Harthra's by my lonesome. But wasn't in me, then. No sir. Seeing the Green Man's smile, and seeing that Henry held true in his hands? Shit, just to be breathing after that mad dash between bullets and dynamite? Here was one to ride the river with if ever there was.

"Reckon you must've left her there," I told him.

He just nodded, saying, "You're just daisy, Jane Canary. You know that?"

Goddamn, must've blushed at that like some little thing. He just laughed that infectious laugh again and put that long barrel back out the window, ready to start the rain again.

"You just watch that lobby and them stairs. Hold them off, if you can."

And I watched him for a spell before turning back to see that ruined lobby for whoever might dare come at us. And I told him, then, "I'll hold them off until Hell freezes over or you say different."

And I would've, too.

EIGHT

Wasn't long after what the shooting plumb stopped. First, sounded like the Green Man must've beefed every pistoler in Cheyenne, it did. But when I looked back at him, saw the way he kept up the searching with them eyes and feelers of his, well, I right expected Somers and his boys had pulled back. Regrouping, I reckoned. Taking toll of the cost our frantic twosome took on their well-heeled party. And was a quite a toll, yes sir.

After a bit, the Green Man drew back that Henry and leaned against this little dresser under the window, them stalks keeping their vigil even as he settled for a breather.

We must've sat there like that, quiet and waiting—his stalks on that road, my eyes on that lobby—for close on to twenty minutes before I turned around to say something. And damn if it wasn't right then we heard Somers' voice rolling up from the street.

Was halfway to dark when he yelled up from some hiding spot. "That was a mighty fine run you had there," he hollered. And I saw the Green Man's stalks searching them shadowed storefronts and alleys across the way.

Well, whatever I'd been about to say was lost, right then. The Green Man didn't say nothing, neither. Not right away. I could see he was doing some quiet reckoning—watching Somers with them stalks, taking tally of what that boy was doing and how many was left with him.

"Looks like you got yourself holed up," Somers hollered at us from far off. And even though I couldn't see him, and even though he was least a hundred yards off, I could hear his voice shaking. I could hear the deep breath he struggled to take before yelling back, "Looks like you got yourself surrounded."

Was then the Green Man spoke up, calling back in some even voice, calm as the open sky, "Reckon we'll have to get ourselves unsurrounded, then, won't we."

Was a space of silence then, like the Green Man's voice had done the job for him, driving them boys away with sand rather than lead. And when Somers spoke up again, sounded like he was even thinking on running.

"Think about the girl, space man," he yelled up from his hiding. "Neither of us wants her hurt, none. Don't want no repeat of the fight my boys gave you back out at that hut, do we?"

The Green Man was staring at me, then. And I could see he was thinking about that fight at the sod hut. How I'd taken some waddy's bullet. About how he massacred them boys what did me, too. But was a wry twist what cracked them thin lips of his. Was a might surprised at that, I was, but glad to see it all the same.

Then, snarling, he called back, "Wasn't a whole lot of fighting, as I recall. Was a lot of dying." And he let them words hang in the air over that Cheyenne street for a long spell before turning his head up toward that window and bellowing out some kind of terrible space-man shriek. Like something out of some nightmare, it was. And damn if that didn't roll up and back down them streets outside, setting off horses and men alike running from the sound of it.

I reckon my face must've gone a shade of white on hearing that terrible noise, too. Like once on when I first heard it in that barn a lifetime before. But wasn't no trace of fear in me, none. Not then. Was exciting, if anything. Was a thrill I felt all the way down to my toes—all curled up in my boots, they was—when he let out that shriek. Was my murdering angel setting the fear of God in them boys outside. Goddamn! Wasn't nothing us two couldn't win right then.

And all of a sudden, I saw them stalks of his twitch and point some different way. Them tips bent at the floor. And like it was some practiced dance, he leapt up, mated that scope with his eye, and bent that barrel straight at the boards beneath his feet. Then, without so much as a pause in his beautiful fluid moving, he squeezed that Henry, putting a shot right between his boots. And, damn, if that shot wasn't answered but some surprised holler and a thud downstairs.

I ran onto that balcony and bent my own rifle over that wrecked railing just in time to watch some beefed gunslinger topple forward, his hat rolling across the lobby like some tumbleweed in a breeze, the hole in its crown matching the one in the top of his head.

And standing there on that balcony, I heard the Green Man yell back out that window, "I wouldn't go sending nobody else in, boy, lest it's you and you mean to end this!"

But was only silence what answered him. And the Green Man crouched again under that window, his back against that little dresser. And after what felt like a good long while, he looked at me straight. Was dim in that hotel, and what little light there was come from that fading sun gone down behind the town but still I could see myself plain in them eyes, reflected. Standing apart, through some doorway, that Springfield of mine held in imitation of how the Green Man carried his Henry.

And after a spell, he asked me, "Was that Somers in the alley? The same Somers?"

I nodded, not finding my words right away. Hadn't the Green Man known it would be? Hadn't he worked that from some boy out behind the sod hut? Shit, hadn't he recognized his voice well enough just now?

But I knew why he was asking. Wasn't no kind of confirmation he was looking for. Was some kind of confession. Some little admittance what I knew who was hunting us. What I knew but didn't put a bullet in him when I had the chance.

So I just shook my head, hoping the dark on that balcony would shadow my shame some. Hoping them feelers of his wouldn't divine out no more than he right knew already. But I couldn't suffer under them black eyes for long, my ghost shining in them. I told him in some low voice, barely a whisper, "I couldn't shoot him."

He just nodded and let his head fall back against that little dresser. And I remember him saying, all quiet, "Reckon I've no such reservation."

Was dark outside by the time I stepped back into that little room. Was tears fighting at the backs of my eyes, there was, but goddamned if I'd give in to them. Shit, didn't even know right what I was close to crying for. Or why I didn't beef him in that alley. Fuck Somers! Fuck him and all them hired guns following at his heels. Was one of his what put this bullet in me, after all. Was one of his what threw that dynamite, taking the hearing right out of my left ear. Shit, was him what took else from me, too, if you recall. Took it on a blanket under some black Wyoming sky, all lit up like Christmas with that thick band of stars. But, God, if it was just for that one moment, maybe that was reason enough not to beef him. Somers might be bunko. Shit, he might be fucking married. But in that moment, with us so tangled up and clumsy under them million candles in the sky? Was a sweetness, then. Was a sweetness I could still feel between them thighs of mine in that moment between dreaming and waking, when your blood starts pumping afresh and all manner of your parts wake from their slumbering. In that moment, them Marthas he moaned was mine alone. And them kisses and them gentle caresses wasn't never for some other woman. Was then he was mine and I was his. And all else what happened since? None of that could take that moment from me.

The Green Man watched me in the doorway but didn't say nothing for a spell. Instead, he set down that Henry and checked the bullet hole that last gunslinger done put in him. When he opened up his shirts to look on it, well, I reckoned it wasn't so bad after all. Little more than a graze. But still he lifted a bloodied finger up from that wound so some moonlight caught the silver of it.

"Might've been a mistake coming to Cheyenne," he said. And I remember him turning to face me, some thin smile turning the end of his lips.

I shook my head and dropped to the floor next to him, my Springfield on the boards beside. "Next time, you listen to me, understand?"

"Yes, ma'am," was all he said to that.

In the space between us was the Green Man's big space-man gun. And after a little while of that thing poking its hilt into my thigh, I reached down and plucked it right up. Was a sight heavier than I would've guessed. Felt like a solid fucking piece of steel, it did. And wasn't hot like you might expect something what shot fire to be. Was downright cold. Like the man what wielded it.

And I expect that got me wondering what the Green Man had been thinking for a while now. So I asked him, "You think they'll keep coming?"

Was closing up them shirts, he was. Said, "Expect they won't come in the dark. Not knowing what I can see and they can't."

But I shook my head at that. "No," I told him. "I mean the Boones.

The posses. You think they'll keep coming? After we get out of this mess?"

He didn't answer right away. Expect he didn't right know what to say. Looking back, I know he'd been thinking about that same thing for a while now. But maybe there wasn't no answer for it. Or maybe he just wasn't sure how much of his mind to share. Either way, took him a while to tell me, "Vengeance begets vengeance, Jane." And that I knew. Knew that all too well, didn't I? Was a young thing and might not've put them thoughts to words but I knew it well enough. Saw it in Piedmont. Saw it in the Gray Man. Seen it in my own self both times.

But, like I said, was a young thing. So I told him, "Wasn't us what started this. Was that murderer Jeb Boone."

The Green Man just nodded at that. Might've been the closest he'd come to getting his ride home, what before Jeb fouled that flying engine all a cropper. Might've been the closest a human come to beefing him, too, for all I knew. But if he was thinking on that, I couldn't tell.

No, I just remember him taking that gun of his out of my hand and setting it beside. "Got to think beyond your guns, Jane," he said to me, "There's a sight more to life than vengeance."

And ain't that all he'd got from riding with me? Since he pulled Jimmy off me in that barn or since I done stabbed a gray man in that ship? Ain't vengeance all I'd repaid him with since he first handed me a pistol, aiming me at Jimmy, and had to finish it himself?

You know, mister, was a lot the Green Man did for me. And I did every bit I could think of for him, when he'd let me. But I knew this wasn't what he wanted. Like back at that sod hut when I'd caught him watching them stars, hunting for home among all them candle lights. This wasn't living.

So, for the first time in all our riding, I told him, "Thank you."

He looked down at me. Wasn't nothing else reflected in them oily eyes this time. Not in that dark. Was just him.

"What for?" he asked.

I remember letting my head drop against his shoulder right then. Queer thing, that. All them months together, all them times we was back to back or on the run, was a precious few we ever actually touched. Such that feeling my ear against his sleeve, hearing my hair scrape against the flannel covering that hard flesh underneath, was right exciting. Damn if my heart didn't feel high pitched and thin at that. Damn if my heart didn't love it.

"What's it like up there?" I asked him.

I saw him set his Stetson on top of that little dresser. And I heard his head settle back against the drawer. "Dark," he said. "Lonely. Not so different than down here."

And that I knew, too. Been plenty of times I'd been like that settler what proposed, in his fashion, back at Independence Rock. When I'd needed people. When I'd been desperate for them. Was like that after Daddy died. After Somers and my falling out at the rails, too. Shit, was plenty desperate when the Green Man found me at Harthra's, that's for sure. But not now. Never been darker, maybe. But lonely?

"I ain't lonely," I told him.

"No," he said. "Me neither."

And right then? Well, puts a blush on me to even think on it. That Green Man of mine was a quiet one. Was a private one, wasn't he? We'd ride for hours without saying a word. Hell, at that sod hut, we went for days sometimes. But right then, I reckon we'd said all there was to say. Maybe ever. And without saying nothing else, that Green Man pushed me off that arm I was leaning on and put it right around me. Pulled me right up to him, too, such that when I put my head back down, was against his chest, it was. I could feel the reeds of his bone shirt. I could feel the rise and fall of his breathing. And although I didn't hear no heartbeat there, I could hear the wind in his lungs, like the wind on the plain. Blowing hot but a relief all the same. Lifted you up, that wind did. Lifted you right on to the stars if you let it.

And that's how we spent our last night together. In some shot up hotel, backs to the wall, guns at our sides. And me wrapped up in my sleepless Green Man, safe as I ever felt in my whole life.

Was home that night. For the last time.

NINE

I slept deep in those arms, I did. Deep enough I remember dreaming I was back at Harthra's ranch, working with them boys what weren't no more. Dreaming Bess was kicking and playing in them fields and Mister Harthra was sitting on that porch of his, his green face shining under that huge sky.

But I don't reckon I remember this dream because of all its sweetness. No sir. Was this unease to it all. Like if I let the sweetness steal me away for a spell, some blackness would creep up on me. Was like I was being watched from them grasses or hills all around. Except wasn't that Gray Man haunting me, this time. Wasn't even no memory of Jeb's ambush, none. Was something I knew well hiding out of sight. Like something I forgot or didn't right pay attention to. And was these nerves in me would go all aflutter after some romp with them boys or chasing after Bess. When that blessed spell broke and that shadow drew close. Would make my heart race. But I wasn't afraid none. Was in my Green Man's arms, wasn't I? Was wrapped up in my murdering angel. Never mind no shadows waiting for us outside in the night. Wasn't no force what could harm me there.

I stirred just once all night. Was right dim in that room, what with no one fool enough to light them streetlights between Somers' posse and us. Was just some weak glow from a street over, or maybe just from that sky full of stars running overhead like a river. Whatever it was, was just barely enough light for me to make out the Green Man checking that bandage around my waist, seeing it was still square on me after all that day's jostling.

When he saw I was waking, he looked at me for a spell. Some kind of sad look on that hard face of his. Then he closed my shirt—his shirt, if you recall—over that bandage and told me, "Never you mind that." And like that was some ever-after, I fell right back to sleeping until morning.

I woke then because I felt the Green Man moving, getting into a crouch under that window what he was shooting and spying through the night before. Was right fucking cold in that room, I tell you. That first breath of mine billowed up like some fucking boiler steam it did. And, shit, if shivers didn't race through me. Was getting near winter in them parts and was the taste of snow in the air. Even the clanking of wagons down below echoed up cold.

The Green Man done put his duster across me at some point during the night. And I was right thankful for it, you better believe. I remember pulling that thing up tight, covering every frozen inch I could squeeze under it until was just my nose and eyes and braids peeking over that worn collar. And as I watched the Green Man peek them long stalks and them black eyes over the sill, spying on the morning scene down in that street, I took in his smell off that leather thing. Was the stink of Mustangs and gunpowder and some bitter sweat like no musk I ever smelled off Somers or Bill or no white skinned man. Was the scent of my Green Man, it was. And I breathed deep of it, I tell you.

After a while, I spoke up, saying my hot words right into that collar to warm me. Asked him, "What you see out there?"

He didn't look back at me, none. Just watched the street with them eyes and feelers—seeing more in a blink, I reckon, than ever some dead eye might've picked out whatever the spell. But he didn't waste no time in answering me, neither, and, with what he said, well, that warmed me up right quick.

"Reinforcements come during the night," he told me. "Somers' and the handful of his we left him are across the way in a feed store. Just three of them. The marshal and his are a little father back. Reckon they're waiting to see if Somers can play out. But he's been deputizing by starlight, seems. Might be a dozen of his scattered around."

My blood kicked up at that, it did. Was fifteen men he was talking about. Near on as many what we faced the day before and that we just

barely squeaked out of. But, shit, if it was just fifteen I reckoned the Green
Man could tell you this part of the tale himself, couldn't he?

No sir, wasn't just them fifteen, as I reckon you're guessing. Shit, reckon you might even know this part of the story already, else you wouldn't
come calling on me that first time, would you? Was all over them frontier
papers, what happened that morning. If it'd just been them fifteen and
we'd done fagged out of Cheyenne, maybe it wouldn't have been.

No. The Green Man sat back against that little dresser and picked
up his Stetson off the top of it. Took to brushing it across that flannel of
his—all idle like—as he kept on, saying, "Them ain't the reinforcements.
Them come in from the north about three hours ago. Must've sent for
them soon as we come riding into town." And then, I remember, he took
to looking at that hat all careful like. Like he hadn't seen it in years. Like
he couldn't right recall where he done got it. "That marshal must've had
some idea of the trouble we'd cause," he said. "That Somers wasn't man
enough to tame it."

Then he sat quiet for a spell. Waiting. Wanting me to ask about it.
And fidget as he did with that hat, he never looked my way until I spoke
up. If he had, them words wouldn't have been necessary.

"How many?" I asked him, talking over that duster collar for the first
since I woke.

He gave up looking on it and fit that hat around them stalks and set
it low over them big black eyes of his. Was lost in shadow, they was.

"Thirty or forty cavalry," he said. "A couple big guns in wagons.
Gatlings, I reckon."

Well, stopped my heart cold to hear that. Was them cold wagons I
done heard on waking, I reckoned. War wagons. Like them soldiers used
to clear the plains of Injuns. Maybe against fifteen we might've fought
our way out. But against how many? Fifty or more? With them fast guns?
Shit, we was plumb fucked.

"What do we do?" I asked him. And for a while he didn't say nothing.
Didn't even lose himself in that silent talking he did sometimes. No, he
just sat there quiet. Lost.

"That marshal's keeping his back," he said. "I reckon them army boys
will do the same. At least until Somers does or doesn't get what he's come
for." And at that, he locked them black eyes on me like some kind of

predator. But wasn't him what made my skin crawl right then. Was my own self. Was remembering Somers in that alley, claiming he'd come all this way and done all he'd done just to keep me safe. To rescue me from the Green Man. Made me think, too, of how I done looked the first time that marshal saw me, bundled up, just come back from dying, all in the clutches of a Green Man riding right out of some tall tale.

So I said it plain. Better that than let it steam up in me to festering. "Until he gets me, is what you mean."

The Green Man didn't say nothing at first. Just watched me until I had to look away.

"That what he's come for?" he asked me. Like he didn't fucking know. Hadn't he tortured some boy right on to death to find that out? Hadn't he gotten every answer? Goddamn, I hated him making me fess up like this. What had he told me, huh? What of that torture had he said to set my fucking mind at ease when I was fretting over Somers' fate. Squat's, what.

But the Green Man was barking up the wrong pecker pole, this time. And I done told him so. "He says he wants me safe, though I've got my fucking suspicions," I told him, tapping that metal bandage round my gut as I did. "He's come for you, too," I kept on, "and you know it."

"You think Somers cares at all if Moses Boone sees me dead or no?" the Green Man asked, his eyes still all but hid in the shadow of that Stetson. "That boy's done tried to save you from me twice now. Ain't that right? You think you'd have a bullet in you if he'd been in that posse what bushwhacked us at the hut?"

And, truth is, I'm still not right sure how to answer that. But the Green Man was right in saying Somers done tried twice to pull me away—first outside Piedmont and then, yesterday, even while all was being shot to Hell around him. But what the fuck was I supposed to say? Somers had come gunning for my Green Man so he might as well have been gunning for me. Fuck him. I'd done left him in Piedmont like I'd meant to leave every bit of Martha. What right did he have to come calling after the girl I was now?

But, turns out, I didn't need to answer the Green Man none. See, was right then Somers piped up, yelling up from somewheres under that window for all of Cheyenne to hear.

"You still up there, space man?" he hollered. I remember his voice was all creaky, like them was his first words since waking. But my Green Man didn't say nothing back. Just sat against that dresser searching out that boy with them bug stalks of his while his hands did the work of snatching up that Henry and loading it a fresh cartridge.

"Reckon you are," Somers called out. "Reckon you know, too, that some fellas come down from Laramie last night to help make sure you don't burn your way out of Cheyenne like you did out of Piedmont. Or like you did up at the Platte, ain't that right?"

The Green Man held that rifle across his chest, he did, and squinted as tight as I ever seen him. Reckon he was doing them numbers, right then. Was ten bullets in that cartridge. Was three of Somers' boys hiding in that feed store. But even if he could draw them out, was there bullets enough—was there red fire enough in that Green gun of his—to best the host arrayed against us? If them soldiers moved in, wasn't no walls or bullets or red flashing death what could stop them all—or their Gatlings—before the two of us ended up beneath snakes.

But he kept quiet, all coiled up like he was ready to spring through that window even if he wasn't right sure how much of him might make it back.

Meantime, Somers kept on, hollering up, "There's an army waiting for you. For both of you. But it don't have to be no die-up. Don't have to be no more blood spilt over no goddamn cattle rivalry. We can all walk away from this." Then he paused for a long spell. Long enough I thought the Green Man was about to speak up. But before then, Somers picked up again, yelling, "I got a proposition for you, space man. I reckon you ought to hear it."

The Green Man smiled a bit at that, he did. Was false, but a smile. And, after all that quiet, he yelled back, "Why don't you just step out where I can see you and tell me all about it?"

I remember sliding out from under that duster and creping closer to the window. The Green Man shook his head at me but I didn't care none. If we was facing some devil's bargain or was about to meet our bloody ends, wasn't no bit of me willing to ride shotgun to my own funeral.

Somers got to talking again just as I settled in under that sill. Said, "You've got the jump on me often enough, I reckon I'll keep my head down this time."

"Then say your proposition," the Green Man hollered back. "And

make it quick. The day's young and I don't mean to waste the measure
of it talking to you."

And as I watched the Green Man right then, seems that false smile of
his started to fade. Was some kind of plan forming up in that brain of his,
tickled all by them stalks scanning the street and the men waiting down
in it. I tell you, mister, watching the Green Man like I was, was almost
like I could see all them deputies and soldiers and horses and guns down
there my own self. Through them stalks of his. Like I could see them
shining in them black eyes.

Well, Somers didn't waste no time. And to his credit, I reckon that
meant his offer wasn't no bullshit but was some plan he done dreamt up
proper without no gun to his head.

"You come out of that hotel there. Both of you," Somers called up.
"You let Martha Jane go with the Marshall and his and you come with
me back to see Moses. Let the two of you discuss what happened to that
son of his without need of any more falling under your guns or ours."

The Green Man let out some wicked cackle at that. "Ain't seen one fall
under yours yet, Somers!" he roared. And damn if his voice didn't echo
around in that little room like a gunshot.

But, I tell you, Somers has some surprises in him, that day. The first of
which was them fighting words he traded right back to the Green Man,
getting under his skin faster than I reckon either us expected he could.

"Seems Martha Jane fell under our guns just fine, space man," he
hollered.

Well, the Green Man's lips tightened up right thin at that. Tight to
the point they near vanished all together, silencing him forever.

And after what seemed an hour of quiet, "I'll do you one better," the
Green Man hollered back, his voice booming but without no hint of that
commanding echo he could put in you. "How about I'll meet you in the
street," he said, "just us two, and we'll put this past us for good."

Was some commotion below us at that. Was some chuckling, too. I
reckon them what saw us the night before knew well it would be Somers
bleeding in the dust at the end of it. Them army boys right thinking the
opposite.

But was Somers' second surprise, then. Wasn't no bit of shaking in
his voice, none, when he spoke back up, saying, "I reckon that sounds

fair. Fair enough if it spares Martha Jane and the rest of these boys down here what just want to go home to their wives and children." And then, I swear, was like I could see Somers through the Green Man's stalks, all crouched behind some feed bags what so the Green Man couldn't pick him off with that scoped Henry. Crouched but not cowering, if you take my meaning. Wasn't none of the fear in him what I saw when he was begging under the Green Man's guns in Piedmont. Was something different now.

"But we do it my way," he kept on. "We do it proper. No queer tricks. And Martha Jane stays clear of it."

I leaned close to the Green Man, shaking my head. Wasn't no way this could go well. The Green Man would beef Somers and then every gun in Cheyenne would rip him to ribbons. But he wasn't paying me no mind. No, he was lost in his, he was. And like to prove my point, the Green Man bared his teeth right then. Like some wolf about to growl or some Injun ready to scalp. And through them tight things I heard him bark back, "Best think careful on that proposition, boy. I ain't all hat and no cattle. I meet you in that street. I'll have you for breakfast."

"I'll be ready, space man," Somers shouted back.

The Green Man all but snarled, I tell you. Started away from the window, standing as he went. But was something of an animal in him as he walked, hunched a bit, ready to pounce and slaughter.

I went right after him, never mind if I was visible through the window or along some sharpshooter's barrel. And I didn't waste one breath, neither. I snapped at the Green Man's back, "I ain't trading one die-up for another. You go out there and lay him low, there a whole mess of deputies and soldiers what're going to gun you down in that street."

He didn't turn none. Just kept on into that wrecked hotel lobby, saying back at me, "Oh, I expect they'll find me right lively."

"Goddamnit!" I yelled. "They'll find you right the fuck dead!"

Well, he stopped at that, turning near the top of them stairs and waiting for my blood to cool. And what could I do but stop my stamping after him. Wasn't no words left in me, then. Wasn't no choice, neither. If the Green Man went outside, or if they stormed in, was the same end to this tale.

"There's a play here, Jane," he said. And I remember him standing there, long and thin without that duster hanging off him. And in that bone shirt, with its splatters of silver and red blood, and them two fingers missing off his left hand, and them stalks just nigh to scrapping the ceiling—he was quite the specter. If ever was a pale rider, he was right there in front of me. And if ever one could face odds such as these, was my murdering angel.

"This ain't living," he said. And I remember him stepping toward me, wrapping me all up in shadow. And he put them hands of his on my shoulders and told me, "There's a play here. A way to keep you safe. At least for a spell."

I ain't ashamed to say, tears broke through right then. Tears because I couldn't imagine no world without my Green Man in it. And if he went out into that street, what else could come from it?

"He ain't going to fight fair," I told him. "I don't know how but he won't."

"Neither will I," was all he said.

"I don't want you to go out there." I told him. "Let them storm the hotel. Or let's shoot our way out the back where their lines might be thinnest. We bested the goddamn Gray Man, didn't we? What's the fucking cavalry next to that?"

And, goddamn, he smiled at that. And them big black eyes of his widened a bit, showing me and all around reflected in them.

I wiped some of that shame from my eyes, right then. But I told him, desperate as I was, "We'll get gone from here and find you some flying thing. I promise." Then I remember sucking some wet breath in, blubbering out, "Jesus, we ain't even supposed to be here. That goddamn doctor couldn't even pluck out my bullet."

That smile of his wrinkled some. "Ain't nothing else for it," he said. "Somers is giving us a way out and I mean to take it. And when the shooting is through, Jane, we'll put this town behind us."

"But—" I started to say but he put one of them long fingers against my lip and quieted me good.

"However it goes," he told me, his voice just barely a whisper, "you lay low at Doc Crowder's place for a spell, understand?" Might've been less than a whisper, even. Might've been some quiet words in my mind, like the way I done seen him speak to that horse of his. "And when all's blown over," he kept on, "we'll meet back at that sod hut. You reckon you could find it again?"

I reached up and pulled his hand away from my lips. "If you tell me to meet you in Hell, I'll find the fastest trail there."

He frowned, then, and took a step away. A step back toward them stairs and the street and the shooting.

"I reckon you would, at that," he said.

TEN

He was down them stairs after that, fixing that Henry over his shoulder and checking that big space gun in its holster. Even stood in the middle of that lobby for spell, hand over that hilt, practicing whipping it up and out faster than a blink, pointing that fat barrel at some imaginary Somers in one of them hotel windows.

And was right then I realized, no matter how this shooting ended, was blood I couldn't bear what was going to wet the streets of Cheyenne.

"Can you wound him?" I asked from the top of them stairs. "I mean, can you win the shooting but not kill him?"

The Green Man stopped his practicing right then and looked back over a shoulder at me, his gun all drawn and ready. "That what you want?" he asked.

I started to say something. I don't know right what. But seeing the Green Man draw put some fear in me I can't right explain even today, how many years later.

And he turned toward me, then, shucking that big gun as he did, too, and said, "How are you wanting this to go, Jane?"

"It's not that!" I shouted. And I remember running down them stairs to him. "Boy's all balled up, is all," I told him. "Thinks he's out to rescue some damsel he ain't got no right to. Like to think he knows what all that cocksucker Jeb Boone died for, too. But he don't." Oh, I don't think I was being right clear. Not right sure what I was wanting to say. Just that Somers was a fool, not some desperado. "That ain't Moses Boone out there's what I mean," I told the Green Man. "That ain't the boy what put a bullet in me."

The Green Man nodded, he did, and turned off. "Seems he put worse than that in you," was all I heard him mutter as he started away. And damn if that didn't kick up some heat in me. So I chased him down to that hotel door and stopped him just shy of stepping out into the street. Was soldiers and deputies plenty we could see through them glass panes already—and them us, I reckoned from they way they backed off. But I stopped him short. Begged him plain, I did, them tears creeping back, "Please, don't do this."

And, at that, he just pushed right past me like I was some biddy on the street. Not so much as a downward look. Just pushed on by like some stranger passing on a child.

Was some kind of commotion when he stepped outside, mister. And I tell you, was a bit of me what expected them bullets to fly soon as his boots hit them boards. I remember my hand settling on that cavalry pistol in my belt, even, waiting its turn to trade a shot back at them what meant to beef us. But them soldiers and all else kept theirs shucked and so did my Green Man. He just walked straight to the edge of that boardwalk and stood there, blinking in that new sun while a whole host backed off a pace, taking their measure of him.

I come through them doors a spell later, blinking too but without so many of them boys measuring me. Hell, was one of them few times I don't remember feeling no mean or hot looks on me from so many men. For some, they might've seen some victim. Some young thing carried off by a space man. But for them what knew better, was some longrider they saw in me, goddamnit. Was some girl what put her share of theirs in the grave yesterday. What burned that fort on the Platte to the ground and butchered its gray devil. Was a cold killer they saw in me—some shadow of that green thing what stood ready to beef them all.

And right off, I saw Somers. Was coming out of that feed store all slow like. Was watching that Green Man all suspicious, like he wasn't right sure the Green Man would keep his word and play this fair. And for my part, I wasn't right sure, neither. Never did one face down odds such as these and win by playing it straight. Shit, wasn't no bit of the West won by straight play at all. Hadn't Jeb showed me that? Hadn't Crazy Horse and the Green Man, too?

But the Green Man didn't move to shoot him, none. Just tipped his hat and stepped down into the dust. And at the last he turned and watched me on them boards. Watched me step right near the edge so what with me on them and him off, we was near eye-to-eye. Was a hard look to him, then. Hard like I done seen him so many times before killing. And was a kind of terror what come off him, keeping all them soldiers and else back a pace.

He stepped right close to me. Close enough his shadow blocked that slanting morning sun and swallowed me up. And I remember this tingling what shot through me as he reached up and swept them fingers of his whole hand through my hair, stroking it off my forehead and down until they come tangled near my braids. He didn't smile none but was a warmness then between us. A sweetness I ain't never felt since.

Then he done told me, for the last, "I'm sorry."

And before I could right ask what for, he turned to them soldiers what was keeping back from us, and said, "Boys, you'll want to hold her."

Shit! Even I heard them words rattle around in my head and they wasn't meant for me. And before I could step off any which, a handful of them boys in blue grabbed me up, taking hold of me by the arm and the back of the neck, stealing off my pistol and Springfield, trapping me where I stood sure as the Green Man once done in that Alcova saloon with that voice of his.

I struggled and fought and tried at biting and all else but they locked onto me right good. What little blood I could draw under my fingernails wasn't enough to buy my freedom and after a spell, wasn't them what occupied me none, anyways. Was the Green Man stepping out into that road like some gunslinger in a story. Never a look back. Never no sign he was even hearing all what I was screaming and barking after. Was chaos in my brain, see, and an equal measure of it what was spilling out. But, truth is, I can't recall a word of it. Was nonsense I was spouting. The calling out of some yack. Or, maybe, the mad banter of a bandit carried up to a hanging.

But, mad as I was, I can't forget what I saw then. Oh, and Jesus right knows it, I've tried. Not much of praying in me, ever, but I've prayed a hundred times to still them memories of what come next. Like to still the memories of finding Bill with his head blowed open nigh onto fifteen years later—and that I know you've heard tell of. Shit, I was even praying right then, to whatever god would hear it. Jesus Almighty or even them savage gods what I saw that berdache and his Lakota praying too before we rode on that Platte station. Any old prayer to stop what was coming.

And was like some queer quiet fell over all the world. The Green Man stopped his walking and stood straight as death in the middle of that Cheyenne street, the sun shining behind him over the top of some low building, putting a glow on them stalks and that long body of his. Somers, too, stopped some hundred yards off out front of that feed store, his back to some chapel at the end of the road.

Except, in that quiet, I could hear the Green Man talking clear as if he were standing right there besides. Heard him say to Somers, "Hope you're better with that iron than you are with your pecker, from what I hear."

Was some nervous chuckling from around us, then. Well, except them holding me as they was in the Green Man thrall, wasn't they. But that chuckling didn't last and quick the quiet was back. And I heard Somers say, "Just what are you playing at, space man?"

And damn if he didn't look uneasy, standing all in the Green Man's sights. All that confidence I done imagined I could see through the Green Man stalks once on? It was plumb gone. Here was the Somers I knew well. A little shaking in his voice, a lot a shaking in them hands. And who's to blame him, huh? More than most, he'd seen the Green Man's quickness and lived to think on it. Back outside Piedmont the Green Man near killed him twice, and for a sight less than he'd done to us the last few days.

But the Green Man stood straight and sure as anything I ever saw. Was a force of nature, he was. And was more than him being some otherworldly thing. Was what he was capable of and that he knew it. Something most of us struggle to figure and never quite know, I reckon. Had that in spades, I tell you. And that alone was reason enough the Green Man should've beefed Somers in a blink.

Should've, anyways.

"I mean to kill you," The Green Man said back at him. "And when I fell you, I mean for Jane and me to walk free. That clear?"

And that last he said looking all around at them deputies and cavalry down out of Laramie. Wasn't none of that voice in what he said, neither.

Just that awesome menace he could put on any ordinary word.

"Jane?" Somers said, like he done never heard that name before. "You done bushwhacked her mind, too, space man? You convinced her she's someone she's not?"

But the Green Man just smiled at that, he did. Said, "Seems you beat me to that one, boy, when you took to confusing her for your wife."

Somers tightened up a spell at that. Some of that shaking fell out and with each deep breath he seemed a little more sure, a little less ready to fall apart. But before he could say else, or even work himself up to some great anger, the Green Man spoke again. And this time, wasn't just words I heard in that quiet morn.

"I ain't wasting no more on talking on you, Somers," he said. And then, in that wicked voice of his what could stop a room or drive it off some cliff, he said, "You either put your bullet in my heart or ready yourself for worse from mine."

And all that madness in my head calmed right then. And all that crazed blubbering I'd been spouting was done gone. My head was clear for the first since them soldiers took me. And in the blink before they pulled their guns, I don't think my heart struck a single beat.

Not until the shooting.

As with all the Green Man done, it was fast. But I swear I could see and hear every detail. Was the wind whistling down the road. Was the sound of that metal gun pulling through the leather as the Green Man unshucked it. And a blink, after, was the sound of Somers' pistol clearing its holster, too. But long before his barrel come up, was the whip-snap of the Green Man's space gun. Twice, now. Boom! Boom! Fast as shit. And them red shots cleared the space between them faster than any bullet, I reckon. Faster than the hand of the fucking almighty!

But wasn't one of them shots what struck Somers. No sir. Was one, each, what passed to either side of him, leaving little singe marks on that boy's shirt by their passing. And a blink later, was each what punched through one of them church windows, blowing out them crudely painted glasses and knocking the heads clean off two sharpshooters taking their aim on the Green Man down the road. Was them surviving two boys we'd left with Somers after yesterday's shooting, each meaning to end this pursuit proper if Somers failed at his draw. Seemed the Green Man's keen stalks found them out, house of God or no. Found them out and laid them low.

But wasn't no third shot I heard from the Green Man's gun. Not before I heard the crack of Somers' pistol. Not before I heard that bone shirt across the Green Man's chest shatter from the shot.

Was then . . .

Sorry, mister. Reckon this ain't something I've much told, before. I told Bill about this, once on. But I reckon no other until you, besides. Talking about it now? Well, it ain't no simple thing, is it? Brings it all back. Makes you live it all over, it does. Shit, I suppose I live it all over every night when I close my eyes, don't I? But it's another thing to go on telling someone about a thing like this. Makes it a sight more . . . real. Like it just happened.

See, I done seen the Green Man shot—or worse—before. But was something about the look of him this time. Something in the way his face went all . . . went all loose, like. How his jaw dropped and them stalks drooped until them tips near bent close to touching his forehead. And how, for just a little moment, his hard stance got soft. Like the steel in them muscles was switched out for water.

Was then he collapsed. Fell right on his side, them black eyes turned up to that young sky.

And . . .

Goddamn. Been thirty fucking years. Long enough a grown woman shouldn't blubber about such things.

And . . . was then his eyes clouded right up. Like they was reflecting some overcast heaven. Except, wasn't no cloud in that cold sky that morning. Just the pale reflection of clouds in them once-oily eyes. Them eyes where I done seen so much.

Goddamn . . .

I felt them soldiers' grip on me slacken some, like them words the Green Man put in them melted away quick as he did. And was right then, too, I felt all manner of evils and angers and hates swelling up in me. Nigh on to exploding, I was. I thrashed against them slackening grips. I screamed and I bit and I pulled, fevered to bursting across that street to my Green Man. To grab up that fallen gun and lay low the whole world in its red fire. I wanted to burn the West to cinders, right then, leaving all traces of us and them what stood against us as ash. And I'd leave Somers until last. And, in his dying, I'd open such a door to Hell that I could pull my Green Man back across the chasm. Else dive in my own self and swallow the fires with him.

But them soldiers, addled as the Green Man left them, wasn't no yacks. They kept hold of me well even as I threw all the hate I could against them. And them I did claw and bite this time. But they took hold of me, all the same. And right good, too. Threw me down on them boards and crushed me under them, pinning my bloodied arms beneath their knees and crushing my shoulder's square to the wood with their spurred boots.

And pressed there, I saw Somers stand over my Green Man. Was the shakes back in him, to be sure, like he couldn't right believe how close he'd come to it. Or what he'd done in the blink them boys in the church had bought him. But was some hate in his eyes, too. Some hate I hadn't seen before. Some hate I reckon the Green Man and I had put there when we left him for dead outside Piedmont.

And over the sound of my own grunting and the noises of them boys pinning me, I heard Somers say to my fallen angel, "You ain't so goddamn much now, is you?"

And was my last sense gone at that. I tell you, all them torn feelings I had for that Somers? They melted right the fuck away. And with every bit of life left in me, I screamed such bile across the dust at that boy, that murderer: "You're yellow! You're yellow and I should've let him kill you back in Piedmont!" And by the time that boy turned to face me where I lay pressed under them soldiers, I kept on and told him plain, "Because I'm going to kill you, Somers. You hear? I'm going to find you and I'm going to rip your fucking throat out!" He even tried to say something to me, then. God knows what, though, because I spat at him every vileness I could muster. And I promised him, "Every time you turn around, you better expect to see me. Because one time I'll be there. I'll be there! And I'm going to kill you, Somers! I'm going to fucking bury you!"

Was then I felt them soldiers grab hold of my braids, pulling my head to the side. And right thereafter, all went black.

ELEVEN

Now, mister, you might think this here's where the story ends, eh? What with the Green Man beefed and me captured.

Well, it ain't. And I wasn't.

See, I woke to see some bright red light shining through some greasy damn windows. Was the setting sun, I reckoned. Setting on all the world, maybe. Hell, might've welcomed it, then, if it was the Armageddon. If them trumpets was sounding out across the West. But was just the sun and was just some filthy fucking windows.

I lay there for a while, not moving a lick. My head throbbing something terrible. Must've been near cracked open, it was. Was some heat around the left side of my skull, and some weight I could feel in my hair what must been a mat of blood all clotted up in it. But I didn't move to feel it, none. Nor to see where all else I was right bruised up from the manhandling them soldiers boys gave me.

No sir. I just lay there watching that sun move on down that window from one greased streak to the next for what felt like days.

Was awake enough. But wasn't no life in me, there. Wasn't nothing. Maybe you've been in a like spot, mister, with all cause for getting up and living right knocked out of you? Maybe you've had something taken from you which you couldn't right go on living without? If so, I'm sorry for you. I truly am. I reckon every man or woman the world over's been in that spot—or will be. The terrible price of living, ain't it? To live through others dying? Shit, was only fifteen years old, wasn't I, and was already a price I was tired of paying.

Must've been an hour or more I lay there looking at that window before I brought myself to rolling over and facing that room. Was Doc Crowder's place, it was, and I expected it. Dark and dirty and full of that brothel smell what sickened me once on. But terrible as that place was, was worse by volumes that day, I tell you, because my Green Man lay out on a table next to me. Not four feet off, he was. Except he wasn't, of course. Was a forever away, wasn't he? Might as well have been back in the sky he come from as laying right there, cold and dead and graying.

And as long as I lay there staring at that window, I reckon I spent as much time laying there watching his unmoving remains. That green skin was darker, some, like that shining silver blood what flowed through it was sunk away and gone. Them pitch, oily eyes was all cloudy and fogged gray as a storm, except still, without no lick of swirling in them. And them long stalks was laying flat on that table, limp sticks lying by some fire.

Was else to mark him dead, to be sure. Was some crudely stuffed hole in his chest, packed with rags to keep off the bleeding. And was his slack jaw, laying open like he was screeching out some last unhearable trill maybe only that queer horse of his could hear. But more than all that, was some emptiness where he was laying. Wasn't no time I ever been in his company there wasn't some power to his being there. Some terror or some awe or some frightening fucking coldness. Or some sweetness what you never saw coming. Was a force of nature, that Green Man was. But was like the waters stilled, lying there. Wasn't no motion on the surface to speak of the storms that fella once whipped up all around. Wasn't nothing to tell of all what he was. Just some empty spot in the room where my murdering angel ought to have been.

After a long while, my heart on to breaking, I remember noticing he was still wearing his boots. And I can't right tell you why but for a spell that lifted my spirits, it did. Shit, was even his notched Stetson on a table just behind. And there, too, was his Henry and that space gun and his Colt, that little pilot's knife, and that duster we done left in the hotel. Even my Springfield and my cavalry pistol was there, besides.

And behind all that gear was a long metal strip leaning against the wall. Was that bandage what had been wrapped around my guts for better than a week, it was. And on seeing that, last, some life come back to me.

Sat up fast as I could manage and had that shirt pulled up to show my belly quick as I could. And sure as shit, was just my bare skin there. Not even a scar to mark where that bullet tore right through me and just about spent my life on them Wyoming grasses.

Not a goddamn scar.

You understand me, mister? Wasn't but a week ago I'd been headed below snakes when the Green Man scooped me up and put that bandage on. Pulled me right back from the brink, it did. Shit, might've brought me back from well on past it, for all I could reckon. So maybe you'll understand what I was thinking when I jumped down off that table and snatched up that bandage. Was metal, that was plain, and was stiff, to be sure. But was a flexible thing, rigid as thick leather but thin as paper, it was. And I didn't have no right idea at all how it worked but I'd seen it wrapped around my belly long enough I expected I could reckon it out. Was desperate to reckon it out.

I took that long bandage and made to setting it on my Green Man. If it could bring me back, why not the same for him, huh? Oh, must seem silly to you. He was dead after all, wasn't he? Been dead all day, so it seemed. But so might I've been out behind that sod hut, once on.

So I took to clawing back the Green Man's clothes all frantic like. I pulled on that bone shirt until it gave enough I could push it beside. And I tugged at that flannel underneath until them button's popped off onto the floor like so many shell casings. And there, beneath all that, I pulled out them foul rags and revealed that torn hole in his chest. The hole in his heart. And on seeing it, I began to cry something awful. Was a terrible thing, seeing that. That green skin all split and cracked up like some dried up river bed. And in all them tears and splits, and the hole made between it all, was some paste of silver stuff. The dried up remains of his living, it was. Shit, reckon I knew I was on some yack errand, there. Seeing that ugly hole in his flesh? Reckon I knew what was done was done and no shiny metal wrapping could stick life back into that stilled flesh.

But I kept on. What else could I? Kept on until I was pressing that bandage down against his chest with one hand and trying to slip the ends of it under him with the other. And was a lot of tugging and pulling on his body, it was. A lot of fussing what saw me right hugging his chest to roll him up so I could thread that bandage beneath. And all the while, was my vision clouded and wet with them damn fool tears. And when all was all, and I had that bandage pulled end to end, stretched far as it could around his narrow chest, wasn't nothing I could do to bring them ends to sticking together. See, hadn't been no seam I could ever see when that thing was on me. And no matter how I tried to join them ends, wasn't nothing I did where they didn't just fall apart as soon as I let them.

Was then I lost it. Lost it plumb proper, too. Collapsed right on him, I did. And God fucking knows how long I was on him, crying out enough for a lifetime. Enough my knees gave way, after a spell, and I fell right to the floor beside, knocking his arm off the table with me so it hung from the shoulder down to right near the floor. And that I hugged, I did. And would I could've squeezed some life back into that mangled half-a-hand what hung there, well, the Green Man would be right here today telling you this tale. But wasn't no magic or prayer or fancy space toy to make that happen. Was just some girl hanging on to the last of what was left her.

Well, my blubbering was right starting to slow on its own when Doc Crowder come into that room and caught me weeping on his floor. And seeing that bandage now hung halfway down next to me, he said, "Little late for that, ain't it, girl?"

I remember snapping at him in some quiet little voice, "Fuck you." But was a snapping all the same.

"Fuck you," I remember saying again before he got another word out. Was the best I could manage, that. But manage it I did. Was a time when some losing like this would've rendered me right witless. When Momma died with that stillborn in her arms, or when I woke to find my daddy gone, wasn't no clear thought I could say to no man for a long while. Was getting hard to that losing, I reckon. To paying that price. Never used to it, no sir. Just ask them folks what saw me after Bill was shot and they'll tell you true. But was getting harder to it, I was. Harder than I used to have been.

Doc Crowder stepped over me and looked down with as close to a pitying look as I reckon he was able. Was a coldness to that doc. Must've been why the Green Man liked him so. And standing there, he picked up the Green Man's Stetson and rolled the brim between them fingers of his like he done never felt a proper hat before.

"Some of them boys the marshal deputized and some of them from

Laramie tried to pick him clean, they did," the doc told me. "But that marshal brought him back to me with all his. Said he reckons whatever earthly remains there was, you'd the better claim to. If that Moses Boone or his want to collect trophies, reckon they can barter with you."

Was then I really thought about what done happened in that street. The shooting and the screaming and me thrashing about. If there was trophies to be had, reckon I was the biggest purse of all, wasn't I? The hoodwinked white girl in the thrall of that green devil.

So I asked him plain, "What about me?" Oh, my voice still all warbly but was some tingle in my heart telling me wasn't all time for mourning. Wasn't out of them sights just yet, was I? Asked him, "How come I ain't some trophy? How come I ain't rotting in some cell with no deputies leering on me?"

The doc just shrugged. "You're just a girl," was all he said.

And like to finish his thought, the door to that shack opened right then and some soldier stuck his head in, eying me sitting on that floor, tear soaked and pitiful all clinging to the Green Man's arm. And wasn't no bit of concern in them eyes, none. No bit of worry what the girl who burned Platte Bridge Station was woke. Reckon was just some biddy he saw on that floor.

"Y'all right in here, doc?" he asked. And was the shadow of another boy I saw falling across him as that door inched open a hair more. Might not have been in prison, none, but didn't mean they wasn't keeping an eye on.

Well, the doc didn't waste a beat, did he? Spread his hand in some disbelief and told that boy, "I look all fucking right to you? Seems I got me a corpse and a bloodied up little girl on my hands now don't it?"

Well, that boy backed out quick, I tell you. And for that, I was plenty glad. Might not have been one of them what held me while the Green Man and Somers faced off but was a plenty strong reminder that wasn't nothing I done to stop that shooting.

But was this business of me being some harmless girl what was more on my mind. And I told old Doc Crowder, "I ain't no little girl."

And without looking on me ever a bit, he said back, "Don't you think I know that?" And after a spell on, told me, too, "Better to let them keep on thinking you're some hoodwinked little biddy. Better they don't see the whirlwind you are."

I took to wiping them tears away, then. Might well have been some river down my cheeks and around them puffy eyes. But I cleaned myself up, I did, and I let that doc help me back to my feet, shaky as my legs was. Some whirlwind, eh? And I remember him taking me beside and setting me in a rickety chair. Was like that day I first met the Green Man, it was. When he done left me lonesome at Harthra's ranch, surrounded by them dead boys, and I had my mourning. Was a point when you got your fill of it out of you. When you'd let out so much of that hurting you can finally see clear again. Least for a while. And in that rickety chair, sitting next to the Green Man's body, now fussed with as much by me as Somers' bullet, was then that clearness of thinking come back to me.

"Where's the bullet?" I remember asking the doc, trying my damnedest not to look at him.

He shrugged and took to straightening the Green Man's shirts. "Reckon it's out in the street somewheres," he said. "Went clean through."

Well, I suppose I can't blame the doc for missing my meaning. But, see, was right then, with my head finally clear, what I was seeing things I hadn't seen before. Things no little girl would've seen but what maybe I should've.

"No," I told him. "Was a bullet in me once on. I'd see it."

And was a long spell before Doc Crowder answered me. Stood there fixing the Green Man's clothes and right avoiding the question. But after he'd fixed that bone shirt and patted the Green Man's chest, he walked around to that apothecary littered with drawings of green men's insides and all their queer tools. And from some tiny square drawer he plucked a little warped bit of lead, flattened some on the end and caked in the creases with blood.

He come over and set it next to me, right near the butt of the Green Man's Henry. And plain as he was talking about the weather, said, "Come out sometime yesterday, I reckon. The bandage is what removed it." Then he paused, some, and that pitying look of his became a sight more true. "I found it when I took the bandage off this morning."

I wiped away some lingering tears, then, and stared for a while at that tiny thing. That little bit of lead what just about left me bleaching in the sun.

I started to say, "I don't—" but nothing followed it out. I didn't understand. I didn't want to. What I mean is, did the Green Man right know the bandage would work it out? Did he want us to get caught in this here trap? Was that why we rode through them towns on our way south? Shit. I didn't want to know the thinking behind it. The thinking I'd seen the Green Man working out all the ways back in that sod hut and again just this morning. No sir, what was left of Martha in me wanted to close my eyes to the lot of it.

I remember squeezing my eyes shut to fight back some fresh tears. "Why'd he bring me here?" I asked, not so much to that doc as to God almighty. "Why to fucking Cheyenne? He done tried to abandon me once on. Back when the Gray Man was on us. But if this was some play of his to let me off again . . ."

And I'm glad to this day Doc Crowder was a cold one. Saw me struggling with the notion and he pressed on, damning how I felt or what I wanted to hear. And better I knew the truth, I tell you. Better by a mile.

"Abandon you? Jane, he ain't never wanted to leave you off. Brought you here to mend you. Got himself shot for the trouble of it." And damn if he wasn't standing over me like some school marm explaining a plainness to a child. But those words he spoke was true and I knew it. "This business of gray men and green men, of their flying ships and their guns?" he said, "theirs are the old ways, Jane. A fading way. Ain't no lick of the future in it? Ain't no way for you to live."

I remember staring at the Green Man's body, then. Was some anger in me, to be sure. But not for him. Was for me being a goddamn yack. He'd told me as much back at the hut, hadn't he? "This ain't living" he'd said. Except he wasn't talking about himself. Was talking about me. On the run, with as little life ahead as behind.

"He wanted you safe," that doc said. And didn't I know it. Had he ever done else? In Piedmont, among them Lakota, in Alcova, at the sod hut and else in between? Seemed was all he'd ever wanted excepting some goddamn flying engine.

And, Jesus, if that didn't bring it all back to me. Thinking on that engine of Mister Harthra's what started it all.

"All this on account of a goddamn flying ship," I said all quiet, like to myself.

And I remember doc shrugging then. And some little smile cracked them flat lips of his. And he said to me, "All this on account of you."

And, mister, I tell you, was right then I reckon I saw myself clear. All them times I'd watched men seeing me afresh? Well, this here was when I saw my own damn self. I got out of that rickety chair and went over to my Green Man. And standing there over his graying corpse, I thought back to one of them first things he told me. To something what's rung true my whole life. About how you can't count on no man. And was then I realized I ain't never learned that lesson, had I? Even when I faced down that Gray Man, was the need for my Green what held me up, wasn't it? Been ever leaning on him. Been counting on the Green Man for plumb all.

But time was up for that. Was high time for me to end this my own self. Like the Green Man done told me at the start.

So, without saying nothing, I snatched up the Green Man's Henry and his Colt from where they lay on that table. And I took the Green Man's holster and set it on my hips. Plucked up his Stetson, too, notched and stained and all, and set it on my head, letting its shadow swallow up as much of me as it could. And, at the last, I took up that pilot's knife, the one I done killed that first Gray with, and damn if I didn't start off for the back door of that shack with a quickness.

Doc Crowder, he made to stand in my way. Said something like, "Now don't throw away what he bought you, Jane. Ain't no one going to come after some girl. Might be they reckon you were his prize, see? Not some he rode the goddamn river with. You go out all heeled and full of piss, they won't hesitate to put you down this time. Was plenty what wanted it at the first."

But I didn't have time to be talked out of it. I asked him, "How many waiting outside? Just them two?"

Doc took my arm, then, making to stop me, and said, "Them boys ain't the ones what done your Green Man."

Well, I took his hand right off me, then, and asked him, straight, "But you know where to find the one what did, don't you?"

Damn if he didn't just shrug at that, "I reckon all of Cheyenne knows that," he said.

Well, I just squeezed that little knife tight, feeling that blade slip in and out on my thinking, and I told that doc, "Then stay out of this—I don't need you for what I got to do."

TWELVE

Wasn't a soul what could've kept me from where I was headed. Not far off from that shot up hotel and that blasted out store was a saloon what lit up that night with soldiers and deputies and all else celebrating the end of some devil in their midst. And from them same dark alleys where yesterday we traded fire with them after us, reckon I saw about every fella what watched the Green Man fall under Somers in that street. And was a few I come across in shadow and evening coldness what wouldn't forget me none, neither. Wasn't an innocent soul in Cheyenne, that night.

No. And wasn't long, neither, until I found myself right where I needed to be. Was the dark of some hotel in the quiet hour before the sun reclaimed the sky. And wasn't hardly a sound to be heard in Cheyenne. Even them still celebrating their part in the day's murdering was far off and quiet all, sleeping in their whiskies or on their whores' tits. Was just the sound of snoring peeking through them hotel doors to tell me which rooms to pass on by. At this last, was one thing them romances with Somers done taught me what I had to be thankful for. Wasn't a snort in that boy's sleeping to wake him or her what lay with him.

So when I found a quiet door, I took a long breath, thinking to steady myself. Except I found wasn't nothing to steady. Maybe, once on, I had to fight to keep the sand in my belly. To keep off them shakes. But was a stone there now. Big as Independence Rock, it felt. And waiting there, before my stepping in, I remember thinking on that last time I saw the Green Man living. Was capable and knew it, wasn't he? Shit. Was my time for that now.

I slipped into that room, letting that Henry lead the way in the dark. And there, in a dim pool of light cast by some weak lamp across some tiny bed, was Somers, fast asleep—that same simple boy what tumbled down that hill so long ago, wanting me to shin out with him. Wanting me to forget all he'd done to me. And in the dimmer light, still, past him, was some red-headed thing, curled up against the cold. You might think that would've raised my blood to boiling, that. Seeing some biddy in his bed. But time was long gone for that manner of caring, mister. This here was the man what felled a Green. My Green. He was due his prizes, those he done already collected and the rest what were coming, all the same.

I settled up near the foot of the bed, my back to the wall, and kicked the footboard hard as I could. And damn if them two didn't jump like some horse wasn't crashing through the goddamn window. But they saw me quick enough. And that Henry I had trained on them, too. Well, on Somers, anyways. So you can understand, maybe, that once up to sitting, Somers kept his lips tight, watching me like I was some phantom come to claim.

"Reckon I told you I'd be coming," I said, my voice all cold as the air what misted up at my speaking it. And while that biddy was looking between him and me, all balled up and right to start up her screaming, I tossed her that pilot's knife, I did. Tossed it right into the hammock them sheets made tween her knees. And I told her, cutting off any howling she was about to spout, "Clean that blade."

Well, she picked it up without even thinking, I expect, and tried to see it clear in that dim light. Was all covered in black, seemed—though was a trick of the light, not like it was, once on. "What's on it?" she started asking. But fool as he was, sometimes, Somers wasn't all yack.

"Blood," he said for me. And at that, that biddy did her little wailing, dropping that thing right back on them sheets. About right through them.

"Quiet, now," told her. And for the only time in that room, I let that barrel drift away from Somers. Put it right on her, I did, and asked, surprising my own self, "Name ain't Martha is it, girl?"

I remember, she was looking between Somers and me in a right panic. And moving away from both of us in that bed, she squeaked out some simple, "No."

And this I told Somers, then, "That's right fortunate, ain't it. Not sure if you could handle some plague of Marthas." And in the silence what followed, I reckon our eyes had some long conversation our mouths could've never talked through. Some long, looking talk about things gone and long since said. About cries out in the night and some long ago tangling of limbs. And about them betrayals done time and time again—by both of us—what led to me pointing the Green Man's rifle at the man what once loved me under the Green Man's stars.

"Girl," I told that biddy, though it was plain she was my elder in years, not in living, "It'd be in your best, I reckon, for you to fag on out of here now. Somers and me got a matter to settle." And when she made to grab up her sundries off the floor, well, I stopped her right quick. Told her, "No, missy. I reckon buff suits you just fine."

And in the blink when she got to thinking about slipping through them cold streets in the suit what her momma made her, I reminded her, "Ain't the first bad decision you've made, is it girl? Don't let it be your last."

And, mister, that redheaded thing was gone in some mad scramble, I tell you. Right leapt over the bed, she did, tears springing up to muffle her blubbering. And right good she did, too. Wasn't no part of me what wanted to harm her. I would've. But no part of me what wanted to.

So was just me and Somers in that little hotel room, then. Wasn't much different from that the Green Man and I shared a night before, neither. Except wasn't no Green Man now. Was just Jane.

I told him, when that girl was, gone, "Seems you had yourself a man for breakfast, Somers. My man. So I hope you got your elbow bent plenty and your pecker polished just fine, last night. Because the time for merriment is right spent."

I remember stepping a bit closer to him. Right up to the end of that bed where that dim lamplight crept up under that Stetson and fell on my face. Was something in my look what must've surprised Somers, then. And I remember thinking, when was the last this boy done took a good look at me? Was it that night we tangled under them stars? Was it when he come after me in that camp outside Piedmont? Sure as shit hadn't been since then. Not what I could see. Because the girl he was seeing now must've been plumb different from what he was expecting. I've long wondered how things might played out if he'd just opened them eyes before right then.

But never mind all that. Ain't no way of knowing Somers' mind any more than there is of knowing the Green Man's, is there?

Well, now what it was just us alone, I asked him, bile burning my throat some as I did, "How does it feel to be paid to do Moses Boone's dirty work?"

And, to his credit, Somers mustered up all the sand he could, right then. Yes sir, what with some spurned lover bearing a rifle on him, I reckon he mustered up a fair amount, indeed. Said back to me, "For killing that green skin? Felt good."

Was just some slow nodding I had for that. And a warning. Told him, "Pretty unhealthy job."

I nodded toward that little knife and said, "Why don't you get to finishing what that slut of yours couldn't manage."

Well, he never took his eyes off me, or that rifle, none, but he reached over and plucked up that knife. And he told me, "You ain't got no beef with her."

And that's true. Like I told you, I didn't want to hurt none what didn't earn it. And that I reminded Somers, too, saying, "Let her go. Ain't going to regret that, too, am I?"

But for that, the boy had nothing to say back to me. What could he? Once on I showed that boy mercy and he paid that back in blood. Wasn't going to make that mistake again.

No, he just started looking at that knife, turning it over in his hands, letting the light shine off them smears of blood all down that blade and handle, too. And after a spell, he asked me, "Who's blood is this?"

"Hard to say," I told him. "Might be a couple fellas." Then I jammed that rifle toward him, making him jump in bed where he sat, buff as his biddy except for the sheet covering him. "Now why don't you wipe that thing off before I add yours to it."

Well, his eyes were back on me in a blink, I tell you. And he done started wiping that knife clean straight away on them sheets. And was right then something must've occurred to him. Something what I seen occur to plenty others since I started riding with the Green Man. About how there was only one way this was going to end.

"That space man made off with you," he told me. "Moses gave me an opportunity, he did. What so I could rescue you."

"Because I needed rescuing?" I asked him, that Henry adding weight to them words. "Because I'm some little girl?" I kept on, them flames long simmering in me now rising up like some bonfire, ripe for a host of savages to parade around. Wasn't no girl no more. Hadn't been since maybe Martha was pinned in that barn, so long ago. A lifetime ago, it seemed. Longer still.

"I don't count on no man to rescue me," I told him, through gritted teeth.

"Martha Jane, it ain't like that," he said.

And damned if that didn't seal his fate, I reckon. As concerned as I'd been about that biddy keeping hush before, I let fly with my own screaming right then, loud as dynamite in that tiny room. I leaned close so that dim light could catch all my face and I asked at a holler, "Do I look like Martha Jane Canary to you?"

Well, Somers flew back aways from me, he did. Right back up against that flimsy headboard he must've been banging against not so long before.

And with that heat blown out of me like some sudden steam from a boiler, I leaned back, saying almost to myself as much for him, "Reckon I ain't been her for a long time. Sure as shit ain't no Martha."

And when his terror settled down some, and when it was clear from listening what my yelling ain't alerted everyone in the damn hotel to my vengeance, I saw Somers swallow hard. Hard enough to get some sand back what I must've spooked out of him. Saw him thinking there for a spell, too. He was right to reckon them words careful, see? Was each breath what might be his last.

"So you're Jane now," he said. And I knew he was thinking back on what the Green Man told him in the street that morning. And looking on me with some pleading eyes, he kept on, saying, "Can't you see he's done something to you?"

And I tell you, he picked them words right proper, he did. Helped me see my Martha was long gone. Done put her to bed. Left her back in some hills north of the Platte, I reckoned. Or in some sod hut lost somewheres north, if else. No, wasn't no bit of that girl left in me. Wasn't no Martha what could've rode among them savages and gone to war. Wasn't no Martha what could've shot her way through Cheyenne at a space man's clip. And sure as I live and breathe right now, mister, wasn't no Martha I was once on could've stood in that room, her finger on that trigger, and stare down him what killed her Green Man.

Was Jane now. All Jane. Come calamity or come calm, was myself and none else. At last.

"He ain't done nothing to me," I told Somers, then. "He helped me be something to myself, is all. And that's a kindness and a sweetness you and old Moses Boone can't take away by killing."

Somers held that knife up, all cleaned on them sheets he done already soiled, and slowly he held it out toward me. I pointed that Henry down between them legs of his to show him where he could drop that blade. Damn if he didn't flinch, thinking I was going to shave off his bits with some high caliber.

He dropped that knife and backed off in that bed, again. And in slow words, he told me, trying to calm me, I reckon, "I know you ain't going to kill me, Jane."

Was a queer thing hearing that name through them curly lips. Wasn't none of the sweetness I'd heard so often from the Green Man in his saying it. Was just some unbelieving, like was some made up thing he couldn't quite reckon. Like me standing there, gun on him and all, was something he couldn't put his head around.

"I've done my share of killing" I told him. "And more."

"Likely you had your reasons, too," I remember him saying, his hands held with them palms up in some kind of pleading. "Like you had your reasons for killing Jeb and them with him. Probably needed killing."

"Like as you had yours for killing the Green Man," I told him. "And we all's got to pay our due for it, don't we?" And at that, I remember thinking to myself, What if Jimmy ain't found me in that barn? What if the Green Man ain't come looking for that ship when he did? What if Jeb had kept his business with Mr. Harthra on the level. Jesus! What if Somers ain't been married? Was reason in all these for any manner of killing what followed, wasn't there? Reason same as led me to hunting down that gray fucker what took my Green Man or for them what caught us at the hut to put one in my belly. Seems little reason's enough for killing. And killing then is reason enough all its own self.

But was time enough of talking, I reckoned. Seeing Somers all un-shucked in that bed reminded me of a time when he sure could cut a swell.

Fine as cream gravy, he was. But wasn't none of that I could see in him now. Was just the coward what stood over my Green Man. And, damn, if the bile didn't burn at thinking on that. And damn if them tears didn't want to break through, washing that image away.

I tell you, mister, was the moment I started to doubt what I'd come to do, right then. I tightened up that rifle against my shoulder. And there, them doubts faded right out. Didn't need no fancy scope for this shooting, just sand enough. And that, I had in spades.

"Tell me true now, because it just might be your last opportunity," I told that boy, "you come for him or you come for me?"

Was tears in his eyes. Some little wetness trying to hide behind some toughness. And as honest a thing as he ever said, he said right then. I've never doubted it. "Come for you, Jane," he said. "Only ever come for you."

"Well, that was a fool thing," I told him.

Somers let his hands down then, he did. And damn if he didn't seem all calm all of a sudden. And I'll never forget him telling me, "Go on, then. Fall apart."

And that's how little that boy knew the Jane I'd become, ain't it? "Ain't falling apart," I told him. "Just putting you behind me."

You know, mister, one of the last things my Green Man told me, just the night before, was got to think beyond your guns. And damn if that ain't the God's honest. I've seen over a whole lifetime what harm and foul guns can bring on a man. But I know, too, there's some you got to put to the bullet. So maybe the Green Man was right. Shit, I know he was. Got to think beyond your guns, indeed.

Just not yet.

And when the crash of hammer and powder, bone and bullet was all quiet again, was like a weight lifted. Like I'd been cleansed in some little crick where my sins done run off like black blood into the eddies.

Promised my Green Man not to waste my life on vengeance, I did. And I kept that promise. Didn't waste another second of it. And I walked out of that room without a lick of regret.

THIRTEEN

When I got back to Doc Crowder's place, was just some red sky starting to glow overhead. And was a dust of snow what fell in the night, too, brushing that whole town with some thin powder shining back like wet strawberries. This here was my first day without the Green Man at my side. The first day I was Jane, all alone.

Them streets was hushed, all, with just the hammering of some distant smith or the bray of some far off horse to upset the quiet. Was a new world, there. Cold and young and lonesome, it was. But damn if there didn't seem to be some queer hope to it all. Like some weight long forgotten was remembered in its lifting. And though I knew folks would be looking for that dark-haired girl what once rode with a Green—and right soon, too—wasn't no hurry in me. I'd put a whole lifetime behind me, hadn't I? Had a whole lifetime ahead, waiting.

But when I got close enough to the doc's place to see it clear, well, I saw plain something was queer. Them two soldiers what was set to watch it, and who I done slipped around just hours on, was lying still as posts on the dirt, their blood done staining that fresh powder. And was right then I heard a rush of horses not far off. Was making down an alley, I was, when I heard that galloping. And just as soon, I saw a mess of riders pass on by the docs, yelling all about rounding up a posse. Seems some whore saw herself a ghost. Seems blood was right let all over Cheyenne. And, while some smile was creeping cross my lips, heard them riders call on they wasn't hunting for no girl. Was a Green they was after. Or the ghost of one.

Tell you true, my heart skipped a beat at that. Wasn't no fear, understand? Was the pace of action, it was, set for running and shooting and all else I've come to see as the result of dying and such. I unshucked that Colt, too. Felt heavy, it did. Since the Green Man first put that thing in my hand, ever it felt heavy. Except today that trigger sung when I touched finger to it. Flexed just a enough so I knew I could bend it. Wasn't ever no railroad tie in my grip, again. And mister, let me tell you, in nigh onto thirty years since that day, I've let that goddamn gun do some singing.

But was nerves afire in me, then. And when them riders done passed by, I ran up to the shack fast as them legs would carry me. Could see plain them boys was shot. Shit, was holes in them big enough to put your arms through. And was a just a blink after, too, I saw was holes in the door from the shooting. Shooting what must've come from inside. And I'd ridden' with the Green Man long enough to know, was his big space gun what punched them holes. Burned right through that door and on through them boys what stood outside it. And for just the smallest moment, mister, I found myself wondering, what for that doc would take up shooting. Especially with the Green Man's gun. Wondered that, anyways until I noticed wasn't no window in that door. No way to know if you were shooting true.

No way for a man, anyways, what with no bug stalks to feel it out.

I was through that door like a fucking bolt, I was. Through it so fast I about knocked myself cold on a post when I come in. And there, inside, was the doc sitting in that same rickety chair I'd been in just a few hours before. Seemed he was coming to grips all the same. But I'd no mind for him. See, because was then, too, I saw the Green Man's table laid bare and all his gear—and what was left of mine—was gone.

I ran over to the doc and took him by the shoulders. "Where is he?" I asked, my voice right on to cracking with nerves. My heart about ready to fall out between my knees. "Someone take him? Was it the marshal? Did Boone send more boys?"

But that Doc Crowder? He was cold, like I said. He didn't answer my panic with the like, none. He just sat back in that wobbly thing and met my eyes square. Said, "No one took him, Jane."

"Then where the fuck is he?" I snapped. And damn if I didn't know the answer before the doc could tell me.

"You ain't listening," he said. "It's a strange thing about them Greens. Not all their bits are in the same places as inside you and me. Why, you might think you shot a man in the heart. But it might be, not every man's heart's in the same place."

And at that, I looked up at them strange sketches of green men and their guts. And damn if I didn't feel right yack my own self. Shit, I couldn't tell what none of that was on them sketches. But didn't need to, did I. Was my ear against the Green Man's chest in that hotel, wasn't it. Had the truth of it right there in front of me, too. Or, I should say, I didn't. The Green Man was gone. And wasn't no enemy what carried him off, neither.

"Where is he?" I yelled at the doc, all of a sudden frantic to get out of that shack and ride. Ride in whatever direction would bring me back to my Green Man.

"Jane, we talked about this," he said, all calm and quiet against my raging. "He knew you'd follow him to hell. And if you had, hell's where you'd be. He means for you to be safe, and safest of all without him."

"Where?" I asked again. And this time, was my turn to be calm. To show him this wasn't no little girl's tantrum. Was something else. Something I don't care to put to words—don't know if I could if I tried it. Was home when I was with him, remember. And if he'd come back from across that abyss, well, how could I do else but go after him.

"Gone," he said. And that was that.

Was like I done woke up from some dream, right then. I took off on foot fast as I could. First to the livery to see Bess stalled up all lonesome—the Green Man's horse gone. And then, for a short spell, I done run every which way through that town, looking down all them streets and alleys for sign of his passing. But, of course, there wasn't none. And as them minutes got longer, and that sun started to break the horizon, my heart calmed. If the Green Man meant to get gone, wasn't no force in creation what could stop him. And for all them what would chase after him, running Moses Boone's fool errand to its last, well, was a pity for them. The Green Man would leave them bleached in some badlands far off. And that I knew they'd never catch him, well, that filled my heart, it did. Filled it right to swelling. Because maybe he wasn't going to be at my side, but so long as he lived and breathed in this world, well, reckon that made the whole West home enough for me.

Was across town when I stopped my running, standing in the weak morning shadows of that unfinished building the marshal what showed us when we come into town. Bare timbers, mostly, without no skin to speak of. Not even a shingle to make a roof. But still, was the tallest around.

So I slung that Henry over my shoulder and made to climb. Was scaffolds enough to make it with no trouble. And by the time I was crawling up onto them third-story timbers, was the sun broke over the horizon, spilling its light all across the plains every which. And was in every which I started looking, hunting for some speck moving against them dry fields and grasses.

And when I didn't see nothing with my own eyes, I took that Henry to my shoulder, let that scope cup my eye, and started looking all the closer. Was like miles of distance melted away in a heartbeat, it was. And among all them queer symbols what ringed what I was seeing, was one what kept moving as I did. Until I reckoned how to move in its direction, anyways. Was like an arrowhead leading me across the landscape toward something. And when I found it, that little symbol centered all in that scope, was then I found my Green Man. Little more than a black dot against the sunrise, miles and miles off. But the shape of that horse and rider—and them stalks barely visible in that sunlight—was well plain to see. Was my Green Man, goddamnit. Living and breathing and riding away.

And at the last I saw him, he stopped for a spell, like he could feel me watching him even from far off. Maybe with them stalks of his. Maybe with something in that there scope. Whatever it was, he stopped all the same. Like to wave back at me. To beckon me on. To wait for me to get Bess and ride out to him. To ride on together until we found a ship or until we escaped Moses Boone or all manner of outcomes. Just to ride, in silence, so long as we could.

And that moment he stopped there? Well, seemed to last forever, it did. But likely was just a heartbeat. A last look back across the plain at the town what nearly killed him—or thought it did. A look back at his daisy Jane who showed him the goddamn elephant.

He come to me like a prayer answered. Now he faded into that sun like a dream at waking.

And he was gone.

And that, mister, is how the story ends. With the Green Man rode off and me perched on some high vantage in Cheyenne, lonesome but needing no man. And with all them forces of Jeb and Moses Boone, the Gray Man, and Somers and all else put behind. Was victors, we was. Was the stuff of them dime novels, I reckon. And was a sight more to come, to be sure. Was still old Moses Boone out there, bent of revenge for us killing his murdering son. But, I tell you, right then I knew I could take all comers. If old man Boone wanted me, well, I reckoned he'd have to come fetch me his own goddamn self. And when he did, was going to be Jane he'd find. And right quick.

But wasn't time for that, then. Not for a long while, if ever. No sir. Then was time for moving on. In all manner of ways. Part of me wanted to stay in Cheyenne and settle matters with that marshal and them soldiers, too. What was left of them, anyways. Matters what would likely be blamed on the Green Man alone. But the better part of me knew I had to keep on. Was done there, wasn't I? Done put that town to the bullet and was ready to put it behind me like so much else.

But where to go? I didn't right know. Certainly didn't expect I'd ever end up in Dakota, that's for sure. But was a long life I done went off to from that high vantage in Cheyenne. Was a scout for Custer and rode with Bill Hickok. Fought my share in Injuns—even some I once fought with, to be sure. And a lot else, besides, what you probably wouldn't right believe, mister. Well, excepting you've believed this tale. But however else my life might've gone, if I'd kept on as Martha, it wouldn't have been a shadow of the like I lived as Jane.

Was like old Doc Crowder said. What would come a time when this world of covered wagons and flying engines was overtaken by tomorrow. When there wouldn't be any Greens left in the West. But I reckon there's at least one still roaming them hills and plains. Maybe his stalks ain't so tall or his draw ain't so quick. But there ain't nothing in all the West what might stop my Green Man from living.

What's that now? Did I ever see the Green Man again? Did I ride back to that sod hut and find him waiting?

Mister, reckon some stories are just for me, entire.

No sir, we'll end this here. Not with me and him finding no flying engine or what with me getting some final vengeance on them Boones.

It ends what with scores settled and escapes made. With me and Bess headed off together, as ever. And with me right become Jane, and Martha right put behind, forever.

Daddy told me, follow the sun west. So I would. See it all. See the elephant. But the West wasn't all, was it? And wasn't just west that setting sun pointed toward, neither. No sir. Was up in that sky, too. Up where the Green Man come down from. Up where it traded places with them stars come nightfall. And unlike most folks, I wasn't one to just look up at that flickering firelight and wonder or make up stories about them shapes they frame out.

See, I'd ridden with a green man. My Green Man. And damn if them stars wasn't more than lights.

So I'd follow the sun. Follow it right on up into the sky.

ABOUT THE AUTHOR

JD Jordan lives in Atlanta, Georgia with his wife, Ellie, and a whole bunch of kids. He's a huge scifi nerd but, despite the contents of this novel, never purposefully sat down to watch or read a Western until the Green Man rode into his imagination. Now he can't get enough of them.

This is his first novel.

You can find out more and follow in Jane's footsteps through the real locations and events of this book at o-jd.com.

CPSIA information can be obtained
at www.ICGtesting.com
Printed in the USA
LVOW12s0937061116
511834LV00001B/209/P